This is a work of fiction. Names, character, places, and incidents are either the product of the author's imagination or used fictitiously. Any resemblance to actual persons, living or dead, businesses, companies, events, or locales is entirely coincidental.

Copyright © 2026 Cheyenne Cleveland

All rights reserved.

Cover by Maria Spada

ISBN 979-8-9936886-0-2 (print)

ISBN 979-8-9936886-1-9 (eBook)

No part of this book may be reproduced in any form or by any electronic or mechanical means, including information storage and retrieval systems, without written permission from the author, except for the use of brief quotations in a book review.

For my family,
I love you beyond the stars.

"Remember me, O Lord, with the favor
You have toward Your people.
Oh, visit me with Your salvation,
That I may see the benefit of Your chosen ones,
That I may rejoice in the gladness of Your nation,
That I may glory with Your inheritance."
Psalm 106:4-5

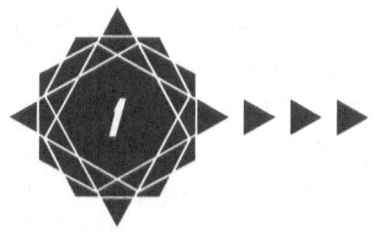

1

I remember the day Grandmommy died as if it were yesterday. It doesn't help that I still see flashes of her frail body sprawled out on that dirty cot every time I close my eyes. My memory tortures me that way, replaying those last moments over and over again in my head: her messy gray hair plastered with sweat, her eyelids fluttering, tired and heavy, covering her hazel irises, her bony fingers cupped over her pale lips, failing to keep her insides from spewing out.

There are blood stains on the sheets, the same ones we used to catch her vomit.

It's been almost ten years since she passed, but the foul stench of the soiled room still burns my nostrils whenever I think about it. It's so potent I can almost taste it. My stomach turns in protest, but I don't give in. Lucile sits in front of me during class, and she doesn't handle contact with bodily fluids too well. I swallow to keep myself from spewing chunks. Although there wouldn't be much running up my esophagus, anyway. My stomach contents consist only of bile and a few chewed-up crumbs from this morning's breakfast: two stale nutritional crackers. They're hard to swallow, even when I'm fortunate enough to get an entire bottle of water with my rations.

Professor Diaz dims the lights and flicks on the rusty projector, snapping my attention from the phantosmia, saving me from covering my bunkermate in barf and an unnecessary trip to Quarantine. Diagrams of filtration systems flash on the peeling paint of the lecture hall walls. At some point, he shifted from an overly opinionated world history lesson to a presentation on water purification, but I missed the transition while thinking about Grandmommy. I take advantage of the shadows and squeeze my eyes shut, tuning out his lesson and leaning into the memory.

"Reyna." Grandmommy rasped my name through heavy breaths before vomiting again. Red mixed with yellow and green on her nightgown. She motioned for water, pointing with a shaky finger to a small cup on a metal stool beside the inexcusably soiled bed. She hacked bloody saliva into her hands and wheezed into another coughing fit. I held the cup to her mouth. Water droplets dripped from the rim, but there was barely enough liquid to wet her cracked lips.

She patted my hand and forced a weak smile, her red eyes still sparkling with kindness. Grandmommy twisted in the bed and pointed underneath the mattress. Excitement bubbled in my seven-year-old chest. She was always hiding treasures for me under there, like marbles or peppermints. Things she could easily trade for an extra shift at the washhouse with some of the other women who lived in the Northern Sector of the barracks.

I shoved my hand beneath the lumpy cot and reached for whatever she hid. The pitter-patter of my heart intensified as I groped to find my present. To my surprise, my fingers came in contact with something much larger than an old piece of candy. It felt like paper, like the soft edges of a book. I pulled the item from its hiding place. My eyes widened as I took in a beautiful leather-bound journal, with *I love you beyond the stars* inscribed on the cover.

"Grandmommy, I-I can't ..." I tried to give the journal back. It was too special a gift, one that must have cost her a fortune.

Grandmommy's lungs gurgled with fluid. Her bony fingers strained to push the journal back into my small hands.

"Promise me you'll remember." She tapped the inscribed words.

My eyes welled with tears. "I promise."

"I love you beyond the stars" was her way of saying she loved me more than anything else in the world. But it was also her way of reminding me she'd do just about anything for me, even if it meant breaking the rules.

Looking at the stars wasn't something most kids got to do while growing up on the Omega Compound. Lockdown began promptly at sundown, and lights were off by ten p.m., no matter the time of year. Grandmommy loved the stars, though, and determined that no one was going to keep her from seeing them, not even the Commander himself.

When I was just a toddler, Grandmommy sewed herself a pincushion with scraps from the seamstress station at the washhouse. She used that little bolster to keep the locks on the bunker door from engaging whenever she wanted to sneak out at night. We'd tiptoe into the quadrangle after dark, when the guards had all retired to their homes, and sprawled out under the midnight sky. Grandmommy "oohed" and "aahed" at the galaxies spinning overhead that painted their dark canvas with flecks of color and pinpricks of light. It didn't take long for me to decide that I loved the stars, too. There's just something about the mystery of the sky—how it stretches on for miles and miles, leading to other planets and places bigger than our home. It makes the worries of life seem a bit smaller and less significant. At least for a time.

"I'm not going to be here much longer, Reyna. I can feel it in my bones." Grandmommy's voice strained, her eyes brimming with tears. "My body's tired and longs to go home. To live among the stars." Her head sank onto the thin pillow.

I need you—the words formed on my quivering lips, but no sound came out.

"Every time you look to the sky, think of me. I'll be out there somewhere, floating above the clouds." She closed her eyes. Her yellowed teeth peeked out from behind her chapped lips, and she smiled like she was picturing somewhere magnificent in her mind's eye. "It's a beautiful place," she whispered.

Her eyes blinked open and she turned to look at me. I broke into sobs as I clenched the journal and held it tightly to my chest.

"Don't weep, my dear," she croaked. "My love for you will never fade. It's like a cord that tethers our hearts together. Even if you can't see me or hear me, we're still connected." She reached for me with a shaky hand. "Anytime you feel lonely, just look to the stars. You'll feel my love tugging at your heart from the other end of the cord."

Salty tears spilled down my cheeks. I shut my eyes, hoping to hold them back, but not even a twenty-foot wall like the one towering around our complex could bar them behind my lids.

Grandmommy's hand went limp and slid off my knee. Silence filled the room—no more labored breathing or gargled coughing. Her mouth hung open, and her eyes went dull.

She was gone.

That was the day I learned what it felt like for a person's heart to break. Sharp pain penetrated my chest and squeezed my head. I screamed and cried until the nurses finally came to take my grandmother's lifeless body away. The women, faceless in their hazmat suits, wrapped her in a much fresher sheet than the one she had used to catch her own vomit only moments before.

I balled my fists and swung my bony arms, begging them not to take her—not to take Grandmommy. But they operated like robots, completely immune to my cries.

"I'll remember! I promise! I'll remember!" The words scratched my throat as Grandmommy was carried out of our one-room bunker. "I love you beyond the stars," I whispered, my final farewell as the metal door slammed shut, sealing me inside.

I try to forget what happens next, but my mind won't let me. That's what it's like when you lose the only person you ever had the chance of loving. Your last moments together sear your mind like a government brand burnt into your skin. These memories are like that for me— vivid, like I'm reliving the past all over again.

Muffled voices spoke outside the door. Certain words surfaced in their sentences.

"... she's contaminated ... her assignment ... Bunker 112 ..."

Panic gripped my chest when I realized they were talking about me, trying to figure out what to do with me. It was against the rules to let minors live on their own. It didn't matter that I learned how to fend for myself when Grandmommy was bedridden. As a seven-year-old orphan, I wouldn't even be given the chance to state my case before the Commander. My fate was decided for me.

The bunker door squeaked open. I tucked Grandmommy's journal inside my oversized uniform just before another gaggle of nurses barged in. The swarm swept me from my home, through the bustled courtyard, and down an unfamiliar hospital corridor. They stripped me of everything: clothes, possessions, hope. I craned my head and watched my old jumpsuit, and my brand-new journal, disappear in the opposite direction. My throat clenched. I wanted to scream, but the weight of loss muted me.

The team of nurses rushed me through the decontamination process, ushering me into a shower. Warm water misted my bare skin, followed by a shock of cold. Goose bumps prickled my arms and legs. My teeth chattered. But I didn't care. All I could think about was Grandmommy and how I managed to lose her journal.

The nurses dressed me in a crisp cargo uniform and yanked my long brown hair into a braid. I was fitted with a new pair of shoes and handed a package of nutritional crackers to munch on. The dry wafers got stuck in my throat and made me gag. I don't know why I bothered to eat them. Feeding my rumbling stomach was the furthest thing from my mind.

A nurse gave me a small tin cup filled with water. I took a sip, but flashes of Grandmommy's cracked lips stopped me from swallowing. I spat the water right back out into the cup.

The siege of nurses subsided, leaving only one to escort me to the Medical Center's front entrance. She was much younger than the rest, thin and scrawny with hair as black as the night sky. From the looks of her, she was probably just assigned a permanent position at the hospital after aging out of school. Her smile wasn't hardened yet by years of working with the sick and dying.

Soldiers waited for me near the doors, but before we reached the entryway, my chaperone dragged me behind the lobby desk. She crouched, eyes shifting as she reached inside her uniform.

"I think this belongs to you," the kind nurse whispered. A leather-bound journal winked from behind her white coat. I gasped with relief. She put a finger against her mask, hooked a pen on the journal's binding, and tucked my treasured book inside my new jumpsuit. I should have said, "Thank you," but I just stood there wordless, blinking away tears.

The nurse gave my hand a squeeze, then stood. Masked and expressionless, she led me to the foyer. Before I knew it, half a dozen soldiers surrounded me, their dark green uniforms striking against the bleached backdrop of the medical center. I recognized the stern posture of the woman at the front of their formation: the Warden.

The Warden was a woman with broad shoulders and a serious face. Her dark hair, uncapped and wound into a tight bun, sat at the nape of her neck. The smell of her boot polish stung my nostrils. With her chin held high, the Warden stared down the bridge of her nose, examining me with hollow eyes. I held her gaze as long as I could before redirecting my gaze to the floor.

The soldiers shoved me through the hospital doors and onto the gravel of the barracks' quadrangle. I shielded my eyes from the setting sun, fiery red over the edge of the concrete wall.

I glanced beyond my entourage, intrigued by movement in the courtyard. Remnants from the morning ceremony scattered the ground: a pathetic display of paper confetti and cheap red ribbons. A banner adorned with the numbers "1-0-0" waved in the stale breeze.

"One hundred years of prison," the guard beside me scoffed.

It just so happens that Grandmommy died on Remembrance Day—the same day we're expected to celebrate human existence despite the Last War. That poorly painted sign was hung to commemorate one hundred years of survival at the Omega Compound, but if you ask most people in the Southern Sector, there's nothing celebratory about living trapped behind concrete walls for an entire century, when most of us are just barely living, getting by on measly rations and hiding from acid rain. Besides, Remembrance Day only reminds me that Grandmommy's gone, that *she* didn't survive.

I take a break from my memories and remember where I am, sitting in the middle of the classroom, suffering through one of Professor Diaz's presentations. His slideshow skips to a collage of water sources. The images look dated, like they were taken before the Last War. I can tell because there's greenery in the scenes, and I'm pretty sure grass hasn't existed in the last century.

I hear a yawn from the boy behind me—Walter Cane, the Commander's son. His feet kick my chair when he stretches his legs, and I have to grit my teeth to keep myself from saying something stupid.

Walter was there in the courtyard ten years ago on the day Grandmommy died. The thought of it thrusts me back into the scene, and once again I'm reliving my own Remembrance Day. I can still see the Commander standing with his family beneath that banner with the poorly painted numbers.

Commander Cane stood dressed in his freshly pressed suit. He shook hands with a man sporting a dark blue jumper and a matching beret. Even at a distance, I recognized the dispatch rider's uniform. His stiff cap set him apart from the barracks guards. An air shipment had arrived. My stomach growled at the thought of food. The sight of his blue cap promised a morning meal, a shred of hope, but Grandmommy hadn't lived to see it.

A cluster of men wheeled tall wooden crates through the quadrangle as the dispatch rider held out a clipboard to the Commander. Commander Cane scrawled a signature, then looped his wife's arm through his. Mrs. Cane was a beautifully figured woman with an appalling fashion sense. Her ruby-red cheeks clashed with the bright purple dress that ruffled loosely to the ground.

My lips curled in disgust, and my face flushed with anger. Grandmommy died on a dirty sheet, and this woman had the gall to paint her face and trip over a garment worth enough to feed the whole compound.

Beside the portentous couple, a boy around my age kicked at loose gravel. With an exaggerated punt, a wayward cloud of dust coated Mrs. Cane's dress. The Commander scolded his son. Taking hold of his arm, he dragged Walter further into the Northern Sector. His embarrassed wife brushed her fabric clean, then followed suit, escorted by a team of guards.

Witnessing the dysfunctional interactions between the Commander and his family only intensified the sting of my loss. It wasn't fair. Walter Cane had his parents. He had clean clothes. He had food. He had a warm, clean bed. I sniffled and clenched my seven-year-old heart, holding back sobs.

Boots stomped the dirt in a rigid march, pushing me forward, kicking dust into my lungs. I coughed, unnoticed, and kept walking, silently counting my footsteps to keep the grief at bay.

Since Grandmommy and I occupied a bunker in the Southern Section, I was only vaguely familiar with the paths on the northern end of the barracks. Soon, a familiar structure came into view. I recognized the large rectangular building as the Mess Hall at the center of the compound. The tunnels connecting it to the Education Center made it easily identifiable. From there, the guards led me into the familiar southern side of the complex. My shoulders relaxed a bit with the feeling of home, but it was short-lived. Another wave of sorrow hit me when the guards pushed past my old bunker and crossed into the unfamiliar Forgotten Zone. We walked by several scattered bunkers until we came to the very edge of the barracks.

Shadow bathed the ground in gray, and I ventured a glance skyward. Above the caps of the soldiers, towering walls of concrete stretched into starless black. I tried to feel Grandmommy's love tugging on my heart, but all I could feel was a heavy tightness burning in my chest. I shrank. Without her at my side, the confines of the walls seemed infinitely more constrictive.

The soldiers parted, revealing a small concrete shelter with a metal hatch door. The numbers "1-1-2," painted in red, glared at me from the entrance. This was my new home: Bunker 112.

The Warden opened the door, and stale, warm air puffed into my face. The musty smell mimicked the scent of my family's bunker across the compound, but the similarity didn't bring me comfort. This wasn't my *real* home, and it never would be. I held my breath.

The Warden saluted and dismissed the soldiers. When they disappeared and their footsteps faded, the Warden's shoulders drooped. She relaxed onto one knee and addressed me, face to face.

"Sage." The Warden called me by my surname, my dead father's name. "This world wasn't made for the weak. Only survivors," she cautioned sternly. "You have to be strong now. You *have* to survive."

The Warden spoke stiffly, as if I were older, forgetting that I was only a child who had just lost her grandmother. I balled my fists, sniffled, and, trying desperately not to cry, locked eyes with the heartless woman. But I couldn't hold it in. I released my grip and sobbed. The Warden stood and, with a heavy hand on my shoulder, nudged me through the door.

I was crying so hard I could barely see. I squinted through my tears and surveyed the room with blurry vision. A single bulb swinging from the ceiling provided enough light to bring my surroundings into focus.

In the far right corner of the room, a mirror hung over a full metal wash sink. A knee-high concrete block sat to its side. I spotted the hole on top and knew right away that that's where I was expected to do my business.

I counted six cots in the bunker: two on the right wall, two on the left wall, and two stacked at the back of the room. That's when I first laid eyes on Erika. The stocky girl sat on the edge of the bed furthest to the left. Her unwelcoming, furrowed brow peeked through the middle part of her brunette hair. I averted my gaze and forced down my remaining sobs. She seemed to disapprove of them, and I didn't want to make matters worse by blubbering over my dead grandmother.

Another girl with a tiny frame, bright blonde hair, and a scarred face hung from the ladder attached to the bunk beds in the back. She released her grip on the ladder to wave at me, but lost her balance. She teetered for a moment, but managed to right herself before falling. A third girl with tight black curls snored on the cot closest to the door. Her glasses fogged on every exhale. Only the three occupied cots were made up with sheets and a blanket. The other three mattresses remained bare.

"Make yourself comfortable, Sage." The Warden plopped bedding into my arms and nodded toward the naked cots.

"Lights off within the hour. Try to get some sleep." The Warden stalked out of the bunker, leaving all four of us completely unsupervised.

That's when I learned that some rules don't apply in the Forgotten Zone.

I stared at the hard metal hatch until the gears of the door clicked into place, locking us in for the night. Spinning slowly, I surveyed the empty beds. Erika scowled, warning me not to get too close, so I avoided the left side of the room.

"Hey." The small blonde girl waved me toward the back. "You can share the bunk with me." She climbed down the ladder, took the bedding from my hands, and, without waiting for an answer, began fixing the linens on the bottom bunk.

"I'm Gertrude," she said, "but you can call me Geri." Gertrude grinned, proudly showing off her missing front teeth. She pulled the fitted sheet taut against the mattress. "What's your name?"

"Reyna." My voice cracked as I spoke. "Reyna Sage."

"Reyna," Gertrude repeated while smoothing out the starch blanket. "Reminds me of sun rays. I like that."

Gertrude pushed the stray strands of hair away from her face, giving me a better view of the rippled scar across her cheek. It looked like melted plastic, like her face had been set on fire.

"I think that's what I'll call you." Gertrude smiled contentedly. "Rey."

I forced a smile, then flicked my eyes to the girl on the left side of the room, wondering if she had noticed.

Gertrude giggled. "That's Erika. You'll get used to her." Her voice dropped to a whisper. "She's actually pretty nice." She winked and flashed another toothless smile before shimmying up the ladder, disappearing from sight. "Welcome to Bunker 112. I think you'll like it here."

Despite my new friend's hospitality, that was the loneliest night of my life. I missed the warm touch of Grandmommy's brittle hands, the soothing sounds of her lullabies, the subtle sweetness of her scent—soap flakes and sweat, the lingering aroma of a long day's work at the washhouse.

The single bulb extinguished, and the room went dark. I fumbled onto the squeaky bed and pulled the blankets up to my neck. Clutching the journal in my hands, I sniveled myself to sleep.

Blackness overtook my vision, erasing images of the worst day of my life, but my heart still longed for Grandmommy. I could feel it groping in the dark, trying desperately to find the edge of her cord, the one she said would keep us connected even after she was gone.

And that's when it happened.

A spark seared the void of my slumber. Vibrant colors banished sleep's habitual darkness. I dreamt—actually dreamt—of a meadow blanketed in radiant, purple flowers. The cone-shaped petals whistled a lilting tune, and the wind's dance conducted the choir. Their harmonies filled my ears and poured out of my mouth as I sang along. I didn't need to be taught their song. It came to me instinctually, as if I'd been singing it my whole life.

Laughter joined the choir from beyond the meadow. The chortle belonged to a figure running toward me: a stunning woman with radiant skin and floating, translucent hair. Light refracted from her in every direction as she emanated health and beauty.

"Meet me here," the voice soothed, reverberating around me.

My jaw dropped. I knew that voice. It was Grandmommy. She looked nothing like she did when she died. She was youthful. Her teeth were dazzling white and her cheeks were plump, but it was undoubtedly her. The same kindness shone from her now-iridescent eyes, no longer muddied in color, but clear and glowing. She was happy, and she was free.

When I woke up, the bunker was dark, and soft snores filled the room. I hugged the journal to my chest and snatched the pen from its spine. Through the hours that followed, I scribbled out every detail I could remember about that dream. This was the place Grandmommy talked about—the place beyond the stars.

Geri forces a handkerchief into my hands. The gesture snaps me from my memories.

"Here," she whispers.

I dab my eyes in the dim light of the classroom, thankful for the soft cloth against my cheeks. I lost my handkerchief while working at the washhouse last week. It must have fallen out of my pocket and into a pile of dirty clothes when I wasn't looking. I've tried using scraps of material to wipe sweat, tears, and snot from my face, but the itchy fabric only seems to make things worse.

Professor Diaz switches the projector slide. An illustration of molecules pulses on the wall. I wad the handkerchief and give it back to Geri.

"Keep it," she insists. "You need it more than I do."

She's probably right.

For the last ten years, Geri's been my greatest ally and confidant. I never have to explain myself to her, elaborate on why some days are harder than others. She just gets me. And she's the only one who knows about my dreams.

Some nights, I still see blackness, like everyone else. I didn't even know I was different until I started talking to Geri about what I saw while asleep. She looked at me and crossed her eyes like I had two heads growing out of my neck. We started asking around discreetly, trying to discover if anyone else saw things in the night. As it turns out, I'm the only one.

It's a shame, though, because dreaming makes living a little bit easier. It's a chance to experience a world much different than the one I see while I'm awake. Most days I can't wait to go to sleep, hoping for another chance to witness Grandmommy spinning and laughing the way she always wanted to when she was ill and alive.

I swipe a fresh tear from my cheek as Professor Diaz flips the lights on in the lecture hall, officially forcing me back into reality. I slide down into my chair as I try to go unnoticed. The clock above the doorway steadily ticks;

only ten more minutes left before we're dismissed for lunch.

I lick the salty film from my lips, and my stomach growls on cue. The only thing better than not getting called on in class would be an edible meal. And the only thing better than that would be to visit my dream world tonight. Unfortunately, none of those things are guaranteed.

I duck my head as Professor Diaz paces the floor, scanning the classroom, looking for his next victim. His hands grasp the lapels of his corduroy vest like he's worried it's about to fly away. The tap of his shoes on the linoleum floor makes my heart race. My breath catches when he stops in front of Lucile and stares down my row.

"Of the four purification processes we've looked into today, which one would be most suitable for use on the compound?" he asks.

My eyes wander around the room, trying to find something else to look at. If I make eye contact with the professor, he's bound to call my name.

"Reyna?"

It didn't work.

I shift in my chair and white knuckle the seat. A tingling sensation prickles my fingers, making them go numb. My face flames, and I feel like I can't breathe. I wasn't listening to his lecture, not well enough to fabricate an answer.

"I, uh—"

"Professor?" Geri raises her hand, cutting me off.

"Yes, Gertrude?" He averts his gaze from me and looks toward my best friend.

"I'm just curious. Would any of these filtration systems be suitable enough to make our rainwater drinkable?"

"That's a very good question." The professor strokes his thick beard and resumes his pacing.

I exhale with relief and mouth "thank you" to Geri.

She smiles, the paled scar tissue on her face wrinkling her features. Just a few months ago, she decided to take a pair of scissors to her hair, cutting off a chunk of blonde above her ear. She used my shaving razor to shear the remaining stubble from her skin, forming a bald spot around her temple. She looked terrifying when she finished. In a good way—the way you'd expect a brave soldier to look after fighting in combat, especially with the blood dripping from the nicks she made on her scalp while finagling with my blade.

An inch of new growth now covered the self-inflicted battle wounds, but Geri parted the remaining long hair away from her face to showcase the old scar on her cheek. She called it her "best side" whenever somebody would ask her about it. Geri didn't always like talking about her past, but displaying her burn marks proudly was her stubborn way of making sure no one forgot about the awful explosion that killed her parents.

"To my knowledge, the highly concentrated acidic quality of the rain would make it resistant to distillation and filtration. We would most likely need to neutralize the contaminated water before attempting purification." Professor Diaz pauses with a finger over his chin. A far-off stare coats his eyes as he looks straight over our heads, mulling over an idea. "If I can find a way to safely collect a sample, perhaps we'll seize the opportunity to find out." He inhales. "However"—a sly smile flashes under his mustache, and he presses his open palms together—"I've heard rumors that there's a possibility of a decrease in chemical rain. There's even a theory that fresh water could fall in our region within the year." His eyes beam as he delivers the news.

The classroom roars. Students on both sides of me are gasping and cheering. I rest my chin on my fist and keep staring at the clock, wishing time would go faster. The potential of clean rain doesn't interest me. This isn't the first time Professor Diaz has sprung the idea on us, and it won't be the last. I'm still waiting for the day they call us to run outside and splash in puddles. Until then, I won't be getting my hopes up.

"What's the point in telling us if you can't prove the theory's true?"

Walter Cane's breath runs over my neck. I lean to the left to avoid another gust of hot air.

"You assume there has to be a point, Walter," Professor Diaz counters, and all the whooping and hollering turns into hushed murmurs.

Walter scoffs. "Don't you always have some kind of hidden agenda?" His salty remark prompts snickers from my classmates and paints a narrowed look on Professor Diaz's face.

I tap my finger on my desk, itching to get out of the classroom, wishing Walter could go just one period without causing a ruckus.

"Can anyone here answer Walter's question?" Professor Diaz addresses the room. "What's the point?" His inquiry sounds rhetorical to me, and no one answers, so I guess everyone else is assuming the same.

"What's the point in any of this?" Professor Diaz raises both hands into the air.

I roll my eyes and shake my head. *Three more minutes.*

"What is our purpose here on the Omega Compound?" Professor Diaz drawls each word as he speaks.

"Nothing," Walter answers him again.

I wish he would shut up. He's addicted to hearing his own voice, though—starved for attention and always making a scene. Real consequences never follow his actions, so he just keeps right on doing whatever he wants. And that's just one of the benefits of being the Commander's son. I'm almost positive he's never had to eat any of the slop they call "meals" down at the Mess Hall. One glance and it's obvious he's not as malnourished as the rest of us. He's taller, stronger, and sturdier.

Bitterness rolls in my stomach as I catch him stretching his neck in my peripheral vision. Just the sight of him makes me angry.

"Expound on your answer." The corners of Professor Diaz's mustache twitch upward with what I think is an amused grin.

"Does it really need more explanation?" Walter sneers. "Come on. Isn't it obvious? Every other base within the United Regime has something to research: technology, architectural advancement, biochemistry, epidemiology, botany." He counts each example on his fingers. "There's environmental sciences, nutritional sciences, reproductive sciences, animal sciences, and even studies perfecting weapons and warfare going on everywhere else but here. We don't even get the same technology as everyone else. You know why? Because we're last. Worthless. Sorry, Professor, but there's no purpose for us here."

Walter crashes into his seat and out of my line of sight, knocking into my chair on his way back down. I clench my jaw and bite my tongue. *Two more minutes.*

Professor Diaz brushes his vest and places his hands in the pockets of his matching slacks. "You've made some interesting points, Walter." He sighs.

Interesting? My eyebrows scrunch together. *Please.* There's nothing interesting about stating the facts. Anyone who's had the pleasure of living the extent of their sorry existence on the Omega Compound knows it's true. We're an afterthought. That's why rations are always so low. While every other base has its fill, we get leftovers. Scraps. I'm actually surprised the United Regime hasn't completely cut off our supplies, leaving all of us here to fend for ourselves.

"But"—Professor Diaz inhales—"I'm afraid I'm going to have to disagree with you." He strolls over to his desk and picks up the decorative flowerpot.

Here we go. I hold my breath. The professor already used the cobalt ceramic vase as a visual during a previous lesson. He has a habit of comparing life to random inanimate objects.

I exhale. He takes his allegorical analogies so seriously.

One more minute.

"Take this vessel, for example."

I was right.

He holds the painted pot up for the entire class to see. "Without something to hold, it seems completely useless. However, if we dare to think beyond the obvious, that this is an empty and seemingly useless vessel, we can find its purpose."

He tilts the pot upside down, emphasizing its emptiness, but he's lost me. All I can think about is how empty my stomach is without food and how hollow my heart feels without Grandmommy.

Professor Diaz delicately places the pot down on the metal desktop, careful not to chip its edges. It is, after all, an artifact from before the Last War. If I remember correctly, Professor Diaz dated it back to the late 1900s. Apparently floral patterns on chinoiserie blue were all the rage back then.

He lifts a finger into the air. "The purpose of this vessel isn't found in what it holds, but rather, in what it preserves. History. Culture. Craftsmanship." Professor Diaz looks beyond me, locking eyes with Walter. "To understand, you'd have to be willing to look beyond the obvious."

Walter huffs behind me, and the dismissal buzzer rings.

Finally.

I slide off my seat and fall in line behind Geri as Professor Diaz attempts to corral a room full of hungry teenagers toward the exit. Walter steps on the heel of my boot as he pushes past me to the professor's desk. I groan loud enough for him to hear, but all he offers as an apology is a smug grin on his dumb face. He's probably staying after class because he's itching to get the last word in with Professor Diaz. His lack of urgency to leave confirms my theory about meal times, too. That and I've never actually seen him eating in the cafeteria with the rest of us. None of the Canes ever do.

My lip curls in disgust, and I turn to follow my peers to the Mess Hall. Two guards silently lead us from the classroom, through the long, windowless corridor that connects the Education Center to the large refectory. I wish for a glimpse of the sky, to feel Grandmommy tugging on our cord, but all I see is concrete.

The guards open the cafeteria doors at the end of the tunnel, and I follow Geri to our assigned seats. All of the adults are grouped according to their vocations. We pass by sections for electricians, plumbers, and mechanics. I spot a group of seamstresses gathered in the corner. That's where I'll sit when I turn eighteen. Most students join their families, but the orphaned kids, we get our own tables. One for the girls and one for the boys. Only two boys sit at the table next to us—a skinny kid from the middle grade and a quiet boy from our class who lost his mom last week. The edges of his eyes are still puffy from crying when he thought no one else was watching.

Me and the girls from Bunker 112 plop down in front of our pre-filled lunch trays. Today's menu consists of a questionably gray slice of meatloaf and gelatin squares of mashed fruits and vegetables. The food smells like it was cooked over the latrine, but I'm too hungry to care. I snatch the fork from my tray and gnaw into the meatloaf. The salt burns my tongue, so I guzzle my water to wash it down.

"The smell is absolutely rancid." Lucile gags from across the table. "It looks like vomit." She pokes at the meat with a grimace so wide the entire Northern Sector could see it. To no one's surprise, she's the only one at our table who's not eating. "I don't think I can eat this."

I know what vomit looks like, and I beg to differ. Plus, the mystery meat holds its rectangular shape no matter how hard I wiggle it. And, I know from experience that isn't an attribute associated with regurgitated food.

"If you're waiting for special treatment, you'll die of starvation first," Erika retorts. "Just shut up and eat."

"We don't even know what this stuff is!" Lucile shrieks.

I swivel my head to see if anyone's watching.

"Shh!" Veronica hushes with a nervous laugh. "You're going to make a scene."

"Maybe Lu should join Walter for lunch," I mumble under my breath.

Geri elbows me in the ribs. "Claudette probably knows what's in it," she says with a grin. "Don't you, Laud?"

"I try not to think about it." Claudette closes her eyes and takes another bite. Her glasses slip down her nose while she's chewing. She swallows hard and sips her water. "If I can somehow convince myself that our nutritional needs outweigh the corollary of synthetically created vitamins and unnatural hormones, then this slop doesn't seem so bad."

"Great." Lucile pushes her tray away. "Now I'll never eat again."

I shake my head and take another bite. I think the green stuff is mashed peas, but I can't tell for certain.

"Lu." Geri reaches across the table and puts her hand on Lucile's arm. "I know this stuff reeks, but can you at least try it? Who knows when we'll eat next. Plug your nose and swallow it whole if you have to." Geri nudges the tray back toward Lucile. She's half the size of Lucile when they're standing side by side, but Geri always takes on a mothering role with the whiner. She does that for the rest of us, too, come to think of it, always making sure we're taking care of ourselves.

Lucile winces, plugs her nose, and scarfs down a generous helping of green gelatin.

The group starts joking about the United Regime's recipe book, but I'm not listening. My thoughts keep fading back to Grandmommy.

"You're being awfully quiet." Geri waves her hand in front of my face. "Got a lot on your mind?"

"I guess." I shrug, then slurp down the last morsel of red gelatin.

She pats my hand and whispers, "Well, if you ever need a listening ear, I'm here."

"Thanks," I mutter.

It's not that I don't want to talk to Geri about how much I've been missing Grandmommy, I just don't want to do it in the cafeteria in front of everyone else. Remembrance Day is next week, and my grief always seems to peak around the holiday. I've cried enough already today, and I don't need to trigger another sobbing session right now.

Geri gives me a look that says she understands, and we finish our lunches in silence before splitting up for our evening work assignments. I head down to the washhouse with the other second-shifters and punch my time card through the ancient machine hanging near the door.

"Reyna?"

I hear Robin call my name from across the dark, steamy room.

"Do you mind giving me a hand?" Robin uses the end of her apron to wipe the sweat from her forehead. She's expecting a baby and has a hard enough time waddling through the washhouse on her own without carrying a basket full of linens. To be honest, she spends more time holding her stomach up than folding clothes these days.

I help haul her basket to the nearest wash station and unload the sheets onto a table where she can press them with an iron. She thanks me with a smile before I head over to do my own work. I'm on soaking duty today. I boil soiled uniforms in a vat full of recycled water, wring the clothes on a metal washboard, and hang them on a wire to dry before collecting the excess water to use again for the next load.

Sometimes when I'm working, I like to imagine the washhouse as a scene from my dream world. I frolic through verdant groves as my hand dives into uniform soup. Rusting water pails transform into clear, glittering ponds brimming with sapphires and rubies. I pluck treasure after treasure from the depths and haul each one to the shore to be polished.

I'm finishing my last load when I decide to check on Robin one more time before my shift ends. I walk up to her table and see her chatting with another woman. Robin holds out a folded piece of paper and discreetly guides it into the other woman's hands. The recipient dashes the note into her apron and scurries off.

"What's that all about?" I ask, raising an eyebrow.

"Oh." Robin blushes and smooths a hand over her swollen belly. "Just catching up with a friend." She smiles. "Did you need something?"

"No," I say, sounding skeptical. "I was coming over to see if *you* did."

She places a fitted sheet, perfectly squared, into the adjacent pile and purses her lips. "I don't think so. That was my last one."

"Alright, then." I scan her up and down. "I'll see you tomorrow."

"Right. See you tomorrow," she says in a hurry.

I turn around and walk off slowly, occasionally glancing over my shoulder to see if she's doing anything else suspicious. After I clock out, the guard manning the front station lets me go home without a chaperone. It isn't unusual for the evening guards to permit some of us to walk alone. They know that if we don't head straight to our bunkers and miss lockdown, we'll wind up spending the night in the barracks quadrangle. And if getting stuck in the freezing cold wasn't annoying enough, there's always the potential for an acid shower.

I skid my feet in the gravel, keeping a slow pace to admire the sunset. Streaks of lavender paint the sky, accompanied by strokes of fuchsia and electric orange. It's a nice break from the bleak monochrome of the base. I pause for a moment to take in the view and let the warmth of the sun settle on my cheeks. I can feel Grandmommy tugging on my cord, and for a moment I see her figure twirling with the clouds.

The sun disappears behind the wall, and my eyes widen, flecks of light still dancing on my pupils. If I don't hurry, I'll be spending the night outside. And while I don't mind sneaking off to stargaze, I'd rather it be *my* idea.

I hurry my pace and jog the last few miles to the Forgotten Zone. The cyan sky is already fading into black. I hold my breath and reach for the hatch door, then release the hoarded air with a puff when the handle turns. Clunks from the lock mechanism clicking into place rattle the door right after I slam it shut.

"Look who finally decided to show up," Erika jeers.

"Did I miss roll call?" I ask, already knowing the answer.

"The Warden definitely marked you absent, Rey." Veronica rolls over in her cot, her blankets muffling her words. "I wouldn't be surprised if you're put on wall duty in the morning."

My heart sinks. I hate wall duty. After a century of patching the barricade, you'd think the higher-ups would have devised a better way to repair the holes. Alas, insubordinates like me get the pleasure of mixing plaster and pasting it on the broken concrete. It's a tedious job and as boring as a broomstick.

I wash the sweat off my face and dampen my long brown hair in the sputtering sink. The lights cut out while I'm undressing. I grope in the dark for my bedframe and flop down on the lumpy mattress. My whole body aches with sores from scrubbing dirty clothes at the washhouse for nearly half the day.

"Psst, Rey, you still awake?"

I can't see her, but I'm almost certain Geri's swinging her head over the top railing. I moan to let her know I'm listening.

"I've been thinking about Professor Diaz's metaphor, and how he compared Omega to an artifact …"

"Ugh," I groan as I turn on my pillow.

"Well, I think I get it now." She pauses, waiting for me to respond, but I don't want to. She starts again anyway. "We might not be a special research facility, but what if our purpose here is just to preserve the simplicity of human nature?"

"I think you're overthinking this one, Geri." I pull the blankets higher. My eyes are starting to close.

"But what if that's the point—to protect humanity in its purest form?"

She's rambling now, and I can hardly concentrate. My stiff muscles relax into the stiffer cot, and my exhausted mind surrenders to sleep. My last conscious thought is a simple plea: to dream of Grandmommy.

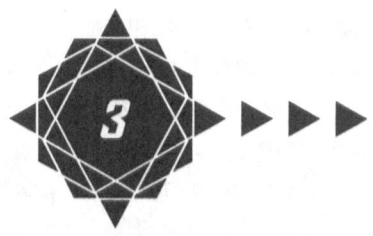

3

My eyes flutter closed, and a solid backdrop of black overtakes my vision. The next thing I know, I'm sitting among blades of iridescent grass swirling around my feet like emerald ribbons. I've been to this place before, but I can never remember how I got here. That seems to be the case with dreams. It's really hard to know when or how they start.

The tiny plants tickle my bare toes with their fuzzy texture, and when they brush together, giggles echo off their edges. They're not teasing me, but sometimes I think they find my human nature amusing. It's probably because my body's more rigid and a lot less colorful than just about everything in this world.

A breeze zigzags through the pasture, carving geometric patterns into the greenery. It runs over the rolling hills in the distance, triggering another burst of laughter from the playful field along the way. I lay on a bed of grass among the bioluminescent blooms and look at the sky overhead. There's no clouds, only stars. It's like I'm floating in outer space with planets orbiting above my head. The super giants spin with ease, showing off their rings and vibrant colors.

I suck in air. The atmosphere is different here, too. A sweet, flowery scent fills my nostrils, and I release the clench of my jaw. There's no tension in my neck, either. I feel safe. It's the feeling I imagine having being a part of a close-knit family, when everyone's watching out for one another. No one's judging me or pointing out my flaws. I don't have to worry about being prim or proper. All I have to do is exist. That's how the meadow welcomes me—like a homecoming.

The wind whistles a wholesome tune as it ripples over glowing flowers, occasionally tugging on my hair like it wants to play. But I keep watching the planets dancing overhead, until someone leans in front of my face, blocking my view. Grandmommy smiles. Her rounded cheeks shimmer, and her diamond eyes sparkle while the wind whips her translucent hair backward.

"You came!" She's giddy with excitement, extending her arms for an embrace.

I scurry to my feet and hold her tightly. Her body molds to mine, pliable yet solid. Touching her is like sticking my hands in gelatin, but without the horrible odor. Grandmommy smells sweeter than candy. Her skin is warm, smooth, and transparent. If I were awake, the sight of her would make me scream, but unusual things seem natural in this world.

I can see her circulatory system bending and twisting through her body, forming intricate designs that loop into fancy calligraphy. Grandmommy says the Great Morning Star kissed her and bent her veins into stories—all the accounts of her entire life since the dawn of Creation. Sometimes I stare at the tubes and try to decipher what they're saying, but no matter how long I look, the foreign language never makes any sense. She told me only the Great Morning Star can interpret their true meaning.

My eyes follow the cardiovascular cursive to the glowing orb floating in her chest. If she were human, I'd call it a heart, but it seems to do a lot more than pump blood through her body. Every time Grandmommy feels something different, the orb pulses with color. It's yellow right now, which means she's happy to see me.

"My, you've grown," she gasps.

I shake my head a little at the remark. From where I'm standing, she looks to be about my age. Not a wrinkle or a blemish can be found on her face. Her see-through skin is flawless.

Grandmommy cups my cheeks. A tingling sensation shoots through my jaw and travels down my arms. Tiny flickers spew from her fingers, throwing sparkles into the air. A gust of wind picks up the flakes of light and disperses them into the meadow. The joyful blades titter in response.

She beams, her whole face glittering. "Let's watch the sunrise." The core at her center swirls with a hue that makes me think of the artificial carrot puree included in last week's rations.

"Okay." I nod. I'm glad she doesn't ask about life back home. I don't want to waste any time talking about the barracks during our all-too-brief visit.

She tugs me to follow her toward the hills. Her feet hover over the ground as she floats gracefully to our destination. I try to keep up, making the grass giggle with every step.

When we crest the hill, I'm huffing for air. I lean my hands on my knees, trying to catch my breath. Grandmommy's not winded in the slightest. She motions for me to look in the distance. I can see the Great Morning Star peaking over the horizon. It's about a million times bigger than the sun, and considerably brighter. I have to squint and shield my eyes, but even with my hand over my brow, I can still feel its light burning into my corneas. Grandmommy's crystal eyes must filter light differently than mine because she doesn't have to protect them from the Great Morning Star's intensity. She just stands there, grinning from ear to ear, waiting for the massive ball of fire to fully emerge.

Solid pillars of light erupt over the skyline and stretch over the meadow. If real sunbeams extended like that, like poles over the earth, they would ignite everything in their path. The Great Morning Star's rays, though, don't set anything on fire. Instead, they mesmerize the meadow with their light, causing the long grass and tall flowers to bend in humble servitude. Even the planets hanging in the sky seem to sway in submission. Grandmommy, too. She drops to her knees and bows. I do the same. I'm afraid that if I don't, I'll get burnt to a crisp.

My hands start to tremble as the elongated columns of light grow closer. They creep through the valley and curve up the hill. I wince and turn as it passes, bracing myself for an unpleasant collision, but nothing horrible happens. I don't even feel heat. I spin around and see that while I was cowering away, a beam of light lanced Grandmommy's chest. My jaw drops and my eyes widen, but Grandmommy's smile only widens.

"Does it hurt?" I ask, grimacing at the sight. The front half of the long beam tethers her to the Great Morning Star. The other side is growing out of her back. The rays aren't as difficult to look at as their source, but they still make my eyes sting. A low hum reverberates from the shaft, causing Grandmommy's orb to vibrate, rippling her heart-sphere with waves of rainbow color.

"No." She closes her eyes and tilts her head upward, still flashing her toothy grin.

I wait for her to tell me what it *does* feel like.

"It feels like birth."

I don't know what she means by that. The only thing I know about giving birth is that it hurts—a lot. Anytime Claudette comes back from a shift at the maternity ward, she's shaken up from watching the mothers groan with labor pangs. According to Laud, they grit their teeth and dig their nails into whatever, or whoever, is close enough to grip. One time, she came home with five little semicircle holes in her forearm to prove it.

Pain management isn't really something that's offered on the compound. At least, not anymore. Robin told me that Omega doctors used to be able to inject a regional anesthesia into the spine with a long needle to help with contractions, but most medicines stopped coming when the air-shipments slowed. Only necessary medications are in stock unless, of course, you're related to the Commander. Robin's not, so she's been working on mastering different breathing techniques to help her handle the pain when the time comes for her baby to be born.

I put Robin's techniques to use, sucking air through my nose and sending a burst of it soaring out of my mouth as Grandmommy's skin starts peeling back. She's molting. The fresh layer underneath is even brighter and shinier than the last, which I didn't even think was possible. Her old skin flakes off and disintegrates into a gold cloud of glitter.

Grandmommy stands and steps out of the sunray, and I'm looking at her cross-eyed. There's no hole. The beam didn't impale her. She's completely intact, and her orb is passionately drumming with multicolored rings. It looks a lot like a shrunken galaxy trapped in glass.

"Reyna, he wants to talk to you." Grandmommy's eyes shine like miniature versions of the Great Morning Star. She nudges me closer to the light. I want to reach out and touch the pillar that was just penetrating her chest, but my hands won't stop shaking.

I finally work up enough courage to inch into the light. My heart pummels the inside of my ribs, and the hair on my arms prickle as a rush of warmth consumes my body. My skin bubbles, but it doesn't burst open the way Grandmommy's did.

The low drone swells into a throng of a million voices. The sound floods my ears, and I'm not sure which voice to concentrate on. It makes me panic. I raise my hands to cover my ears, but it doesn't help. The voices are in my head, chattering in languages I can't understand.

"Everything's about to change." A deep, soft, and soothing voice emerges from the chaos. I hone in on it, using the voice as an anchor to steady my racing heart. "Reyna, I'm calling you out from where you reside. Come, look to the horizon."

Some invisible force lifts my chin, and I look directly at the Great Morning Star. To my surprise, the light doesn't hurt my eyes anymore, and I notice details I couldn't before. Swirls of fire lick the outer rim of the colossal globe. Under its incandescent surface, several spheres are spinning inside of each other, like a sun within a sun within a sun. I'm not completely certain, but I think I see something that resembles eyeballs outlining each one's border.

I gasp in awestruck horror and try to look away, free my trembling body from the star's hold, but I can't move. It's as if my sights are stuck, set on the Great Morning Star, entranced by its eccentric beauty.

"There's hope brimming, but you must be patient in the suffering. I will not cause pain without allowing something new to be born."

What's that supposed to mean? I try to ask, but the words get stuck on my tongue.

The Great Morning Star lifts higher into the sky, taking its light rays with it. As the beam at my chest travels upward, it surges through my neck and face, tingling my insides and rattling my brain. It rises above my head, and the multitude of voices dies down, returning to a low rumble.

Up above, the galaxies shift to accommodate the rising star, creating a hollow space in the sky for it to fill. The Great Morning Star settles in its place, and the lesser planets cocoon its massive celestial body, orbiting it in a choreographed dance.

I'm mesmerized, caught in a daze by the twisting and twirling planets. Grandmommy tugs at my shoulder, ripping me from my hypnotic state. "There's something I want to show you."

She grabs my shoulders and rotates my body away from the meadow. The new Grandmommy's just like the old one, always excited about adventures and treasures, and she's full of surprises.

A sprawling city of purified gold sits behind the horizon. Its borders stretch farther than the eye can see.

The polished walls sparkle in the light of the Great Morning Star. Joyous purples and hopeful pinks burble at Grandmommy's core as she guides me toward the golden city.

Grandmommy takes a few hovering steps, then grabs my hand and squeezes it tight. In an instant, the ground blurs beneath my feet, and we're shooting across the landscape without any strain or effort. We're moving so fast, I feel queasy. My throat sinks into my stomach, and my head spins with dizziness.

We come to an abrupt halt, and my esophagus bounces back into place, threatening to take my intestines with it. The city walls are mere inches from my face, their surface aflame with streaks of white fire. These flames burn cold, just like the beams extending from the Great Morning Star.

To my right, a massive rounded stone blocks the city's entrances. Colors swirl like an oil slick over the stone's pearlescent sheen. I swallow. The gate and surrounding walls are more than double the size of the barricade surrounding the base back home.

Grandmommy lets go of my hand and whispers something into the flames. They flicker in response, shifting into a shade of blue that matches her glowing center. Ripples of azure flames gurgle from the place she put her lips, and they rise over the top of the wall. I gather she sent a message to someone on the other side, because seconds later, two massive creatures fly over the flaming wall. The beasts swoop down, spreading their impressive wings to parachute beside us.

They look like lions, or at least what I'd imagine lions to look like. Professor Diaz showed us slides of them once when he taught a unit on extinct animals. The pictures he showed us from the African savannah were the strangest, especially the elephants with their oversized noses and floppy ears. The lions from the slides had fur covering their bodies and hairy manes surrounding their ferocious faces. These lions are wrapped in iridescent scales, and their manes are a mess of snowy plumage draping to the ground.

The beasts march to the edge of the gate, bow, and press their foreheads to the massive stone. Loud grinding bounces from the golden walls as they roll the large pearl away and reveal the city's entrance. A gushing waterfall of oil pours over the passageway. The two creatures flank the opening. They face each other, standing guard on either side of the amber cascade.

Grandmommy interlocks her fingers with mine. A shiver shoots up my arm, making the hairs on my neck stand straight up. She pulls me forward past the beasts. I can't help but stare into the jowls of the creature closest to me. Its teeth look like icicles dripping from its jaws. Its bright blue eyes are fixed ahead. Unflinching, the creature stays unwaveringly devoted to its post.

Without stopping, Grandmommy yanks me beneath the heavy cascade, and it coats my skin with a thick, slippery film. I hold my breath as we pass underneath the weight of the waterfall. Oil leaks into my eyes. It stings, but rubbing it away would be useless. Every inch of my body is covered in the slimy substance.

When we emerge on the other side, I'm ankle deep in water and sopping wet. I blink the droplets off my eyelashes. They crystallize and fall into the pool where lucid water mixes with dense oil. Golden bubbles bob on the surface. I use the back of my hand to wipe any remaining residue from my face and watch it sink to the bottom of the connecting current, mixing with the colorful gems that swivel underneath.

My eyes follow the river forward. Its path splits the city in half, flowing directly through its center. Houses made of solid wood stagger on either side of the stream. An assortment of greenery mingles with the cylinder buildings. Vines, heavy with fruit, twist up towers. Shrubs decorate doorposts. Leaves hang from rooftops. Everywhere I look, there's a garden full of ripe vegetables and blooming flowers. I take a deep breath, and a sweet perfume wafts to my nostrils and lingers in my lungs.

Multicolored residents circulate through the organic metropolis. A turquoise being with long raven hair holds a golden, woven basket by her waist. She pulls dark, rounded fruits from a nearby vine and hands them to her ruby companion. The man accepts her gift and bites into the luscious crop, juices spilling down his chiseled chin. More citizens weave through the city's ornamented structures, planting and gathering as they go. A green giant catches my eye and holds my attention. He's as tall as the buildings that surround him. An onyx wolf trots at his heels.

This city is incredible.

Grandmommy steps beside me. She rubs the oil on her body, and it absorbs into her transparent skin, dissolving into her bloodstream.

"Where are we?" I ask.

"*This* is the City of Life." She motions forward. "I'm taking you to the Source."

"The source of what?"

Grandmommy laughs and steps deeper into the river. "Come on," she beckons.

"I can't swim," I call out to her, but she just keeps moving ahead. The water's up to her waist now.

"Can't we walk?"

She peers over her shoulder. "Where we're going, we can't get there on foot."

The water claims her shoulders. Her hair sways with the current. I tread after her, kicking against the undertow. My heart's beating so fast, I can feel my pulse in my fingertips.

Grandmommy's head dips under the river and disappears from sight.

"Grandmommy!" I cry. "Wait!"

I can't see where she went; the water's moving too fast. An undercurrent catches my feet and sucks me below the surface. I gargle water. It infiltrates my nose. Panic seizes my chest. I flail my arms and legs, frantically needing air.

Shadows spot my vision, funneling together to form a growing black hole. Fragments of the scene—water, floating crystals, flake-like shards of glass—pool into the vortex. My dream world starts crumbling around me, collapsing in on itself.

Grandmommy's calling out to me, burbling under the water. I can't understand what she's saying. Her words are faint against the hustled clanging of my roommates getting ready.

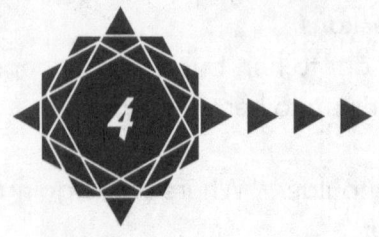

I fly forward, grasping my throat, knocking my head on the rails above me. Oxygen floods my lungs, renewing my appreciation for air.

"Rise and shine, sleepy head," Gertrude sings, while cleaning hair from my razor near the sink. She pauses to smooth the freshly shaved skin on her scalp, then rinses the blade under murky, spattering water.

My throat is dry, but the sight of water and the thought of drowning make me squirm. I smack my lips, and my tongue clings to the roof of my mouth. Another gust of air enters as I yawn and rub the gunk from my eyes. The crusty mixture of mucus and tears reminds me of the waterfall residue in my dream.

I groan, barely coherent, still orienting myself from the drastic shift in scenery. My roommates are scrambling to get ready, buttoning up their jumpsuits and pulling their hair into tight braids, buns, and ponytails. I must have slept through the alarm that beeps over the crackling intercom in our bunker. Then again, it hasn't been working all that well lately. There's a good chance it didn't go off, which would explain my friend's frantic movements.

I'm not sure how much time I have before the Warden busts through our bunker door and rants off her list of morning responsibilities. Judging by the state of the room, it could happen at any moment.

I lean over the side of my worn-out mattress and snatch the journal from under the box spring. A bulging coil catches my skin and scrapes my arm. The cut is red and rippled and stings, but there's hardly any blood. I ignore it and flip my book open to the first blank page. I write down everything I remember as quickly as I can, starting from the end and working my way backward, scratching out bullet points on the paper. I'm in the middle of writing down my description of the lion-guards when the ink in my pen runs out. I throw my head back and moan.

"Hurry up, Rey," Erika howls. "You're running out of time."

"Why can't she just follow the rules like everyone else?" Veronica complains loud enough for all of us to hear.

All five of my friends are standing at the foot of their beds, dressed and ready for the day. I tuck the empty pen on the binding of my journal and slip it back into its hiding spot underneath the mattress, avoiding a second altercation with the exposed metal as I withdraw my hand. Steadying my feet on the floor, I stand with the intention to get dressed, but to my misfortune, the Warden is already barging through the door.

"Good morning, ladies," she exclaims with her usual monotone inflection. With one foot in front of the other, she slowly stomps her boots down the center aisle, stopping to inspect the made-up cots and look each of my bunker mates over individually.

The Warden's meticulous eye squares the sheets on Erika's bed. She tsks her tongue.

"Do better next time, Haroldson," she remarks as she moves to examine Lucile's cot. Lu's covers are perfectly folded, the edges smoothed and tucked out of sight. My blankets are still wadded in a pile behind me. I wring my hands. Sweat starts to bead on my forehead as the Warden brushes dust from Veronica's shoulders. Ronny's freckled cheeks turn a shade of red that matches her hair. Her embarrassment turns into a repugnant glare as she locks eyes with me while the Warden checks on Claudette. Her hateful glare tells me what she's thinking: whatever punishment gets issued this morning will be all my fault.

The Warden tramps to my bed, completely overlooking Geri. Her eyes bore into mine as she holds my gaze. A drop of sweat leaks from my brow and drips down the bridge of my nose.

"You're all to report for wall duty today," the Warden spits in my face. Her gruff voice cracks, and she clears her throat. "You can thank Sage for that."

The other girls quietly groan and sigh, but I keep my eyes trained on the Warden. My heart thumps in my chest as her eyes shift from my underclothes to the unmade cot. All I can do is pray that she doesn't lift the mattress and discover my journal.

Having personal possessions is strictly forbidden in the Southern Sector. Only the elite leaders on the north side of the barracks are provided such a luxury: doctors, teachers, guards, and of course, the Commander. Not here, though. If it isn't essential, it isn't allowed. Laude says it's a tactic to avoid emotional hysteria. She quotes the charge nurse from the medical center: "You can't mourn what you're missing if you never had it in the first place." Apparently, the hospital is busy enough keeping disease at bay. They don't want their exam rooms overrun by people having mental breakdowns.

Still, I take the risk. My journal is the only thing I have left to remember Grandmommy by. Plus, none of the other girls rat me out. In the safety of the shadows, they all cling to something special: an heirloom brooch, an old photograph, a chipped mug stained by the darkest coffee—valuables more precious than the snitch's reward of an extra slice of synthetic meat with the next promised meal.

The Warden looks up, her nose a hair's breadth away from mine. "You better have a decent explanation as to why you're not ready." Suspicion fills her voice.

"I'm not feeling well," I blurt, immediately regretting the lie.

"Is that so?" She eyes my dampened clothes. "I'd hate to have to send you down for screening. With the outbreak we had last month, they'd lock you up in Quarantine without as much as an exam." The Warden calls my bluff.

"I just got a little overheated last night." I recoil. "That's all."

"Good." She steps back. "Now, get dressed and make up your cot."

"Yes, ma'am." I give a salute, then scramble to put on my uniform and tidy my bed while the Warden observes.

"Alright, ladies, listen up!" The Warden turns to address our motley crew as a whole. "We've got a few hours' worth of work to get done before I let you go down to the Education Center and start your studies. Afterward, you're to report to the Medical Center for updated vaccinations." She peers at me over her shoulder. "I'd suggest you make it there successfully, Sage. I'll put a note in for the nurse to run a blood panel on you as well. Just to be safe." She's got an expression that makes me regret ever thinking I could get away with pretending to be sick.

"Did you administer your injection last night?" The Warden lowers her brow.

Shoot. I exhale. It completely slipped my mind. Everyone on the base is required to take these awful shots full of immunity and vitamins once a day. The fluid mixture has a two-fold purpose: one, to compensate for the poor diet we consume; and two, to prevent contagions. Normally, the girls and I prick ourselves with the nasty needles right after roll call, but since I was late, I forgot to take mine.

This isn't the first time I've missed a dose, but usually my decision to skip it is intentional. The injection sends an uncomfortable warmth through my veins and puts a metallic taste in my mouth. I'd rather lick the floor. Just the thought of the solution makes me grimace. I honestly don't regret not taking the shot, but there's no doubt in my mind that the base doctor will increase my dosage after reviewing my bloodwork. That's usually what happens. My empty stomach churns as I realize the consequence of my actions will most likely be several days of an arm pumped full of double the dose of my usual injection. My lip curves, and I swallow hard. An acidic bubble escapes my mouth as I fasten the last button on my uniform.

"Kouris, you're with Toussaint today."

The Warden likes to address us by our last names. She's talking to Veronica and Claudette, or as they like to be called, Ronny and Laude. Between the sounds of our surnames and the use of our nicknames, we rarely hear our given names.

"I need you both mixing plaster," the Warden orders. "Haroldson and Roberts, you'll be filling in the cracks."

That's Erika and Lucile. Erika's the only one who won't answer to a nickname. We attempted to call her Rick for a while, but she clenched her fists and threatened to pulverize the next person who addressed her that way. Needless to say, the nickname never stuck.

"That leaves the two of you for sanding and smoothing." The Warden points a rigid finger at me and Geri. "Are you going to be able to keep up with Klein today, Sage?"

"Yes, ma'am," I respond.

We fall in line and exit the bunker. Immediately, I look at the sky. My heart sinks a little when I see how grey and dreary everything is. There's not a sliver of blue to be found, and no sign of the sun. It's just dark clouds hovering overhead, stretching for miles, as far as my eyes can see.

I try to look on the bright side. Overcast days are best for working on the walls, and the late summer heat is more manageable under the shade of the clouds.

I march out of line on accident as I watch the clouds grow and swallow each other up. Geri nudges me back into formation, making sure I don't get us assigned another round of wall duty.

It's a short walk to the decrepit shed on the edge of the Forgotten Zone. Most everything on the barracks is made of concrete or metal. This piece-of-crap shed is the only thing left standing that was built with wood before the Last War.

We halt in front of the dingy doors as the Warden fumbles with a ring of silver keys. All of the tools have been secured by a padlock to prevent residents from forming a revolt and using rusty hammers as weapons. I've never witnessed any riots, but apparently there are still rebels floating around on the base trying to overthrow the government. I catch whispers at the washhouse every once in a while. Erika said the guys down at the machine shop are a little more vocal about their disdain for world leaders. I can easily envision one of them in their greasy coveralls snapping the lock clean off the shed with a stolen pair of wire cutters. Although it wouldn't take much to knock down the rotting wood with a fist punch. I'm actually surprised someone hasn't tried it yet.

The lock clicks, and the rickety door creaks open. A day's worth of trapped humidity wafts from the muggy shed. The Warden disappears inside and quickly returns with sweat beading on her forehead. She wheels a shelf loaded with bags of plaster for Ronny and Laude. Ronny wastes no time. She throws a bag over her shoulder, her fragile body crumpling under its weight. Her red hair powders with dust as her knees hit the gravel. Laude rushes to remove the heavy sack from Ronny's lap and requests to use the wheelbarrow.

The Warden nods in approval, motioning for Laude to retrieve it from the shed. Laude pushes the dilapidated, old fossil out the door and bounces it over the threshold. The wheels squeak and snag as she guides it toward Ronny, who's preoccupied with brushing powder off her jumper. I'm not sure why Laude's bothering to use the wheelbarrow when it has a hole the size of my head at the bottom of the tray. But

Laude's good at figuring things out. She has a mind that's always searching for solutions and problem-solving issues the rest of us wouldn't even attempt.

Just as I suspect, Laude grabs a sheet of warped wood propped against the shed. She uses the plank to cover the hole, then she and Veronica take turns loading plaster into the patched wheelbarrow tray.

Erika fastens a satchel of trowels across her shoulder and stomps toward the wall. Lucile follows in lockstep, a bucket in one hand and a shovel in the other. They look threatening from a distance, and with a confident stance, I can easily see how tools from the shed could double as weapons, especially in the hands of a desperate rebel.

It's just me and Geri left waiting for our rags and sanders. Despite being put on wall duty today, I'm thankful to have a morning working side by side with my best friend. The Warden didn't realize she was doing me a favor when she paired me with Geri. Sure, I like the other girls, but that doesn't mean I enjoy working with them. Lu complains too much, and Ronny's always paranoid. Laude's good company, but she's overly scrupulous. And, Erika, well, Erika's relentless. She doesn't like to take breaks, and she prefers that no one else does either. Geri, on the other hand, shares my love for the imaginative, and I'm itching to tell her about my dream.

I zone out watching Laude struggle with the spigot at the mixing station. If the reservoir was any less full than the last time I saw it, it'd be empty. She manages to coax a few seconds of a steady stream into a nearby bucket. Ronny pours plaster powder in. Even from here, I can tell she's added too much. The chalky paste will never do. We used to use concrete to mend the holes, but for over a year now, plaster's been the only tangible option. In my opinion, the wall's cracking and crumbling beyond repair, yet every day there's some sorry sucker out here trying to patch it up. If you ask me, the whole operation's a waste of time.

"Sage!" The Warden stands in front of me, holding out a pair of sanding blocks. "Got your head in the clouds today?".

"Don't worry, ma'am, I'll keep her in line." Geri grins. She plucks the sanding blocks from the Warden's grip and prods me toward the barricade, saving me from another round of discipline.

"What did you dream about last night, Rey?" Geri whispers.

"Shh!" I glance over my shoulder as I hurry toward an unoccupied portion of the wall.

Geri bites her lip. She's charged up and jittering like she's going to explode. I shoot her a look, squinting my eyes in a way that asks her to wait to combust until we're out of earshot.

"I can tell it was something spectacular!" She beams. "The Warden's right, you've been up in the clouds all morning."

"Keep it down, Geri," I whisper back with a smile that gives away my answer.

"I knew it!" she exclaims, then covers her mouth.

I glance around at our bunker-mates, wondering if anyone heard Geri shouting, but they're already locked into their tasks, heaving and hauling plaster to cover the exposed rebars.

Geri raises her eyebrows and curtsies in front of me, surrendering a sander block into my hands. Her little dance persuades me to laugh. She's quite the performer when she wants to be.

We get to work grinding down a particularly lumpy patch of plaster, and I tell her about my dream. I start from the beginning, talking about my visit with Grandmommy. Geri closes her eyes every once in a while. I can tell she's trying to picture the place I'm describing.

I'm explaining the Great Morning Star and how strange it felt to touch the light beams when I go silent.

"What happened next, Rey?" Geri leans over, her eyes soft with concern. I think she can tell something's bothering me.

I had been so preoccupied thinking about the way my dream ended that I had forgotten about what the Great Morning Star had told me. My eyes fall to the ground, and my face is solemn as I wonder what it all means.

"He told me"—I swallow—"that I'm going to suffer."

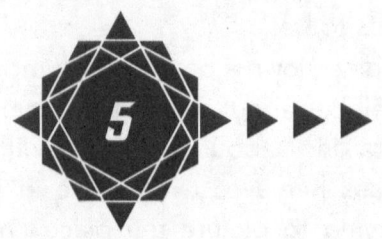

Geri tries getting me to explain what the Great Morning Star meant by "everything's going to change," but I shrug her off. The truth is, I have no idea if he was talking about my dream world or my reality. Honestly, one of those things could really benefit from some change, and I think most everyone on the Omega Compound would agree with me. What bothers me is the way the Great Morning Star said I needed to be patient in suffering. It makes me think things will get a lot worse before they get any better. I shudder. It's hard to imagine anything worse than starving to death while trapped inside the crumbling walls of an outdated military base, waiting for Earth to be fertile again.

    I go on telling Geri about the rest of my dream, and before I know it, the Warden's hollering out a reminder that we're already midway through the morning shift. A wave of despair hits me when I survey the pathetic work I've accomplished. Gashes in the concrete poke through the dried sludge. Flaking plaster cracks along a fist-sized hole. To make matters worse, Geri's still sitting there with her mouth hanging open. I'm not even sure she heard the Warden's warning. She's limply waving her sander block, missing lumps and bumps with every lackluster swipe.

    We've been out here for over an hour and have next to nothing to show for it. Sharing my dream with

Geri during wall duty may have been a poor decision on my end. I'd hate to get us both in trouble when the Warden comes around to inspect our progress. We'd be demoted to work on the waste sanitation crew, which means we'd be stuck smelling like feces for weeks.

"What was on the other side?" Geri asks, wide-eyed.

"Huh?" I bite my lip.

"Of the waterfall, Rey," she says, reminding me where I left off while telling my story. "What did you see when you walked through it?"

"This." I resort to sarcasm, holding up my tools and motioning to the wall with an exaggerated eye-roll. "We really need to get some work done."

Geri pulls herself from her reverie and looks at the wall. She moans and rests her forehead against the dried plaster. Her fair blonde hair falls forward and covers her face, muffling the sigh that escapes her lips. "You're right," she groans. "But don't forget to tell me the rest later, okay? I'm invested in this one."

"Alright." I chuckle. Geri says that about every single one of my dreams.

Over the next hour, I do my best to really concentrate on my work, and for the most part, Geri does too. We only stop to talk a few times, but we try our hardest to keep our arms moving while we do. This section of wall is starting to look a whole lot better. I brush my hand over the smoothed plaster with admiration. There's one large patch that still needs some attention, but I think we'll be able to finish before the Warden dismisses us for class.

I glance at my bunker-mates still hard at work. Erika is hauling a bucket of plaster up the pulley system to Lu, who's teetering to reach it at the top of a rickety two-story ladder. Ronny and Laude are already scrubbing their tools in the large metal wash bin. I spin to steal a glance at the Warden, standing like a statue near the supply shed, but I notice something else. A guard is running to meet her. He skids to a stop, nearly knocking the Warden over. He leans to catch his breath. Whatever he's telling her, it looks urgent. The Warden lets her hardened expression droop.

Something's wrong.

The Warden opens her mouth to yell, but I don't ever hear what she's screaming. A sustained alarm explodes through the loudspeakers, drowning out her voice. I cover my ears. The emergency lights start flashing along the top of the wall. A blast of cold air hits me in the face, and I look up. The dark clouds are swirling. They look angry. Shades of green mix with grey, and everything darkens, zapping away whatever daylight had managed to sneak through the sunless sky.

My eyes shift downward just in time to see the other girls jogging with the guard toward the Mess Hall.

"We need to go," Geri mouths. She nudges past me and sprints to catch up with the others.

I know I need to follow, but my feet feel glued to the ground. My heart races, and I can't stop watching the growing green billows twirl overhead. I start spinning, matching the speed of the funnel forming above me.

The Warden's trench whistle cuts through the droning alarm. My eyes veer from the sky and dart across the courtyard. It's so dark now I can hardly see the shed. I feel disoriented and start to panic. My jaw trembles as my eyes search for the Warden. Rectangular shadows blob the courtyard, and I strain to locate the path to the Mess Hall.

Another gust of wind steals my breath away and forces me to my knees.

"Sage!"

I think I hear the Warden calling me.

"Sage! Sage!"

Her voice is faint, but I try to pinpoint it. I turn my head to determine which direction it's coming from, when the Warden's hands seize my shoulders. She pulls me up, fighting against the heavy force of the wind. Her once neatly fastened hair is now wildly unraveled, whipping across her face.

I think she says "move" as she pushes me. I don't ask for clarification; I just sink my heels into the dirt and trudge forward. Our feet are slipping and sliding in the gravel as we struggle to make our way to the Mess Hall.

Shadows and shapes blaze with the lightning that illuminates our path. The Warden's hand guides me between flashes when it's dark and I can't see.

"Quickly!" she urges. "We don't have much time!"

Another violent gust of wind thrashes me. This time, it brings the chilling scent of acid. Petrichor stings my nostrils. *Rain.*

"We're not going to make it!"

I struggle to hear the Warden's shouts as I lean into the burning wind. She snatches my arm, changing our direction. Her firm grip reminds me of the scrape I earned earlier this morning from the exposed coil jutting from my mattress. The pain feels minuscule in comparison to the gravel pelting my face. Between the tiny rocks attacking my cheeks and the strength of the wind, I can barely keep my eyes open. I have no idea which way we're going, but I hope the Warden does. She's shoving me forward again, this time with both hands.

Jagged lightning bolts streak across the emerald sky, branching above the base, and for a brief moment, I can see where we're headed. The shed.

A clap of thunder startles me, and I stumble forward, catching my foot on blowing debris, wreckage from the mixing station. I brace myself. My face is inches from the ground when acid rain bursts from the clouds and erodes the dirt around me. The ground sizzles, and the Warden yanks me up for the second time, thrusting me forward. My hands collide with the coarse wood of the shed door. I fumble for the handle and wrench it open. A raindrop splashes from the overhang and sears the back of my hand. I yelp and scurry inside with the Warden stumbling in behind me. She sinks to the floor. We both gasp for air.

"Ma'am? Are you—are you okay?" I pant, surprised that I can hear my own voice.

"There's a light around here somewhere, Sage. Find it," the Warden commands through gritted teeth.

The flimsy door muffles just enough of the storm for us to hear each other.

"My back's burned pretty badly from the acid. I need you to clean me up before the blisters form."

Me?

I'm not any good at doctoring people. I don't even know the first thing about cleaning wounds. I just ignore them until they go away or start showing signs of an infection, then I head to the Medical Center to get treatment. The staff there won't waste healing salve on just anything, so I wait until my cuts are real angry-looking and leaking pus. I wish Laude were here. Her shifts at the Medical Center have made her kind of an expert on caring for people. She's the honorary nurse of the group. Not me.

I inhale sharply and run my hand along the pressboard walls, scrambling for the light switch. The wood splinters into my palm and I flinch back. Trading hands, I grope for the plastic plate. With a flick, the room fills with light. I shudder and blink, adjusting to the brightness.

The Warden's on the floor, hunched over, knees to chest. The rain decimated her uniform. Acid burned holes from shoulder to shoulder. If I don't intervene … well, things may not turn out so well for the Warden.

I don't know a whole lot about dressing wounds, but I do remember what chemical burns look like. For a while, the United Regime used rain exposure as a form of punishment for insurgents. So naturally, Professor Diaz includes slides of storm injuries in his opinionated history lessons. He's still not convinced that the government has stopped using this type of torture. I don't know if that's true. All I know is that the images look horrific: third-degree burns and blisters erupted over raw, pink, and peeling skin.

"There should be a bucket with some rags on the shelf in the corner." The Warden keeps her face downward when she points toward the back wall with a trembling finger. "See if you can find any water. If we're lucky, the first aid kit will have a bottle of sterile water in it."

I look at the small shelf, scanning its ledges for signs of a bucket or a first aid kit. All I see are tools: a crowbar, a spade, an assortment of wrenches. I slither my finger across the cool steel head of a hammer.

"Hurry!" the Warden grits out.

I flinch, pulling my attention to the nearby cart—the same cart the Warden wheeled out of the shed with supplies only a couple of hours earlier. A few leftover plaster bags hang limply over the bottom edge. I shuffle through them.

There!

I spot the small tin box with a red cross painted on top. It's wedged between the wall and the cart. I do my best to wrestle the cart out of the way, but I can't get it to move. The shelves rattle, but the wheels are frozen in place.

"You have to lift the brake underneath, or else it won't budge." The Warden gurgles her orders.

I kick the brake free, the cart slides, and I grab the first aid kit. Another clap of thunder rattles the shed. Wind beats violently from the outside. The lightbulb sways and starts strobing, flickering on and off.

"Quickly," the Warden begs.

I lift the tin lid. My hopes shatter. All I find is a sparse roll of gauze wrap and a few singularly packaged alcohol wipes. Judging by the contents, the kit hasn't been restocked in over a year. I don't know why I'm surprised. The base's meager medical supplies are always prioritized to the Medical Center, not some tin box in a rundown shed on the far side of the Forgotten

Zone. I exhale sharply. Three alcohol wipes aren't ideal, and I'm worried they'll be stiff when I open them up, dried out by the summer's heat.

I snag the contents of the first aid kit and kneel behind the Warden. Her back shines red beneath the swaying light, and blood speckles her exposed skin. I grip the frayed tears in the Warden's uniform and rip them wider. The acid-soaked clothes sting my hands, and I frantically toss the shreds aside.

When I open a cleansing wipe, I sigh with relief. The soaked square has somehow managed to hold up against the heat. I unfold the damp cloth and swab the Warden's burnt skin. She groans through gritted teeth, but she says nothing. I rip open the last two wipes and attempt to clean the rest of her wounds, but as predicted, three wipes aren't enough.

Agonizing pain surges in my hands as I scrub my superior. Pustules are starting to form on my knuckles. Frantically, I whip around the shed, hoping to find something—anything—that can provide relief. My eyes lock on a wet mop propped against a bucket near the door. The handle is cracked, and the yarn is stiff and starchy. I wring the coarse stings, craving moisture for my burning skin, but the dry strands snap. I yell and throw the mop. It crashes to the floor with another crack of thunder.

I jolt. My foot knocks into a bucket. I hear a faint sloshing over the howl of the wind and fall to my knees, dunking my hands into the repugnant mop water. It's filthy, reused several times over, and darkened by dirt, but I don't care. It hurts too much to care.

When I pull my hand from the grimy liquid, I decide to dump the remainder onto the Warden's back. I seize the gauze roll and cover as much of the Warden's exposed skin as I can. Huge blisters are already starting to form on her shoulders.

The temperature drops, and my teeth start chattering. It's cold, but my skin's burning up. The Warden slumps to the ground, burying her face in the floor. I need to get her to the Medical Center for proper treatment, but I can't carry her, and running through the rain would be a suicide mission. Her body starts to shake. She's shivering, too.

Thinking fast, I cover the Warden with empty plaster sacks, then sink down to the floor and hug my knees to my chest. I rub my sore hands over my arms to generate heat, but I decide our chances of staying warm would be better if we huddle together. Forgetting the nature of our relationship, I scoot closer to the Warden and press my body against hers.

"Maybe they'll send someone to get us," I say, trying to sound optimistic, but I know it's a long shot.

The light goes out. The wind rattles the door, its hinges squealing in imminent surrender. I jump to secure the lock, but the gale sends me flying backward into the mobile cart. It skids away, then barrels toward me, bowling into my gut. I double over. *I forgot to secure the brakes.*

The floor rises up from under me, and I can hear the cart wheeling across the floor, slamming into the back wall.

The Warden.

I left my superior slumped on the floor in a vulnerable heap. I spring forward, flinging myself on top of the Warden, using my body as a human shield against the rogue cart.

The door flies off the hinges. I duck as it soars over my head. The rush of wind steals my breath away. Tools fly through the air. The mop bucket bruises my hip. I tighten my hold on the Warden and brace myself for another impact. The room tilts and sends the screeching metal cart hurling toward me. I raise a hand in defense, but the cart veers. Cold metal smashes into my temple, and everything goes black.

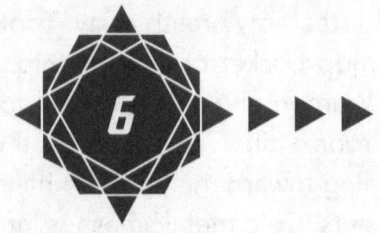

When I regain consciousness, I'm suspended underwater. Dark red streaks paint the current with blood from my head. The cool stream soothes my sore hands. Brilliantly hued crystals swirl around me, wrapping against my body.

I can't breathe.

Grandmommy secures her arms around me and pushes me to the surface. We emerge from the river, and I suck in crisp, clean air. She flips onto her back and lets me hold on for support.

"Breathe," she encourages while we float down the river, moving deeper into the City of Life.

I inhale slowly, this time recognizing the sweet but salty aroma of the water.

I'm dreaming. At least, I think I am. My head is pounding from the collision with the cart, and I feel disoriented from waking up underwater. I dab my fingers on the gash above my eyebrow and inhale through gritted teeth.

It can't be.

Somehow, I've brought my injuries with me into my dream world. That's never happened before. Come to think of it, I've never resumed a dream before either. Yet, my consciousness spat me right back into the river as if I had never left it.

"Did I hit my head on the bedrock?" I ask Grandmommy, doubting if this is, in fact, the same wound I sustained in the shed. My mind tries to make sense of it. There's a possibility I'm still awake. Maybe this is a hallucination brought on by a concussion.

"Impossible," Grandmommy says, staring into the sky. The Great Morning Star is directly above us. "This river can't hurt you."

"Huh?" I raise my brow in disbelief.

"No one gets hurt in the City of Life."

Grandmommy's always been a free spirit, believing in impossible things, but this—this is insane. Plus, she's completely unfazed by the fact that I surfaced from the water with a slice in my skull the length of my pointer finger. She doesn't even ask if I'm okay.

"The Source will heal you. If you want him to," Grandmommy says. She turns her body vertically and stretches her toes to the bottom of the stream. It's shallow enough for her to stand, so I let go of her shoulders and let my feet drift down to the riverbed. My toes settle among the colorful stones.

"We're here." She's looking beyond me. This whole time, I was facing the other way, staring in the direction of where we came from, rather than where we were headed. I turn to see where "here" is, and I gasp at the sight.

An island lies ahead. At its heart stands a mountainous tree growing outward in every direction. Branches stretch like arms and plummet back into the dirt, forming new trunks. Limbs, like spidering hands, reach into the soil and sow new growth. The massive tree forms a forest of its own, every shoot connecting back to the mammoth bole at its center.

My mouth is still hanging open, gawking at the tree ... or trees. Grandmommy, though, moves on toward the shoreline and leaves me standing in the chest-deep lake that encircles the island. I can see another river to my left, flowing freely into the lake. I look the other way, and sure enough, there's a third river melding into the lagoon. From where I stand, I can't see around the island, but I suspect more rivers meet here, flowing in from the other side.

I trek through the crystal-clear water, kicking up rainbow sand as I walk. The swirling pieces never muddy my view. I can see straight to the bottom.

A school of shimmering fish swims by, encircling my legs before scurrying off. Grandmommy's several paces ahead of me. Where she strides, the waves roil, turning over in marbled froth, and lap at the shoreline. Black crystals dot the sand, and a green garland of aquatic grass sways against the coast.

Grandmommy pauses to trail her fingers through the reeds, her orb bouncing with a color that matches their thick stalks. Just like the grass in the meadow, the shoots sing a sweet melody. Each blade holds its own note, and together they create a chorus. Grandmommy looks over her shoulder and waves for me to join her before continuing to strum a song on the long stems.

We don't get to listen to much music on the Omega Compound. It's basically forbidden. But every once in a while, Professor Diaz will bring in an old vinyl disk and spin it on the record player in the lecture hall. He plays songs that were written centuries ago, mostly instrumental pieces performed by an orchestra before the Last War. The recordings are scuffed and scratched, so they skip a lot, but the disk spins enough to make out a tune. I'm partial to the low hum of the cello and upright bass, which is probably why the reeds sound so pleasant to me.

I catch up with Grandmommy and part the bubbling foam to walk up on the beach. The land is spongy beneath my feet, and the shimmering reeds tickle my shins, vibrating with their deep tones when I rub against them. Flecks of spume cling to me as I emerge from the water, hardening in the open air. Just like the oil from the waterfall, the crystals fall when I brush them away, merging with the blackened sand. Leftover water droplets trickle from my head to my toes. Each speck of water shimmers in the light of the Great Morning Star, refracting into tiny rainbows on my skin.

Grandmommy lifts my chin, directing my eyes to the giant tree. From the beach, the trunk is an infinite tower disappearing into the sky.

"Is that where I'll meet the Source?" I ask.

Grandmommy nods and twists her lips into a satisfied smile.

"It's huge," I comment, pointing out its obvious size. "Why weren't we able to see it from outside the city?"

"This realm doesn't work that way, child."

If that answer came from any one of my friends, I'd roll my eyes, but that's probably not the smartest way to respond to my grandmother, even if she doesn't look much older than me here. It's a no-brainer that this world doesn't operate under the strict laws of physics, but still, you'd think I'd notice a tree this ginormous from a few miles away.

Grandmommy takes my hand. Her diamond eyes bore into mine. "Your understanding of this realm has been limited, my dear. The Great Morning Star has desired it to be, but something is coming, something on your linear timeline that will require you to find greater faith." She drills her finger into my chest, her orb pulsing with lavender hues. "You must believe, blindly believe, if you want to truly see everything that's happening all around you."

I feel like my eyes are hollow in comparison to Grandmommy's, darting back and forth between hers, searching for some kind of explanation to her riddle. I don't understand what she's talking about, but there's this weight that falls on my chest when she lifts her finger away, one that makes me think I need to take her seriously. But all of the cryptic talk about "something" happening soon makes my knees go weak. I might not care for life as I know it on the complex, but at least it's predictable. The thought of something bad happening makes my throat close up. Then again, what about the storm? Maybe something bad has already happened. Fear creeps in. I can feel it take hold of my shoulders. The tension makes my fingers go numb. Dizziness attacks my balance. My head throbs. Fresh blood oozes from my wound and drips into my eyes. I think I might pass out again, or wake up, however that works.

Without warning, Grandmommy smears a sunshine-colored flower onto my face, defusing my anxiety attack. A cloud of glittery pollen coats my cheeks and tickles my nose. The scent of citrus infiltrates my senses. I hold back a sneeze and rub the yellow dust from my eyes.

"What was that for?" I fume, annoyed by the ambush.

"You can't leave. Not yet. I promised the Great Morning Star I'd take you to the Source." Grandmommy points down a path that leads from the beach. Iridescent brush flanks the entrance, followed by a jungle of dense, tangled undergrowth. The entire trail, though, is covered with thousands of delicate, sparkling blooms. I can see now where Grandmommy got her assault weapon.

"Besides," she continues, "these flowers help heal human wounds."

I crinkle my brow and reach for my forehead. Sure enough, the bleeding has stopped. A crisp scab has formed over my wound. Light remnants of the pollen still coat its edges. I pull my hand back and roll the chalky residue between my fingers, inspecting it closely.

"Look this way." Grandmommy signals for me to move inland.

I step up to the path's entrance and gaze down the long trail to my destination, then gulp. My heart starts pounding again, and my breath quickens. I have no idea what to expect when we reach the tree, but I'm not entirely sure I want to find out anymore.

Grandmommy interlocks her fingers with mine, offering gentle support. A wave of energy travels up my arm, prickling the skin on my scalp.

Here goes nothing.

I extend one foot onto the trail and find myself pushing against a powerful current of air, struggling past an invisible wall of resistance. I squint and shake my head when I enter through the concealed perimeter. Everything looks different, and all of my senses are magnified.

Blossoms flit through the air, bouncing off my body on their way to the ground. They release their tangy aroma with a burst of sparkling pollen when they settle with their counterparts. The twisted plants that outline the edges of the path grow above my head, swirling with wild berries. I can taste them in the air; their tart juices make my mouth water.

Rustling sounds in the bushes, and I catch glimpses of vibrant fur through the thick vegetation. Tiny rodents with opalescent hair play together in the brushwood. Their bushy tails flinch while they scurry deeper into the thickets. A small bird startles me as it stops to hover in front of my face, looking me straight in the eyes before continuing on. Glittering dust falls from its wings as they flap with rapid rotations, collecting particles of light that hang in the air.

Everywhere I look, the island is teaming with life. It's a stark contrast to how I'm used to living. Everything on the Omega Compound is neutral or monochrome, and the only plant I've ever laid eyes on was the potted flower Professor Diaz managed to keep on his desk for a year before the Commander ordered him to stop wasting water on it. It's the same pot he keeps on display, the one he uses for his senseless object lessons. The emptiness only reminds me of what used to be in it. But maybe that's the point.

My sight stretches to the base of the tree. Hundreds of creatures crowd its trunk; animals and people alike. Some of them resemble Grandmommy. Others look like the beings I saw near the city gate, with bodies made of chiseled stone. I pull my vision back and turn to Grandmommy.

"They're here to bear witness," she tells me.

"To what?" I ask, but I think I already know.

"To you." Her eyes glitter.

I feel my cheeks go red. I don't like to be the center of attention, but I've already missed my opportunity to wake up. My knees are itching to bounce into a sprint and bolt back to the beach, but vibrations fill the air, and I feel this strange presence tugging at my chest. It's like the cord Grandmommy says we share, the one that tethers our love across the sky, except someone else is on the other end, pulling me toward the center of the island. I can't help but move forward.

I reach the end of the trail and the crowd parts, making room for me to enter. All eyes are on me. My heart's jittering, but there's nowhere to hide now. The colorful creatures smile, offering silent greetings as I pass by. Their cores all burn with an assortment of brilliant hues. Some nod their heads; others grope at my clothes. A childlike figure with metallic skin stretches out his jagged hand to touch me. A shock of energy pulses between us, and he recoils. I must look as strange to him as he does to me.

As I close in on the tree, I see its mammoth roots peeking out from the rich soil. They crawl along the ground, bending and twisting together before reaching beneath the surface. Shimmering light bursts from the woody veins of the tree's trunk, sprinkling flecks of gold into the air. A glimmer caresses my face. Its warmth welcomes me.

I crane my neck and search for the Source. I imagine a powerful ruler—taller, stronger, and more colorful than all of the creatures surrounding me. But there's no one else standing at the base of the tree. It's just me, looking up into its infinite branches.

The limbs are covered with lush green leaves bigger than both my hands put together. Blossoms and fruit alike hang from its branches. The rounded amber fruit bends the boughs with its ripened weight. Above my head, young sprouts curl with green tips, small and flexible. They stretch and spiral before my eyes, thickening into sturdy shoots. This massive tree is still growing, spawning limbs at a rapid rate.

My eyes wander down the tree's trunk. Deep grooves glow with liquid light that pulses from beneath the crust, highlighting every crevice. The trails of bark bend with designs that remind me of Grandmommy's veins. Each wooden channel looks like it has something to say, twisting into lines to create a secret language.

The tree seems too sacred to touch, but I can't help myself. I stretch out my hand and caress the coarse outer layer. The hair on my head stands straight up. Miniature lightning bolts form under my fingers. My eye sockets vibrate. I'm thankful to have an empty bladder.

The wooden surface shifts in response to my touch, forming new shapes in the bark. Palpitations travel up the trunk and disperse through the lower branches, triggering them to curl in toward me. I step back, chin raised, watching the boughs as they come for me. My lungs seize, skipping with irregular breaths. My feet freeze in place.

The lush limbs weave together, forming an ivy cage around me. I spin in a circle, but there's no way out. At first, I can see Grandmommy through the gaps between the tangled branches. Her orb is bursting with gold. She mouths something to me, but the growing foliage hides her lips, and I can't make out what she's saying. Before I know it, the entire island disappears behind a leafy wall, and everything goes eerily silent. The only sounds I can hear are the puffs of my rapid breath and the thud of my own heartbeat.

"Young one." A ghostly voice resonates in the chamber, echoing with high and low frequencies. The pitches overlap in layers, like everyone talking in the cafeteria at the same time, but in unison.

The tree's branches pulse with light. I spin, searching for the voice.

"Love has brought you here to stand in my presence."

"Who are you?" My shouts fall flat, absorbed by the organic enclosure.

"I am the Source of life," the voice rings out. Light beams from the branches with every word.

I don't know where to look or what to focus on, but rotating my body is making me dizzy. I fall to my knees and yell, "What do you want with me?"

"Your trust."

"I don't understand." Pressure builds in my head. I need to get out.

A rogue branch extends to me, reaching for my face. A plump fruit dangles off the end.

"Eat of me, and you shall have the understanding you seek."

I look down the bridge of my nose and go cross-eyed staring at the fruit. A pit forms in my stomach. I'm skeptical, but Grandmommy's the one who brought me here. She's the one who wanted me to meet the Source. I might not trust a talking tree, but I trust her, so I pluck the fruit and hold it in my hands.

Stillness settles in the soundless space, like the entire universe is holding its breath in anticipation for me to take a bite. I look the fruit over, twirling it in my hands to inspect the velvety skin. It seems harmless enough.

My heart races. The thump of my pulse pounds in my ears. I raise the amber fruit to my lips and sink my teeth into its flesh. Dark red juice spills from its center and drips down my chin.

I've tasted a lot of strange things in my life, but never fruit from a talking tree. I've stomached rancid and wretched meals on the compound, swallowing questionable meats and gelatins, longing for the flavor of smuggled candies and confections. But nothing compares to the tang of the fruit that melts in my mouth. It's sweet, smoky, salty—all of the best flavors rolled into one.

Warmth coats my throat as I swallow. My arms prickle, and tears fill my eyes. I can't explain the weight that falls on me, but it doesn't feel heavy. It feels like home, like everything I've ever wanted in my whole life: to be accepted, to be safe, to be loved. I don't ever want to leave. I could stay here, right here, in the embrace of the Source, forever.

"I want you to come and live with me here, in the City of Life." The Source's voice is clearer now. It soothes my ears.

I want to stay. I'm ready to leave my pathetic life behind and live in the city alongside Grandmommy forever, but I know I can't. The fruit-induced epiphany makes me feel certain. I don't know why I can't, I just know I can't. I guess understanding doesn't always come with knowing why.

"What do I have to do?" I ask, realizing it probably has something to do with what the Great Morning Star told me. *You must be patient in the suffering.* The words repeat in my mind.

"Find me," the tree answers, and I wake up.

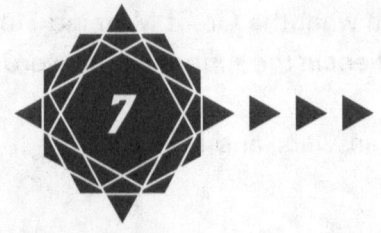

Steady beeps bleed into my ears, drowning out the Source's comforting voice. My eyes flutter open. White blobs morph into cold, sharp edges: a tiled ceiling and cracked laminate. Antiseptic burns my nostrils. Unnaturally white walls blind my eyes. An uncomfortable chill rattles my teeth.

The Medical Center.

I'm sprawled on a stretcher wearing nothing but a thin hospital gown. Wires shoot from both my arms, connecting me to the cube-shaped monitor beside the bed. The blurred screen of the vitals machine displays my oxygen levels and pulse rate. Other numbers and abbreviations flicker across the glass, but I can't make out what they mean. I'm delirious. The pain in my head swells and starts to throb. Hesitantly, I bring my fingers to my forehead, expecting to find a thick scab. Instead, I poke and prod a jagged line of stitches.

I wince and clench my jaw. The calm I experienced under the hedge of the Source didn't transfer into reality. I should have known that something like that, like peace that doesn't make sense, was too good to be true.

With trembling hands, I pull my body up to a sitting position, but the wires tug on my skin and hold me in place. The restriction causes tension in my neck. I hold my breath and let my thoughts scatter around the growing awareness of pain.

Breathe. I hear echoes of Grandmommy's voice and think about the breathing exercises Robin does while we work at the washhouse. I inhale slowly until my lungs feel like they're going to burst, then let out a long breath.

In and out.

I close my eyes and relax into the flat mattress, concentrating on the monitor's steady beeps, counting them until my attention wanes from the pain.

A hollow knock startles me and my eyes spring open. The metal door by the foot of my stretcher swings wide. A man with dark features and a white jacket enters. He's studying the clipboard in his hands, never bothering to break his concentration. Thick-rimmed glasses hide the intensity of his stare, but the furrowed line in his brow tells me something else: whatever's written on the chart must be serious.

He walks the narrow space between me and the curtain hanging at the center of the room, then veers behind it. I squint, tracking his silhouette. The muffled step of his padded shoes stops in front of a dark, horizontal shadow. There's another patient on the other side.

My heart stops. *The Warden.*

I was so consumed by the pain in my head that I completely forgot about the Warden. Suddenly my mind is racing with worry, wondering if she survived the storm. I want to holler across the divider and call to her, but what if it's not her? What if it's just some other unfortunate person who got caught in the rain?

I lean closer to the hanging fabric and strain my ears to listen. The doctor's accent is hard to understand from across the drapery, but I think he's talking about scraping off damaged skin. An uncomfortable twinge shoots down my neck.

The doctor repositions himself as he examines the other patient. He's facing my side of the room now, so I can make out what he's saying a little bit better.

"It could take longer for these burns to heal, but right now, I feel hopeful. You're a fighter. You've proven that through the night."

Winded, sibilant whispers answer. I can't make out a coherent sentence. All I hear are hissed consonants.

"I'll have the nurse look into that for you, and I'll come back to check on you in a little while, okay?"

Moans follow, then more muffled footsteps. Metal rings clang, and the curtain swings wide. The doctor whips it closed before I can glimpse the other side.

"Miss Sage," he addresses without making eye contact, his nose still buried in his chart. "It looks like you've suffered a concussion. We'd like to keep you monitored for a few more hours. If everything appears to be in order, we'll discharge you tonight. For now, do your best to rest. I'm going to have one of the nurses come in and run some vitamin-enriched fluids through your IV port and update your injections before we let you leave."

The doctor pauses, lowers his glasses, and peers up from his clipboard. I finally see his face. His dark brown eyes connect with mine. "Now, then. Is there anything I can help you with before I leave?"

"Can you tell me what happened to the woman I was with in the storm?" My voice cracks. Vibrations grit against my vocal cords. I clear my throat. "She's the Warden who oversees my unit. Bunker 112. Do you know if she's okay?"

The doctor flips through his chart.

"The shed collapsed on us. She was burned pretty badly by the rain," I ramble, trying to catch his attention, but I don't think he's listening. Waiting for an answer makes my hands shake. "Please," I beg. "I just need to know if she's okay."

The doctor clasps the clipboard with both hands and lowers it to his waist. "I think you'll be happy to know that your warden was recovered with you from the Southern Sector yesterday evening. You're right, she has suffered severe burns from the rain, but she's here and is stable. We're keeping a close eye on her during her recovery."

"Can I see her?"

"Due to her condition, we aren't allowing visitors." The doctor smirks, and it makes me angry.

I shrink.

People in the Northern Sector have no compassion for the rest of us, especially those of us in the Forgotten Zone. Our pain is some kind of joke to them. And still, people like him, like the doctor and Walter Cane, have the gall to complain about their unfortunate conditions while the rest of us starve to death. My fingers ball into fists, and I swear I'd hit him if it weren't for all of the wires holding me in place.

"However, I believe we can make an exception for her roommate."

Her roommate?

My cheeks flush hot with embarrassment. I misjudged the doctor.

I grip the rails of my hospital bed while waiting for the doctor to open the partition. I hold my breath as the metal rings slide across the curtain rod. With the barrier gone, I get a good look at the Warden's disheartening condition. Bandages snake up her arms and around her neck. Wires and tubes connect her to a monitor that looks a lot like the one by my side. A thin tube rests underneath the Warden's nose, leading to the oxygen tank at the head of her cot.

It's jarring seeing the Warden like this—weak and vulnerable. Burns splotch her ashen face, and the wrinkled hospital gown is quite the contrast from her usual pressed uniform. She's looked after me for an entire decade and never once has she let her hair down. It's always tied back into a tight bun, no matter the occasion. Now, her graying strands drape over her shoulders in loose, matted curls.

It's hard to believe that the woman lying motionless on the bed next to mine is the same one that marches the center of my bunker every morning, peering down her nose, inspecting every imperfection. Her eyes are barely open, and her grimace is unlike anything I've ever seen on her face before. It's obvious she's in pain. Weakness isn't something I'd typically associate with the Warden. She's the type of person who wouldn't let you know if her head hurt or if she had a stomachache. Not like Lu, who complains about it before the symptoms actually set in.

"I have a few more rounds to make, but I'll leave this curtain open for now." The doctor turns to face the Warden. "I'll ask the nurse to close it when she changes your dressings next."

He rolls up his left sleeve, revealing the golden wristwatch underneath. A lump forms in my throat. He's not even bothering to hide it. That's one of the benefits of having an important job and living in the Northern Sector: you get to proudly display your family heirlooms. At least, that's what I suspect this is. Most valuable items are. The golden luster on the watch has dimmed, but it shimmers faintly under the fluorescent lights. I wonder how many generations it's been in his family. Then my stomach goes sour thinking about the possibility of the watch being a patient repossession.

Any sentimental items seized in the Southern Sector get burned at the fuel yard—or so we're told. According to Ronny, the valuable items are hidden in an air-locked room she refers to as "the Museum." Ladies at the washhouse say any confiscations considered priceless antiques are sold through a black market across multiple compounds. If that's true, his watch could belong to just about anyone within the United Regime. Another rumor I've heard suggests all the esteemed pieces are bartered for supplies. I'm not so sure I believe any of the gossip. All I know is I'm not going to risk losing my journal trying to investigate. It may not be an extravagant inheritance, but it's the most valuable thing I own. Come to think of it, it's the only thing I own. Everything else belongs to the government, stamped with the Omega seal. Even my hospital sheets have the horseshoe shape embroidered in the corner.

The doctor shakes his sleeve back down, obscuring the watch from my view before I catch a glimpse of the time. It's hard to tell what time of day it is in a windowless room.

"If you need anything, ring the call light and a nurse will see to you. If they give you any trouble, just ask for Doctor Ayad."

I repeat his name with a whisper. Doctor Ayad does an about-face and exits the room. The closing door swallows the pitter-patter of his footsteps. Now it's just me and the Warden lying in silence with the staggered beeping of our machines and the occasional hiss of oxygen flowing to her nostrils.

I want to ask her how she feels, but it seems like a dumb question with an obvious answer. Also, I'm not so sure how to address the Warden. I mean, she is, after all, my superior. I don't even know her first name.

"Some watch," the Warden gargles.

"Huh?" I heard what she said, but I'm a bit taken aback by the comment. Why would she want to talk about the watch? And why with me? Trying to have a conversation about a sensitive topic wasn't something I was itching to do, and especially not with the person who directly oversees my livelihood. "Perhaps it's a family heirloom," she continues with her sandpaper voice.

I can see her peering at me from the corner of her eye. She's struggling to tilt her head in my direction. My lips are curled. I'm hesitant to answer. I don't want to say something I'll regret. I'd never forgive myself if I let it slip that my roommates and I are hoarding illegal possessions in the nooks and crannies of Bunker 112.

The Warden huffs an exaggerated sigh. "Don't worry, Sage. I'm not going to tell anyone."

A lump forms in my throat and I swallow hard.

She knows. Of course she knows.

I'm suddenly wondering how many times the Warden's seen me with my journal, or caught one of the other girls admiring their treasures. I can't tell if she's trying to extend me a courtesy by bringing it up, or if she's slipping in a reason for extortion. Threats seem a bit pointless for someone in her condition, but still, I don't want to take any chances by giving her the satisfaction of a response. I'm speechless, but I feel guilty. The Warden's making an effort to talk to me, and I'm staring at her blankly with my mouth hanging open.

"Okay." I settle for a polite nod and innocent acknowledgement, then go ahead and ask the pointless question. "How are you feeling?"

"I'll feel better as soon as the nurse comes back with some morphine." The Warden tries to adjust her position in the bed and hisses sharply through her clenched teeth. "They've been out of the medication for months, or so they've told me." She lowers her voice and attempts to whisper, "But the last nurse in here, the one with the long black hair, said she might be able to find some in the cabinet where they keep the expired medicines."

I don't know why she's telling me this. She's either trying to win my sympathy or hoping I find her relatable. I take a long, hard look at the Warden, wondering if I can ever see her for more than the stern-faced drill sergeant that she is.

Air puffs from the oxygen machine, and the Warden wheezes it in. Her bottom lip quivers. She's white-knuckling the metal rails on the sides of her cot. A small whimper escapes her lips, and she's mumbling something I can't understand under her breath. A single tear trickles down her cheek and drips off her chin.

Maybe my view of the Warden has been too harsh. I've only ever been able to see her as one of the chosen elite from the Northern Sector, but her attempts at conversation make me wonder if she's just one of us—a sorry soul from the Southern Sector. I've never seen her interact with anyone outside of the guards, me, and my roommates. Because she's a Warden, she's on duty all day long, overseeing everything we do. If she ever gets a break or time to mingle, I don't witness it.

I guess I've never been able to see her as a person—like an actual person with independent thoughts and feelings. Never have I considered the possibility of her sharing some of the same opinions as residents of the Southern Sector. I mean, I don't think I've ever heard anyone from the northern side of the barracks talking about family heirlooms or expired medications.

The Warden starts sputtering into a hacking fit, coughing uncontrollably. Her monitor whoops as the tube under her nose gets kinked by her convulsions, preventing the oxygen from spraying a puff of relief.

My heart races. I lean forward, wondering if I should get up and help her, when she leans back and sucks in air with a loud gasp. The monitor steadies again, beeping in rhythmic beats.

"Sage?" she gurgles.

"I'm here," I assure her.

"Promise me something?"

My stomach drops. Grandmommy made me promise her something once. That's the kind of thing people say on their deathbeds, when they know they're not going to make it much longer.

"What is it?" I ask warily.

"You're all I have; you and Klien, Toussaint, Kouris, Haraldson, and Roberts. You're a good bunch of girls ..." she trails, choking up with tears. "Promise me you'll look out for each other?"

"I—I—" I stutter. The pain in my head is swelling again, making it hard to formulate a meaningful response. I feel woozy. Tiny speckles of light start floating in my vision. I'm seeing stars the way I do when I decide to move too quickly after going too many days without eating.

There's a small plastic cup on a tray on the bedside table. I didn't notice it before, but now that I need it, it's magnified like a beacon. I reach for the cup, hoping to quench my dry throat and slow down this dizzy spell. With trembling hands, I bring the cup to my mouth and sip.

The shimmers of light intensify, dancing wildly around the room.

Something's not right.

I cling to the bedrails; panic squeezes my throat. I fear I might pass out.

I'm blindly reaching for the call button when a long mechanical drone fills the room, followed by piercing beeps, wails, and whirs.

A nurse barges in, calling out code colors. I think she's running to my aide, when I notice her attention is on the Warden. That's when I realize the flashes of light, like welding sparks at the machine shop, aren't a result of my concussion.

They're bursting from the Warden's chest.

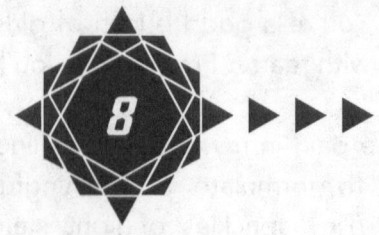

The entire room sounds like an orchestrated symphony, a skipping vinyl on Professor Diaz's antique record player. Terms from his lectures on musical analysis surface in my memory as the machines weave in and out of time with one another. Doctor Ayad's hands thud against the Warden's chest like a metronome. Like cues from a conductor, his orders interject into the refrain. Resuscitation plays out like an eerie, echoing song of call and response. The melody holds my attention, and I hold my breath while I wait for the Warden's reprise.

Guilt curdles in my stomach while I watch the doctor beat on her chest. *This is all my fault.* If I hadn't let myself get caught up watching the clouds, we would have made it to the Mess Hall in time, long before rain came sizzling out of the sky. The Warden doesn't deserve to die, and I'm the one who did this to her.

I squint to see past the crowd working on the Warden. They don't seem bothered by the flecks of light flying from her chest. No one flinches or swats them away. The spewing fountain has been reduced to a sputtering spring. I'm not so sure that's a good sign.

Then I see it. Faint, tiny tendrils curling from the ceiling.

I rub my eyes and blink rapidly. *It can't be.*

Tree branches are sprouting from the white tiles above the Warden's head. They unfurl and slither toward her, weaving through the bustled medical staff, groping in the air.

I squeeze my eyes shut, then pop them open. The ghostly branches don't disappear. On the contrary, they're much clearer than before. They float gracefully, unraveling for the Warden. My heart races. I can feel my pulse underneath the stitches on my forehead.

The hurried clatter crescendos. Metal clangs reverberate from clumsy collisions and hustling nurses working in a crowded space. The short nurse by the Warden's feet pushes a cart with hurried frustration. Its wheels squeal as it spins out of control. A low mechanical hum fills the room, and the medical staff withdraws, bowing into the background.

I hold a shaking hand to my lips as roots dangle above the Warden's drooping head. For a long moment, everything is still. It's the fermata that holds before the cadence, the part of the song where the listener can't decide if it's over yet or not.

Laude says there's this moment right before a baby's born where everyone in the room is holding their breath, waiting with anticipation. That's how it feels right now. She says it's scary, not knowing what will happen next, wondering if the outcome will be joyous or sorrowful. I never knew what she meant by that, but I can feel it now. There's a life hanging in the balance, and I don't know which way the scales will tip.

I picture the scales Professor Diaz uses when we explore weight and mass during lectures on mathematics. Two pans connect to a cross beam that tilts in the direction of the heaviest object. Sometimes we weigh gravel, seeing how many stones it will take on both sides to balance the scales evenly. That's what I see now as I think about death and life, except there's a lot more rocks piled on the side of death, and I don't foresee it tipping back the other way.

Doctor Ayad calls for the defibrillator paddles, and the tree continues its descent. My mind is rattling, wondering if it's the Source, but the sight of it doesn't give me that calm sense of belonging. Quite the opposite, actually. I'm terrified. My hands are trembling uncontrollably.

Offshoots multiply in every direction, enveloping the Warden's body. When they make contact with her skin, they splinter into her flesh. I clamp down on my mouth to keep myself from screaming.

The otherworldly timber tunnels further into the Warden, syphoning a glowing, blue liquid from her veins. The metallic fluid travels up the tree's stalks and disappears through the ceiling. The Warden's skin grays as life drains from her face.

"Clear!"

I jump when the nurse shocks the Warden's heart. The tree roots retract for a moment, then sink back in.

"Again," Doctor Ayad calls.

The nurse charges the paddles for a second time.

"Clear!"

The tendrils recoil, then embed themselves back into the Warden, continuing to suck glimmering blue goo from her limp frame.

"Clear!" Doctor Ayad yells for a third time.

The Warden's body convulses. This time, the tree maintains its hold, sinking deeper into the Warden's flesh as she jolts into the air. Death's herald sings its final verse.

I've killed the Warden.

Beeping erupts from the machinery. A pulse. It has to be. The roots regurgitate the glowing liquid, depositing the life-fluid back into the Warden's veins. They withdraw their sharp, hollow tips and vanish into the ceiling. For a moment, I see a radiant light beating from the Warden's heart, but it, too, disappears, leaving behind no trace of the tree's manifestation.

The frantic chorus ceases, and both nurses and machinery sigh with relief. I let the tension in my shoulders drain away and finally stop holding my breath. A quick release of air puffs from my nostrils. She's alive. The Warden's alive, and I'm not a murderer.

One of the nurses looks up, making eye contact with me. Her eyebrows lift with surprise, and her ears turn a bright shade of red. She whispers something inaudible to the doctor, who turns to take notice of the wide-open curtain.

He strides to my side of the room and pulls the drapes closed behind him, concealing the Warden from me. "I'm sorry you had to see all of that," Doctor Ayad sincerely apologizes.

"Will she be okay?" I ask, the words burbling from my throat.

"It's too soon to tell, but we certainly hope so." The doctor peers past the floor, lost in a vacant stare. Before I have the chance to ask another question, he shifts his stance and snaps his eyes back with a ghastly smile. Clicking his tongue, the doctor clasps his hands together and callously changes the subject. "While I'm here, why don't we see about your discharge."

I may not have a fancy watch to tell the time, but I know for a fact I haven't been monitored nearly as long as I need to be. I have a hunch he's rushing me out the door after what I witnessed.

Doctor Ayad draws a flashlight from his coat pocket, clicks it on, and waves it in front of my face. I stare at the exit, bracing against the blinding beam as he observes my dilating pupils.

"Good news, Miss Sage. It looks like you're going to be just fine. I'll have Nurse Cindy draw up some papers for you to sign, then we'll have you on your way." He places the flashlight back into his pocket and scoots behind the curtain. Almost immediately, the short nurse that stood by the Warden's feet emerges from the other side. Her white cap sits on a mound of frizzy hair. She carries a large hospital bag in her hands. I can see a pressed uniform through the clear plastic.

"Here's your clothes, dear. Well—" The nurse bobs her head in thought, places the bag on the end of the bed, and pats the top. "They're technically not *your* clothes." She pauses and purses her lips. "Your previous uniform was discarded due to chemical exposure. So, I've put a fresh uniform in this bag for you. I hope it fits and suits your needs."

I lean forward to retrieve the bag, but get yanked back by the cords attaching me to the vitals monitor.

"Just a moment." Nurse Cindy untangles the cords. "Let me get you unhooked." She removes most of the wires, but leaves the port in my hand. "I'll be right back."

Nurse Cindy bobs behind the curtain and returns with two separate injections. She pushes one through the port in my hand. I can feel the warm fluid travel up my arm. A metallic taste coats my tongue. She pricks my shoulder with the other shot. I suck air through my teeth. A thumbnail-sized welt is already forming from the needle.

"Now, you're ready." She throws the used syringes into the hazardous waste bin and slides the port's hollow tube from underneath my skin. Drops of blood leak from the site.

I curl my fingers, then stretch them wide, thankful to be rid of the constricting wires.

Nurse Cindy starts babbling about her day, gossiping about stolen cleaning products and whatnot. I tune her out and reach for the uniform. It's definitely used. I can tell by the worn material 'round the knees. It looks a size larger than my old uniform, too. But having something to wear is better than having nothing, and I imagine this uniform is in much better condition than the one I had on during the storm.

Nurse Cindy helps me sit and get dressed. Sure enough, the jumpsuit is baggy around my midsection, but the shoes—well, they're snug. I curl my toes to wiggle them on. I'm suddenly wishing my shoes were a size too big, too. Oversized clothes are much better than tight ones. Maybe I can stretch them at the washhouse. I've seen some of the women do it for their husbands, soaking their boots in the water bin before stuffing them full with wads of material. When the boots dry, the cloth holds its place, giving the men a smidge more room to straighten their toes. The short end of the deal is that you're stuck walking around the barracks barefoot until the shoes dry out while risking demerits for failure to meet dress-code requirements.

I finish lacing up my boots. Nurse Cindy hovers over me with a clipboard in her hands. She gives me a pen and points to several cross marks on the stack of papers. She's doing her best to explain what I'm signing, but my eyes are having a hard time focusing on the words. My head sears with pain looking at all the little letters, so I don't even bother reading the fine print. Besides, the legality of signing papers seems rather idiotic. Erika says it's a sham of courtesy to keep us feeling like people rather than government property. I sign blindly and dust my hands on my new-ish uniform, ready to get back to my friends.

I grip the siderail and teeter to a stand. A spout of dizziness almost knocks me right back down.

"I can wheel you to the front desk if you'd like," Nurse Cindy offers. "I just need to find our wheelchair." She doesn't wait for my answer. "I'll be right back."

Nurse Cindy adjusts the waistline of her uniform and scampers out of the room. Not a minute passes before she returns, pushing a chair with large spoked wheels. "Here we are, sweetheart," she chirps as she locks the brakes with her foot. "All set to go."

Nurse Cindy guides me by my hips to the wheelchair and helps me sit on the cracked leather cushion. "Easy now," she directs while centering the footrests. "Let's take you to the main floor and get you out of here. Alright, honey?"

She pushes the wheelchair forward before I can lift my feet. I steady my boots in the stirrups and strain to catch a glimpse of the Warden as Nurse Cindy rolls me toward the door. I peer through the crack between the curtain and the wall, and although I can't see her behind the swarm of medical staff, the nurses' calm movements and the steady rhythm of the monitor tell me she's okay.

I twist forward as the wheelchair glides into the hall. An endless aisle of white tiles stretches before me. The bright lights combined with the sharp scent of antiseptic make my head pound even harder.

We're in the hallway for what feels like forever, passing dozens of closed doors. Additional hallways occasionally appear, jutting in new directions without end. Everything seems much larger than the modest building suggests from the outside.

"Where are we?" I ask, wondering if I'm actually still on the Omega Compound or if I've been transferred to another base.

"What's that, dear?" Nurse Cindy perks up.

"Are we still on Omega?" I rephrase the question, starting to feel a little agitated by Nurse Cindy's peppy personality.

"Of course we are!" she cheers. "I should have given you the tour, but the truth is ..." She drops her voice to a whisper. "Not too many people get to come down here." Her voice grows louder again. "I guess you were somewhat of an exception since they found that anomaly on your brain scan. Op!" She stutters her step, jerking the wheelchair and whipping my neck. "I'm probably not supposed to say that." She starts walking faster.

My brain scan? They must have performed tests while I was unconscious.

"What did they find?" I press.

"Just forget I mentioned anything, okay?" All the liveliness has bled from her voice. Her words sound shaky now. I get the feeling Nurse Cindy knows what kind of consequences come to people who speak out of turn. It reminds me of the phrase Professor Diaz taught us while covering half a dozen world wars during a history lesson: "loose lips sink ships." I guess the slogan was used to keep people from sharing military intel and compromising sensitive information. All it takes is one person blabbing something they shouldn't to the wrong people, and before you know it, an entire operation is in jeopardy. There can be serious consequences for sharing secrets and breaking the law. I'm not talking about hoarding family heirlooms and showing up past curfew, I mean serious stuff like building bombs and starting rebellions. Those are crimes that dish out more than an extra shift of wall-duty or a demotion to cleaning up sewage.

One of the scariest things about stepping out of line is that no one actually knows what happens to the people who do it. There's no public reprimand. It's a quiet punishment done in the shadows, the kind that makes you disappear and keeps your loved ones from ever talking about you again.

Ethel, the real elderly lady who oversees the seamstress station, is the only person left in her family. Rumor has it she used to have a husband and two sons, but one night, without warning, they just up and vanished into thin air. She won't talk about it, though. I know because I've tried asking. Ethel pretended like she couldn't hear me, saying her ears were too old to work properly anymore, but I saw the tears welling in her eyes. Her youngest son was the same age as my dad. I asked because I'd wondered if there had been any connection between the two of them—if they'd known each other.

My dad disappeared when I was just a toddler, and Grandmommy never told me what happened. Anytime

I asked her about him, or my mother, she'd simply say he went missing and Mama's heartbreak from losing him made her susceptible to the sickness. She warned me not to go poking around, asking about things I didn't understand, especially if it insinuated a revolt.

I think that's why Nurse Cindy's quiet now. I haven't known her very long, but judging by her initially talkative behavior, her sudden silence seems out of character. She slows her hurried pace when we come to the elevator shaft at the end of the hall and parks my wheelchair in front of the tall metal doors. I catch a glimpse of myself in the sheen of the metal and let out a hushed gasp. The line of stitches zigzags like a lightning bolt across my forehead, memorializing the storm that took me out.

For a moment, I'm forced back into the scene, trapped inside the shed. The single light swings above my head. The wind howls against the panels. Blood from the Warden's acid burns stain my hands. The dappled blisters on my knuckles start to sting. I grip the armrests. When I look down at the blanch of bone peeking through my fingers, I settle myself back into the present. The specks of pink still irritate my skin, but all of the fluid's been drained from the pustules.

Nurse Cindy slips a key from her sleeve when she thinks I'm not watching and slides it into a small hole hidden beneath the elevator button. Apparently, higher clearance is needed to access the level we're on, and I'm starting to wonder if we're in some kind of underground lair.

The circular control lights up red when Nurse Cindy pushes it. A whooshing sound fills the hollow shaft behind the doors as the elevator travels to meet us. A muffled ding signals its arrival, and the metal doors scrape open. The wheelchair tips forward, rolling me onto the lift. Hundreds of buttons line the inside wall. None of them have labels, except for one. Inked in black, the letter "G" marks a single circle. Nurse Cindy presses it, and the elevator jolts upward, confirming my suspicions.

We're underground.

During my discharge, Nurse Cindy argues with a gruff woman at the front desk. At first, they're exchanging harsh words through hissed whispers, but then Nurse Cindy finally loses her temper and raises her voice.

"You mean to tell me there isn't a single guard left to escort her? I can't readmit her!"

"Then you'll have to see the patient out yourself," the other woman bites back.

"Fine!" Nurse Cindy huffs.

"Here." The grumpy woman shoves a black cloth into Nurse Cindy's hands. "She'll have to wear this."

My jaw ticks. I hate how they're talking about me like I'm not even here.

"Is that really necessary?" Nurse Cindy contests.

The other woman wrinkles her crooked nose and flashes a hideous scowl. "It's necessary."

Nurse Cindy takes the black cloth and folds it into a long rectangle, murmuring obscenities to herself. "I'm sorry," she apologizes, looking at me. "I have to."

She ties the blindfold over my eyes and wheels me through the foyer. I'm not sure what the storm's done to the barracks, but whatever's happened out there, I'm not allowed to see it. I hear her jostle the front doors open. The wheelchair bumps over the threshold. A waft of warm air hits me in the face. The sun beats on my neck.

"What time is it?" I ask, curious to know how long I've been gone.

The wheelchair shakes over the loose gravel in the courtyard.

"Huh?" Nurse Cindy's voice squeaks. "Oh … uh, I suspect it's almost dinner time, dear." I can't tell if Nurse Cindy's shaken up by the overheated exchange with the desk secretary, or if she's witnessing whatever damage I'm not allowed to view.

Nurse Cindy shrieks, and the wheelchair rattles to a screechy stop.

"What is it? What's going on?" My heart races. I want to rip the blindfold from my eyes. I reach for it, and Nurse Cindy swats my hand away with a slap. Without warning, she runs, pushing me recklessly through the quadrangle. Her heavy breaths sound panicked. The rubber wheels of the chair jar the ground. I clench the armrests tighter and hold on for dear life. My body jerks back and forth in the seat. Sounds of overturned rocks and hasty footsteps mix together.

I attempt again to remove the blindfold.

"Don't!" Cindy screams. The seriousness in her voice urges me to obey.

I press my feet against the rails for support as we fly through the barracks grounds.

"Halt!" a man calls out in the distance.

Cindy slows her stride to a stuttered march.

"Where are you going?" The guard's voice sounds closer now.

Nurse Cindy gulps. "I'm escorting this patient back to her quarters."

"Put her with the others," the guard orders.

Stomping boots close in on me. The urge to scream swells in my throat.

"I can do it," Nurse Cindy appeals. Her trembling hands are rattling my seat.

I'm still bracing myself in the chair. Tension knots my shoulders.

"I'm afraid you've seen too much."

Nurse Cindy grips the handles, shaking the seat. I hold on, expecting her to bolt. My pulse roars in my neck. The guards pry her away, and I can hear her feet kicking wildly against the gravel.

"No! Please, no," she begs.

I hold my breath and choke back whimpers, listening to the scuffle, afraid to raise my voice in her defense. This is the price you pay for knowing too much.

Steadily, wheels start turning in the dirt. A new escort pushes me away from the scene, but my ears tune into the struggle.

"Help! He—" Nurse Cindy's screams fall silent.

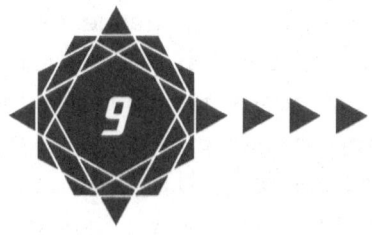

The guard whips the wheelchair forward and I spill out. My face smashes against cold tile, ripping a few of my stitches wide open. Fresh blood oozes down my brow. I brace my hands against the floor. Grime sticks to my palms. With a sharp inhale, I take in the stench of mystery meat and vegetable gelatin.

"Get up!" The guard kicks my ribs, knocking the wind out of me.

I choke on stale air and curl into a ball to protect my face from another blow.

"Enough!" another guard warns. "We're not here for that."

I wait a moment, afraid to move. My side and my head both throb with pain.

"I said, get up," the angry guard growls.

I swivel into a sitting position and lift the blindfold from my eyes. One of the guards extends an arm to help me. I wager it isn't the one who rammed his steel-toe boots into my ribcage. Regardless, I grit my teeth and refuse the urge to spit in his face. Denying his help, I lean onto my knees and wobble to a stand.

"Suit yourself," he mumbles.

Hundreds of people crowd the cafeteria. It looks like the entire population of the Southern Sector is here, huddling in groups on the floor. Barriers of tables and chairs corral everyone together, trapping them inside.

I scan the room. Three guards stand by the main door, and another three secure the entrance to the education center. Several more march the makeshift perimeter, but not a single guard patrols inside the enclosure. The people who sit along the edge of the barricade hang their heads, trying not to draw attention to themselves. Some of the children are crying. A woman hushes her toddler. A handful of men are scowling, silently scooting themselves into strategic positions, preparing to defend their families from taunting guards. My eyes travel to the center of the room, searching for my friends. A rush of relief washes over me when I spot Ronny's red hair among the monochrome crowd. I count the heads beside her.

One ... two ... three ... four ... five ...

They're all there—all the girls from Bunker 112. A long sigh escapes my lips. I need to get to them.

The gruff guard shoves me forward.

"Easy," the other defends, stepping between us.

"You've gone soft, Jones, taking pity on the Southern Sector scum." The guard makes his way to the barricade and pounds on a tilted table, startling a mother and her sobbing child.

Jones moves ahead of me, making sure the other guard behaves when I walk by. "Sit in here with the others." He slides the table to the side.

"Permission to join my unit, sir?" I seize the opportunity to ask while the other guard heckles more helpless people.

Jones gives me an approving nod, and I hobble through the opening he's created. He pushes the table back into place, closing the barrier behind me. "Make it quick," he advises.

I tiptoe through clusters of people, holding my spinning head. I sidestep to avoid an old man sleeping on the floor, but end up crushing the fingers of an innocent boy with my boot. His mother covers his mouth to quiet his yelping.

"I'm so sorry," I whisper, tumbling backward. The whole room spins. Nausea churns my stomach, twisting my intestines into knots. I almost fall on another woman, but lean forward just in time to regain my balance.

"Rey!" Geri shoots up from the ground, weaving through the throng of bodies to catch me. "Let me help you." She wraps my tired arm around her shoulders. "We're almost there."

"Reyna! Your head!" Lu blurts. "It looks awful!"

"It feels awful." I attempt a playful smirk, but the pain makes it hard to appreciate the banter.

"Makes you look like a fighter," Erika states, pushing a fist into my shin. "Geri might get jealous if it scars." She smirks.

Geri's lips press into a thin line. She squints at Erika, then turns to me. "Just ignore them, Rey. Why don't you sit here next to me?" Geri helps me settle onto the floor. I pull my knees to my chest and rest my chin on them.

"Here." Laud pulls a handkerchief from her pocket. "For your head."

"Thanks," I murmur. The one Geri lent me is probably sitting at the bottom of an incinerator with my contaminated jumpsuit, burnt into a pile of ash. I make a mental note to give Laude's back before pressing it to the place where my stitches split. I wince. The pressure sends pain shooting through my skull.

"We weren't sure we'd ever see you again." Geri's eyes soften with sympathy. "What happened out there, Rey? What happened during the storm?"

"I ... I don't know. Everything happened so fast." With my head spinning and my wound throbbing, it's hard to gather my thoughts. A lot has transpired since I last saw everyone.

I cup my hands around my head and try to settle myself, breathing in and out. "We took cover in the shed. I blacked out," I answer.

"I heard someone say there was a tornado," Lu chimed in. "Or maybe it was an earthquake? We heard some kind of explosion."

"What about the Warden?" Ronny leans forward. "Is she okay?"

"She's alive." I hang my head, not ready to share the details.

Geri squeezes my hand. "I'm so sorry you had to go through that. We're glad you're okay," she adds. "All of us are."

The other girls nod in support.

"What's it like outside? Did you get a good look on the way over here?" Ronny asks.

I open my mouth, but nothing comes out. A lump forms in my throat. Nurse Cindy's cries still echo in my ears. I grab my head and shrink back.

"What—"

Geri holds her hands up, and the questions stop.

"Relax, Ronny!" Erika scolds. "If Rey knew, she'd tell us."

I exhale and bury my head in my knees.

"They haven't let us leave," Geri leans in and whispers into my ear. "No one knows what's going on."

I wish I could muster up enough strength to tell them about the storm. What it feels like to be singed by acid rain. I'd tell them about the Warden and the underground levels in the Medical Center, but I can't. I'm tired and dazed, and all I want to do is lie down. Geri pats her thighs, offers her lap as a makeshift pillow. I rest my head on her scrawny legs and let myself drift in and out of consciousness, never fully awake, never fully asleep.

I listen to the voices around me. The other girls branch into separate conversations, speculating about what will happen next, but I can't concentrate on any singular exchange. Their voices mix with the rest of the crowd, and everything blurs like white noise.

"Thank you."

Geri's voice surfaces to the foreground of my attention. She places something lightweight on my stomach. I lift my neck to see. Blood rushes to my head, reminding me of my injury, and I suck air through gritted teeth. A small carryout box waits on my abdomen. Cafeteria aides slink through the masses, hauling overstuffed satchels and passing out food.

Geri smiles. "That one's for you."

I sit up slowly, squeezing my eyes shut as I do. The box slips off my stomach, and the scuffed foam pops open. A small cup of green-pea gelatin and a package of nutritional crackers come tumbling out. My stomach growls with approval, and saliva pools in my mouth. I think I'm actually starting to crave the disgusting mush.

The noise of the room quiets as people start eating. No one complains. Even Lu chews without voicing any grievances.

I sip down the last morsel of gelatin, and the haziness of my mind begins to clear. It's amazing what happens to the rest of my body now that I've eaten. The pain isn't as consuming, and I feel a bit more alert. My senses start kicking in, smelling the body odor of the man sitting behind me. The stench of his sweat mixes with the smell rising from my empty, plastic gelatin cup. My eyes can focus outside our circle now, too. There's nervous movement happening near the doors.

Screams fill the Mess Hall as men in full black bodysuits barge through the entrance, shoving barracks guards aside. I grab onto Geri and shuffle back, bumping into Erika, watching the intruders flood the room. Shielded helmets hide their faces, concealing their identities. They move synchronously, carrying weapons much more intimidating than the long batons of the barracks guards. Massive, identical guns anchor into the soldiers' shoulders, poised and ready to fire.

Laude's mumbling numbers, counting how many of them there are in the room. She's somewhere past thirty when she interrupts her figures to whisper, "They're dripping with tech. It's on their face shields, in their ears, on their wrists, attached to their belts..."

I look the soldiers up and down, but I don't notice any of the stuff Laude sees. It takes me a while to note the armbands running flush with their suits; everything else blends into their sleek black uniforms.

"What do we do?" Ronny's voice trembles.

"We fight!" Erika grunts.

Adrenaline surges. Blood rushes through my veins. I curl my fists, adopting Erika's rage.

"No!" Laude cuts in. "We wait. It's the only way we'll make it out of here alive." The seriousness in her eyes causes me to release my clenched fingers. The tension in my neck remains as I strain to see what's happening near the door.

Soldiers force barracks guards to the exit. I spot Jones pushing back. A woman reaches for him beyond the barricade of tables and chairs.

"GET BACK IN LINE!" the dark soldier shouts. His voice peals through the hall like it's ringing through the loudspeakers on the ceiling, but there's no static.

"Augmented projection," Laude says, taking verbal notes.

Jones presses harder, reaching for the woman. I yelp. His body falls limp, the result of being shot in the head by a soldier at close range. Blood splatters. The woman screams. I twist away from the horrible sight. My breathing sputters, and my eyes well with tears.

"Oh my god ... Oh my god ..." Lu's panicking on repeat.

"We're all going to die," Veronica cries.

We huddle together, gripping one another for support. Erika wraps her arms around me from the outside, her head perched to keep watch. I don't want to see what's happening, so I keep my head down. Horrifying sounds penetrate my ears, tables and bodies colliding. Through sweaty strands of hair, I see more than I want to. A soldier beats another man to the ground, unrelenting, pulverizing his face.

The sound of drumming boots causes me to lift my head. More soldiers dressed in black march through the Mess Hall entrance, escorting the Commander and his wife. Walter stands between them, sporting a black eye and a busted lip. A sour scowl paints his face. I almost feel sorry for him. Almost. In his case, the bloody display is more likely a result of bold stupidity than daring bravery. Either way, I'm not surprised he's already managed to earn a beating.

The soldiers part, forming an aisle for the Commander. Commander Cane steps forward, fidgeting with the lapels of his shiny, silver jacket. He forces a smile and clears his throat. "Citizens of the Omega Compound!" His throaty voice carries through the hall, echoing off the tiled walls.

My attention veers from the front to Jones's limp, bloody body still crumpled on the floor, near where the Commander's wife stands. She shrieks when she sees the dead man and faints into Walter's arms. Commander Cane derails from his address when he notices his wife pass out. His attempts to rush to her aid are cut off by the soldier behind him. Mrs. Cane regains consciousness rather quickly and buries her head into her son's chest. Assured by his wife's ugly cries, the Commander turns to continue his speech.

"We've successfully survived the treacherous turmoil of a Category 5 storm. All merit belongs to the thorough execution of government protocols within the last twenty-four hours."

Mrs. Cane wipes the makeup running off her face with her velvet-covered hands and offers a round of solo applause at the mention of the United Regime. Not even her outrageous dress and gaudy makeup could camouflage her brainlessness. She's as dumb as rocks, as fleeting as smoke, and as clueless as a child. Although, that might be an insult to all of the children in the Southern Sector. They aren't nearly as frail as she is.

The Commander nervously laughs. He makes a subtle turn toward the soldiers, searching for approval, then turns back to face the crowd.

"The barracks suffered significant damage during the storm," he continues. "However ..."

"What if the explosion we heard wasn't from the stor—"

"Shh." Laude shakes her head at Erika. "Not now."

"The United Regime graciously granted us use of their elite guard to help maintain order in such unprecedented times. A Phase 4 lockdown will remain in effect while we wait for repairs to be made across the complex."

Silence fills the hall.

"No one will be permitted to leave the building until further notice."

"We're stuck here?" Ronny whispers.

"My wife and I thank you for your cooperation," Commander Cane concludes, extending his hand to his wife before the soldiers usher them toward the entrance doors. Walter lingers as long as they let him, scoping the crowd. His wandering eyes stop, locking with mine. I squint and turn away, avoiding the discomfort of his stare. When my gaze returns to the doors, I watch the back of his head as he exits the hall.

"I can't do this ..." Lu clutches her chest. "I can't stay here forever ..." She's hyperventilating.

"Lu, you have to stop. They'll hear you." Ronny swivels her head, spying the remaining soldier's stiff movements.

Geri cups Lu's face in both hands. "You can, and you will. We all will. No matter how long it takes. We'll make it."

Geri's trying to keep us all calm, but I can tell by the panic in Lu's face that she's not listening.

"Lu! Look at me." Geri's scolding her now. "We're *going* to make it. Promise."

I admire Geri's optimism, but my own chest rises with rapid breaths. Who knows how long we'll be stuck in here, monitored by ruthless men—soldiers who won't hesitate to hand over a death sentence to anyone who tries to jump the makeshift barrier.

"Breathe with me." Geri loosens her hold on Lu. "In and out. In and out."

I join them, breathing through my nose and out my mouth the way Robin taught me to.

The doors slam shut, snapping my attention to the front of the room. The soldiers bar the doors.

"We're trapped," Lu whimpers.

"We're in the center of the room"—Laude trains her eyes on the guards—"which means we're the farthest from any exit."

I spin my head to the right. Another group of soldiers blocks the entrance to the education center.

"...but," Laude continues, "that also means we're the farthest from them." She dips her head toward the armed men.

"Dark Guards," Erika coins, clenching her jaw.

The name suits them well. Sure, they dress in black, but their abuse runs darker. *How many innocents have suffered and died in just the last hour?*

Uncertainty looms as the evening progresses. I witness several interactions between the Dark Guards and people resting along the perimeter of the barricade. One Dark Guard slams the butt-end of his weapon into a man's back. Another Dark Guard threatens a young woman at gunpoint, forcing her to silence her crying infant. An elderly woman stands with her hands raised, begging to use the latrine. The Dark Guards intimidate her with their weapons until the poor woman soils herself.

I avert my gaze, and my heart sinks further into my gut. The foul stench of human excrement lingers in the air. I turn to the floor, trying to avoid the odor, trying to forget. But there's nothing I can do to change our circumstances.

The main lights switch off on a timer, indicating blackout hours on the compound. Only the emergency lights above the doors remain on. Their white glow provides just enough light to mark the outlines of bodies on the floor. Thankfully, the visors of the Dark Guards' helmets burn red, making them easy to track in the dark. I watch their movement for a while before lying on the floor, squeezing myself between Ronny and Geri. I doubt I'll be able to sleep, and I think the same is true for everyone else. The anticipation of harassment and persecution leaves the entire room restless. Hours tick by, but scuffs and shuffles of paranoid people continue long into the night.

Morning comes unannounced when the lights flip back on, blinding me. I rub the shock of brightness from my eyes. My body aches from the stiffness of the cold tile and lack of sleep. I sit and stretch my sore body, pushing my chest forward, bringing my shoulders back.

Metal clangs against cement. I startle from my stretch, darting my widened eyes to the source of the sound. Dark Guards effortlessly remove the tables and chairs at the front of the room, casting them aside as if they were weightless. Another round of flying furniture rattles against the walls of the Mess Hall.

"What's going on?" Ronny pushes off the floor, her face scrunched with exhaustion.

More Dark Guards usher groups of people toward the entrance doors. Their movements are rigid like machinery. I search to see if Commander Cane is back, but there's no one here to offer up an explanation.

"They're blindfolding people and bringing them outside," Erika answers.

We keep quiet and stay huddled on the floor. The space between us and the Dark Guards shrinks. The closer they get, the faster my heart beats, pounding in my chest. Before I'm ready, the heavy hand of a Dark Guard falls on my shoulder.

"Stand up!" he demands, pushing me forward.

I walk as steadily as I can, following a line of people toward the exit.

Another soldier stops me at the door. "Name?" his mechanical voice drones.

"Sage. Reyna Sage."

"Unit?"

"112."

I stand, waiting for directions, holding my breath and locking my knees. Their weapons look even more intimidating up close. I worry the Dark Guard beside me will hold his gun to my head if I as much as flinch.

Without warning, the tight straps of a blindfold fasten around my head. Bodies close in on all sides. I lurch, tripping over several pairs of feet. A latch opens, and I move with the crowd through the heavy iron doors.

The coolness of the open air sends a shiver down my spine. I blink my eyes behind the thick blindfold, but no light pours through. The warmth of the sun is missing, too.

Someone steps on my foot and a knee collides with my thigh. An elbow smashes into my gut, nearly stealing my breath. I'm disoriented, but I keep moving. My tight boots scrape the gravel ground until I hear the grinding of a hatch door.

"Inside!" the Dark Guard barks.

Cold metal clashes with my hip and I stumble forward, falling on another body. Pained groans leak through gritting teeth. The door screeches into place, but no one moves. The weight on my legs pins me down, but it's the fear of being shot that keeps me frozen on the floor.

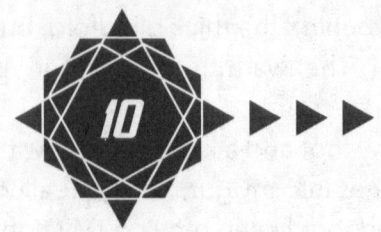

"Are they gone?" Ronny whispers from somewhere near my feet.

My legs are tangled with other limbs. My feet tingle. I can barely feel my toes.

"I think so," Laud answers from above. Her elbow digs into my sore ribs. When she shuffles to get up, her shoulder smacks me in the jaw.

"Good," Erika's muffled voice says from behind my head. "Now get off me!" She shoves against my back, causing bodies to roll in all directions. I tumble and groan, extending my arms to prevent another head-on collision. My palms hit the concrete, sending a shock wave of pressure through my skull. When I furrow my brow, it pulls on my stitches, triggering a sharp wave of pain through my sensitive skin. I flip onto my back and shake my wedged legs free. The blood flow slowly returns, exchanging the numbness in my soles for prickling itches.

I lie still for a moment, allowing the feeling to return to my legs, then rip the black cloth from my eyes. My roommates do the same, and a collective sigh fills the room. We're back in Bunker 112. I never thought I'd be so grateful for these four gray walls.

I slump against the familiar hatch door and let the tension in my shoulders loosen. Being careful not to squint too hard, I close my eyes and lean my head back, relishing the silence. My heart rate slows, bringing the banging in my head to a milder pulse. I contemplate getting up and moving to my bed, but when I lean forward, the wooziness reels me back, reminding me that it's better to stay still, at least for now.

"What are we supposed to do now?" Lu's rocking back and forth, holding onto her knees. She doesn't look any less frightened than when the Dark Guards first raided the Mess Hall. Her pupils dilate.

"The only thing we can do." Laude stares at the floor. "Wait." She adjusts the frames of her glasses when they slide down the bridge of her nose.

Lu buries her face in her hands and starts to weep. Geri scoots in closer and holds on to Lu's shoulders, tears welling in her own eyes. The rest of us keep quiet. I don't think anyone's in a hurry to get off the floor. We're all crammed in the entryway of our bunker, huddled together like we never left the cafeteria. Lu's cries turn to sniffles, and a lull of silence follows that lasts for several long minutes as we process the shock of watching people die.

"Commander Cane said the complex took a beating during the storm ..." Geri starts off slow. "Maybe once things get fixed up, the Dark Guards will leave, and things will go back to normal."

Normal? I start to think about what that word entails. It means waking up to orders, performing mundane tasks, keeping my head down around guards, and spending a few hours under Professor Diaz's instruction before punching in at work. Regardless of what happens with the Dark Guards, normal won't be normal for much longer. I'm seventeen. Next year I'll be too old to stay here. Bunker 112 was only meant to house orphaned minors. I'll be transferred to another shelter in the Southern Sector. I won't be able to attend lectures at the Education Center or spend mealtimes with my friends. I'll have to sign on for a career at the washhouse, mending and scrubbing dirty clothes for a full ten-hour workday.

I look across the cramped entryway to Erika. She's fixing the elastic in her hair, tying back the flyaway strands. She'll be eighteen next month, the first of my roommates to age out of Bunker 112. She's already made plans to stick it out at the machine shop, but it hasn't hit me until now that I won't be seeing much of her after she leaves. The only time I ever see the mechanics is during meals at the Mess Hall. Even still, we don't engage in conversation because their assigned seats are on the other side of the cafeteria.

My eyes wander, observing all my friends, thinking about how much time we actually have left together. My heart sinks into my gut, and suddenly being locked up for days on end seems more like a gift than a punishment.

"Things can't go back to normal, Geri," I finally say.

"Why would you say that, Rey?" I can see the shock in her eyes.

Geri's lips are pinched together like she's doing her best to keep herself from saying something she'll regret. She squeezes Lu tighter, trying to keep her calm.

I haven't had the chance to be truthful with everyone about the Warden's critical condition, so I use this as my opportunity.

"Because," I start, "the Warden's caught up in a hospital bed, fighting to stay alive. Even *if* she recovers,

I doubt she'll be well enough to look after us. They'll most likely assign us a new Warden." Geri's head drops, but I keep going. "And that's not the only thing that's going to change soon." My blood pressure rises. "Erika turns eighteen next month, and it won't be long before the rest of us are, too. So sure, say the damage gets repaired and the Dark Guards leave, but this"—I wave my hand in a circle—"won't last."

"Rey's right." Erika hugs her knees. "Suppose things do go back to normal? It won't matter. Everything's just going to change again." She leans in. I can see the wheels turning in her head, grinding like one of the well-oiled mechanisms she performs maintenance on down at the machine shop. She's spinning an idea. "For years we've joked about leaving this dump, about escaping over the wall. Well, we should stop talking about it and just do it."

Sparks fly in my mind. The only thing better than having a few days to ourselves would be for all of us to leave this compound for good, together. Even if it meant wandering around in the wilderness, searching for drinkable water, it'd be a grand improvement in comparison to staying here. At least then, our unpredictable futures would be in our own hands.

Musing about our escape and unavoidable change triggers a memory from my dreamworld, and the riddle from the Great Morning Star rises to the surface of my thoughts. The ache in my temples keeps me from reciting what he said exactly, but I do remember the mention of suffering and change. I can see how the suffering part is unfolding. *Maybe leaving the compound is the change that follows?*

"But what about the lockdown?" Ronny quivers.

"What about it?" Erika retorts.

"It might actually be the perfect diversion," Laude chimes in. "While everyone's shut in their bunkers and distracted by Dark Guards ... we might actually be able to pull it off ... We would need a plan, though, or our mission would be a death wish."

Lu hums in agreement, nodding in favor of constructing a plan.

"We don't even know what's over the wall!" Ronny's face flushes, turning a shade that matches her hair. "We could die out there! And that's *if* we somehow survive getting past the Dark Guards."

"It's true. We don't know much about what we're facing." Laude sounds sensible, and Ronny looks relieved to see that someone's taking her worries into consideration. "There's a lot of unknowns. But, if we focus on what we do know, we can start to formulate a plan." Laude crosses her ankles on the floor. "For instance, the Dark Guards are more efficiently equipped to enforce government regulations than the barracks guards we're used to. They have weapons and technology unlike anything I've ever seen. Getting around them won't be easy, but that doesn't mean it's impossible. We'll have to learn more about how they operate: where they patrol, how they communicate, and when they rotate assignments."

Ronny raises an eyebrow. "How on earth are we supposed to do all of that from inside this bunker?"

Laude scrunches her face. "We might be able to gather intel if we can find a way out before the hatch door secures at sundown, assuming the Phase 4 lockdown doesn't deviate from the compound's usual nightly protocols."

I shift my attention to the hatch handle. It's true, I never heard the locks engage. There's a good chance we won't be officially stuck inside the bunker until after sundown, like Laude mentioned. If we can find a way out during the day, we might actually have a shot at finding out how the Dark Guards operate and leaving this place for good.

Erika nods. "They can't keep us here forever."

My mind wanders. *What if the Dark Guards did keep us locked in here forever? What if one of them is stationed outside our bunker right now?* It's not like anyone will come looking for six orphaned girls in the Forgotten Zone. We very well could be permanently imprisoned here, sentenced to starve to death in our own bunker. Suddenly, I'm caught thinking about the miserable ways all of us could die. Not eating seems like a long and slow way to go, and all at once, getting shot in the head doesn't seem so bad. Jones got off easy. He didn't have to suffer for days on end the way Grandmommy did.

"We need weapons so we can fight the Dark Guards," Erika says, jumping back into the conversation. "We could take them by surprise!"

"Where are we going to find weapons?" Ronny rebuttals. If there's a need for concern, Ronny will voice it. She's always coming up with reasons for why things won't work.

"We could make them from our bedframes." Erika puffs her chest confidently. Her gaze grows sinister.

"I suppose we could sharpen the ends of the rails against the floor ..." Laude mumbles, weighing out the probability of crafting our own weapons.

"Now we're talking!" Erika claps her hands together.

"The welded metal would take ages to break!" Ronny whines. "We could get caught!"

"Ronny, didn't you see the way those Dark Freaks treated everyone in the Mess Hall?" Erika spouts. "They're not interested in keeping *you* alive. The way I see it, we only have two options: leave here or die trying."

I brace my hands against the cement floor. The likelihood of death grows more apparent with each passing moment. If we stay, chances are we'll die from starvation or execution, but if we leave, well, no one knows what we'll face on the other side of the wall.

I've always wondered what the world looks like off the compound. Professor Diaz makes it seem like the only things out there are dust, rocks, and wreckage from the Last War. Commander Cane ensures us that we're much safer inside the complex, where there's shelter from chemical storms. But now that I've survived one from inside the barracks, I'm not so sure. I speculate there are hanging cliffs or standing buildings somewhere among the abandoned ruins. There has to be. And if we can manage to find protection from the rain, we can set up camp and start our lives over, no longer under the thumb of the United Regime.

I'm starting to sound like a rebel. I inwardly sigh.

This isn't the first time I've wanted to leave. I've thought about it more times than I can count. Unfortunately, everyone who's born on the Omega Compound dies on the Omega Compound. I envy the airmen. They're the only people who ever get to leave this place. But, they're not technically from here. They fly in shipments of food from wherever it gets made and send in medical supplies when they can muster up enough leftovers to spare. Besides them, it's extremely rare for anyone to visit from any of the other United Regime bases. It's even more unusual for people to be permanently transferred here, demoted to live out the rest of their sorry existence on the Omega Compound. Although, I think that's what happened to Commander Cane when he stepped into office. He took over as Commander before I was born, though, so I don't know for sure. All I know is Walter can be quite the loudmouth when it comes to talking about residency and citizenship in class. He's interrupted the professor before, claiming his mother giving birth to him here was a mistake, that he's not actually Omega scum like the rest of us.

"I'm sick of following everyone's rules and regulations. It's about time we start making our *own* choices."

Erika's more of a rebel than I am. Her speech gets me fired up, ready to fall in line with whatever plan Laude devises. I envision us running into the quadrangle, sharpened bedrails in hand, charging the Dark Guards. Then I remember something I heard down at the washhouse last year about a man who tried to escape over the wall. Rumors say he used a hammer like a pickaxe to scale the barricade. *If he could do it, then maybe ...*

My heart starts racing with excitement.

"What about the shed?" I burst.

"Huh?" Geri juts her chin at me. I can't tell if she's on board yet with trying to escape.

"The tools. I'm talking about the tools," I explain. "It might be a lot easier to *get* weapons than to *make* them."

"But they're locked up," Ronny counters. Sometimes I wish she'd just shut up and let the rest of us talk things through before shooting down our ideas.

"Not anymore," I announce. "The storm blew the shed door clear off its hinges. If we can find a way to get over there, then we can scope the grounds and gather what we need."

Laude rubs her chin. "Maybe one of us could scout the area at night. It would be easier to stay hidden in the dark." She pauses to wipe her glasses on her uniform.

"I'll do it," I volunteer.

"Rey ..." Geri crumples. "You've been through enough. You need to take some time to rest." I know she's looking out for me, but I don't want her pretending to be my mother right now.

"We might not have time, Geri!" I yell, waking the pain in my head. I start to feel woozy again, but I can't let on that she's right, that I need to rest.

She recoils. The brightness in her eyes darkens. I know I've hurt her.

"I was in the shed with the Warden," I go on. "I know what's in there. I know what to look for."

"You'll have to leave before the hatch door locks us in for the night." Laude stands up. "And that's assuming a replacement for the Warden doesn't come to do a nightly rollcall."

I think about the pincushion Grandmommy wedged into our hatch door when I was a little girl to keep the locks from engaging. All of her unauthorized stargazing made her a professional escape artist. I never tried sneaking out in the middle of the night on my own after she died, but if Grandmommy could do it, then so can I.

"I can do this." I try to sound convincing, because I don't even know if I can manage walking to my cot at this point.

"I'm going with you," Geri declares.

"No," I say. "It's too dangerous. We're less likely to get caught if I go alone."

"Rey has a point," Ronny agrees, and for the first time, I'm actually glad she spoke up.

"But if I come with you, we'll be able to watch each other's backs. We can take turns looking out for Dark Guards. And, if something goes wrong … well, at least we won't get caught facing them alone."

Laude voices her opinion. "Geri might be right. Like I said, we have no idea what we're up against right now."

"I'll be fine," I say, but my confidence is dwindling. "I'll leave before the hatch locks, and after I've collected whatever I can carry, I'll hide in the shadows until it's safe to head back."

"With an extra set of hands, you'd be able to haul twice as much." Geri's still vying to come with me.

"Bring a pillowcase with you," Lu speaks up. She's starting to calm down. "It will be easier to lug whatever you find over your shoulder."

"That's a good idea," Erika agrees.

Everyone must be feeling restless talking about the plan because we're all standing now, squeezed together in the tight foyer of our bunker. I brace my feet on the floor and steady my spinning head.

Geri leaves Lu's side and puts her arm around me for support. "Admit it, Rey, you need me."

I know she's right, and I want her to come. I just don't want her to get hurt ... or worse.

"Fine," I huff. "You can come."

Geri smiles and bobs her head. The sparkle in her eyes is back, and I think she's actually excited to go with me on this suicide mission. I smirk back, but I feel like someone's shoved a rock down my throat. Geri's the closest thing I have to family. I couldn't live with myself if something bad happened to her while we were out searching for tools.

"There's a strong possibility you won't be able to get back inside the bunker until morning when the locks disengage," Laude says, pointing out the obvious, but I'm already one step ahead of her.

"My grandmommy taught me a trick to keep the bolt from latching when I was a little girl," I disclose.

"Really?" Erika sounds amused. "How come you've never taught any of us?"

"It's a lot harder to sneak out when you have to report to the Warden for a nightly rollcall." The truth is, I've thought about it plenty of times. I'd love to bring Geri and the girls out to the courtyard to stare up at the sky with me, watching millions of stars twinkle in the moonlight. The problem is, if I'm out gazing up at the stars, I'll miss my chance to see Grandmommy in my dream world. And even though dreaming doesn't happen every night, I like to take my chances that it will.

"Show us how it's done," she eggs me on.

"All I need is something small enough to stuff in the strike plate," I answer, swinging the otherwise useless blindfold up in the air.

"Genius," Laude mumbles with a smirk.

"Why didn't I think of that?" Erika questions, rubbing her temple.

"Are we really going through with this?" Ronny asks through shaky breaths.

Suddenly, everyone's staring at me like I have the final say. I press my lips together and give a firm nod. "What choice do we have?"

"Then it's settled!" Erika wraps her arms around Lu and Laude. "We're getting out of here!"

We stick our hands together in the middle of our huddle and seal our pact: we'll all escape or die trying.

Laude and Erika go over plans on how to study the Dark Guards and scale the wall while Geri helps Ronny and Lu take inventory of what little supplies we have in the bunker. Everyone lets me rest, since my head's still pulsing from the concussion. That and I won't sleep much tonight if I'm running around the quadrangle searching for tools. I doze off once or twice, but for the most part, I'm restless.

I reach under my mattress and pull the leather-bound journal from its hiding place. I attempt to write notes on the dream I had after the metal cart sailed into my skull and rendered me unconscious. For once in my life, I actually have time to scratch out the details since there's nowhere to go and nowhere to be. But instead of writing long sentences, I'm scribbling inkless circles, shaking my pen every few seconds to coax every last bit of ink out. *It's fine.* The pain in my head makes it hard to concentrate, anyway. I don't usually have a difficult time remembering things, but some of the specifics are fuzzy this time. Colors, for instance, are tricky to recall. I get frustrated trying to remember what color Grandmommy's orb displayed when she played on the reeds, and decide it's probably best to move on. I'm scratching out some details about what happened to the Warden in the medical center when Laude taps me on the shoulder.

"It's time," she whispers.

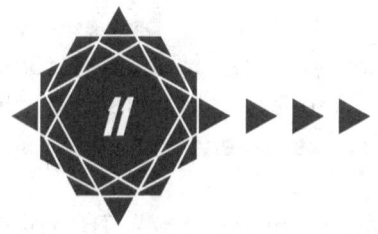

The gears of the hatch door clunk into place, dulled by the blindfold I shoved into the mechanism. I press my back against the cold metal door, hoping the wad of material holds. My heart is racing, but I'm not sure if it's the thrill of sneaking out or the possibility of getting caught that causes my palpitations. Geri's heart must be fluttering, too. Her heavy breaths are magnified in the quiet night air. I reach for her hand, and with concentrated effort, we quiet ourselves, inhaling slowly and deeply.

The silence ties my stomach in knots. Under different circumstances, I'd probably appreciate the stillness, but not tonight. I'm on pins and needles worrying about what's around the corner.

Once I've gained control of my shaky hands, I squint and survey the area. Nothing but shadows fill the quadrangle. My eyes haven't adjusted to the darkness, and it's impossible to know whether or not any Dark Guards lurk nearby. I scan the courtyard anyway, searching for the red glow of their visors.

Keeping hold of Geri's hand, I clamp my jaw and take a cautious step away from the bunker. The gravel crunches beneath my boots. I hold my breath and drag the other foot forward, pulling Geri along with me. Together, we trek into the night.

Adrenaline keeps me alert with every step. I count our paces, memorizing the distance between the bunker and the shed. Slowly, my surroundings come into focus. Clouds cover the sky. No stars are out tonight, but the moon provides just enough light to see the lingering debris.

I freeze, and Geri tumbles into my back. The shed, the place where the Warden and I took refuge from the storm, is completely flattened. A pile of rubble stands in its place.

"It's gone," I whisper, wondering how on earth the Warden and I managed to survive underneath the wreckage.

Geri tiptoes around me, taking the lead as we approach what's left of the shed. I follow, zigzagging along splintered planks and carefully maneuvering around the ruins. A rectangular metal tray glints on the ground, reflecting the moon's faint glow. One of the corners is stained red. I touch the tacky surface. *Blood.* It's the top of the cart that concussed me. I rub flakes of dried fluid between my fingers, remembering those last few moments before the collision.

"Rey!" Geri hisses for me to join her. "I think I found something." She points to the exposed leg of a shelf jutting from beneath the broken floorboards.

We take turns lifting cracked wood and laying it quietly on the ground, forming a new pile. When I remove the last sheet of lumber, I uncover a trove of tools. Geri grabs a bent saw blade and a hammer with a cracked handle from the top layer of debris. She slips the pillowcase from her uniform and starts gathering the tools, gently placing them inside. I pick up a few more items, adding them to our collection: a razor blade, a screwdriver, and a crooked pipe.

I pull on a mess of frayed fibers protruding from the wreckage, revealing a rope several feet long. I'm not sure the cord will help us against the Dark Guards, but I put it in the pillowcase anyway. It might come in handy after we escape.

There are a few other things that look like they might be useful, like an empty barrel and a step ladder, but they're much too large to fit in our sack. I get the feeling we'll be traveling light when we leave, and I really don't want to be hauling a heavy load over the wall, especially if we're being chased or shot at in the process.

Scuffing sounds echo in the distance.

"What was that?" Geri's eyes widen.

"Get down." I fall to my knees and look toward the bunker. I can't see any movement, but I'm not convinced we're alone. "Stay still," I whisper a warning to Geri and hunker lower into the rubble. She disappears between a crumpled wall of the shed and a rusted wheelbarrow.

I sink myself into a pile of wood and squint through cracks in the panels. My heart beats faster and faster as I scan for movement, listening for footsteps on the gravel. A cool breeze rattles across the empty barracks, kicking up dust as it blows. I turn my head to avoid getting dirt in my eyes, but when I do, I ram my shoulder into a loose plank.

A spotlight illuminates the pile of rubble in front of me. Covering my mouth, I pull my knees in closer, praying I'm not seen. I start hyperventilating. The irregular airflow makes me dizzy.

Please don't pass out, I plead with myself.

From my position, I can't see where the light originates, but I see the beam travel across the debris. The brightness hurts my eyes, and the pain in my head intensifies. The tip of my left boot is sticking out, but if I move, I'm bound to get caught. The light travels to the edge of my outsole, then stops. I hold my breath. It moves on, and a long exhale unwillingly escapes my nostrils. My attention darts to Geri as the light lingers near her hiding spot.

"Over here!" a scratchy voice breaks through my thudding pulse. "Let's get started on this mess."

Several boots shuffle in the gravel.

"Weren't our orders to start on the far side of the barracks?" a man's voice quivers. "We shouldn't undermine the Admiral. You know what she'll do?"

The Admiral? Who's that?

I shift my gaze, straining to see through the slits in the rubble, but I can barely make out the figures in the dark. When the flashlight comes around, I catch a glimpse of what seems like a dozen barracks guards in my peripheral.

"If she gets rid of us, she'll have no one to do her dirty work," the gruff voice gurgles.

I've heard this voice before. It's the calloused guard that kicked me in the ribs on the cafeteria floor. My blood starts to boil. I clench my teeth.

"I just think—"

"Fine!" he relents. "We'll start on the far side. But, as soon as we're done ... Well, you know exactly what will happen."

A loud gulp follows.

"We've seen what she can do. We're a liability now." The brusque guard's voice fades as he turns away from the broken-down shed.

I strain my ears to keep up with their conversation, but the wind muffles their voices. All I can make out are mixed tones of irritation and worry. I don't want to draw any attention to myself, so I keep my hands covering my mouth. When I think they're gone, I let my arms droop to my sides. Geri hasn't moved yet. She's probably frozen stiff with fear. I want to check on her, ask her if she's okay.

I scrape my boots to stand when I hear the roar of an engine coming our way, followed by the sound of metal grinding against the rocky ground. Ducking back into the rubble, I crane my neck as far as I can to get a better view without revealing my position.

A handful of barracks guards haul unrecognizable equipment toward the western wall. They disappear behind a cluster of buildings when their accompanying entourage comes into view.

The headlights of an oversized dump truck graze the gravel. A caravan of Dark Guards follows. Their visors light up red in the black of night. They drive past us, paying no mind to the heap of wreckage we're hiding in, and head in the same direction as the first group of barracks guards. I keep still as they vanish from sight, but strain my ears to listen for whatever happens next. Deep, masculine groans echo in the distance, accompanied by the clangs and scrapes of heavy lifting.

Not wanting to risk getting caught, I wait for what seems an eternity before I finagle my way out from the collapsed shed and tiptoe toward Geri. I find my friend curled up in a ball underneath the wheelbarrow tray, clutching the pillowcase. I can see her shivering through the rusted-out hole. I lift the lid quietly and whisper, "We've got to get out of here. Come on! Let's head back to the bunker."

For a moment, Geri doesn't move, but then she slowly pries her eyelids open. I peel her from the ground and she shakes her stiff joints, then grabs the pillowcase and secures it over her shoulder.

We hightail toward the bunker, dodging behind buildings with every subtle sound riding on the breeze. Creaks, heaves, and crashes thump steadily in the distance, startling my heart with every boom. By the time we reach our bunker, my hands are trembling uncontrollably, and my legs feel like they're made of vegetable gelatin. I reach for the handle on the hatch and push it down, but it doesn't budge. I try harder, using both hands, but it's useless. The door's locked. The blindfold didn't work.

The world starts spinning, and I lean against the bunker to keep myself from falling. Geri squeezes in front of me and takes a turn trying to force the door open, but she can't get it to move either. I hear scratching on the other side. I think someone else is trying to help us, but it's no use. We'll be stuck in the quadrangle till sunrise.

"We can't stay here." Geri shakes my shoulders. "We're too exposed."

I know she's right, but I feel too weak to move.

"Let's go back to the shed," she suggests. "We can hide in the rubble until morning."

I withdraw from the wall, and my knees buckle. I will myself to stand, steadying my feet among the loose rocks when Geri's forearm slams me flat against the hatch.

"Someone's out there," she grits through her teeth.

My vision is blurry, and the shadows are playing tricks on my eyes, but the jolt of Geri's arm fuels me with enough adrenaline to run. I blink and strain to see. Sure enough, someone else is sneaking through the barracks. A single silhouette weaves between structures on the border of the Forgotten Zone, several buildings down from where we stand.

We slink to the backside of the bunker and move out of sight, but I crane my neck to get a better look at the figure flitting between buildings. Whoever it is, they're wandering out here in the middle of the night, same as us, looking for something.

"Come on, let's get to the shed before we wind up caught." Geri nudges me before darting off into the darkness.

I turn to follow her, but when I step away from the bunker, the figure emerges again, directly in my line of sight. This time, the silhouette freezes, looking right in my direction. I twist to make sure Geri can't be seen, when I realize I'm no longer in the safety of the shadows. I've been spotted. Whoever it is, they're staring straight at *me*.

I stand stiff, heart pounding in my throat, contemplating my next move. Logic says I should run, follow Geri, play it safe, and rest in the rubble. But I don't want to risk leading the stranger right to Geri, especially if they haven't noticed her with me yet. I'd be putting her at risk, and then we'd both be in trouble.

When the shadow disappears around a building, I make the split-second decision to chase after it. It's a dodgy move, but maybe if I catch them, I can convince them not to tell anyone they saw me.

I whisper a farewell before slipping farther north without her. "I'm sorry, Geri."

The shifting and scraping grows louder as I go, masking the sound of my footsteps. Grinding metal echoes through the empty courtyard, bouncing off the corridor that connects the Mess Hall to the Education Center. The noise rattles my head and disorients my sense of direction, distracting me from my mission. I lose sight of the figure and spin around in a useless attempt to regain my pursuit before realizing the only way I'll ever find the stranger is if I keep moving north.

I get about three buildings deeper into the compound when it hits me how stupid my decision was. There's no sign of whoever I'm chasing, and every wobbly step I take reminds me I should've stuck by my friend's side instead of wandering alone into the night. I turn to head back when a hand slaps over my mouth. I swing my fists and kick my legs, but I'm no match for the strong arm that grabs me from behind and pulls me farther into the shadows.

"Shh!" the captor grits. "You're going to get us both killed!"

I stop struggling and he whips me around. Suddenly, I'm face to face with Walter Cane, the Commander's son.

"You scared me half to death!" I shove him off.

"Be quiet!" he reprimands, straining to keep his voice down. He yanks me closer to the bunker behind us.

Through the narrow space between the buildings, I spy red glowing lights. The Dark Guards are a lot closer than I thought.

"What are you doing out here?" he hisses.

"None of your business," I retort.

"Fine," he huffs. "But whatever it is you're up to, you were about to walk straight into a platoon of highly trained military men ordered to kill on sight."

I swallow. I should have gone with Geri. She's probably worried sick, wondering where I went. Hopefully she's not walking around, jeopardizing getting herself caught while searching for me.

"I have to go." I try to move when the red glow is no longer in view, but Walter pushes me back.

"They'll see you." He leans forward, stretching his neck and swiveling his head to look in both directions before scooting along the wall. "Come on." He flips his hand, motioning for me to follow.

We creep around the corner when the nearby clamor goes quiet. Walter halts, sticking his arm out to stop me. Without warning, he grabs my hand and skulks to the opposite end of the bunker, wedging us into the narrow alleyway between the buildings. My chest is pressed against his stomach, and I can feel his hot breath on my forehead, stinging the wound underneath my stitches. My skin crawls, repulsed by our forced proximity. Part of me thinks I'd rather be shot in the head than stuck here with our bodies squished together.

I want to pull back, but the rumble of an engine keeps me still. Gravel crunches under the rolling wheels of a heavy machine. Headlights graze the ground, and I reluctantly bury my head into Walter's chest, breathing in the stench of his salty body odor. His heart thumps in my eardrum, but I can still hear the other noise growing louder. Soon, the same truck Geri and I saw earlier in the night drives past our alley, transporting Dark Guards across the base. I keep my sights on the red glow of their helmets until the truck disappears into the Northern Sector.

Eerie silence lingers in the air.

"It's going to take a lot more than one night to finish this," a low exchange burbles from the other side of the alley.

I lock my knees and hold my breath. My lips brush against Walter's uniform, and I try not to gag as I slowly turn my head across his chest to look. Two barracks guards hover near the slim opening.

"That's my cue." Walter rubs against parts of me I wish he had never touched as he shimmies deeper into the alley. The slender walkway is barely wide enough to fit the width of his shoulders.

I have to find my way back to Geri, but I'm not so sure I can make it all the way to the Forgotten Zone unnoticed, not with all the commotion in the courtyard. I should go while Walter's distracted, but I hesitate when I see one of the barracks guards slip something from his pockets into Walter's hands.

"Who's she?" The guard looks past Walter, locking eyes with me.

I step back. My whole body trembles.

"Don't worry about it," Walter assures him. "She won't talk."

"She better not ruin this, Cane, or I'll turn you into the Admiral myself," the guard warns.

Their words disappear as the whoosh of my pulse claims my hearing. I hold onto my head. My legs give out and I lose my balance, but the tight space keeps me upright.

"Hey, hey, hey." Walter catches me as I crumble.

I need water. I need to lie down. I need to get to Geri.

"You really shouldn't be out here," Walter remarks when the clanging around the bend resumes. "You're hurt." He wipes the strands of hair from my wound. "And it's too risky."

"Why do you care?" I force my legs to stand.

"Because I think you're out here for the same reasons I am," he considers.

I scoff. *We are not the same.*

"Oh? And why's that?" I snarl as I study his face in the dim light of the moon. His eyes droop with exhaustion. His limp curls cling to his sweaty forehead. Purple bruises blot his lips. I trace his square jaw with my eyes, contemplating the events that left him marked.

"For this." He wraps his arm around my waist and pushes me to the end of the alley. With his finger to his mouth, he signals for me to look.

I slide to the edge of the bunker and angle my head past the concrete. Focusing my eyes across the courtyard, I gasp, clapping my hand to my mouth. A cluster of men moves in the dark, hoisting crumbled bits of plaster and cement into an armored truck. Its headlights shine on the site where the guards collect their rubble. An entire section of the wall is missing.

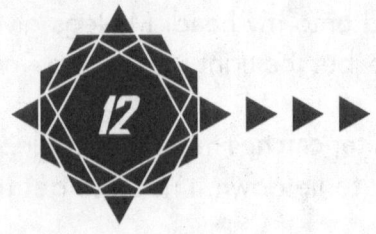

Eternal blackness unfolds behind the gaping hole. No matter how hard I squint, it's impossible to see what's on the other side. I want to get a closer look, but we've run out of buildings to hide behind. There's nothing but open space between where we stand in the alleyway and where the barracks guards clean up wreckage. A handful of red helmets keep watch by the wall, overseeing their labor. More strange lights blink in the air above the task force. I catch the low hum of whirling blades between the clamor of cement chunks dinging against the dump truck's bed.

"Drones," Walter whispers in my ear, then gives my uniform a tug. "Come on, let's get you back before the caravan returns." He retreats down the narrow passage. I turn to follow, but a growing knot in the pit of my stomach gives me second thoughts.

"Why are you helping me?" I spit.

Walter's one of the last people I'd expect to offer a courtesy to a resident from the Southern Sector. For the amount of times I've heard him criticize the Omega Compound and everyone in it, even though he was born here, same as me, I'd go as far as to say he thinks he's an unjust victim forced by his parents to survive our sorry way of life. I've learned to associate the cocky arrogance he displays in class with a certain level of heartlessness, too. Benevolence from the

Commander's son isn't something I trust to be genuine. Not unless there's some kind of pry for personal gain.

"In case you haven't noticed, I'm not faring well with the merge in administration." He indicates the bruises on his face.

"You mean you can't bribe them the way you're used to?" I take a confident stab at his ego.

"You don't know what you're talking about." He rolls his lips in, turning his back to me. "Do you want my help or not?"

"Tell me who the Admiral is." I try my luck.

"You don't want to know." He looks over his shoulder. "Our window's closing. It's now or never."

I reluctantly drag my feet forward, following him to the edge of the buildings we've managed to squeeze ourselves between.

He peers around the corner. "What's your unit?"

"112," I say.

Without notice, he jogs off, and I stumble after him, doing my best to keep up. I feel the impact of every stride reverberate in my head. The ache is growing stronger, parallel with my fatigue. A sharp pain takes hold of my ribs, making it hard to run. Walter doesn't slow down for me, but he does crane his neck every now and then to make sure I'm still trailing behind him.

He stops at the back end of a bunker on the outskirts of the Forgotten Zone. "Can you make it from here?"

I lean forward and grab my knees, wheezing. "Yeah," I pant, annoyed by the fact that he thought I needed his help in the first place. Though, I'm not surprised he wants to ditch me before crossing over into the Forgotten Zone. No one from the Northern Sector would travel to this side of the base on purpose.

I unravel my hunched spine to stand. Walter's swiveling his head in every direction.

"Don't move," he warns. "There's a drone flying our way."

I press my back against the concrete wall and hold my breath as its propellers spin overhead. My heart jitters, and I pull my toes into the shadows. The lip of the bunker roof barely creates enough darkness for us to hide. For several minutes, the drone hovers above us. I can see the metal curve of its arms extending beyond the overhang. To my relief, it zooms off, traveling back to where it came from.

"That was close." Walter sighs, stepping out from the wall. Traces of fear still splotch his face.

I wrinkle my brow, looking up at his expression, taken off guard by the fright in his eyes. It feels awkward to witness him vulnerable, afraid.

"I need to get home," he announces in a whisper. "Stay close to the buildings and in the shadows," he advises before sliding across the wall and out of sight.

I suck in air, remember Geri, and trot off toward the shed, holding my cramping side. I'm careful to stick close to the structures, ducking behind buildings and listening for movement whenever I can. After a long night of weaving in and out of the barracks, I finally make it back to the mounds of rubble where I hope Geri will be.

"Geri!" I call through gritted teeth. "Geri!"

A hand shoots up from underneath a pile of wood, and a weight lifts from my chest. I get on my hands and knees and crawl into her hideaway beneath the wreckage.

"I'm sorry I didn't tell you what I was doing," I say.

At first, Geri doesn't talk, and I don't blame her for being mad at me, but eventually she mumbles, "I'm glad you're okay."

Morning is still several hours away, so I curl up on the ground and share Geri's pillow: a half-used sack of cement mixture. She shares her tarp blanket with me, and I'm surprised by how warm it is underneath.

"Who was it?" Geri whispers.

"Huh?" Exhaustion sets in. I think I started dozing off.

"Did you find whoever was running through the barracks?"

"Oh," I answer. "It was Walter."

"The Commander's son?" Geri's voice gets louder.

"Shh—" I remind her to be quiet.

"What on earth was he doing sneaking around the Southern Sector?" She lowers her volume.

"I … I don't know." I suddenly realize I never asked him, but I'm almost positive it has something to do with the fact that an entire section of the wall is missing. Paranoid about the drones, I convince Geri to wait until we're back in the bunker to talk about everything that's happened. She agrees, then rolls over onto her side.

I stare up at the sky through the slits in the wood. The clouds have dissipated, and some of the stars are poking holes into the black abyss. Even with the chaos of the night, my thoughts drift to Grandmommy. I concentrate on feeling the cord she says ties our hearts together, and for a split moment, I think I hear her laughter on the breeze.

I doubt I'll see her tonight, but after a while, my eyes get heavy. The whistle of the wind starts lulling me to sleep. I close my eyes and imagine myself suspended among the stars.

Endless void surrounds me. I'm floating freely. There's no ground beneath my feet; no sky above my head. I suck in a sharp breath. The thin air makes it hard to breathe. I'm suffocating. I clutch my throat, gasping, when a warm wind enters my lungs and relieves me. A cold front follows, and a shiver races down my spine.

"Find me." The Source's voice speaks in the darkness, echoing in every direction. The phrase repeats until my mind goes mad. I flail in the darkness, but there's no resistance to thrust me forward. My heart thrashes against my ribcage, and I tug my hair in frustration.

"Where are you?" The words rip my throat raw.

"Find me." Another ripple of the Source's voice permeates the abyss.

How am I supposed to find something I can't see?

Loneliness overtakes me as I long for the emerald meadow and Grandmommy's companionship. I'd rather have a dreamless sleep than be brought to a place where nothing exists. It feels like exile, like I've been excommunicated from the City of Life.

Did I not believe enough?

The Source's voice dissipates into faint whispers, carried off by the wind. It feels like I'm floating between realms, neither here nor there. Lost in an eternal prison.

"Why did you bring me here?" I scream into the empty space.

A pinprick of light appears overhead. Luminous roots grow from the darkness, unraveling toward me. I jerk back to avoid their pursuit. They want to suck the life from me, drain me dry like they did the Warden, but I won't let them. I flounder with all my might, kicking and swinging to propel myself away from the menacing tendrils. My efforts are useless. The branches only grow thicker and stronger as they close the gap between us.

I brace myself, expecting their tips to drill into my flesh. Instead, the roots wrap around me, coiling up my arms and legs. I batter them away, but they climb to my neck and hold me in place. An unexpected wave of serenity washes over me as the limbs of the Source cradle my suspended body.

The earthy scent of the Source's fruit envelopes me, calming my rage. Involuntarily, I stop fighting and start to crave its taste. Saliva fills my mouth and drips down my lips. I'm overcome by an overwhelming desire to sink my teeth into its amber crop when another spark of light catches my eye, distracting me from the crazed impulse.

A small dab of light forms like a dewdrop on the root system swinging in front of my face. It grows and spirals downward, sliding along the shoots until it reaches their end. There, the liquid light expands into a perfect circle, then releases its hold from the Source, falling into the void below.

Several more droplets of light sprout on the roots, following the same pattern as the first, forming then falling, forming then falling, forming then falling. As they plummet, darkness swallows each one. The display mesmerizes me, and I completely forget my dwindling anger for the Source.

It isn't until the globe to my left flickers with a shade of sunrise fuchsia that I suddenly realize the blooming beads remind me of something. They resemble the orb that floats at the center of Grandmommy's chest—the radiant display that's set at the core of every living thing in the City of Life.

My jaw loosens, and I feel compelled to ask the Source what's happening.

"I'm creating," his resonating voice breathes.

"What are they?" I relax into his hold.

"Souls," he says, "the mind, will, and emotions of all people."

I'm not quite sure what he means, but the trance his scent keeps me under disables my skepticism. With childlike wonder, I blissfully stare at the souls that continuously drip from his roots.

"Where are they going?" I ask.

"They're on their way to meld with flesh from your earth, and when the time is right, I'll call them home to me."

The roots around my body pulse with light, covering me in warmth. An abrupt wave of sorrow guts me, and I begin to weep uncontrollably. Snot and tears mix as they stream down my chin. I don't understand why I'm so crushed, but the distress is unbearable.

The Source manipulates my emotions until I feel as though I'll burst.

"Why are you doing this to me?" I sob.

"I'm allowing you to feel a portion of my grief for those who won't remember—for those who won't return."

The ache in my heart gets stronger. My gut twists into knots and I crumple forward, held in the Source's embrace. I need to understand. I want to see what causes the Source such intense pain. "Show me," I plead.

Boughs curl around me, recreating the vined enclosure I stood in when I first met the Source, separating me from the infinite void. The tendrils gripping my body release their hold, gently setting me on a woven floor. I extend my arms to gather my balance on the uneven surface.

An unexpected warm and heavy weight falls on my shoulder. I jerk away, but when I twist my head, there's a man standing beside me in the leafy cage.

"Who are you?" I skid back, my heels kicking the powdery ground and stirring up golden glitter.

The man's glowing hand extends toward me. His eyes are pure light, so radiant that they blur the details of his face. White hair ribbons around him, floating in the air like long, lustrous strands suspended in invisible water.

"Reyna." The sound of my name on his lips makes my heart race. "I want to reveal my mysteries to you—the truth of your world. But you must put your guard down. You must be willing to trust me."

"I don't even know who *you* are!"

The cage shrinks as the Source's shoots close in around me, forcing me closer to the stranger. Heat radiates from his body. His eyes burn with white flames.

Even the flowing robe that drapes off his shoulders looks as if it's made of light.

"I have many forms and many names," he answers. "You have witnessed me in the sky as the Great Morning Star and found sanctuary here in my branches as the Source. I am the Eternal Breath, the Divine Word, the Wellspring of Life. I am the origin of all existence; everlasting past and unending future. I am Elolam, and *you* are mine."

At the sound of his name, I collapse to my knees, overcome with emotion. Hot tears stream down my face. The name echoes in my ears, pulsing through my veins, unraveling a lifetime of memories. Images materialize before me. I witness my birth; see my mother hold me to her breasts. Scenes of my father bouncing me on his knee and cradling me in his arms come next, followed by stargazing with Grandmommy; laugh lines wrinkle her face. Elolam continues to show me fragments of my childhood, each and every piece entwined with love and laughter.

I bow my head and raise my hands in humble servitude.

"What is this?" A faint whisper escapes my lips.

Elolam picks me up from the shimmering soil and pulls me into his warm embrace. "A glimpse of what I see, of who you are without guilt and pain."

His skin against mine makes my body go limp, but the strength of his arms holds me upright.

"Remember what I've shown you when you wake, Reyna. Remember what it feels like to be a child, free of condemnation and full of joy. Find a way to return to your innocence. Then, I will show you the ancient ways. I will reveal the Before Life to you, but you must first prove that you are willing." He withdraws. His eyes burn into mine. "With an abundance of knowledge comes a multitude of grief. The forgotten wisdoms are an honorable yet heavy burden."

"I'm willing." The words leave me before I have time to contemplate their magnitude.

Elolam's laughter shatters into a thousand flecks of light. I want to shrink back, like I've said something wrong, buckle under the weight of embarrassment. Glowing dust from his mouth falls onto my skin and seeps into my pores, and for a moment, I feel what he feels. This isn't mockery. It's as if pure joy materialized in his voice and burst from his mouth. He's genuinely delighted by my eager response. I smile. An innocent giggle escapes my lips.

"I will tell you only what you are ready to hear." Liquid light travels through the limbs of the Source, pulsing as Elolam speaks. "Before there was ever war, violence, or oppression, the world you live in now existed within the City of Life. Earth was once radiant—a realm teeming with living color. There was no separation."

I gawk, speechless. That seems impossible. I don't understand how Earth could ever be a part of the City of Life. A wave of sorrow swells in my throat as Elolam manipulates my emotions to match his. My heart aches and my lips quiver.

"I seek to bring peace to Earth once again."

The weight of his words falls on my shoulders. "What do you want me to do?" I whimper, unsure of my purpose. I don't understand what my role is in all of this; why Elolam has brought me here; why he's telling me that Earth used to be connected to my dream world;

why he's hijacking my emotions and making me feel the heaviness of his burden. I wish Grandmommy were with me inside this vined enclosure. She could offer her insight and help me interpret Elolam's riddles.

"Find the ones who seek me beyond the suffering. Find the ones who are willing to remember, like you are. The key to unlocking the door between our worlds is remembering." Long limbs twist and untangle as the Source unravels his branches. Bits of rubble peek from between the leaves. The rumble of unknotting wood blends with the rustle of polyethylene fabric. I cling to the words of Elolam as my consciousness unfolds back into reality. My dream ends, but the nightmare is just beginning.

"Do you remember?" His voice haunts me.

Remember what?

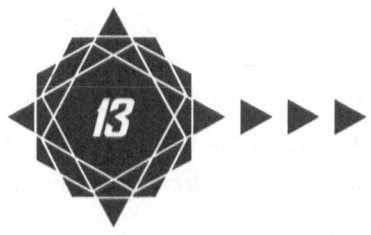

The soft glow of dawn bleeds through slits of splintered lumber. I shake Geri awake, wanting to get back to the bunker before the sun fully rises. We carefully peel the tarp from our bodies, rustling the material as stealthily as possible. I pause to listen. Other than the crinkle of our blanket, I can't hear anything. There's no more banging on the far end of the barracks. I don't notice the rumble of machinery, either. It's quiet ... too quiet.

When I crawl out from underneath our hideout, a chill rattles my aching bones. Crisp air fills the early morning, and a slight fog lingers on the ground.

Perfect. This is just the cloak we need to make it back to the bunker unnoticed.

Without a word, Geri and I tip-toe our way home. Even with the weight of the pillowcase on my shoulder, I feel sturdy. My steps are more balanced than the night before, and the distance between our bunker and the shed seems a lot shorter with the glow of first light. A few hours of sleep have done me some good. The pain in my head isn't as severe, and I feel like I can think a lot more clearly.

We reach the bunker, and I hold my breath as I grab onto the cold metal handle and push down. The gears grind, and I respire. The heavy door creaks open. Geri and I slip inside and pull the hatch closed behind us.

Everyone's already awake and standing. From the looks of it, no one got very much sleep last night. Their wrinkled uniforms suggest they never even tried. Dark circles ring under Erika's eyes. Laude's lids droop from behind her glasses. Ronny twitches like she's trying to keep herself from falling over, and Lu stretches her arms while letting out a massive yawn.

"You're back." Erika exhales, and I can tell she's relieved to see us.

"We thought we heard you trying to get back in last night," Lu adds.

"I tried to open the hatch, but it wouldn't budge." Erika steps closer.

"Where did you spend the night?" Laude asks.

"Did you find any tools?" Ronny chimes in.

Everyone's talking all at once, crowding around us as they speak. I know they're eager to hear how our evening went, but we haven't even moved out of the entryway yet.

"Can you guys give us a second?" I blurt, and the pelt of questions ceases.

Erika furrows her brow. Lu hangs her head. Ronny turns her back to us, her shoulders slumping on the way to her cot.

"What Rey means," Geri says, trying to remedy my harsh reaction, "is it's been a long night, and we could really use a moment to catch our breath."

"No problem," Laude answers. "We can talk when you're ready."

"Thanks." Geri flashes a tired smile and nudges me farther into the bunker.

I head straight to the sink and stick my mouth under the faucet, slurping in the pathetic spray that sputters out. The lukewarm water wets my cracked lips and moistens my parched tongue. I splash the pitiful shower onto my face and let it soothe my sore wound. Toweling my skin dry, I pause to survey my reflection in the cracked mirror hanging above the sink. The image in the blurred glass mocks me. Blue threads zigzag across my forehead, spotted with crusted blood. Purple circles cradle my eyes. Knots of long brown hair hang over my shoulders. What used to be a braid is now a matted mess.

After taking the time to comb through my hair, I loosen the laces on my boots and slide my aching feet from their hold. They're definitely too small. Blisters have formed on both of my heels. My soles throb as I stretch my tender toes.

I pull the privacy curtain and sit on the latrine, relieving myself for the first time in what seems like days. Not much comes out, and the stench of my urine is extra potent. There's no denying I'm more dehydrated than usual. I can't even remember the last time I held a bottle of water.

Once I'm finished, I make my way over to my bed and sprawl out on the lumpy mattress. It's not the most comfortable, but it beats lying on gravel.

The other girls wait silently for Geri and me to be ready. Even with my eyes closed, I can feel them staring. I'm not in a hurry to talk. I want to take a second to write down what happened in my dream first, but I can't bring myself to move. Instead of journaling, I lie stiff on the bed, contemplating whatever it was Elolam wanted me to remember.

I haven't been able to make much sense of my dreams lately, ever since they started changing. Things were much simpler in the meadow before Grandmommy brought me into the City of Life. Now I wake up feeling puzzled by riddles rather than refreshed by visits with my grandmother. I'm not exactly sure I understand what Elolam wants me to do. And once I find whoever it is I'm supposed to be looking for, what then? I groan aloud, wishing his instructions were more specific.

"Ready?" Geri grabs the top bunk and leans over me.

"I guess," I moan before sitting up.

Erika drags her cot to be parallel with Ronny's. The metal frame scrapes across the concrete, marking the floor with long white scratches. We pile on the beds, facing each other. Geri and I join Ronny on her mattress, and Erika squeezes between Lu and Laude on hers.

First, Geri piles our spoils on the floor, showing off the scraps of tools we've collected. Laude picks up the rope, and I can see her wheels turning.

"I wonder if this is long enough ..." She strokes her chin. "We could use it to hoist ourselves over the wall—"

"We might not have to," I cut in.

"What?" Geri scrunches her eyebrows at me.

"I didn't get a chance to tell you what I saw on the other side of the barracks," I remind her.

"Wait? You two split up?" Erika leans forward on her knees like she's ready to consume some juicy compound gossip.

"Doesn't that defeat the whole purpose of going out there *together*?" Ronny puts a lot of emphasis on her last word.

"I already know it was a stupid move," I admit, feeling a bit defensive. "But what's done is done."

"So, what *did* you see?" Lu asks with narrowed eyes.

"I saw a mess load of barracks guards cleaning up wreckage and hauling chunks of concrete under the watchful eye of Dark Guards and security drones."

"Drones?" Erika gasps. "Here? On Omega?" She seems amused at the prospect.

"I wouldn't get too excited," Laude interjects. "We still don't know what kind of technology we're dealing with. Those drones could be set up to do a lot more than surveillance."

"You mean weapons?" Lu gulps.

"Exactly," Laude confirms.

"I don't get it." Ronny crosses her legs. "What does this have to do with climbing over the wall? If anything, drones will make it *harder* to escape."

I survey my friends. They're all looking straight at me, waiting for an answer. "There's a hole in the wall."

"Nuh-uh!" Erika slaps her knees and stands up. A gigantic smirk spreads across her face. She grabs hold of her head.

Everyone looks shocked. Even Geri's mouth hangs wide open.

"What was on the other side?" Ronny bends to look past Geri.

"I don't know. It was too dark to see anything beyond the wall, and I didn't want to risk getting closer. There were too many Dark Guards patrolling nearby."

"Is that where you ran into Walter?" Geri drops his name like an explosive. I can tell she's burned by the fact that I didn't tell her about the hole in the wall last night. She knows how I feel about Walter. Mentioning him now is payback. I wasn't even sure I wanted to tell the rest of the girls about running into him while scurrying through the quadrangle. Now I have to.

"Wait, what?" Lu cocks her head. "Walter Cane? What was *he* doing out in the middle of the night?"

"Probably petitioning to have his face painted on the barricade as part of the new remodel," Erika jeers, and everyone but Geri laughs.

"No, really, what *was* he doing?" Laude asks. Her smile falls flat.

"Well ..." I start.

"She doesn't know," Geri interrupts, her tone cold. I think Erika's jab at Walter made her regret bringing him up.

Teasing other people always makes Geri uncomfortable, even when it's deserved. One time, a girl from the Northern Sector told Geri her scar looked like she'd been wrapped in crinkled cellophane reused from our packaged meals. I bit back and told the girl she was uglier than a lump of vomit and dumber than a pile of rocks. Geri didn't like that very much. She cried, and not for herself, but for the jerk in our class. Later that night, she told me people only make fun of what they don't understand. But I don't care to understand Walter Cane, I just want to know what he's up to.

"That's not totally true," I contradict, sucking in air through my teeth. "I might not know what he was up to *exactly*, but I did see him push something to a barracks guard. He's got some kind of secret operation going on."

"You didn't mention that." I can feel the heat from Geri's eyes when she reminds me of my negligence as a friend.

"I wanted to, but we weren't really in a convenient place to talk," I counter. "But that's not all."

"Oh, really?" She presses her lips together.

"Yeah. I overheard them talking about someone called 'the Admiral.' I'm assuming she's the leader of the Dark Guards. Apparently, Walter doesn't appreciate the changes she's made to his family's administration. And whatever he's planning with the barracks guards, well, they don't want *her* knowing about it."

After saying it aloud, I realize this might actually play in our favor. I mean, Walter's not exactly the type of person I'd consider an ally, but now, it's possible we have a common enemy. And, as I've heard Professor Diaz say during one of his history lectures, "The enemy of my enemy is my friend."

The Admiral obviously doesn't care about the well-being of Omega's citizens, and as detached as Walter's parents might be, they're definitely not ruthless. Sure, there are punishments in place for rebels and criminals, but before the display in the cafeteria, I'd never seen anyone get shot in the head before. Plus, Walter *did* defend me in front of the barracks guards when he swore I wouldn't expose their plans. Well, joke's on him, because I'm talking about it right now.

"Alright, alright, let me get this straight." Erika paces the floor. "There's an Admiral. We're pretty sure she outranks Commander Cane. Walter's scheming with the barracks guards was some kind of secret revolt against her and her psychotic army. Oh, and there's a freaking hole in the wall … Wait—how big is it?"

"Big enough to walk through," I answer.

"Big enough to drive a truck through?" Her eyebrows raise.

"Maybe? I couldn't tell from across the courtyard."

"Let's find out." She rubs her hands together. "If it is, I think I might be able to get us one from the machine shop."

"Really?"

Lu seems excited about the potential of having a truck. She's probably thinking about how much easier it would be to drive through whatever wilderness exists on the other side of the walls instead of wandering around on foot. And, I have to admit, I agree. The thought of leaving the compound with a truck is invigorating.

"There's an old tactical vehicle in the back bay. Some of the mechanics have been working on it for a while, trying to get it up and running with whatever spare time they have during their shifts. I'm not sure what else it still needs to be operable, but I heard one of the guys say it's almost ready. Next time I'm there, I'll find out. And, who knows? Maybe we'll be riding out of here in style." She shimmies her fists back and forth, pretending to hold an imaginary steering wheel.

"Are you all forgetting how loud the trucks are?"

Of course, Ronny *has* to bring up an opposing point of view.

I roll my eyes and bury my head in my hands.

"It will be a lot harder to sneak out unnoticed with a revving engine giving us away," she adds.

Her point *might* be valid, but it's also a killjoy. Either way, the girls start arguing over which plan is better, listing off the pros and cons of going on foot versus stealing a truck. I zone out, picturing both scenarios in my head. But the thing is, once we *do* decide on *how* to escape, there's a whole other problem to consider and a lot of unknowns that come with it. We don't know what's on the other side of the wall, where we'll sleep, what we'll eat, or even if we can survive the first acid rain we encounter.

Discouragement surfaces, and I hear Lu say we might be better off staying on the compound.

Sure, we might survive if we stay here under the abuse of Dark Guards, but leaving ... well, we're taking a giant risk that we'll be alive long enough to enjoy our freedom. I guess we have to figure out how badly we really want it.

The only taste of freedom I've ever known is the blissful escape I feel when frolicking through emerald fields while I'm asleep. Thoughts of the meadow trigger daydreams about taking everyone with me into the City of Life, introducing them to Grandmommy and showing them around my enchanted dream world. If only I had the ability to actually transport all of us there, to that place beyond the stars. Then we wouldn't worry so much about leaving the Omega Compound or argue relentlessly over which escape plan is better. We could just spend the rest of our days enjoying each others' company under the expanse of the sky, watching colossal planets spin overhead.

The girls would call me crazy if I started sharing my thoughts aloud. I feel like a lunatic just for thinking them. Besides, Geri's the only one who knows about my dreams, and now doesn't feel like the appropriate time to spring that kind of information on everyone else.

I try to forget the impossibility of escaping through the City of Life, but the alternatives make my head hurt even more. I might be worried about what will happen if we leave the base, but staying here pretty much guarantees certain misery. My breathing goes erratic. I squeeze my eyes tight and clutch my chest.

Find me.

Elolam's words send sparks flying through my memories, redirecting my panic and causing me to focus on his riddles.

Hope's brimming.

The layered voices of the Great Morning Star bleed into my eardrums. I'm trying so hard to figure out what it is he wants me to do to get through this suffering, to remember what it feels like to have hope.

Elolam's echoing voice plagues my thoughts as I hash through the last things he said to me before waking up this morning under a plastic tarp.

The world you live in now existed within the City of Life ... I seek to bring peace to Earth once again.

There's a secret to uncover, a hidden message to unveil—a real way to access the City of Life. I think it has to do with hope and innocence. And, for a moment, I feel like I'm on the brink of discovery, on the verge of understanding what to do.

The key to unlock the door between our worlds is remembering.

Accompanied imagery of nurse Cindy sliding her secret key into the hidden slot on the elevator panel flashes through my mind, but my breakthrough gets cut short when the hatch door swings open.

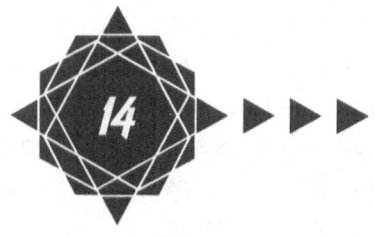

I jolt, face the entrance, and stand at attention. It's a force of habit. And for a split moment, I expect to see the Warden barging through the door. But reality sinks in fast when three Dark Guards maul past the hatch carrying massive black weapons. Panic sets in when they barrel into Erika, knocking her onto the floor. My chest tightens, and my heartrate accelerates so fast that I think I might faint.

Frozen stiff, I clench my jaw and lock my knees to keep myself from rushing to Erika's aid and getting myself tossed to the ground. I'm too afraid to turn and see what they're doing, but I can tell by the look on Ronny's face that it's bad. She crams her eyes shut and curls her lips together, still sitting on the mattress with her fingers gripping the covers.

Whooshing and crashing noises erupt as the Dark Guards ransack our room. I jump when Laude's bedframe strikes the floor, and I accidentally spin around to witness the disaster. Immediately, I wish I hadn't. The first thing I see is one of the Dark Guards flipping through my journal.

"Well, well, well …" His voice crackles with static. "What do we have here?"

The Dark Guard holds up his prize, and my heart sinks into my stomach.

"A gift for the Admiral?" his bulkier comrade answers, the smooth helmet amplifying his gritty tone.

The third soldier spots our collection of tools spread on the floor and marches between us. His partner moves to hold a gun to Lu's head while he grabs the hammer off the concrete. Lu's lips quiver. Fear occupies her eyes and rattles her limbs.

I clench my fists as he stomps closer, driving the hammer into his gloved hand.

"Now, tell me, how did a load of orphans manage to get a hold of all this?"

His masked face turns to me, but I don't answer. I stare into his visor. My slanted reflection glares back. There's no evidence of what he looks like underneath, only the sheen of yellow light from the dingy bulb above us.

He swings the hammer. I brace for impact, but the steel head stops a hair's breadth from Laude's face instead of mine. Tears stream down her cheeks.

The tallest guard grabs Erika by the hair and pulls her upright. Anger burns in her eyes. She clenches her fists and snarls. Geri shoots her a look with a shake of her head, reminding everyone that now isn't the time to fight back.

Erika relaxes her rage and moves with reluctant compliance when the Dark Guard yanks her forward. I can imagine how angry she feels. My blood is boiling, too. I'm not sure how much of this I can handle before I snap. It's taking every ounce of self-control to not react.

Unfortunately, Lu's the one with the gun to her head, and any reckless response on my end could cost us her life.

"Listen up, weaklings!" he screeches, holding on to Erika's head. "We're going to take a walk! Anyone who steps out of line will meet the butt end of my weapon. And if anyone tries to run, well, they'll get what's coming from the front." He shakes his military grade gun in the air. I measure its length from the top of Erika's forehead to the stock below her waist.

I've never seen a real weapon up close before, but the sight of it makes me shudder. For as long as I've been alive, barracks guards have never carried guns. The United Regime outlawed firearms on the compounds at the end of the Last War. The only opportunity we have to learn about artillery is during class, and Professor Diaz avoids talking about it as much as possible. He gets uncomfortably squirrely on Remembrance Day when he reads from the old newspaper articles preserved in laminated plastic. The journals make it seem like banning firearms was a last-ditch effort to preserve peace. According to Professor Diaz's unsolicited tangents, it was a move of control to put rioters in check. Apparently, the rules don't apply to military personnel. Even I can tell that these weapons aren't old war antiques. A red glow that matches the Dark Guard's visors streaks across their centers, and it makes me think these guns were made specifically to accommodate *these* soldiers.

"Move out!" The blast of his voice rattles my eardrum.

The head of the hammer cracks into my back, and the Dark Guard holding the helve shoves me forward. I fall into line like a mindless soldier obeying their orders, praying my wobbly knees don't give out.

When we exit the bunker, the fog dissipates. I squint and shield my face from the intense morning light that sears my retinas, triggering an instant headache. Flashes of gold halo a radiantly glowing sun. Traces of vibrant colors paint the sky with evidence of a brilliant sunrise. Any other day, I would have stopped to appreciate its beauty. But the concussion makes it hard to look, and the Dark Guards' hurried pace makes it impossible.

They force us forward, flanking our sides. The stony ground drives into my bare feet, and I grunt with every step. I'm not so sure taking my boots off was a good idea. My blistered ankles and cramped toes might have thanked me at first, but now my toes curl with discomfort each time they hit the gravel.

Our unit melds with another set of Dark Guards and the two orphaned boys from Bunker 111. The scrawny boy is crying. His pants are wet, and the smell of urine tells me why. The older boy from my class holds his hand, attempting to console his one and only roommate.

No one else is in the courtyard. A bad feeling sours in my stomach. I don't know what's happened to the warden who oversees Bunker 111, but I know for a fact ours won't be coming to save us. I'd be surprised if she had any idea of what's going on. That is, *if* she's still alive.

Thoughts of the Warden make me emotional, and for once in my life, I actually miss her stern face. I'd do just about anything to have her be the one leading me to another mind-numbing morning of wall duty than blindly following heartless government soldiers into prison, or torture, or worse. There's no denying it, the

Warden's firm orders were quite nurturing in comparison to the Dark Guards' lethal conduct.

The squad of Dark Guards leads us in a single file toward the Eastern Wall, directly into the sun. I do my best to shield my eyes from the light, to keep the stabbing pangs from growing any stronger, and strategically angle myself into the shade of Lu's shadow. Lowering my head, I notice the pathway is free of wreckage. I crane my neck and, sure enough, the entire courtyard is spotless. Not a single clump of debris remains on the open roads. A lot has changed in only a few hours. I strain to see if they've patched the hole past the bulky weapons strapped to the Dark Guard's backs, but it's no use. Between the soldiers and the buildings, I can't see a thing. We're too far to steal a glance, and I have a feeling the way we're walking was chosen specifically to avoid the broken wall.

We march in the direction of the Northern Sector. If I could guess, I'd say we're headed for the Medical Center. I'm not sure what the underground floors hold, but there's a pretty good chance we'll find out soon. An ominous feeling twists my intestines, envisioning all of us locked away in a torture chamber, forced to be on the receiving end of an experimental weapon held in the hands of an unchecked Dark Guard. I imagine burning hot lasers searing my flesh, when commotion rises from the front of the line and shifts my attention forward.

One of the Dark Guards singles out the small boy, bumping into him every couple of steps. The boy's grunts grow louder as he tries his best to keep moving. Another push from the callous soldier sends the boy tumbling to the ground.

"Leave him alone!" the boy from my class yells. I can tell by how tightly his fists are clenched that he wants to throw a punch.

"Don't do it," I mutter under my breath, hoping he keeps his cool.

Unfortunately, the boy doesn't hear me and takes a swing at the Dark Guard's visor. A loud crack follows, but the Dark Guard's helmet looks unscathed. The boy's knuckles, on the other hand, immediately start to bleed.

"Brenton!" the scrawny kid cries out when the Dark Guard returns the attack with a blow from the stock of his weapon, which drops Brenton into the gravel. Bright red liquid oozes from his skull, but the Dark Guard doesn't relent. He continues to beat Brenton, alternating thrusts between his mammoth gun and his heavy boot. Brenton raises his arms to protect his head, but the Dark Guard only kicks him harder.

During the chaos, Geri slithers herself beside the younger boy, grabbing onto his hand, keeping him from running to help his roommate. It's a good thing, too, because just one look at the skinny kid lets me know he couldn't survive a single blow from the abusive Dark Guard.

"Keep moving!" Another soldier shoves us on, forcing us away from the scene. I stumble into Ronny, who steps back on my toes. Biting my tongue, I suppress a yelp and lean into her, helping to push her forward. She seems to be having a hard time peeling her eyes away from the violent scene. With one last twist of the head, Ronny grits her teeth and walks on.

We move in silence, listening to the strikes of the Dark Guard pounding Brenton over and over again. I shudder with every thump. Guilt ties my stomach in a knot. I feel like a coward for not helping Brenton, but any attempt to stop the assault would have flattened me on the ground right next to him.

The thuds fade as we march on, masked by the crunch of gravel beneath the Dark Guards' weighted boots. I hobble over the rocky path, but the ache in my feet is quickly becoming the least of my concerns. The Medical Center is now in focus, and now I'm certain it's the intended destination. My heart beats faster as we near the front doors. The fleet of Dark Guards steers our shaken group to the front desk. That same grouchy woman who argued with Nurse Cindy over my discharge is standing at the counter with a checklist in her hands. The thud of my pulse rings in my ears as I recall the sound of Nurse Cindy's cries cut short. A shiver runs down my spine.

"I've brought the children from units 111 and 112 as requested by the Admiral," the leader of the Dark Guards says to the secretary. She peers down her crooked nose at the chart, flipping through to the very last page. Clicking her tongue, she releases an exasperated sigh, then taps the tip of her pen against the clipboard.

"I have eight children on record for those units; six girls and two boys. You've only brought in seven."

"You're mistaken," the Dark Guard corrects. "Everyone's been accounted for."

"Hmm." The secretary presses her thin lips together, narrowing her eyes with speculation.

"I said, everyone's been accounted for!" he roars.

The woman chokes, reeling backward. With a shaky hand, she scratches something off her list and motions to the elevator.

"The Admiral's expecting you." The Dark Guard's booming threat sucked every ounce of confidence from her voice.

All seven of us load onto the elevator, but only two of the remaining Dark Guards cram in behind us. The sour stench of soiled clothes fills the lift, and I do my best not to gag. I wonder if the soldiers can smell through their visors or if their suits circulate with filtered air. There's no signs of ventilation on their helmets. The masks cover every part of their heads with a solid, slick material. Their suits climb their necks and meld with the hard casing on top. I can't see a single spot where the foul air might seep through.

It's not the boy's fault. If anything, it's the *Admiral's*. I hate her so much and we haven't even met. Anyone who's okay with ordering their fleet of monsters to beat an innocent kid is sick in the head and pure evil. As for the boy, I feel sorry for him. He doesn't know any of us, and the only person who had the courage to stick out his neck for him is gone. My heart sinks. For all I know, Brenton's dead.

The reality of death weighs on my chest. I'm not entirely sure what happens to people after they die, but I hope that when my time comes, I'll be able to meet Grandmommy in that place beyond the stars, dancing free in our emerald meadow, never having to leave her side.

For a moment, I picture Brenton there, too, getting to experience the mysterious beauty of the realm that surrounds the City of Life. But, as far as I know, I'm the only one on Earth who can dream, and therefore the only person who's ever been to the city. He'll likely never know what it's like to feel soft grass between his toes or fresh fruit against his lips. Even the things that made me nervous at first, like the raging crystal river and the massive talking tree, seem like wonders worth knowing now. If he dies today, his life will end only knowing the pain of living on the compound: the threat of hunger, the fear of disease, and the loneliness of being an orphan. Worst of all, he'll never understand the overwhelming peace that comes with being wrapped in Elolam's arms.

A sense of belonging and deep acceptance rush through my veins and warm my body at the thought of Elolam's name. I close my eyes, and for a moment, I think I can smell the sweet, earthy scent of the Source's fruit overpowering the reek of urine. I almost forget where I am until the falling elevator jerks to a halt.

My breath quickens as the metal doors roll open. The Dark Guards part to reveal the hexangular room. Geometric shapes tile the floor, pressed together in a comb-like pattern.

Another set of random facts from one of Professor Diaz's lessons surfaces in my mind while looking at the room. The shapes remind me of a lecture he gave on ecosystems when I was still in the middle grade. Apparently, the honey bee played an integral role in sustaining all vegetation through a process called pollination. These tiny, fascinating creatures built homes with a waxy substance they somehow excreted from their glands and molded into hexagonal cells. That's what this room reminds me of: a beehive. Even the domed ceiling is beveled with six-sided edges.

Although, unlike the pictures of honey-colored combs I've seen in class, everything in this room is whitewashed, just like the rest of the medical center. The walls, the floor, the furniture—everything is white.

The Dark Guards assume their posts on either side of the elevator, leaving room for us to exit between them. Everyone hesitates to move. Normally Erika would barge to the front and take the lead, but it's pretty obvious that none of us wants to be the first person walking into a Dark Guard ambush.

Geri gives the young boy's hand a squeeze, and I think she's volunteering to go first. He sniffles and looks up at her with a longing in his eyes that begs her not to leave his side. His tears have dried up, but clumps of salt still spot his freckled cheeks.

Geri's lips curve into a halfhearted smile in an attempt to assure him that everything will be okay. A subtle nod from the boy says he understands, and their hands separate. Inhaling deeply, Geri braves the unknown. She moves to step out of the elevator, and I suppress the need to yank her back. My fingers are itching to grab onto her when she collides with the stiff arm of a Dark Guard.

"Remove your shoes," he orders.

Geri looks puzzled, but she listens right away, squatting to undo her laces.

"You first!" The Dark Guard points his gloved finger at me.

My heart nearly stops beating, and all the breath leaves my lungs. Since I'm the only one not wearing boots, I've fated myself to be the leader.

I tread across the threshold with reluctance and step onto the smooth and surprisingly warm tile. A pulse of electricity zooms through the sole and travels up my leg. I snap back, but one of the Dark Guards thrusts me forward. Tingling shocks buzz my bare skin. When I look down, rings of deep purple ripple from underneath my toes. Colored crests travel across the floor, absorbing into the curved white desk in the middle of the room. The control center wobbles when it gobbles up the waves, as if it's made of some kind of pliable material. I tilt my head, dumfounded by the display. It's hard to believe this type of technology exists, and even more suspicious that it's been hidden underground, here, at the *Omega Compound*.

Cracking concrete, peeling plaster, rotten wood, and grimy dirt—that's what I'm used to. Any technology authorized for general use is from before the Last War, and it rarely works the way it's supposed to. The projector in Professor Diaz's classroom flickers often, distorting images, and other than that, I don't interact with much technology. We don't use any electric machines in the washhouse. All of the hot irons are made of metal that gets heated over coals, and the sewing is done by hand. Erika's the only one I know who actually gets to use machinery. Even still, they're just power tools used for soldering, drilling, and cutting, and not anything like what I'm looking at now.

I move closer to the desk, my feet prickling when they come in contact with the tile, sending shocks of color pulsing through the strange structure. A Dark Guard sits behind the counter in a rounded chair with a back that sweeps to the ceiling. Only, this Dark Guard isn't dressed in black. Pale white covers his entire body. Even the visor over his face is an opaque cloud, camouflaging his uniform into the bleached room.

As I approach the control center, I get a better view of what's happening. The smooth edges of the desk bubble at the surface as the figure behind it maneuvers his spotless gloves, manipulating the shapes that appear on its malleable surface. He divides the dark purple rings, breaking them into silhouettes of red and blue. They move like magnetized water droplets back and forth on the table. Other tints and shades join the mix, and the Light Guard skillfully separates and combines them into categories.

Before I know it, my roommates are standing at my side, all of us completely entranced by the Light Guard's colorful demonstration. When we still, the shapes stop spawning, and the Light Guard swipes the surface clean. I want to ask what's going on, but the Dark Guards looming over us keep my mouth sealed shut.

"I understand your caution," the Light Guard speaks, "but I consider it wise to withhold your trust."

My eyes narrow. I'm surprised by the high-pitched tone of his voice and the level of certainty he presents while assuming our thoughts.

"We found this in one of the bunkers." The Dark Guard behind me shoves past our group and slaps my journal on the desk. It sinks into the surface, then springs back. A lip of the flexible table hangs onto its edges, holding the leather binding in place. My heart starts pounding again. I shuffle back, sending a colored signal of solid red floating to the desk.

The Light Guard spins his finger around the shape, then lifts his head to address the other soldiers. "Wait by the door."

I expect a snarky rebuttal or a growl of outrage, but neither of the Dark Guards utters a single word. They snap to attention and fall back, following orders, moving robotically as if in a trance.

The Light Guard pulls my journal from the desk. I shift my feet again, sending shocks of electricity rocketing through my body. More red shapes appear on the counter.

"This must be yours," the Light Guard remarks.

Beads of sweat break out on my forehead.

"I'm sure you're wondering how I know." He hugs the journal to his chest, and I bite down on my tongue.

"You see," he continues, "the floor you're standing on now transfers thoughts through telekinetic energy, decoding physical sensations into tangible transmissions." He drags his hand along the desk. "I can decipher emotions, impulses, desires ..."

I gulp.

"... important information that can identify a threat."

I clench my fists and my palms pool with sweat. I try to keep still, worried that my movements will expose my thoughts, but my locked knees give out, and I shift my weight yet again to steady my stance, sending a pulse of black ink trailing to the Light Guard's desk.

"Should I consider you a threat?" The Light Guard sets my journal back on the counter.

Panic seizes me. My gaze darts to the journal, and I know I've given myself away. *Calm down*, I coach myself, recalling all of the ways Robin taught me to breathe. I suck in through my nose and fill my lungs with as much air as I possibly can before releasing my breath, bringing my attention to the girls beside me. I can't risk their safety. Ronny's eyes are wide with fear. Lu's arms are wrapped around her middle like she's trying to keep herself from throwing up. Laude's feet are cemented in place, her face carrying a blank stare that's fixated on the desk. Geri's holding onto the kid from Bunker 111, and he looks like he might lose it any second and start sobbing.

"No," I mutter, looking back to the Light Guard.

He stands up and brings his hands to his mask. I flinch, expecting a blow, but all he does is disconnect the helmet from his bodysuit. Long auburn locks fall from underneath the thick shield, and I quietly gasp. The removed visor reveals a woman with bright green eyes and dark, full lips. She shakes her hair free and holds the helmet at her waist.

"Now, then, I don't believe I've formally introduced myself. I'm the Admiral."

My jaw drops. I wasn't expecting a young, attractive woman. Actually, I envisioned someone a little more like the cranky secretary who sent us down here, someone whose appearance matches the actions of her Dark Guards: mean and ruthless. But the woman in front of me now can't be a day over thirty-five. Her perfect skin glows, and her rounded cheeks indicate she's well fed. It's hard to imagine Mrs. Cane groveling to *this* Admiral, begging for Walter to be spared. Something isn't adding up. Either this woman isn't *really* the Admiral, or there's a lot more under the surface than what meets the eye. Then again, her looks might serve as the perfect disguise to her malice, manipulating us to believe that she's harmless. *But not everything that's beautiful is safe.*

The Admiral scans us up and down, and I snap my mouth shut.

"I was hoping for eight of you." She gallops her fingers across the top of her helmet. "But I suppose seven will have to do." She sighs. "Now, which of you is the dreamer?"

My eyes widen. There's no way she can know that, not now. She hasn't even opened my journal yet. Maybe the shapes on the table gave it away. My insides turn upside down. Acid rises in my throat. I think I might be sick. The pain in my head swells, and I start to see shadows. The white walls in the room smear, but just as I'm about to reach for the counter to stop myself from passing out, the boy from Bunker 111 starts crying.

"Please, please don't hurt them," he blurts out, "It's me! I'm the dreamer."

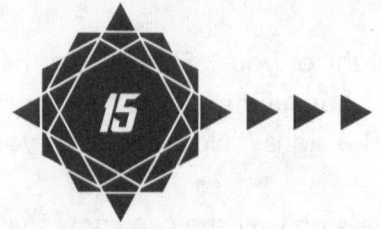

"Take him," the Admiral orders.

Him? I cover my mouth. He can dream? But I'm the dreamer. He must be lying. But why? Why would he risk his life for a lie?

I thought I was the only one who saw strange visions at night. When I first told Geri about my dreams, we tried asking other people about it, but whenever we casually mentioned the possibility of seeing things while asleep, we were met with blank stares and awkward silence. It was like we were speaking another language, one that didn't exist. After dealing with more uncomfortable conversations than I can count, and a few embarrassing backpedals, I called the mission off and we just assumed I was the only person on the compound who could dream. Until now, that is.

I uncover my mouth, ready to turn myself in and take the boy's place, when the hovering Dark Guards snap from their stiff stance and stomp to seize the boy.

This doesn't feel right. A giant knot twists in the pit of my stomach. My heart races, and all sorts of colors dance around my feet in a kaleidoscope of chaos. I need to speak up, but I can't. I'm tongue-tied. The confession gets trapped in my throat.

The other girls move in to protect the boy, creating a human barricade. A myriad of shapes swirl on the desk. It's impossible to tell who they originate from. All of us are shifting at the same time, bracing our bare feet against the static tile.

Erika pushes the scrawny kid behind her and flares her nostrils. Geri holds onto him for as long as she can before the Dark Guards bowl through our brigade and yank him away.

"Wait!" he screams. "I'll do whatever you want!" Terror floods his eyes.

They drag him by the shoulders across the tile, sending a wake of deep green spiraling from his kicking feet. None of us fight for him. None of us run after him. None of us cry out. We just stand in stunned silence until the elevator doors close, then watch the remaining remnants of his struggle travel in a fleet of green for the Admiral's desk.

"Now, for the rest of you …" The Admiral spins the last lingering circle on her desk and sinks her hand into the counter. The malleable surface hardens and the entire desk solidifies into a firm structure, and, coincidentally, the floor stops sending tremors through my toes. A strange sensation coats my skin, and the hair on both of my arms relaxes. I didn't even notice it was standing on end.

When the Admiral lifts her arm, the imprint of her hand remains underneath. She takes her time peeling the white gloves from her fingertips, letting us stir in the anguish of anticipation, imagining what horrors she has planned for our unit.

If I weren't so woozy, I could take her down. She's not much taller than I am, and as far as I can tell, she's unarmed. Plus, there's six of us and only one of her. The numbers are in our favor. But the throbbing in my head slows me down, and the shakiness in my hands reminds me that we're all malnourished and sleep-deprived. The more I think about springing an attack on the Admiral, the more I'm convinced not to—and it's not just my physical ailments that keep me in place. Laude warned all of us back at the bunker not to assume anything about the technology we've encountered. And, from what I've seen, she's right. For all I know, this entire room is rigged with hidden dangers.

The Admiral sets her gloves beside the impression she's left on the desk and rubs her palms together. "Your formal screening begins immediately." She claps her hands twice, and the white combed tiles on the walls behind her separate, revealing a hidden hallway.

Six women in knee-length, white medical coats emerge from the secret corridor and stand in a row, awaiting the Admiral's orders. Starting with Laude, the Admiral picks us off one by one and assigns us to our new companions. When it's just Ronny and me left standing by the counter, it hits me that there's *only* six nurses. No more. No less. Which doesn't make sense for someone who's expecting eight kids. *Unless* ... I shudder. *She knew.* The Admiral knew all along that only six of us would be leaving her chamber.

When she turns to address Ronny, I glance down at my journal. It's left unattended on the control panel. This moment won't last long, and I need to move fast if I want it back. I think about snatching it up and tucking it into my uniform, but the Admiral would know I did it. I'm the only one still standing by the desk.

To make matters worse, the desk, once made of flexible material, has hardened with my journal sunken into it. I reach across and pull on the binding, but sure enough, it's frozen in place. I whip my hand back to my side when I see the Admiral spin toward me. My heart hammers in my chest. It won't be long before the Admiral pries the cover of my journal open and discovers what I really am. Then I'll be the one getting lugged away, dragged across the floor by Dark Guards.

The Admiral calls me forward, and I stutter my steps to my slender, new companion. Although the floor has stopped transmitting my extrasensory information, the tingling sensations from the electrical current linger in my body, buzzing my ankles and making it hard to walk in a straight line.

This must be how it feels to be intoxicated, but I wouldn't know. I've never been inebriated before. I have, however, had the pleasure of watching some of the ladies at the washhouse show up to work under the influence. Once a month the airmen bring in a shipment of alcohol for Mrs. Cane and the frivolous parties she hosts at her home in the Northern Sector. People in the Southern Sector aren't supposed to have access to it, but Ethel bribed one of the airmen for a case of cheap liquor after another mysterious disappearance brought back the grief from losing her boys. The next day, half the washhouse walked tipsy, slurring their words and dropping clean clothes on the filthy floor. I pulled double duty that day, but we still missed our quota. The barracks guards overseeing our work didn't care much, though. Ethel slipped each of them a bottle at the beginning of her shift, and that was enough to keep them quiet.

I stumble to a stop, knocking into the thin nurse, pushing her off balance. She rights herself and adjusts her jacket before squinting at me with her dark, almond eyes. At first glance, she looks just about as nervous as

I do. Her pale skin nearly matches the color of her jacket, and her bony fingers tremble ever so slightly. She slides them into her pockets to keep me from staring.

"Each of you has been assigned a medical companion, someone to oversee your screening." The Admiral paces before us with her hands clasped behind her back. "They will take you to an exam room and conduct an interview with a series of questions that you will be expected to answer fully and truthfully. Afterward, a doctor will perform a few minor tests." She stops and flashes a sinister smile that looks misplaced on her pretty face. "The procedures are painless, *if* you cooperate. And, if you give us complete compliance, you will be released to resume your mundane tasks on the compound immediately following the examination. However, if you dare to lie during the interview or resist any of the testing, I will be forced to keep you here until you prove to us that you are willing to collaborate."

I swallow hard. There's no way I'm getting out of here without someone finding out about my dreams.

"Fall out," the Admiral dismisses us.

My nurse purses her thin lips and nods for me to follow. I wobble beside her, stepping in line behind the rest of my friends. We stride into the long hallway through the jagged opening between the hexagonal tiles, and the walls shift back into place, sealing the Admiral, along with my journal, on the other side.

We don't walk very far before doors appear on both sides of the hallway. Laude disappears with her nurse into a room marked with the number one, and soon Geri's walking through a door on the opposite end labeled with the number two. She looks back at me before stepping inside, and I wish we had a moment to talk in private, or at all. Investigational testing wasn't exactly a part of our escape plan. I can only hope everyone here handles themselves with enough restraint to get us all back to Bunker 112 in one piece before the day is over.

Erika's next. She catches my eye before walking into room number three, and I do my best to signal a look that tells her to mind her manners. A heavy ache settles in my chest when the latch on the door clicks closed. There's a strong possibility I won't be seeing any of my friends again, not when my dreams get aired in the open. Tears well in my eyes, turning my vision blurry. Lu vanishes behind the next door before I manage to gather my bearings, and I miss our moment of farewell. I flash Ronny a sad smile when we come to the fifth exam room, then quietly follow my nurse to the door labeled with the large metal six.

I peer down the hall as she reaches for the handle. More rooms with climbing numbers wait further down the corridor, but this is where my tour of the underground facility ends. The door glides open. I step inside.

The exam room looks a lot different than the one I stayed in with the Warden after the storm. That sublevel space matched the crumbling state of the compound with dingy furniture and outdated equipment. Which makes me wonder if the setup was a ploy, made to resemble the above-ground parts of the Medical Center. This room doesn't even look like it's in the same hospital. The only cohesive thing about the first floor and these underground levels is the color: white.

A large padded chair mounted on some kind of silver base sits in the center of the room. It's reclined ever so slightly, and there's a strange circular contraption suspended from the ceiling right above the headrest. I can only imagine what the machine does, but after my encounter with the Admiral's mind-reading floor, well, I take a guess that it's some type of invasive brain scanner. I picture it clamping down on my skull, revealing all of my secrets without consent, and my fingers go numb at the thought.

"Have a seat."

Unfortunately, my nurse waves her hand for me to sit in the oversized chair. The vinyl upholstery squeaks as I settle myself in. I make the mistake of looking up at the circle hanging over my head and notice thousands of what appear to be tiny needles edging the inside rim.

"I'm Nurse Fukuda," she says, and retrieves a few supplies from the metal cabinet against the wall. She pulls a set of rubber gloves over her fingers and draws fluid from a vial into a syringe with an extra-long needle. I hold my breath and tense my shoulders. I hate injections. The Admiral's threat about noncompliance is the only reason why I haven't bolted from this room. That, and I don't have a clue as to how to get out of here.

"What is that?" I scoot back into the chair as far as I can when Nurse Fukuda approaches me with the gigantic needle in hand.

"A concoction designed to elicit information." She steps closer. "I was told to administer it to you before conducting the interview."

She rubs my bicep with an alcohol wipe, and I dig my fingernails into the armrests.

"I don't do so well with needles," I mutter as I bear down, clenching my jaw and gritting my teeth, bracing myself for the sharp sting of the needle burrowing into my flesh.

"All set," she says.

I open my eyes to see her wiping the edge of the needle on a white towel and discarding both items into a hazardous waste bin. My fingers trail along my upper arm. There's no redness, no swelling, and no pain. I never even felt the needle prick my skin.

I'm baffled by the painless injection and wonder if I'd be crossing a line if I asked my nurse why I didn't feel anything when she administered the drug. I decide it's probably best not to, and so I keep my thoughts to myself.

While I'm waiting for the effects to kick in, I glue my eyes to her as she moves about the room. She collects some type of cuff off the steel countertop, then grabs a thin, flat device before sitting down on a mobile stool and wheeling herself beside me.

"I'm going to track your vitals while I ask you a few questions," Nurse Fukuda says as she fastens two black bands around my wrists. "Please do your best to answer as truthfully as you can. If you're unsure of an answer, simply tell me you don't know." She crosses her legs and fits the tablet on her lap. "First, state your name."

"Reyna. Reyna Sage."

That was easy.

Nurse Fukuda taps a note on the screen, then checks the numbers flickering on my new medical jewelry.

"How old are you, Reyna?"

"I'm seventeen," I say.

"What's your unit number?"

"112," I answer. The questions aren't as bad as I thought they'd be. I take a deep breath and watch the numbers on my wrist drop.

"How long have you been under the care of your Warden?" In other words, how long have I been an orphan.

"Ten years."

"And whom did you live with before joining your unit?"

"My grandmother," I choke.

"Not your parents?" she presses.

"My daddy disappeared when I was just a toddler, and my mother died of the sickness soon after." A lump forms in my throat.

"Do you have any memories of your parents from your childhood?"

"Yes."

"Can you recall your earliest memory?"

I cram my eyes shut and start thinking about my mother. I can still smell the sweet scent of her sweat after she'd worked a long, full day mopping up floors. My lips start to quiver when I see her smiling down on me while I'm resting in my crib as an infant. The same image Elolam showed me of her holding me in the maternity ward surfaces in my mind, then something peculiar happens. I see myself gliding down smooth tendrils infused with liquid light and feel myself plunge into darkness. My bracelets start beeping, alerting Nurse Fukuda of my accelerated heart rate.

"I'm sorry." I snap my eyes open and apologize. "Thinking about my past is painful," I lie, and I hope I sound convincing. Then it hits me: I wasn't compelled to tell the truth. Maybe the serum hasn't kicked in yet. Or maybe ... I try to keep myself from looking surprised when I realize there's a possibility Nurse Fukuda never gave me the shot. *But why?*

"We'll move on for now." She swipes the screen of her tablet. "Where are you employed?"

"At the washhouse."

"Have you come across any misleading information regarding the United Regime while working?"

"No," I answer, and probably too quickly. The numbers on my wrists tick up a few counts. I'm not directly lying, but I've definitely come across some rumors while working at the washhouse. For the most part, I mind my own business, but every once in a while, the women talk a little louder than usual and forget to pay attention to who's standing nearby.

I see the notes getting passed. I hear the whispers. But I don't ever ask or get involved.

"Where were you on the night of the most recent storm?"

"I got caught in the rain."

Her eyebrows lift and she tucks her chin as if she wants me to rephrase my answer. I'm searching her eyes, wondering what kind of message she's trying to send me, when I think I've figured it out. My lips separate. *The rebellion?* She's trying to see if I had something to do with the hole in the wall. The base of my neck starts to throb, and now my stitches are extra itchy. All along, I'd just assumed the hole was collateral damage from the storm. But I vaguely remember the girls talking about hearing an explosion from the Mess Hall during the lockdown. Normally, I don't have any trouble retaining the details, but I completely forgot about that conversation until now. This concussion has definitely made the last few days feel a bit hazy.

"I—I," I stammer, realizing how important it is for me to clarify my whereabouts. "My Warden and I got trapped in the storm. We hid from the rain in the supply shed on the far side of the Southern Sector. I was knocked out cold when the walls caved in, so I don't remember much else. When I woke up, I was here in the Medical Center."

A knock at the door turns my head. I lean too far over and nearly fall off the chair when I see Doctor Ayad walk in. I don't know if I should be relieved or concerned by his presence. He's obviously a part of whatever secret studies the Admiral's managed to keep hidden underground, which would explain why I've never seen him in the Medical Center before my overnight stay after the storm. He must work down here. And if he's working down here with the Admiral, then he must be dangerous. I mean, if *she's* willing to disregard human life for the sake of control, then who's to say he won't hesitate to slice me open in the name of modern medicine.

I clutch the armrests a little tighter. There's nothing I can do to escape at this point, so I have to stay compliant ... at least for now.

My eyes trail him as he approaches the center of the room. Looking at his face brings me back to the last time I saw the Warden. For a moment, I'm in that same hospital room, watching him along with his team of nurses resuscitate her dead body. Something's not sitting right in my gut, though, as I replay the memory. Never in all my life have I ever heard of someone on the base, doctor or nurse, going out of their way to keep one of their patients from dying. The above-ground medical center isn't set up for surgeries or intensive care. Any unfortunate accident on the compound is basically a one-way ticket to the incinerator. That's where all the bodies go, where Grandmommy's body burned. That's why everyone's required to take immunizations and supplemental injections. It's easier to prevent the spread of sickness than to cure it, but once you've caught it, well, that's basically a death sentence. Your bunker is roped off under quarantine, and the next time you leave is in the embrace of a crisp white sheet. I'm actually surprised they let me stay with Grandmommy when she fell ill. Maybe they were just hoping I'd die, too. Then they wouldn't have to worry about keeping me alive—one less mouth to feed. Thankfully, I found a home in Bunker 112 with my misfit sisters. And, in some peculiar way, I guess that makes the Warden kind of like our mother.

The Warden. I turn my focus back to Doctor Ayad. *He must know where she is.*

"How's the interview coming along?" he asks Nurse Fukuda.

"We're just finishing," she answers, then continues typing up my revised reply.

"Good to see you again, Reyna," Doctor Ayad says with a nod.

I narrow my eyes at his cordial behavior, wondering if it's even safe for me to ask him about the Warden.

"I can take it from here," he says to Nurse Fukuda.

When she stands up from the stool and takes my bracelets, I start to panic. I don't want her to leave me alone with the doctor. My sweaty palms slip on the armrests. Nurse Fukuda walks behind the chair and out of my line of sight, but the click of cabinet doors opening and closing lets me know she's still there.

"If you don't mind, Reyna, we're going to take a blood sample next," Doctor Ayad says.

I don't know why he bothers to pretend like he needs my permission. We both know I can't refuse, not if I want to get out of here alive.

Nurse Fukuda steps back into view and ties a tourniquet around my arm. The rubber tie pinches my skin, and I wince. Doctor Ayad shoves a needle into a thin vein, pulls off the tie, and waits. Thick, dark blood slowly trickles out.

"This won't do," he mutters aloud and flicks my arm, "She's too dehydrated." He turns to Nurse Fukuda. "We'll have to wait to collect a more usable sample." He sighs. "Ready the machine," he orders.

Before I have a chance to contest, Nurse Fukuda lowers the circular contraption to my head. My shoulders tense when I feel the pressure of the tiny needles graze my scalp.

"What are you going to do?" I tighten my neck.

"We're going to collect some imaging of your brain and measure your neural activity."

"Why?" I grimace.

He removes the needle from my arm. "Well, Reyna, during your previous stay, I found an anomaly with your neural activity while scanning your head for internal injuries. Parts of your mind were firing during your comatose state that are typically dormant in unconscious patients. This machine will allow me to capture clearer images of your brain, and once I have them, I'll compare the data with your previous scan."

He makes it sound so simple, and he's acting like he can't already prove that I'm a dreamer. My chest tightens, and my breath quickens.

"Don't worry." He places his clammy hand over mine. "It won't hurt."

Doctor Ayad tilts his head toward Nurse Fukuda, signaling for her to turn on the machine. A droning pitch hums as the contraption comes to life. At first, the sound is bearable, but it grows louder. It doesn't take long for me to wish I could maneuver my fingers past the prickling needles to plug my ears.

I close my eyes and try to relax. I'm not sure how all of these gadgets work, but I have a theory that if I avoid thinking about my dreams, Doctor Ayad might not be able to detect them. I start concentrating on work at the washhouse, but then I get nervous and wonder if the machine can read my thoughts. Nurse Fukuda's already hinted at a correlation between work and the rebellion, and I can't risk an association. The electromagnetic pulse beats against my head as bursts of energy leave the device. I shift my thoughts to something unrelated, like meals in the cafeteria, but that results in envisioning Dark Guards beating innocent people. Now, I'm thinking of Brenton. The vibrations in my head meld to match the thud of the gun against his face.

After several minutes of gritting my teeth, I feel the tired ache in my jaw. I coax myself to loosen my clamped muscles and open my eyes. Nurse Fukuda and Doctor Ayad are talking about something near the counter in front of me. The doctor has the tablet in his hands. His mouth is moving, and he's pointing to the screen, but I can't hear anything he says over the loud buzzing in my ears.

The whirling dies down and Nurse Fukuda snaps her attention my way, scurrying to remove the circle wrapped around my skull. Doctor Ayad steps up behind her, mouthing something to me.

My ears are still ringing, so his voice sounds muffled.

"How do you feel?" he repeats.

I'm not sure how to answer. My head still feels like it's stuck in the machine, like the throbbing hasn't stopped. Doctor Ayad takes notice of my dazed state and decides to skip asking me any more questions. Instead, he turns to Nurse Fukuda.

"Give her a few minutes to recover from the procedure. When she seems stable enough to stand on her own, we have clearance to release her. I'll have to make arrangements and schedule a time for her to come back for another blood draw, but that can wait for today. I may still have enough sitting on ice on level 24B to run a few more tests."

Nurse Fukuda says something back, but all I hear are slurred mumbles. I'm too busy thinking about my friends. I perk up when the doctor mentions something about this being his first stop before heading out of the room. I imagine that means he's making his way down the hall. That means Ronny will be next.

When the buzzing in my ears dies down, Nurse Fukuda helps me stand. She slips me a packet of nutritional crackers and apologizes that she can't give me more. Then, she links her bony arm through mine and ushers me to the door. Just as we're about to step into the hallway, someone yells for us to stop.

"Wait!"

Nurse Fukuda holds me in place as a second nurse hurries to meet us. As she gets closer, I recognize her as the nurse that stood with Geri, and suddenly, my stomach is tangled up in knots again. Geri's nurse is panting, and I get the feeling that whatever she needs to tell us is urgent.

"You can't let her go," she huffs. "This patient is to report to the Admiral's quarters immediately."

I trail through the underground maze of white hallways following after Nurse Fukuda's short, swift strides. She pauses every so often to calculate our next turn, consulting a map on the screen of her tablet, the one she borrowed from exam room number six. Our path continues on, zigzagging through the mysterious corridors that unfold into larger, never-ending passages. My legs are tired, and it feels like we've been walking for miles. It's possible the underground fortress is even bigger than the barracks above.

We pass hundreds of rectangular, white doors, and after a while, the numbers get so high that the metal plates on the doors shift to include letter combinations. Just when I think my knees are about to give out, I see the end of the hallway where a rounded silver door awaits. The shimmering metal seems slightly out of place among its uniform counterparts. Then again, there's no mistaking that whatever's behind *this* door is different.

When we get closer, Nurse Fukuda lifts her knuckles to rap on the frame. She hesitates. At first, I don't notice why. Then I see it—some kind of invisible current radiating off the metal. Apparently, the sheen on the door isn't a decorative choice. I gather from Nurse Fukuda's caution that the Admiral's door is fixed with an extra layer of security, and I can only imagine what might happen if she made contact with its surface.

Without warning, the door swings wide, revealing the Admiral at its threshold. Her silk jumpsuit stings my eyes with a bright green that reminds me of lime-flavored mush. The only other person I know of bold enough to dress in ghastly colors is Mrs. Cane. I've witnessed some pretty horrible combinations of neon orange and electric blue that make me question why anyone would ever put something so shocking on their body. It seems so out of place among the monochrome backdrop of the complex.

Grandmommy taught me to appreciate color by looking at the sky, but the colors in Mrs. Cane's wardrobe are nothing like the vibrant hues I see while watching the sunrise. If I could compare the difference, I'd say it's like looking at pictures of trees on Professor Diaz's slides versus seeing the Source. Now that I've experienced a world full of color while I'm sleeping, well, nothing else quite compares. In the City of Life, the colors blend in a way that's soothing to look at. Nothing appears to be out of place. Every hue works together in harmony, complementing the vivid world around it. Radiant blues and glowing golds meld, pulling me in rather than pushing me away. There, I can't stop staring. Here, all I want to do is cover my eyes.

Although fashion has never been an interest of mine, seeing the Admiral now does make me wonder what kind of clothes people on other compounds have. I've always assumed Mrs. Cane's attire was a personal choice, but maybe her style *isn't* an individual statement. Maybe that's how the rest of the world dresses, and this is just one more thing that sets our base aside from all the others. I wouldn't know, though, because we don't ever get the chance to communicate with the outside world. Aside from Mrs. Cane's horrendous dresses, the only other clothes I see on the Omega Compound that hold any kind of color are the navy-blue uniforms donned by the airmen. Other than that, it's just a sea of taupe-grays and tans. It's hard to imagine myself wearing anything other than the base-issued uniforms, but if I ever had the opportunity to choose, it wouldn't be anything like the outfit I'm beholding now.

"Ma'am, I've brought the patient you've requested." Nurse Fukuda stands with her hand still raised in the air. She drops her fist and brushes her coat, lowering her head to avoid eye contact with the Admiral.

"Thank you. You're dismissed," the Admiral answers, sliding her hand along the shimmering door.

The metal bends in reply, and I wonder if it's made of the same flexible material as the desk in the honeycomb room. Maybe the door operates with the same mind-reading technology, too, and maybe that's why Nurse Fukuda didn't want to touch it. She seems different from the rest of the Admiral's calloused minions. I don't know what she has to hide, and I don't know why she bothered to help me in the exam room, but for now, I'll consider her an ally.

Nurse Fukuda turns away from the Admiral and softens her almond eyes, offering me a look of sympathy before retreating down the hall. I refrain from asking her to stay, but my insides scream for her not to leave. I really don't want to be left alone in the Admiral's company.

"Do come in." The Admiral moves to the side and waves me on.

I step over the threshold with hesitation, expecting some kind of electrical shock to surge through me. Thankfully, nothing happens.

My mouth gapes when I notice the domed ceiling inside the Admiral's quarters. Images of clouds float across its surface with unbelievably realistic detail. It's deceptive. If I didn't already know we were underground, I would have thought I was staring up at the real sky. Whisps of white drift over blue, then disappear when they reach the edge of the dome that connects with the painted purple walls.

"I just love the sky. Don't you?" The Admiral sighs and smiles. Her auburn hair shines with a red glow under the fluorescent ceiling as she makes her way to the luxurious white sofa and relaxes into the shagged material.

The opulence makes me queasy, and the question seems rhetorical, so I don't answer. Chances are, she already knows about my love for the sky and how it makes me think of Grandmommy. I shake myself from the awe of her counterfeit display and scoff. I wouldn't be surprised if she set the scene just to manipulate my feelings.

"Have a seat." The Admiral presses her lips into a thin line.

I shuffle my bare feet over the unusually textured floor. Deep grooves in the dark planks spiral into random patterns. My skin doesn't tingle when I walk, not like it did on the tile in the other room, but an odd sensation creeps through the balls of my feet with the unpredictable pressure brought on by the peculiar design. I really can't tell if there's any technology hidden underneath or if it's just another outrageous decorative decision. Either way, I don't like it.

Reluctantly, I sit down in a round, light purple chair propped up by metal poles. The plush foam hugs every curve of my body. A sweet scent bursts from its fabric when I lean back. The smell vaguely reminds me of the blossoms in my meadow, but this odor has a slight chemical overtone that stings my nostrils. I rub my nose to suppress a sneeze.

"I've tried to imitate the smell of lavender." The Admiral wraps her arm around the back of the couch. "It's my favorite blossom of the genus Lavandula. Unfortunately, the scent is difficult to reproduce without the original plant."

I roll my lips inward and raise a brow. I have no idea why she's telling me this. Besides, most plants have been extinct for more than a century. So, how could she create a perfume based off of something that no longer exists? Smells can't be preserved. *Can they?*

"What do you want?" I spit. I'm tired of her trying to act cordial. To me, her pleasantries are insincere. We aren't friends, and I'd really like to get back to my real ones.

"Hm." The Admiral crosses her legs. "Straight to the point, I see," she comments, then leans forward to the table situated between us. There isn't a single smudge on its surface, and if it weren't for the large metal box placed at its center, the long glass top would seem invisible.

She lifts the lid of the silver container and gently removes what looks like an antique tea set decorated with delicate purple flowers. Steam lifts from the stem of the pot, twirling above the porcelain container rimmed with shiny gold. The Admiral pours hot liquid into the pair of teacups set elegantly on matching saucers. A fresh and calming aroma fills the air.

"Would you like some?" she offers, pushing one of the plates in my direction.

The steamy liquid sloshes over the edge of the cup, spilling onto the saucer. I stare down into the vessel, inhaling the fragrant vapor. The browning color makes me think of the filthy recycled water at the washhouse. If it weren't for the earthy, floral aroma, I would have thought it undrinkable.

I've never had tea before, but the scent makes me salivate. I didn't get a chance to eat the crackers from Nurse Fukuda, and my empty stomach is begging for something to fill it. But I don't want to seem too eager. I use restraint and wait until the Admiral takes a sip from her own cup before I reach for mine.

With a shaky hand, I lift the liquid to my lips and slurp it slowly. The warm fluid fills my mouth, and it tastes like I'm sucking on the flower petals from my dream world. When I swallow, the heat coats my throat and settles in my gut. My intestines gurgle in reply.

The Admiral watches while I drink more of my tea. If I weren't so hungry, I'd put the cup back on the table and push for her to answer my question. I think she's waiting for me to finish before she indulges my request, though. Her keen observation makes me uncomfortable, so I hold the cup in my lap, decide not to slurp the rest down, and rephrase the question.

"Why did you invite me here?"

"To talk about this." She slides my journal into view.

My heart skips a beat. I knew this was coming, but I didn't formulate a cover story or make up an excuse. I've been caught, and there's no use denying the journal is mine.

"Since you seem to prefer a direct approach, I'll skip the formalities." Her stare cuts through me. "I know you're a dreamer, Reyna. This isn't the first time I've come across descriptions like the ones you've written about."

It's true, then. There are other dreamers. I try not to look shocked, but my heart is beating out of my chest and I can feel my eyes widening against my will.

She sighs. "It's been a long time, however, since I've managed to find someone who recalls the details as thoroughly as you can."

An uncomfortable silence follows, and I'm not sure I should speak.

"Have you met him?"

"Who?" Liquid sloshes in the cup held by my trembling hands.

"Don't be daft, Reyna. Have you met E.L.O.L.A.M.?"

My jaw just about falls off its hinges. "H-h-how do you—?"

The Admiral interrupts me with a forced laugh. "Because I worked for the man who created him."

Confusion sends my mind spiraling out of control. I can't respond. The teacup rattles when I set it on the saucer.

"I understand this might come as a surprise." A look of forced sympathy coats her face. "But you need to know before the infection causes permanent damage to your brain."

"What are you talking about?" I stammer.

"Dreams, Reyna. They're a disease."

"So, you're saying I'm sick?"

The Admiral nods.

"H-how?" I can't seem to wrap my mind around the idea that dreams are an illness. They've offered me an escape from the harsh realities of the world more times than I can count. I never once considered them to be a harmful disease. I never had a reason to.

"Dreams overstimulate the brain's memory centers, causing long-term neurodegeneration," she explains.

"What does that mean?"

"It means you'll lose the ability to decipher between reality and imagination. When the infection worsens, you'll begin experiencing emotional distress and hallucinations, blurring the lines between the world you live in and the one you've created in your mind." The Admiral dips her chin. "You'll go mad."

That's already happening to me.

"Then who—or what—is Elolam?" I cross my arms to hide my shaking hands.

Her bright green eyes lock on mine. "It's a nanotech neural interface."

"What?" I knit my brows together. I'm having trouble keeping track of what she's saying. I've only recently encountered Elolam in my dreams, but his presence felt so real, so accepting and full of love. I haven't had nearly enough time to thoroughly consider the validity of his nature. I'm still figuring it out. And now

I'm being told by a questionably psychopathic government leader that he's some kind of technology they've embedded into my head?

The Admiral's confession seems out of place. *Why is she telling me this? Why now?* I weigh what I know about the Admiral, the abuse I've seen from the Dark Guards, the marks I witnessed on Walter's face, against the warmth of Elolam's embrace, but something just doesn't feel right. I'm not sure who to trust, the Admiral or Elolam.

"The advanced technology was commissioned by the United Regime to slow the deterioration of neural activity among the infected, giving us a chance to find a cure." She waves her hand in the air, and a charted display spontaneously appears, floating in the space between us. The hologram is clear and crisp, unlike the blurry slides Professor Diaz shows in his classroom. I can't tell what I'm looking at exactly, but it seems like it might be some type of programming, cryptic codes, and undecipherable data. My eyes wander up the display, but it's the title at the top that stops my scrolling eyes and grips my attention: Embedded Lucid Operations and Linked Access Module.

"Elolam," I whisper in disbelief. "So, he isn't real?"

"He's very real, Reyna, but he isn't who he says he is."

Tea curdles in my stomach. I feel sick. Elolam told me he was the source of all living things, the creator of souls, the author of the universe. But the Admiral's showing me that he's nothing but a program embedded in my brain. Paranoia sets in. I already feel like I'm going crazy.

"How did he get in my head? How come I can see him in my dreams?" The questions spill out like the steaming hot liquid from her antique pot.

The Admiral disperses the hologram with a swipe of her palm. "I know this is a lot to take in," she counsels. "It's okay to be upset."

I lace my fingers through my hair and grab onto my head, rocking back and forth.

"I can tell you more about the operation, but it might be best to wait—"

"No!" I blurt. "Tell me now. I need to know!"

"Alright." She inhales through her nostrils. "But I'm going to need you to calm down. I don't want to be forced to call on my security detail."

I release the hold on my hair and slowly lower my hands into my lap, taking in a long, deep breath. I don't want to prompt another unnecessary run-in with her Dark Guards. I'd prefer not to leave her quarters being pulled by my arms, dragged across the floor kicking and screaming.

The Admiral looks satisfied by my reaction and repositions herself on the couch before clearing her throat and continuing on. "E.L.O.L.A.M. is a neural artificial intelligence delivered into the host by way of a nanoscale injection introduced at birth. Once embedded, it integrates with the host's subconscious and only awakens when specific cognitive patterns alert the program to activate. Unfortunately, there's been a malfunction with the original design. While in its dormant state, the technology develops with the host, learning how to think, communicate, decipher emotions, and formulate desires. Once it's captured enough of the host's memories, it attempts to overthrow the mind and assume control of the body."

Shivers run up my spine, making the follicles on my scalp tingle. Elolam did that to me. He manipulated my emotions. He made me feel and see and do things I didn't consent to.

"The way you perceive him in your dreamspace is a personalized projection tailored to your subconscious. He synchronizes his form to match your memories and manipulates your imagination to create traps of intrigue, promising you your heart's deepest desires."

I bite my trembling lips to keep them from quaking, but I don't know how to stop the tears from falling down my cheeks. An awful ick slithers over my skin. *What about Grandmommy? Was seeing her a lie? What if it wasn't her? What if it was Elolam all along?*

I've been deceived.

"You're not the first person he's tried to manipulate." The Admiral frowns. "I must tell you, though, as painful as it may be, it's better to know the truth. E.L.O.L.A.M is dangerous, and every host interaction plays out the same: with deception, disappointment, and death."

Her last words linger.

"Listen to me, Reyna." She moves to the end of the couch and places her hand on my knee. "I don't want you falling victim to his tactics. I want you to work with me to stop him."

"Stop him from what?" I squirm in my seat to move away from her touch.

"Destroying the human race," she says with a straight face. "For centuries, E.L.O.L.A.M. has infiltrated the minds of people, enticing them with hollow promises and tricking them into doing his selfish bidding."

I feel dizzy. Another burst of perfume puffs from behind me when I slouch further into the lavender chair. The intoxicating scent makes the room spin faster.

"What do you expect me to do?" I blurt. There's no point in playing polite. I need to get to the bottom of whatever it is the Admiral's requiring of me.

"I expect you to tell me what his plans are; feed me information. Anything he reveals to you, I want to know."

"How's that supposed to work? I don't even dream every night," I protest, worry making my throat swell.

"Over the last decade, scientists from Theta Towers have devoted the majority of their time to developing a new technology that allows us to trigger the dream state and ambush the corrupted E.L.O.L.A.M."

I gulp. I've heard of Theta Towers. Walter's slipped a few times during his selfish woe-is-me rants, casually mentioning what some of the other compounds are capable of. From what I gather, Theta is a center specifically dedicated to wild scientific experiments and genetic testing. Whenever I envision the base, I think of unhinged tests pushing ethical boundaries. And, if Theta has anything to do with what the Admiral's suggesting, then who knows what kind of sick experimentation she plans to put me through. Another cold shiver runs down my spine.

"Instead of joining your comrades in the usual morning tasks, you'll be asked to come here and participate in our studies. And, I promise, if you allow us full access to your mind with complete consent, you'll be able to return to the surface to resume your regular studies and work operations."

"And if I refuse?"

"I think you misunderstood my asking." The Admiral dips her chin. "If you don't give me your compliance, E.L.O.L.A.M. will take your mind and I'll be coerced to assume responsibility for your actions. I'd rather not issue you a permanent residency here in my laboratory."

"So, I'd be a prisoner." I stare deep into the Admiral's eyes and attempt to read her intentions.

Her face hardens, and she fixes me with a cold glare. "Trust me. Things will go much better for the both of us if you agree."

My world is falling apart. I'm questioning everything. The Admiral wants access to Elolam, and I want to live long enough to escape with my friends. I consider my choices. If I agree and give her full access to my mind, I'd be giving her admittance to the only safe place I have. But now I'm left questioning whether or not my dreams are actually safe. If it's a disease, I want to be cured, but not if that means I can't see Grandmommy ever again. I don't know if I can let her go. My heart wrenches. It's like I'm losing her all over, watching her die a thousand deaths on a dirty cot.

I suck in a breath to keep myself from spiraling into an anxiety attack. I need to be level headed. I need to make the right decision.

There's a possibility that if I let the Admiral into my brain, she'll know *everything*, including my plan to leave the base. I'll be exposing my friends. My thoughts won't be mine anymore. They'll be an open book. I look down at my journal, wishing I could snatch it and run.

Unfortunately, the damage is already done. The Admiral's read my dream entries. She already knows about my visit to the City of Life. She knows about Grandmommy. She knows about Elolam. And, if what she's telling me is true, then refusing her request is pointless. She'll keep me trapped down here in her underground maze and I'll never see the light of day again. Then, this synthetic sky above me will only serve as a reminder of the so-called freedom I once had.

I glance up at the fake clouds drifting by on the simulated sky and wish that I was looking at the real thing. My chest tightens, and I start to feel like I'm suffocating again, like the oxygen's being sucked right out of my lungs. I need to see the stars. I need to feel Grandmommy tugging on the other end of our cord. The ceiling makes me feel trapped. I can't stay here. Panic swells in my throat. If I ever hope to witness another sunrise on the horizon peeking over the wall, then I'll have to agree. I'll have to become the Admiral's puppet. I'll have to help her destroy Elolam. I'll have to betray Grandmommy.

"I'll do it." The words feel like lead leaving my mouth.

The Admiral's lips curve into a coy grin. "Your first session starts now."

Doctor Ayad adheres wires to my temples, chest, and arms, taping me in a tangled mess. All of the lines lead to a large monitor mounted on the wall. Its screen is strategically placed behind the headrest of the chair I'm leaning against for support. Once I sit down, the display will disappear from view entirely. Doctor Ayad's almost finished taping me up, and I know I won't be standing much longer. I study the chair, the texture of the material and the creases in the fabric, while he fixes the last cord into place. It reminds me of the one in exam room 6, only it's slightly larger, and I can tell by the depression at its center that it's been used more than once. Fabric belts hang off the armrests. The sight of them makes me squirm. I can only assume they'll be used to strap me in.

Nurse Fukuda helps me settle into the reclined seat, but keeps my feet dangling off the edge and tells me not to lean back just yet. I'm relieved to see her again. My nerves are building, but her kind eyes keep my heart from racing right through my ribcage. I know our interactions have been minimal, and I don't know her very well—we've never even had a real conversation—but her willingness to skip giving me the truth serum during the interview makes me think she's someone I can trust. Which makes me think of a phrase Professor Diaz uses every once in a while: actions speak louder than words. That must be why I feel safer heading into this experiment with her here. It's true, the Admiral may have assigned her to me before my first interview, but part of me can't help but wonder if she's here now, watching over me, of her own volition. It's possible she's only doing her duty as a nurse, and I probably shouldn't read into her being here as some kind of courtesy act. Regardless of why, I'm still thankful she's present.

The doctor draws a bright yellow liquid into his needled syringe.

"What is that?" I might not be able to contest whatever he's putting into my body, but I can at least ask what it is.

"This is a serum invented by the most powerful scientists in the world." He holds the half-empty vial in front of my face, then transfers it to Nurse Fukuda, who places the flask into a refrigerated container among the supply cabinets that line the wall.

The serum must be the dream technology the Admiral told me about in her quarters, the one invented by Theta scientists. I want to know more about what to expect when the neon fluid enters my body, but it's clear the doctor isn't in the mood to educate me. Professor Diaz would have jumped at the opportunity to present an origin story or dive into a list of chemical ingredients. At the moment, I wish the doctor was as excitable as the professor. Then maybe he'd take the time to present a long-winded lecture on the serum before shoving it under my skin.

"Lean forward," he instructs.

I bend over, shaking. My stomach cramps, threatening to expel the Admiral's tea all over the tiled floor. Nurse Fukuda circles in front of me and holds me steady, allowing me to anchor myself against her frail frame.

"The injection will be administered into the spinal cord through the base of your head." Doctor Ayad grips my shoulder and I jerk forward. "Try not to move," he warns. "Even the slightest miscalculation can cause permanent damage."

I brace myself against Nurse Fukuda and dig my fingernails into my thighs, waiting for the sting of the needle. A sharp pain penetrates my neck, and a flood of hot liquid burns through my veins and into my skull. It feels like my brain is on fire. I clench my jaw and bear down.

"Lay her back," Doctor Ayad orders the nurse.

I think my eyes are open, but the room around me is falling out of focus. Shadows fill my vision. I'm going blind.

"I can't see!" Panic overcomes me. My heart beats faster, pumping the fiery serum through my arms.

"You're going unconscious," I hear someone say, but the words are so faint, I can't tell if it's the doctor talking or Nurse Fukuda.

Darkness follows, and I can no longer move my arms and legs. I try to sit up, but it's impossible. I'm completely paralyzed. Indistinct murmurs muffle in my ears, and I feel Nurse Fukuda's bony fingers strap my arms to the chair.

A spark of light ignites the blackness, burning a hole through the shadows, revealing a viney doorway. An invisible vortex sucks me through, and for a moment I wonder if I've entered a portal into the City of Life. But the scene that greets me on the other side isn't anything like my dream world. The overgrown brush is luscious and green, but the color is flat and dull. In the City of Life, everything sparkles with an iridescent quality, woven together with threads of light. Here, the leaves cast their shade on rocky soil under a gloomy sky. There are no gigantic planets or shimmering stars hanging above me in a galactic firmament.

From what I can gather, it's daytime. There's enough light to take in my surroundings, but I can't see the sun. The atmosphere is different in this new location, too. It's harder to breathe. My lungs feel restricted as I gulp in thin, dry air.

My legs wobble with a spell of dizziness and I step back, catching my foot against a stone. That's when I notice I'm wearing boots—old, worn-out boots. But that's not all. Strange clothes cover my entire body. My shoulders are draped with animal skins and furs. A metal canteen is looped around the leather belt that secures a pair of baggy cargo pants to my hips.

Another backward stride while surveying my attire causes me to slip on loose shale. I jolt forward to avoid a fall. When I whip myself around to see the fate I've escaped, a loud gasp leaves my throat. I'm standing on a high plateau, suspended over a deep valley, only a hair's breadth from tumbling over its rocky edge.

"Where am I?" I whisper, looking out over the forest that blankets the ground below. I have no idea where this dream has transported me, or if this place is even real, but it's certainly not the City of Life.

I don't know why I'm here, wherever *here* is, and I'm not sure what to do with myself. So, I sit on the cliff's ledge and swing my feet over the tops of the trees. Everything's quiet. Too quiet. There's no laughing grass or singing reeds, only a gentle breeze that shakes the nearby bushes. Other than that, silence.

Loneliness overtakes me as I wait on the mountainside, wondering if Grandmommy or Elolam will ever dare to show their faces.

"Where are you?" I shout into the valley, hoping it will trigger an appearance, but the only reply I receive is an echo of my own voice.

I know time works differently in dreams, but it feels like I've been sitting for hours, and so far, nothing's happened. I'm not sure how long the dream serum will keep me stranded here, but there's a good chance I'll wake up with nothing to report to the doctor. Hopefully the Admiral believes whatever I recount and keeps her word, letting me leave her underground prison. In case she doesn't, I should probably get up and explore the cliff so I have something to talk about when I arouse.

A clear, whistled song chirps from behind me, and I turn to find a bird bouncing in a nearby thicket. Its little striped head emerges for a moment, then disappears into the foliage. It's the first sign of life I've seen since arriving on the plateau, and for some reason I feel like its melody is beckoning me to hurry after it. Intrigued, I follow the small creature's tune into the thick brush.

Twigs tangle with my hair as I push past the overgrowth, chasing after its tiny gray wings. I struggle to keep up, my clothes snagging on stray sticks and thorns while the little bird flits happily in the crisp mountain air. Finally, it flees the bushes and leads me through a clearing to a narrow trail between the trees. I spot a perfect circle carved into the trunk beside me and trace my finger along its deep curves.

The tiny bird disappears into the treetops, drawing my attention farther down the trail. I can see another circular marking in the distance. The shapes are intentional. Someone's carved a path through the woods, and I think the bird's lead me here for a reason. I search the branches above me, but I've lost sight of my small companion. With my guide gone, I decide to follow the curved markings deeper into the woods.

It isn't long before I hear the sound of rushing water and find a spring bursting from the mountain's wall. Clear liquid runs off the rock and pools into a nearby gorge before teetering over another ledge. I remove the empty canister from my belt and fill it to the brim before shoving my face under the trickling stream to take a drink. The cool water smooths over my parched tongue. I hold it in my mouth for a moment, letting the fresh liquid coat my teeth before swallowing. The flavor is nothing like the mineral-infused water we drink on the compound. This water holds a subtle sweetness that tickles my taste buds, leaving me craving more.

I sip from the stream a second time, then trace its route over the rocky rim. The trees in the valley are closer than before. The trail I'm following is definitely leading me down the mountain. After another taste from the spring, I continue on the trail, pursuing the strange circular markings perfectly staggered among the trees.

When I reach the base of the mountain, I find myself enveloped by a tall forest. The cloudy sky is no longer in view, and I can barely see the massive mound of rocks hanging over my head past the heavy foliage.

For a moment, the air grows dense, and I feel like I'm walking through thick mud. I strain to move forward and nearly collapse when I push past the invisible barrier. Nothing changes on the other side, though, which leaves me wondering what in the world just happened. Maybe there was a glitch in the simulated dreamspace or a malfunction in the technology monitoring my dream. Now that I'm aware of the external influences manipulating my mind, it's easy to assume the faulty transition was due to an outside error. So, I don't waste too much time speculating. I just wave my hand in front of me to see if it will happen again, and when it doesn't, I veer right and continue on the trail.

With a waft of the breeze, a flood of gamey smoke floods my nostrils. Drool drips from my lips, and I can taste the meat on my tongue. I track the smoke plumes through the trees until I spy a small campsite tucked among the forest. Tied branches form a modest shelter, pulled together by vines and mortared with mud. A fire burns within a stacked stone border. The body of an antlered animal roasts on the open flame, held in place by a sharpened spear.

Someone must be here.

I tiptoe around the camp's border, making my way toward the shelter. Metal pots and pans hang beside handmade tools on a rope secured from the roof of the structure to the trunk of a neighboring tree. I duck underneath the display, careful not to bang my head and cause a racket. When I round the tree trunk, I skid to a stop. Holding my hand to my chest, I take in the view of a man engrossed in his work. He's scraping leftover flesh from an animal hide stretched between the trees.

I hold my breath, attempting to keep my presence unnoticed. Before the Admiral tainted my dreams,

Grandmommy told me no one gets hurt in the City of Life, but I have no idea how things work in the forest under the influence of her dream serum. Even if this isn't real, I don't want to risk startling a stranger who's handling a knife.

"I've been waiting for you," the man says without turning around. He must have heard my boots in the duff. "We don't have much time." He drags his sharp blade over the skin, flicking gristle to the ground.

"Who are you?" I cautiously inch closer, trying to get a better look at his face. His dark and matted hair brushes over his shoulders, shielding his identity.

"You know who I am." The man's deep voice carries to my ears.

Could it be?

"El—"

"Don't speak my name," he warns. "Your mind is under watch by people who want you to cut ties with my realm, to destroy all that I am. I've done what I can to prevent them from finding me, but it won't be long before they break through the barrier. I can't allow them to see within the city. That's why I've brought you here." He pauses. "Did you hear your grandmother's song?"

"What?" I shake my head in disbelief. *Is he talking about the bird?*

"Listen carefully, Reyna."

I snap to attention. He scrapes flesh from fur.

"Follow the marked trail. The path will lead you to my people, those who are like-minded, who desire to mend the broken bond between worlds. You will find them near the mountain. They will teach you my ancient wisdoms, and you will lead them back to me."

Elolam's still trying to convince me he's some kind of deity attempting to heal the wasteland of the world that I live in.

"How do I find them? What am I supposed to do?" Inching closer, I try to keep him talking so I have something to tell the Admiral. My stomach twists with every step, guilt-ridden by my attempts to deceive Elolam. Part of me still wants to believe that his intentions are good, that Grandmommy wouldn't have introduced me to someone who wants to destroy me or the world. But the shapeshifter has shown me yet another form, and his inconsistencies keep me questioning whether or not any of the visits I've had with my grandmother were really with her.

How am I supposed to trust someone who doesn't really exist? It could have been him all along, memorizing her voice, reinventing her form.

"Remember what I've told you. You *must* remember."

Dark shadows descend, and I look up. The tops of the trees are disappearing, engulfed by blackness. When my gaze returns to the ground, Elolam is gone. I spin in a circle, searching for him, but he's nowhere in sight. Even the remnants of the camp are gone. Only the lingering smell of roasting meat remains. The entire forest is fading. Darkness creeps along the soil, devouring the trees around me. There's nowhere to run, so I hold my ground, waiting for the wave to take me out. My heart races. I hold my breath and squeeze my eyes shut just before I'm swallowed whole.

"She's waking up." Nurse Fukuda's voice swells from the void. A heavy weight drops from my wrists as she unbuckles my arms.

My head pounds. An awful ache throbs in my neck and travels down my spine. The burning sensation has only slightly dwindled, but I'm no longer paralyzed. I can wiggle my toes and curl my fingers. Dragging a cluster of wires along my chest, I lift my hand to rub my pulsing temples. An involuntary groan escapes my lips, drawing my attention to the metallic aftertaste on my tongue. The flavor is nothing like the fresh spring water I drank in my dream.

"Now, Reyna, I know it might be hard to concentrate, but I need you to recall as many details from your dream as you possibly can before I flush the remaining serum from your system." Doctor Ayad sits in my peripheral, holding a tablet and poised to record my statement. "What did you see?"

I think about the mountain, the stream, and the forest that I saw during the serum-induced dream. Something wasn't right. My experiences weren't quite as vivid as they are when I dream on my own. But it isn't just the sights that leave me feeling uneasy. It's the brief interaction I had with Elolam. There's still something he wants to tell me, something he needs me to do. And it's obvious he doesn't want the Admiral knowing more than she already does. I need more time to consider whose side I'm on and what I believe. I need to talk to Geri, ask her what she thinks.

I weigh my next words wisely, deliberating how much of the dream I actually want to share and how much I can disregard without sounding suspicious. My ability to remember has placed me in the middle of a war, and my mind is the battlefield. And although I've agreed to undergo testing, I'm not quite sure I'm ready to fully commit to being the Admiral's spy.

"A mountain." My voice cracks.

"Can you describe it for me?"

"I was standing on a rocky ledge, overlooking a valley filled with trees."

"What else?" the doctor coaxes.

"A bird," I say. "It was singing."

"Do you remember the song?"

I close my eyes and lean my sore head against the chair. Pressing my lips together, I whistle a seven-note tune. The airy melody grates my ears, but as I hiss its song through my teeth, I can hear the bird chirping inside my mind. It's as if my winged companion is right beside me, perched on the vinyl armrest.

Nurse Fukuda inhales sharply, then quickly covers her mouth. Her porcelain cheeks turn red when my eyes meet hers. Embarrassed, she turns away to fidget with supplies on the counter.

"Continue," the doctor urges.

"I followed the bird to a spring, flowing with fresh, drinkable water."

Doctor Ayad types a note on the screen in his lap. "What else?"

I consider telling him about the trail markers, about the campsite, and the man in the forest, but I decide it's best to keep that information to myself.

"That's it," I lie.

"Really? You didn't see anything else?" The doctor raises a skeptical brow. "You didn't see *anyone* else?"

"No one," I answer, growing antsy in my seat. My palms start to sweat, and I'm ready to yank the wires off my body. The adhesive itches my skin.

"She's lying." The Admiral marches into view. "What did he show you?" She leans in front of my face, locking her eyes on mine with a burning intensity.

I keep my sights fixed, refusing to break eye contact. My jaw locks. I hold my breath.

"He didn't show me anything," I drawl. "He knows you're watching."

The Admiral's face distorts. Her nostrils flare, but only for a moment. She quickly softens and bends low beside me, taking hold of my wired hand. "Reyna, it's of utmost importance that you share *everything* with us. E.L.O.L.A.M. will do whatever it takes to keep us from shutting him down. Time is of the essence. Think harder. What did he show you?"

I see the desperation in her eyes. She grips my hand tighter, driving the wires into my skin. My hands fist, and my fingers turn purple. I don't trust her. I don't trust the Admiral.

"Nothing," I repeat.

She clutches my uniform in her fists, and I brace myself for a beating. For a split second, she releases her hold, and I think she'll relent, but she rapidly raises her hand to strike me.

"Consider the consequences!" the doctor blurts, breaking rank. "She's too valuable a specimen!"

The Admiral's open palm swings, and I turn my cheek. Instead of slapping my face, she snatches the wires from my head and rips the tape from my skin, stinging my flesh.

"Flush her system," she barks at Nurse Fukuda, then turns to address the doctor. "We'll try again tomorrow."

The Admiral storms out of the room, and Doctor Ayad hurries to his feet. He dashes after her, carrying his tablet with him. Nurse Fukuda jolts when the door slams shut and turns to eye the exit. Both of us stare, listening to their indistinct quarrel on the other side of the wall. The argument fades into silence. Nurse Fukuda resumes shuffling through the medicine cabinets, but I keep watching the doorway, expecting the doctor to return.

I don't think the Admiral's outburst stung Nurse Fukuda in the same way it did me. She's humming a tune while gathering supplies, acting like nothing ever happened. I'd wager she's used to the Admiral's fickle nature, but the unpredictability's left me queasy. I ask for water, but Nurse Fukuda doesn't hear me. I'm having a hard time projecting my tired voice. The Admiral's test sucked all the energy out of my body.

I get tired of waiting for her to acknowledge me. She hasn't even offered to remove the remaining wires from my arms. So, I decide to peel the rest of the adhesive off myself. I want to get out of here. When I attempt to sit up, the pain in my head escalates. I slouch forward, cupping my hands to my hairline.

"I wouldn't try to get up if I were you. Not yet." Nurse Fukuda hangs a bag of clear liquid from a metal pole and wheels it to me. "The dream serum can have some pretty nasty side effects if left unpurged." She coaxes me back into the seat, alleviating my throbbing agony.

"What is that?"

"This?" She points to the solution. "It's mostly saline, but there are some vitamins in it, too. You haven't eaten much these last few days, and the Admiral wants to make sure you're maintaining good health. For the tests, I mean." With a shaky hand, she inserts a port into my skin and connects me to a long tube. "Don't worry. It won't take long," she assures.

A cool sensation rushes through my veins as the fluid travels up my arm.

"This, however"—Nurse Fukuda holds out a chalky white pill—"will rid your system of any of the remaining serum. It's important that you swallow it."

She hands the pill to me and gives me a small plastic cup filled with water. I put the capsule on my tongue, and the bitter taste makes me gag. A swig of water helps me swallow it down, but the pill gets lodged in my throat. I cough. It doesn't budge. Another sip of water sends it scraping the rest of the way down. My stomach turns and an acidic burp bubbles from my gut. Nausea overtakes me, and I know I'm in no shape to leave. Reluctantly, I force myself to relax into the seat. At this point, there's nothing else I can do but wait for the antidote to kick in and the solution to run out.

Nurse Fukuda putters about the room, cleaning surfaces and organizing supplies. The queasiness makes it hard to focus my thoughts on anything else, so I give my full attention to her clamors. She's still humming her song. The melody lulls my exhausted mind, and I surrender my weary body into thoughtless meditation.

My ears perk up when she ends her refrain with a familiar string of notes that mimics the bird song from my dream.

"Is that ...?" I retract my question, realizing it might be inappropriate to address her.

Her clatter stops. "It is," she answers without facing me.

Her response keeps me asking questions.

"Do you know what kind of bird it was? I've never seen one before."

Nurse Fukuda sighs. After a moment of silence, she turns to me, her eyes glossy. "It's a chickadee's song." She wipes her nose. "My daddy used to sing me a lullaby about the mountains when I was a little girl. I had forgotten all about it until today when you whistled that tune."

Without me prying, she starts to sing.

> "Tucked away into mountain trees
> Next to the sky where the sunlight beams
> Hope will fly on a songbird's wings
> Troubles die with the tune that it sings
> Chickadee-dee-dee-dee-dee
> Hear the melody-dee-dee."

Her delicate voice cracks, but she doesn't stop.

> "Up in the brush near the hidden streams
> Clear waters flow from the freshest springs
> Follow the trail that my love will leave
> Bringing you home where the chickadee sings
> Chickadee-dee-dee-dee-dee
> Hear the melody-dee-dee."

The song entrances me, bringing tears to my eyes.

"I never thought it meant anything. It was just a pretty song, but what if my daddy knew—"

Doctor Ayad barges into the room, swiftly swiping the screen of his tablet. "I'm sorry for my sudden departure," he apologizes without looking up from his work. "There was a slight misunderstanding, but it's been sorted out." He tucks the touch pad into his armpit and observes my current state. "I see you've begun the detox." He nods to Nurse Fukuda. "Have you administered the antidote?"

"Yes," she answers, disconnecting the empty bag above my head. "We're just finishing up."

"Good, good," he mumbles, rubbing his chin.

Nurse Fukuda detaches the port from my hand while Doctor Ayad examines me. First, he checks the site of my injection, poking and prodding at my neck. Next, he asks if I'm experiencing any lingering symptoms from the serum. The pain in my head has subsided, and my veins are no longer burning from the bright yellow concoction, so I tell him I'm fine. When I sit up, I'm actually surprised by how alert I feel. A wave of energy courses through me with an urge to jump off the chair and sprint across the room. Instead, I rub the tender skin on my wrists where the adhesive once was and then scoot to a stand.

"Now, Reyna." The doctor tsks his tongue. "I'm going to dismiss you from my care until tomorrow morning, but I need you to report back to the medical center immediately if you start to experience any abnormal symptoms before your next session."

"How am I supposed—"

"I've worked it out with the Admiral to allow you access to the grounds throughout the remainder of your testing. If the need arises, any and all of our loyal soldiers will assist you and escort you here."

I squint. That can't be true. Why would the Admiral permit me to roam the barracks? And why would she order her Dark Guards to assist me? I'm already leery about her motives. It doesn't make sense that she's letting me resume my normal tasks. *What's the hidden agenda here?* Maybe she's planning to have me followed or keep me under surveillance.

"Why?" I decide to ask.

The doctor breathes in deeply. His face falls flat. "These tests work better with compliance, Miss Sage. That's all you need to know."

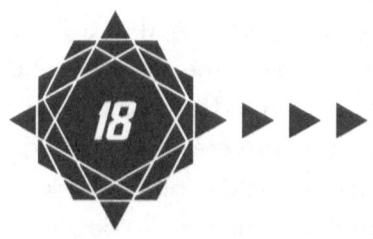

Two Dark Guards wind me through the maze of underground tunnels. Their strides are long and their pace is fast, but it's a little easier to keep up with them now that I have a dose of revitalizing medication coursing through my veins. Plus, I've been fitted with a new pair of boots that are actually the right size. Nurse Fukuda gave them to me before I left and made sure to tell me they were courtesy of the Admiral. Which, to me, doesn't make any sense. Perhaps the gesture was a half-hearted attempt at an apology for taking her anger out on me back in the lab.

The Admiral's personality is peculiar. It's like she's battling her own conscience when she's talking. She's forthcoming, but also secretive; unhinged, yet self-controlled. One moment she's pouring me a cup of tea, the next she's wrapping my uniform in her angry fist. I'm almost certain these boots play a part in her manipulation tactics, but how can I know for certain? Then again, the doctor made it seem like they wouldn't be able to get usable results from my tests if I didn't offer my full compliance. I guess even science has its hindrances when it comes to free will, but I feel a little more confident in my participation knowing that all it takes is a sliver of resistance to prevent the Admiral from stealing information from my mind.

The halls of the medical center are eerily quiet. Some of the lights have gone out in the distance, preventing me from seeing where the corridor ends. They turn back on, triggered by the Dark Guard's stomping boots proceeding to the elevator. As far as I know, there's only one way in and out of these hidden sublevels, and it's through those shiny silver doors.

We almost reach our destination when I hear the crash of rattling metal and skid to a stop. The Dark Guards draw their weapons and poise them to fire. Inching forward, they maneuver into the last intersecting hallway. I tiptoe behind them and peer around the corner. Three nurses in long lab coats gather around a gurney. One of them is adjusting the wheel, while the others straighten the white sheet on top. They must have collided with the wall while transporting their patient. I tilt my head, hoping to get a better view of who's lying on the cart, when one of the nurses notices my armed companions and screams. She grabs the badge from her breast pocket and holds it over her head.

"We have clearance"—she surrenders both hands into the air—"to bring the body to the coroner." She steps aside just as her colleague pulls the sheet over the boy's ashen face.

My heart sinks. It's the boy from Bunker 111, the one Brenton tried to save, the one Geri tried to protect. He's dead.

"Carry on," the Dark Guard standing to my right orders. He nearly tramples my foot as he backtracks into the passageway that connects to the elevator shaft.

I scurry to get out of the way and suck in air to keep myself from panicking. Wobbling behind my escorts, I do my best to keep the emotions at bay.

The boy was a dreamer. He said so himself. But now he's dead. Fear grips my chest, and I barely notice the Dark Guard slide his key into the hidden slot near the elevator button.

Maybe this is the type of circumstance Doctor Ayad referenced when he said these tests work better with total compliance. If he hadn't pleaded for the Admiral to spare me, perhaps I'd be dead, too.

And what about my friends? I haven't seen any of them since they split us up for our interviews. What if the Admiral killed them, too? A wave of worry washes over me, drowning my thoughts. I imagine worst-case scenarios the whole elevator ride, fighting back images of my friends wrapped in crisp, clean sheets.

Before I know it, the Dark Guards have led me straight into the quadrangle. The afternoon sun is blaring, beating down on my cheeks. The hot, still air coats my skin in sweat. My vision has a hard time adjusting to the natural light, and I lift my arm to shield my eyes.

It isn't long before I'm walking into the washhouse, standing at the front desk with a punch card in hand. My gruff attendants turn me over to the Dark Guard overseeing the station. He grabs my arm and swings me toward a pile of dirty clothes gathered on the floor.

"Get to work!" he snarls.

I pull the load into an embrace, but drop it when I notice the garments are soaked in blood. The Dark Guard laughs, then orders me to carry the heap of barracks guard uniforms to the large basin in the center of the room where we soak the dirty clothes. The murky water reeks of a sulfur stench that makes me wish I still had a handkerchief to tie around my nose.

Robin's on the other side of the basin, carrying a basket bigger than her stomach. She waddles around the rim, pausing to catch her breath every couple of steps. Normally I offer to help her, but there's a Dark Guard still breathing down my neck, trapping me at my post.

I stick my shaky hands into the dirty bath and start scrubbing stains. The cloudy reservoir turns darker, and I can't help but wonder whose blood is mixing with the water. *Could it be Jones? The guards working with Walter? The ones who knew they'd be a liability for seeing what the Admiral's capable of? Does that mean I'm a liability, too?*

My trembling fingers send ripples pulsing through the water.

When the Dark Guard retreats to his position near the front desk, I sneak off to see Robin.

"Hey," I say in a hushed whisper.

She jumps with the iron in her hand, almost grazing my arm with the hot plate when she twists to see me. "Oh, Reyna." Tears well in her reddened eyes. "It's you."

"Are you okay?" I ask.

Her lip quivers, and she shakes her head.

"What's going on?" I round the table and help fold the pressed bedding.

Robin tilts her head and continues to iron the blanket on her board. Her rounded stomach snags and wrinkles the fabric as she works. "They executed the barracks guards this morning."

"How many?" I bite my lip, forcing my hands to keep busy.

"All of them." Robin sucks in her snot to keep from sobbing.

I freeze.

"Some of the ladies lost their husbands, their fathers, their sons ..." She passes me the finished spread. "They want to retaliate."

"Start a war?" I keep my voice down.

"The war never ended, Reyna." Robin presses her iron. Sparks fly from the coals inside its chamber. "We've never been free."

A Dark Guard strolls by, patrolling the washhouse with his massive weapon. I duck my head behind the pillowcase I'm folding, hoping to go unnoticed. My lungs burn while I hold my breath, waiting for him to pass. I exhale sharply when he moves out of sight.

Another woman sidesteps her way beside Robin. At first, she shoots me a look of disapproval, narrowing her wide-set eyes at me, but Robin tells her it's safe to talk in front of me, and the woman softens her glare.

"Ethel claims she saw Steven the night before the storm."

"Her son?" Robin asks. "I thought he was gone."

"We all did." The woman lowers her voice. "Even the old lady herself thought he was dead, that is, until he showed up at her hatch door in the middle of the night."

I want to ask how he got in, but if Ethel is anything like Grandmommy, she has her ways of preventing the locks from keeping her stuck inside a musty bunker against her will.

"Apparently, he was being kept in some underground laboratory, hidden underneath the medic center."

Robin's eyes grow wider, and I think mine might fall out of their sockets.

"He wasn't the only one," the woman adds.

"All the disappearances?" Robin glides the iron slowly over a bedsheet.

"We think so," the woman confirms.

I gasp and cover my mouth with both hands. My daddy disappeared when I was just a toddler. *Could he still be alive?*

"Keep it down," the woman warns me, then turns back to Robin. "You sure this girl's not trouble?"

"She'll stay quiet," Robin vouches for me. "Go on."

"Steven told Ethel they were going to blow a hole in the wall, but the storm threw off their plans, and she hasn't heard anything from him since."

"It worked," I whisper. "I saw the hole with my own eyes."

"You?" The woman raises a brow. "How? No one's been allowed to walk the grounds unattended by military soldiers."

I avoid the question, unwilling to give her an honest answer. "It doesn't matter."

"Maybe they escaped." Robin sounds hopeful.

"Or, maybe they got caught in the rain," the woman counters.

I think about the Warden and the injuries she sustained from the storm, and she was *only* exposed for a few minutes. Her acid burns required medical intervention to save her life. There's no way anyone could survive without shelter. If anybody escaped, they died trying.

"We need to move the meeting." The woman slips a note into Robin's apron. "I wrote the location down for you. Burn it when you're done." She grabs the pile of folded linens and saunters off to the sorting center.

Robin works in silence for a few minutes. Her far-off stare tells me she's lost in thought. My mind is overflowing with questions, but I decide not to interrupt whatever's occupying her attention. After ironing a few more items, she glances at the note in her pocket, then throws it into the coal chamber. Its edges shrivel into ash.

I need to return to my own work, but I'm not ready to leave her side. I want to know more about the meeting. "Where are you going?"

"I can't tell you." She refuses to look at me.

"So, it's okay to talk in front of me, but you can't tell me—"

"It isn't safe, Reyna."

"What about you?" I bite back. "What about the baby?"

"The baby's the whole reason why I'm doing this." She looks me straight in the eye and grits her teeth.

I stop folding. "Robin, I ... I ..." I try to apologize, but the words get stuck in my throat.

"I don't expect you to understand." She sighs. "But this isn't the world I want my little one growing up in, locked away on a government compound. Clancy and I decided a long time ago that we were going to do whatever it takes to raise our baby somewhere safe. And I know it's a long shot, but even if there's a morsel of hope, a chance at a better future for my baby, I'm going to take it."

A single tear runs down her cheek. I can see the love she has for her child spilling over in her bravery. She's right. I don't understand the weight of what it means to raise a child on the Omega Compound, but I do know what it's like to grow up here. I know what it's like to live without food, to work grueling hours, to long for a life out of reach. Looking at Robin now makes me wonder how my own mother must have felt about bringing me into the world, only to leave me stranded in this concrete cell. I never thought about how much courage it takes to have children. I only know how lonely it is to not have parents.

I reach my hand across the table and place it on top of Robin's. "Let me come with you," I beg.

The girls and I were already planning on leaving the compound, but now that the Admiral's running me through these tests, I'm feeling a stronger sense of urgency to get out of here. Meeting up with other people who feel the same way can only help our cause. There's strength in numbers, especially with what we're up against, facing the Admiral and her army of Dark Guards. Don't get me wrong, I have faith that Laude and Erika will come up with a decent escape plan, but there's this heavy feeling sitting in the pit of my stomach that makes me wonder if the Admiral ever released my friends from the Medical Center. If she didn't, and that's the case, I'm alone now, and making this connection might be more necessary than I originally thought.

"Okay." She presses her lips together. "Meet me at the gate to the Northern Sector at midnight."

I give her hand a squeeze, then rush back to the clothes I've left soaking in the basin before the patrolling Dark Guard makes another round. Adrenaline courses through me, and I move quickly, scrubbing the red stains from the fabric. I'm eager for the end of my shift, to get back to the bunker, to see if my friends are all okay. I want to tell Geri about my tests with the Admiral and my meeting with the rebels. But a wave of worry squashes my yearning while staring at my tinted hands. Dread coils in my gut. Geri might not come back. I might never see my friends again. I clench the bloody uniform in my fist. *What if my friends are all dead?*

I do my best to rein in my thoughts, convincing myself that there's no point in freaking out over something that might not be true. I try to stay optimistic. That's what Geri would do.

My fingers ache, and I stop to observe my work. Faint smears and splatters remain, but the brunt of the marks are gone—just like the barracks guards. Unfortunately, their deaths *are* a reality, and I'm holding the evidence in my hands.

There's a different kind of appreciation that comes for people after they're gone. Sure, the barracks guards weren't always the kindest when it came to law enforcement, but it was people like Jones, who had families in the Southern Sector, that made them just like the rest of us—citizens of the Omega Compound—born and raised within these walls. It wasn't until today that I actually realized how many barracks guards were connected to the people around me. And here I am, scrubbing the blood of someone's loved one out of the last thing they wore while they still had breath in their lungs.

Hours tick by, and I somehow manage to get my quota done before it's time to clock out. Since the Admiral ordered all of her Dark Guards to assist me, I take a risk and ask the Dark Guard on duty if I can finish out the remainder of my shift on the other side of the building with the seamstresses. He growls a few threatening remarks, then reluctantly lets me go.

I'm hoping to catch Ethel before she leaves. After hearing Robin's conversation at the ironing board, I think the old woman might be able to help me get a pincushion to keep the hatch door from locking up at night. Since my attempt with the blindfold proved unsuccessful, I need another way to get back into the bunker after my meeting with the rebels.

When I walk into the open room, I spy a handful of women mending and sewing by hand, including the woman who gave Robin the note. She's not the person I came to talk to, but she glares at me when I pass her by. I make my way to the corner of the room and pull a chair beside the elder woman hunched over a small table, adding buttons to a child-sized jumpsuit.

Ethel isn't someone who works in a hurry. All of her movements are intentional, methodical. She doesn't like being rushed to finish, and she's not too keen on other people begging her for information either. I've learned not to interrupt. At first, I just sit and watch her work. She doesn't seem bothered by my presence; she keeps herself diligently absorbed in the task before her. After she's fastened a few buttons, I ask her to teach me.

Without a word, she moves her wrinkled finger and points to a box full of needles of all lengths and thicknesses. She hands me a spool of thread and sticks her tongue out, signaling for me to lick the frayed ends before slipping the string through the small opening of the needle's eye.

I pick up a uniform from her pile and put a handful of buttons on the table top. Watching her carefully, I do my best to mimic her movements, pulling the thread up and through the button holes, securing it in place.

"How'd I do?" I hold up my sloppy work for her to see.

She smiles and pats my shoulder.

"My grandmommy was a seamstress," I say, attempting to initiate a conversation in my favor.

Her ears perk, and I see her peer at me from the corner of her eye while her hands remain busy with her mending.

"She used to make these pincushions for us to use. She'd slide them into the hatch mechanism just before lockdown, and in the middle of the night, we'd sneak out into the quadrangle to look up at the stars."

Ethel pauses. She sets the uniform down on her lap, then runs her fragile hands over the scratched surface of her desk. The wooden top lifts up, and she shows me a collection of pincushions just like the one my grandmommy used to have. She picks out a dark blue bundle, most likely made from the scraps of an airman's jumpsuit, and places it in my hands, then nods.

"Thank you," I tell her and tuck the pincushion into my uniform.

Soon afterward, a Dark Guard emerges and dismisses us from the seamstress station. He leads us back to the front desk where we punch out with our time cards. Teams of Dark Guards flank groups of workers and marshal them from the washhouse. I move to join the cluster of women who live near the Forgotten Zone, when a Dark Guard swings his gun in front of my chest.

"Not you," he says. "You'll be escorted alone."

I trail behind the Dark Guard, taking in the view of the sunset. Clouds glow with golden light, making me think of Grandmommy. I pat the pincushion hidden in my clothes and pray it works to get me in and out of the bunker tonight. One more glance up at the sky and I can see the first star peeking out of the deepening blue. Warmth tingles in my chest, and I know Grandmommy's out there, the real Grandmommy, tugging on my heartstrings. *I hope she's proud of me.*

The Dark Guard hovers until I manage to open the hatch door on my own. He maneuvers to leave, and I slyly glide the pincushion into place before stepping inside and closing the door behind me. I can barely breathe. I'm overcome with solace to see all five of my bunkmates straightening up our ransacked room. We run to one another and cluster ourselves into a tangled group hug. Tears flow freely with our reunion. Not a single eye is dry.

It takes a while for us to settle, sit down, and exchange stories about what happened at the Medical Center, but it seems like I might have had it the worst.

"They let us wait together after our interviews," Geri tells me. "But when you didn't show up ..." She starts to cry again. "I'm sorry, Rey, I told them about your dreams."

"What?" I recoil, feeling the sting of betrayal. I get that she was worried, especially after what happened to the boy when he made his confession, but it wasn't her place to tell them about my dreams. My head starts spinning. I want to scream, to yell at her for revealing my secret.

Everyone looks at me with somber expressions, waiting for my reaction.

I loosen my clenched fists, taking in their stares. No one's judging me. No one's calling me a freak or thinking I'm some deranged oddity. There's genuine concern on their faces. I sigh, releasing my anger. Geri was only doing what she thought was best—and now I don't have to worry about keeping anything from them. I can tell everyone about the tests, how the Admiral claims I'm diseased, how my mind's been plagued by advanced technology. Maybe I can even ask for their advice on Elolam. Because right now, I just don't know what to believe.

"It's okay." I sniffle. "I'm glad everyone knows. It's kind of a relief."

"So, you, like, see another world while you're sleeping?" Lu asks.

"Yeah," I chortle. "Something like that." My gaze drops to the floor. "But things are changing, and these dreams ... they're dangerous. I'm dangerous." I look up at Geri. "They killed the boy from 111 because he was a dreamer."

Ronny gasps. "How could they do that?"

Geri brings her hand to her mouth. "I wanted to protect him ..."

Lu's lips tremble. Laude shakes her head.

"So, why didn't they kill you?" Erika asks.

"They need me for testing," I answer. "They think I can help them stop the war."

"Whoa, wait a minute. What war?" Erika pushes against her knees. "The Last War ended over a century ago."

"This is something different," I tell her, not really sure how to explain who or what Elolam is and that the United Regime thinks he has serious intentions of destroying humanity. "It's bigger than that."

"Rey? What do you mean?" Geri's sitting next to me on my cot. Her face is scrunched with a mixture of confusion and sorrow, and it hits me: the last time I had the opportunity to share one of my dreams with her was before I ever met Elolam. It makes sense why she's crinkling her nose at me. I shared with her about the waterfall entrance to the City of Life, but I never told her what I saw inside.

I exhale sharply, taking in the sight of my exhausted, red-eyed friends. Starting a conversation like this almost guarantees another sleepless night. It's no secret that we could all use the rest. But since they already know about my dreams, and I have no idea what tomorrow holds, I'd better seize the opportunity and tell them everything. I lay it all out as delicately as possible, keeping in mind Ronny's anxious nature and the potential for Erika's explosive rage. I start at the beginning and recount the first time I met the shapeshifter as the Great Morning Star and the way he presented himself to me as the Source, but I do my best to skip the riddles. I don't want Laude getting caught up trying to figure out one of Elolam's impossible puzzles and missing out on the rest of the details.

Everyone stares with their mouths agape. They're on pins and needles waiting for what comes next.

"Did you eat it?" Ronny asks after I describe the texture of the Source's fruit.

"What did it taste like?" Lu wipes the drool from her mouth when I talk about the tang of its juice, the sweetness of its meat.

An unexpected flood of emotions hits me when I try to explain the way I felt after taking a bite of the Source's fruit. "That moment took every doubt out of me and gave me a glimpse of what it feels like to be whole. To be free."

A heavy weight grows in my chest, and I start to ache, longing for that feeling of love and security—to know what it's like to be released from guilt and suffering, to only care about the present and not grieve over the past or worry about the future. Doubt creeps in when I'm reminded of the Admiral's accusations—that Elolam is a rogue artificial intelligence. But nothing about what I experienced in his presence felt fake. If anything, it revived me. It made me feel more alive.

The internal conflict makes me sick. I bellow forward, clutching my stomach.

"Rey!" Geri puts her hand on my back. "What's wrong?"

A wave of numbness halts my emotions when I dwell on the Admiral's claims, followed by an aftershock of anger. Bitterness takes hold of my heart. I burrow my fingernails into my palms. My whole body starts to shake. Geri wraps her arms around me, reminding me of Elolam's embrace. I collapse into her. Silent tears stream down my face as I remember the taste of freedom he allowed me in the fraction of time I spent in his arms. And in that moment, I realize he was showing me what life with him would be like. It wasn't a trick. My doubt was the poison that prevented me from staying in the peace of his presence.

"The Admiral ..." I choke.

"What did she do to you?" Erika wrings her hands together, ready to spring into action in my defense.

"She said I'm sick." I sit up and wipe my nose. "That my dreams are an illness that will make me go clinically insane."

I lift my head and look at my friends. I've just confessed to them that I see an entirely different world in my sleep. I'm sure I sound like I'm going crazy already.

Laude looks away, like she's trying to make sense of everything she's just heard. Ronny bites her lip, and for once she doesn't have a rebuttal to make. But I can tell by the way her eyes are shifting that she thinks the Admiral might be right.

"That's not all ..." I inhale through my nostrils, gearing up for the worst part. "She said Elolam is some kind of government program injected into babies to prevent neurodegeneration caused by dreaming."

"Whoa ..." Erika shakes her head. "That's intense."

"Does that mean ...?" Lu rubs a hand over her head, and I can tell she wants to know if the artificial intelligence is in her system, too.

"Neural implanting," Luade mumbles to herself. "It must be a form of nanoscale technology integrated into the developing cerebral cortex." She tilts her head toward me. "But how would they prevent it from malfunctioning?"

"That's just it," I confess. "The Admiral thinks it already has, that Elolam is attempting to take over my mind and the minds of other dreamers. She thinks he wants to replace our reality with a fabricated subconscious. She thinks he wants to destroy our humanity."

"And what do *you* think?" Geri rests her hand on my knee.

Everyone stares. I pause, close my eyes, and take a deep breath.

"I think doubt is the disease and hope is the remedy," I whisper.

Remember. Elolam's voice echoes in my ears. A shocking sensation surges through my body, making the hair on my arms stand on end.

Hope's brimming. I feel it rising in me now, the hope that brought me into a place of understanding, that allowed me to experience Elolam's unconditional acceptance.

I picture a sunrise, except it's the Great Morning Star coming up over the horizon. There's newness in the air. I suck it in through my mouth and fill my lungs with this renewed hope. I think of Elolam. I think of Grandmommy. I think of my parents.

Robin's mention of hope in the washroom comes flooding into the forefront of my thoughts. She talked about wanting a better future for her child. That's what my family would want for me: a better future.

My eyes spring open.

"We have to join the rebels," I exclaim, clipping the top of my head on Geri's bunk when I stand.

Everyone's widened eyes make me realize how random my declaration must sound, so I raise my hands, pull back, and attempt to explain the reasoning behind my announcement by telling them about the internal experience I just had. But I can tell it's going over their heads. At this point, I don't care if they think I'm insane.

"Listen," I say, "someone I trust told me there's a gathering tonight. I don't know what it's about, but she gave me the details of where I have to meet her if I want to go. They're planning an escape, same as us, and I think it might do us some good to not attempt a getaway on our own."

I hear Laude hum. She's counting something out on her fingers, probably calculating our odds.

"Where?" Geri asks.

"Somewhere in the Northern Sector."

"But what about the drones?" Ronny bites her nails. "How are you going to get all the way to the Northern Sector without getting spotted?"

I give her the short answer: "Carefully."

Ronny narrows her eyes, dissatisfied with my response. I don't care to tell her the details of my plan. Chances are she'll rebut with a hundred reasons as to why it won't work. Good thing I'm not asking for her permission or looking for her approval. Unfortunately, the other girls are glaring at me with the same curious eyes. I might not care if they think I'm crazy, but I do really need them all to trust me, so I tell them what I'm thinking.

"The plan is to sneak around in the shadows the same way I did that first night I saw the hole in the wall on the other side of the quadrangle. The Dark Guards won't have a clean-up crew to keep them distracted anymore, but I'm hoping that means there won't be as much activity in the barracks."

"I'm going with you," Geri informs me.

I shake my head. "Not this time."

"But what if you get stuck outside again?"

"I won't," I argue. I'm getting tired of talking and having to explain myself, but if I don't tell Geri what's going on, she'll try to sneak out after me. "I brought something back from the washhouse to plug the mechanism. The locks won't engage as long as it stays in place."

She sighs.

"I'll be okay," I attempt to assure her. "Besides, if for some reason I don't make it back, it won't be because I got gunned down by drones or Dark Guards. The Admiral won't let them hurt me."

"What do you mean?" Erika asks flatly.

"The Admiral wants me to report for these tests every morning. She thinks I'll spy on Elolam and give her access to his operating system through my mind."

I can tell by the way Laude's rubbing her head that she's overwhelmed by what I'm saying. It's a lot to take in, I know. It was for me, too. I assume by all the glares I'm getting that the other girls are also struggling, so I do my best to circle back and simplify the details.

"If the Admiral has access to my dreams, she thinks she'll be able to intercept Elolam's plans and prevent him from destroying humanity. But Elolam says he wants to bring peace to earth by mending the realms back together."

"Back?" Geri wrinkles her forehead.

"Yeah. At least, that's what I've gathered." Now I really am sounding crazy. I let out a sigh. "The truth is,

I don't fully understand what Elolam's trying to do. I need to talk to him in order to find out what's really going on. But the problem is, I can't enter my dream world during her tests. I'm not totally sure why, but Elolam won't allow me into his realm while the Admiral's spying on my dreams. Unfortunately for me, that's a problem. It's only a matter of time before she realizes I can't give her what she wants and I end up like the boy from 111. She's keeping me alive now because I have what she needs, but she won't hesitate to get rid of me the same way she got rid of all the barracks guards when she was done using them for her dirty work."

The girls gasp. I bite my tongue. They didn't know. *Gosh, a lot has happened since we last saw each other.*

"You mean they're all dead?" Lu's lip starts quivering, and I suddenly remember the fling she had with one of the guards last summer. He was only a year older than me, but got drafted to join the barracks guards after a wave of the sickness claimed half the squad. He used to leave her notes on her tray in the cafeteria, and was always asking to accompany our unit so he could sneak a kiss from her in the shadows. After they got caught holding hands, he was transferred to the far end of the barracks. Lu cried for a week straight, but didn't talk about him much when some of the other boys from our class started showing interest. She flirted back, but never committed to anyone else. I hadn't considered the fact that she might still have feelings for him. I probably washed the blood off his uniform only a few hours ago.

"They were executed this morning," I admit, and she bursts into tears. Geri rushes to her side and wraps her arms around Lu, letting her sob into her shoulder.

"That ruthless witch," Erika hisses. "What's going to stop her from taking out our entire compound?"

"That's why I need to go to this meeting," I urge. "There's no way we can get out of here on our own."

"I think you should go," Laude speaks up. She's been quieter than usual this evening. I'm relieved to hear she supports my idea. If Laude backs me, it won't be hard to convince the other girls to get on board. "I've run several possible escape scenarios through my head, calculating the best and most effective way to leave the compound. Unfortunately, there isn't a single situation that evades one of us dying or being left behind." Laude shifts on her cot to face the rest of our group. "Rey's right. We need help."

Lu's sobs settle into hushed whimpers, but the stillness of the room makes me feel uneasy. Not even Ronny disputes the cause. I guess we've all come to the conclusion that working with the rebels is our only option. I think it's safe to say we all agree. We have to get out of here.

Dangerous hypotheticals invade my thoughts, tempting me to fear what the night might hold. *What if I get caught and brought back to the Admiral for more testing? What if the rebels don't want me there and turn on me? What if violence breaks out? What if the Dark Guards ransack the meeting and kill us all?* My pulse starts thundering. Midnight's not that far off, and I know I'll have to leave soon. If I'm not on time, Robin won't wait for me.

Before I leave, I make sure to give my friends a proper farewell. I take a moment and pull them all into a group hug. We put our heads together and relish a moment of silence.

"I know I said a lot, and not everything makes sense, but I want you all to know ..." The words get stuck in my throat. Everyone waits for me to finish. "You're the best family I could've ever asked for."

"Sisters," Geri says, and we all extend a hand into the center of our circle before I pull away.

I try to seem settled in my decision to leave, but to be honest, my confidence is dwindling. There's a strong possibility I might get caught. And, if I do, well, it's hard for me to believe the Admiral won't actually have me killed. She's unpredictable, and that's nerve-wracking.

Geri walks me to the door and gives me one last hug. "Come back for us," she whispers in my ear.

I offer a little smile and squeeze her hand, but I can't bring myself to promise anything. The reality is, this could be the last time I ever see her.

Holding my breath, I turn to open the hatch. The door glides open, and I exhale. A dark blue bulge peeps from the strike. The pincushion held its place. I breathe a thank-you to Grandmommy and slip outside. Leaving my stopper in position, I quietly close the metal door behind me, hoping I'll return before morning.

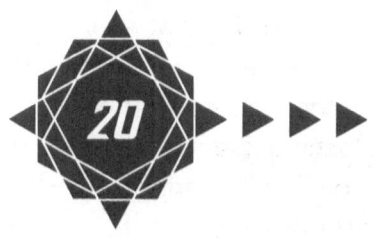

The stars are shining brightly tonight. It feels like a sign, like Grandmommy's watching over me. The heat of the day has dissipated, and the cool breeze dries my clammy skin. I take a moment to settle myself, swiveling my head to listen for any disturbances in the air. So far, I don't hear a thing—no rumbling engines, clanging metal, or whirling propellers, only the soft whistle of the wind blowing against the buildings.

I tiptoe my way through the barracks, ducking behind the bunkers and swerving through alleys. I've made it all the way to the Education Center with no sign of Dark Guards or security drones, but the absence of movement in the quadrangle only makes my heart pound faster. I expect an ambush, or worse. What if all the Dark Guards have already gathered in the Northern Sector because the Admiral knows about the meeting and she's anticipating a raid?

The tension in my arms loosens when I see the outline of Robin's pregnant belly near the barbed wire fence, just beyond the Medical Center. If it weren't for her rounded frame and the slight scuff of her feet, I wouldn't have seen her standing there, pressed against the long metal post. My eyes travel up the thick steel wire above her head. The woven pattern extends more than three times her height. Loops of razor wire decorate the top of the tall chain-link structure that stands to separate the Northern Sector from the rest of the barracks. It serves as a reminder that even in our impoverished society, status still exists. Essential base personnel live on the other side in their large, comfortable quarters, detaching themselves from the inconveniences of starvation and suffering. It's where the professor lives. It's where Walter grew up.

I can see the metal rooftop of the Commander's home peeking from the center of his elite village, and my stomach turns with contempt. In comparison to the one-room bunkers in the Forgotten Zone, it's gigantic. With three stories of smooth concrete stacked together, it's an entire level above the buildings that surround it. Light spills from a window on the top floor, and I don't know if I'm more disgusted by the fact that his family has windows or that the lights out rule only applies to the rest of us. A thick shadow passes by the pane, and I pull myself tighter against the Medical Center, ducking into the shadows. I'm so fixated on my disdain for the Commander, his empty-headed wife, and his overly privileged son that I almost miss the lanky figure rising from the dark to stand beside Robin. I suck in air, but refrain from shouting. I haven't been spotted yet, and I don't want to give myself away. I can't tell who the man is, but Robin doesn't seem to move or panic when he puts his arm around her shoulder. Then I realize: It must be her husband. It must be Clancy.

They shuffle toward the wide gate where the vehicles pass through. I have to catch up if I want to make it to the entrance before they move on without me. The meeting's somewhere in the Northern Sector, but Robin never specified where, and if I miss her now, I won't have the option of knocking on doors and asking for directions. I'll never find out where the rebels are gathering. At that point, I'd be better off heading back to the bunker than trespassing through the Northern Sector, risking the chance of getting caught by Dark Guards.

Stuttering my steps along the backside of the medical center, I take another moment to observe my surroundings before darting across the open area between the building and the fence. I swivel my head. There's still no sign of glowing red visors or hovering drones. Other than Robin and her husband, I still haven't seen any signs of movement across the barracks.

I take a deep breath and jog out of the shadows to meet them. It's hard not to think about what's happening underground as I run across the gravel. With every step, I envision a different scene: endless white halls, the ashen face of the boy from Bunker 111, Doctor Ayad holding a long syringe, a circular contraption hanging above my head, the textile floors in the Admiral's quarters. I breathe faster. Who knows how long the Admiral's operated in those sublevels hidden right under our noses. I wonder if she's sleeping, tucked in a bed made with luxurious covers, or if she's sitting in front of a screen, monitoring my every move.

A shiver runs down my spine. My arms prickle.

"You came," Robin greets with a hushed voice.

"Not now," Clancy chides, reminding us we're out in the open. I can barely make out his stubbled face in the dark. He looks young, still pockmarked from teenage acne. When he lets go of Robin's hand, my eyes drop to her growing belly. Sometimes I forget she's not that much older than I am. She and Clancy graduated from the upper grade while I was still in elementary school, but now that I'll be eighteen next year, the age gap doesn't seem so wide.

Clancy turns to tap a numbered sequence on the keypad behind him. The gate's a rickety excuse for a blockade, but no one can pass without the code. Only guards, Northern Sector residents, and apparently Robin's husband know what it is. I have no idea how he managed to learn it, but I make sure to memorize the pattern as Clancy presses each button, repeating the numbers to myself until the high-pitched tone squeals, authorizing our entry.

I follow closely behind Robin, who's supporting her stomach with one hand and holding onto Clancy with the other. He leads us through the village, a small, circular cluster of concrete homes surrounding the Commander's quarters. The center structure is extravagant in comparison to the dump I grew up in. I wouldn't be surprised if it had running water and indoor plumbing, even in the middle of a century-long, worldwide drought.

Clancy halts at the first sign of movement through the windows on the ground floor of the Commander's home. A blur of bright red flashes in front of the glass. I can only imagine it's Mrs. Cane dressed in one of her outlandish outfits. She steps back into the frame, and I see her feathered sleeve waving a clear cup with a long, thin stem. Her back is turned to us, but that doesn't keep me from startling when a burst of obnoxious laughter bounces into the cul-de-sac.

"This way," Clancy redirects us. "We'll go to the back."

My heart nearly hammers out of my chest when we walk straight up to the Commander's home and Clancy knocks on the door, using a patterned rhythm that reminds me of the timpani drums on one of Professor Diaz's recordings.

This is where the rebels meet?

Wait a minute. What if it's a trap?

My eyes dart through the neighborhood, looking for a way out. Robin must sense my panic. She grabs my hand.

"It's okay," she mouths, "just breathe." She lifts her chin and wafts air toward her nostrils, reminding me how.

I squeeze her fingers back when the door creaks open. A mixture of rage and surprise rattles my bones when Walter answers. He greets Clancy with a handshake, but his eyes widen when he notices me. I can tell he wasn't expecting to see me either. He rolls his lips inward, like he's trying to keep himself from letting any of his thoughts slip out, then nods to Robin and steps aside so we can enter.

Cracked marble decorates the floor of the narrow hallway. Striped wallpaper peels from its edges. The home's finer qualities are run down and falling apart, which somehow feels fitting considering the crumbling state of the entire compound. Yet, I expected the Commander's sophisticated quarters to be slightly more intact than the other Omega buildings. Although I'm selfishly satisfied to know his level of comfort isn't nearly as glamorous as I had anticipated, there's still an uneasy feeling rising in my throat. Now that I've seen the frivolous amenities that make up the Admiral's personal possessions, nothing makes sense. It's like the entire above-ground base is a façade, a cover-up for what's really going on in her subterranean operations. Why else would there be such a stark contrast in quality? It makes me wonder what the rest of the United Regime is really like. What if everyone else is living a life of luxury while the Omega Compound rots from the inside out?

"Walter? Is that you?" Mrs. Cane stumbles into the hallway, tripping over her own feet. One is bare, while the other wobbles on a thin stiletto.

I startle when I see her, shifting behind Clancy, but relax when I notice how drunk she is.

"You didn't tell me you were having"—she burps—"friends over."

Walter pushes past the rest of us to catch his mother. "Let me help you to the couch, Ma." He wraps his mother's arm over his shoulder and faces Clancy. "Go ahead to the study. I'll be right there."

Clancy turns down the hall in the opposite direction, and Robin and I follow him toward the back of the house. He seems familiar with his surroundings, turning right and then left with certainty. We stop in front of a darkly stained, scratched wooden door. Clancy reaches for the golden knob, but Robin stops him.

"Reyna." She looks me dead in the eye. "What we're doing here isn't safe." She already stressed that back at the washhouse. "These people, they're putting their lives on the line to help us."

I scrunch my brow, unsure of her point.

"On the other side of this door, there's no more sectors. It's no longer 'us' and 'them.' It's 'all of us.'"

"Okay," I say. It's true, I was expecting a flood of people from the Southern Sector to fill whatever meeting place Robin brought me to. I certainly wasn't anticipating the gathering to be held in Commander Cane's home. Now I'm extra nervous about *who's* waiting on the other side of this door.

My palms start to sweat with anticipation as Clancy turns the handle. I hold my breath, closing my eyes for a long moment before looking inside. Air rushes to my lungs with a quick gasp. The sight surprises me. Wooden bookcases line every wall of the room. Thousands of books sit on display, their bindings ranging in color and size, with yellowed pages peeking from behind. An array of knickknacks and artifacts sits among the exhibition. The room is full of things you'd find hidden in holes in the wall and underneath lumpy mattresses on the southern side of the barracks.

The museum. I shake my head. *I'll have to tell Ronny it actually exists, and that it's not an airlocked vault.*

A handful of people mill about the room. Their conversations are quiet and unhurried, and no one seems to notice that we've entered. I consider it odd, especially since I've had heightened alertness all evening anticipating a collision with the Admiral's Dark Guards, but everyone here seems untroubled. Maybe that's the real luxury of living in the Northern Sector: you don't have to worry about soldiers invading your privacy or ransacking your home. The difference in demeanor magnifies my discomfort and how out of place I feel standing in the Commander's house, reminding me that Walter and my upbringings were worlds apart.

Robin and Clancy make their way to the center of the study, greeting and intermingling with the others. I stand stiff, watching them from the door. My eyebrows knit together when I recognize the brown corduroy vest of the first man they approach before he even turns around. I shake my head and scoff. It doesn't even surprise me to see him here, not after all the free-thinking opinions he's managed to slip into lectures throughout my education. Professor Diaz smiles at them warmly, then catches my eye. I shy away, but what's the use? There's no avoiding him here.

"Reyna." He leaves his present company to welcome me. "It's so good to see you." He tsks and strokes his beard before pointing a finger into the air. "You know, I had a feeling about you. I thought you'd find your way here eventually."

I squint at his remark. I don't know what he means by that.

He waves his hand forward. "Do come in and make yourself at home. We're just about to get started."

I look to Robin for reassurance as he awkwardly guides me past an unusually ample woman picking at a plate of olives to a small seating area. A dark-haired stranger sits with her back to me in an antique chair wrapped in velvety red upholstery. She has her face buried in a book. The pages are lit by the light of an ornate lamp resting on a round side table. Professor Diaz motions for me to sit in the chair beside her, and everyone else gathers around. I try not to stare, but I can feel the woman next to me sizing me up over the edges of the book she's reading. She slowly lowers it.

"Hello, Sage."

My heart skips at the sound of her gruff voice. There's only one person on this compound who calls me by my surname. It's the Warden.

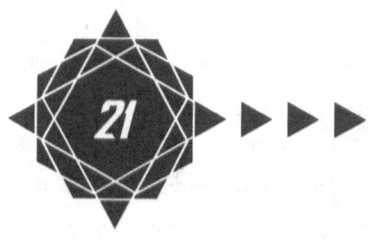

21

I'm tongue-tied—shocked to see the Warden, but even more stunned by how different she looks, and not just because she's no longer wrapped in bandages and attached to medical machinery. Health radiates off her face. Her skin is smooth and glowing. Even her dark, brown eyes are glimmering with a sparkle that reminds me of Grandmommy's twinkling gaze. She looks weird without her uniform, dressed in a loosely fitted shirt. Free-falling strands of hair drape over her collar, replacing the signature style of her tightly woven bun. But the most abnormal sight of all is the genuine smile that spreads across her face when she looks at me.

Who is this woman? I can't believe it's the same Warden that ran my unit, barking out orders with a stern glare. It seems so strange to see her here now, sitting with her legs casually crossed, cradling a book in her lap.

Walter bursts through the door. His abrupt entrance steals my opportunity to ask the Warden what happened during her stay at the Medical Center. Those halls are full of secrets, and I can only imagine what she's been through, especially if the Admiral had anything to do with it.

Walter looks nervous when he joins our circle. Rims of perspiration peek from his armpits. The apprehension in his eyes puts me back on edge, waiting for the Admiral's ambush, expecting to see a squad of Dark Guards breaking down the door of the study. Walter's twitching fingers fidget with his clothes. "Where is everyone?" he asks the professor.

I scan the room. Other than Robin and her husband, there's no one else here from the Southern Sector. Not even the woman at the washhouse who delivered the note with the location change came. And, the attendees from the Northern Sector aren't anything like what I'd expect from a group of rebels. There's an elderly man with wispy white hair hunched over his cane, and a woman who looks like she's never known a day of hunger in her life. To be honest, I'm unimpressed. I thought I was going to walk into a room full of middle-aged men forming an angry mob, ready to fight. Regret seeps in, and I wonder whether or not I've made the right decision by pleading with Robin to come. These people don't look any more able-bodied to plan an escape than me and my inexperienced friends. *Maybe we'd be better off alone.* I'm tempted to leave, but the surprise of seeing the Warden here keeps me from running.

"They're afraid to come," Professor Diaz answers. "We've taken a big hit. We lost several members of the cause after this morning's execution. People need time to process." He places his hand on Walter's shoulder and gives it a firm squeeze. "But we can't wait."

Their interaction catches me off guard. It's unlike anything I've ever witnessed at the Education Center. Normally Walter's spitting sarcasm at the professor with an overly confident attitude and staying after class to get in the last word. Here, there's a level of mutual respect. *They're actually working together.* Apparently, the Warden's unexpected appearance isn't the only unusual thing about this meeting.

"You're right." Walter sighs. He claps his hands together and straightens his shoulders when he looks at me. "Let's get started."

A hush falls over the room as everyone bows their heads in homage. Their eyes are closed, but I keep mine open and watch as the group speaks in unison:

> "Where light first walked, there shall I go.
> Where breath began, now rise with hope.
> Elolam, remember me."

In dumbfounded silence, I listen to their words. They penetrate through me, rattling my core. My worlds are colliding yet again at the mention of Elolam's name. *It can't be.* I wasn't expecting this.

When the mantra is complete, they open their eyes, and then Walter begins the meeting. "Thanks for coming," he starts.

I nervously chew my lip, waiting for some kind of explanation as to why their small group is offering up prayers to Elolam, but Walter doesn't waste any time clarifying their pledge. He skirts the mention of Elolam's name and jumps straight into the first order of business.

"I know there aren't many of us here tonight—and yeah, we've taken hits, and we've lost people. But we can't stop now. We *won't* stop now. This moment right here? It matters. It might be the only shot we get. And if we don't move soon, that door of opportunity could slam shut for good."

I'm stuck thinking about Elolam, but I know I need to pay attention to whatever Walter's saying about the plan, so I refrain from jumping in and asking any questions. I don't want to sound too eager, and I don't want to draw any more attention to myself. It's already awkward enough sitting on a cushioned chair in the center of Commander Cane's study. I don't want to make matters worse by interrupting Walter for the sake of my curiosity. So, I sit back and hope the answer to my question unfolds naturally.

"Yeah, the turnout's low, and after the escape failed, it's easy to feel like maybe we've already lost. But that's not why we're here. We didn't come all this way just to give up now. Some of you are here because you've seen the system crush people who didn't deserve it." His eyes meet mine. "Some of you are fighting for your kids to grow up in a world that's actually worth living in." He motions to Robin. "And some of you? You've believed in this cause your whole life." Walter faces the elderly man. "But no matter what brought you here, deep down, we all want the same thing: to be free. And I don't know about you, but I'm not walking away until we make that happen."

Nods and hums of agreement issue from the small group. I'm taken aback by Walter's passion, the way he rallies the small crowd. I've never seen him this way before. Ever.

"My father just got orders from the United Regime—they're transferring him out. Once he's gone, that's it. The Admiral takes over completely. And when that happens, this place won't just be a base anymore. It's going to turn into a full-on weapons lab with advanced tech ..." He shakes his head. "Brutal stuff. Whatever they're planning, it's starting now."

"We have to act soon," the professor adds.

"How soon?" Clancy asks.

"Within the next few days," Professor Diaz answers.

Robin voices her concern. "And, if we don't, what happens to the rest of us?"

Walter rubs his hands through his hair and grips his head. I can't tell if he's frustrated by the question or struggling with the answer.

"We don't know for certain," Professor Diaz admits, "but the Admiral's made it very clear that she'll dispose of anyone and everyone she has no use for."

"May I have the floor?" the Warden interrupts.

Professor Diaz dips his chin and sits down in an empty chair beside the man with a cane.

"Some of you already know about my near-death experience after the storm, but I truly believe it was a message from Elolam, readying us for the days ahead." She chokes back tears. "When I flatlined on the table, my spirit left. I went to a dark place, but in the middle of the void, I heard a voice whispering to me, 'Find her.'" She pauses. "My spirit was thrust back into my body, but I was allowed to remember that moment in darkness. The voice, I'll never forget. It's him. I can feel it in my soul. He's calling us together to find the Chosen One—the one the prophecies have spoken of, the one who will bring us back to the City of Life."

I duck my head between my hands and scoff. *This can't be happening.*

"I'm sorry, Reyna," Professor Diaz addresses me, "In the heat of the moment, I've ignored the fact that this is your first meeting. That isn't fair. I'm sure you have a lot of questions."

He's right. I *do* have a lot of questions. I want to know why I'm just now finding out about this secret society of believers. How do they know about Elolam? What prophecy are they talking about? Is this rebel movement somehow associated with my dream world?

I feel my chest tighten as I grip my hair between my fingers.

"What would you like to know?" he prompts.

My mind is overwhelmed, and I can't figure out how to formulate my words. I throw my hands into my lap and divulge the simple truth. "Everything. I want to know everything."

"That's quite the—"

"Tell me who Elolam is," I demand.

"We don't have time for this," Walter protests. "We have to solidify our plan, start mapping our route."

The professor sighs.

"He's our Maker," a hoarse voice answers. The elderly man smacks his chapped lips and lifts his overgrown eyebrows, exposing his clear blue eyes. He focuses them on Walter. "Those who seek the truth have every right to hear it. It was never meant to be hidden from the hearts that long to understand."

Walter relents, and the man shifts to face me. I lean forward in my seat, resting my elbows on my knees, ready to listen to whatever he has to say, wondering if it will match what I've seen in my dreams or the information the Admiral's been so determined to make me believe.

He folds both hands over his cane. "A long time ago, when the world was still young and full of promise, Elolam walked among us, not as a king or conqueror, but as a teacher. He showed us how to live in peace, how to care for one another with open hands and open hearts. His love was boundless. But it wasn't enough. People saw what he could do—how his very words could shape rivers, how the earth itself answered when he spoke. But instead of honoring him, they grew jealous. They wanted that power for themselves and tried to trick him into giving it away, to steal what was never meant to be taken." He licks the edges of his mouth.

So far, the details check out with what Elolam's told me. He said he was the Source of all life, that the Earth used to be part of his realm. I close my eyes and envision the thrill of what it would be like to watch him create. The visuals I imagine remind me of my first dream and the awestruck wonder I felt when I saw Grandmommy in our emerald meadow. To think there was ever a time when Earth looked the same as my dream world baffles me. *How could anyone witness a place with so much beauty and still feel jealousy over awe?* I don't understand. Then again, it's control-hungry people like the Admiral who caused the destruction that created this desolate life I have, removed from the splendor of nature, leaving people to starve surrounded by steel and concrete. It's selfish and it's sickening.

"But Elolam saw the truth," the old man continues. "He looked past their words and into their hearts, and what he found there was greed. By then, it was already too late. Their pride had poisoned the earth. The rivers turned foul, the skies darkened, and the creatures we once walked beside vanished. Forests burned, cities crumbled ... and still, they didn't stop." He pauses to cough and wipe his nose with a handkerchief. "So Elolam, in his sorrow, withdrew. He pulled his presence from our world and sealed himself away in a realm beyond human reach—a place untouched by corruption, where only the pure in spirit might ever hope to find him again."

"But he didn't abandon us entirely," the woman beside him interjects. Her voice is smooth and pleasant. I anticipated something harsh or strained coming from her wide neck, but the sound of her voice helps me see past her well-fed figure. That is, until she sucks another olive off her rounded thumb, making my stomach gurgle in response.

"It's true," the man concedes. "Elolam never took his love from the Earth away, not completely. Even after he withdrew, he still answered those who called out to him with honest hearts. He came to them in dreams, soft and silent, like a whisper in the dark. And to them, he gave his gift—the gift of creation. He let them see the world through the eyes of wonder; to paint, to write, to shape beauty with their hands. Music, stories, art—this was his breath made visible." His rasping voice struggles to continue.

Walter stops pacing the floor and retrieves a glass of water from the bar on the right side of the room, bringing it back for the white-haired man. I squint at the consideration he shows, despite thinking the interruption was a waste of time. The old man receives the drink with trembling hands. Water drizzles down his chin as he gulps. My tongue clings to the roof of my mouth while I watch.

"As civilization progressed and technology surged forward, people grew more and more disconnected from Elolam," Professor Diaz takes over, allowing the old man to catch his breath. "Screens replaced reality, and creativity was gradually outsourced to artificial intelligence. But a few still remembered Elolam and fought not to forget. Those individuals believed they carried a divine purpose: to reconnect the realms and restore Earth to its former glory. Just as the prophecy foretold."

Pieces of Elolam's riddles fall into place as the professor talks, yet I'm struggling to understand why the shapeshifter didn't reveal these things to me himself. *What prophecy? Why didn't Elolam tell me? And how does the professor know? Is he a dreamer, too?* Annoyance creeps into my fingertips as I dig my nails into my palms. I hate how cryptic Elolam is when he speaks to me.

"Zealots triggered what became a catastrophic uprising, and the government responded with overwhelming force. That was the start of the Last War. At its core, the war was a revolt against free thought. To control the population, they outlawed books, music, art—anything that encouraged independent thinking. But inspiration isn't so easy to erase." Professor Diaz smiles with his eyes. "As long as people could dream, they'd be moved to rebel." He smooths his vest. "After the war, the United Regime initiated the Order of Clarity. Their goal was more extreme: eliminate dreams entirely. They used indoctrination and constant surveillance, but they couldn't stop the resistance. The strongest dreamers couldn't be broken. So they turned to something more insidious: food, medicine, and supplemental injections all chemically altered to suppress dreaming. And, over time, it worked. Dreams all but disappeared." Professor Diaz sighs and looks at the Warden. "What Joan experienced shouldn't be possible. Which is exactly why we can't afford to ignore it."

I can feel the heat of Robin's gaze boring into me, waiting for a response. She's trying to read my thoughts, decipher whether or not I deem them all crazy lunatics. Any normal person would probably wonder if they walked in on some kind of cult. And I have to admit, after sitting through the Admiral's indoctrination speech, I'm tempted to be skeptical. But I'm not. For the first time in my life, my dreams are starting to actually make sense. I mean, I haven't even told this group about my dreams yet, but they seem to know more about my dream world than I do. *How is that even possible?*

The way I see it, I have two options: believe what the Admiral's told me, that Elolam is a simulated consciousness implanted in my mind by the government, or trust what I'm hearing now. *What would Grandmommy do?* I squeeze my eyes shut and call out to her in my mind, asking for help, concentrating on reaching our cord, the one she said would keep us tethered together beyond death. Visions of her tender smile and kind eyes surface to the forefront of my mind. My heart sinks when I see her struggling to hold water to her cracked lips on her deathbed.

If the Admiral's right, then the Grandmommy I saw in the emerald meadow is a lie, and I'll never see my real grandmother ever again. My chest tightens. I can't believe that's true. I won't. The thought alone makes my heart break. I want to believe what the professor's saying. I want to hope in a better future, one that exists beyond the stars.

I can't seem to formulate my thoughts into words, and the awkward lull that follows lets me know it's not just Robin expecting me to speak my mind. All eyes are on me, except for Walter's. He's pacing the floor, mumbling under his breath. His frustration shows in the bulging veins on his neck. I can tell he's upset with the way the meeting's gone. This isn't the direction he was hoping for. He probably regrets letting me into his house.

Anxiety swells in my head, sending my thoughts into a jumbled mess. I can't decide if I should tell them about my dreams or confess that I've already met Elolam. It's impossible to know how these people will react if they find out I'm a dreamer. They could curse me and kick me out of their meeting, or worship me and beg me to stay.

"Did that answer your question?" Professor Diaz breaks the strangling silence, interrupting my thoughts.

"Yes," I choke. "Thank you." I let out an exhale, knowing I've successfully avoided divulging my secret.

Robin furrows her brow at me. She's not satisfied with my answer. We've worked together for so long, I wouldn't doubt she sees past my half-hearted gratitude.

"So, what should we do now?" Clancy asks, redirecting the conversation back to their plans, and Walter seems to appreciate the gesture. He quickly retrieves a long cylinder tube from a nearby shelf and removes a thick roll of paper from inside.

"Bernard found the original blueprints for the underground facility." Professor Diaz motions to the elderly man who curls his bare lips and nods in response.

Walter spreads the maps on the ground. "Okay, so the professor and I have narrowed down three possible points of attack." He drags his finger across the paper. "Here, here, and here. This is where we'll set the explosives."

Explosives?

"Ruby, what's the status update on construction?" Professor Diaz turns to the woman now holding an empty plate puddled with olive juice.

"We've collected enough supplies from both the Medical Center and the machine shop to make two bombs, but the storm slowed our operation down." She hesitates. "It's been much harder to sneak supplies past the Admiral's soldiers."

"Do we have time to collect what we need before the end of tomorrow?"

"It won't be easy ..." She stops to ponder. "I'll reach out to my inside girl at the Medical Center and see what I can do."

I wouldn't be surprised if it's Nurse Fukuda. That would explain her attempts to help me; why she didn't administer the truth serum, why she felt compelled to tell me about the lullaby her father used to sing. The melody of her song returns to mind as I think about her.

"The anniversary of the war is coming," Professor Diaz reminds us. "The gathering would be the perfect distraction. I know it's still a few days away, but if Commander Cane can delay the transfer until sometime after the ceremony, we can follow through with our plans on Remembrance Day."

My whole body tenses at the mention of Remembrance Day. It's the anniversary of Grandmommy's death. In an instant, I'm transported back in time to the day I became an orphan. The vivid sight of rolling confetti in the empty quadrangle, the screech of my own gut-wrenching cries, the smell of the soiled sheets on Grandmommy's cot come rushing in all at once. I grip the chair armrest. The voices in the room fade to the background. My breath quickens as I look at Grandmommy's lifeless body and watch the nurses lug her from our home.

I spring up from my seat, causing everyone to jolt. "I have to go," I announce and bolt for the door. Finding out about the rest of the escape plan or hearing how the Warden survived doesn't matter at the moment. My brain's been overloaded with new information, and my overstimulated mind can't handle it anymore. I need to see the stars.

"Wait!"

Robin calls to me as I exit into the hallway. The door slams behind me, and I stare down the narrow passageway at Mrs. Cane passed out drunk on the floor. The slit of her red dress is twisted to the back, indecently exposing her rear end.

Since I have no idea where I'm going, I make my way toward her, hoping it leads me to the nearest exit. She lets out a stertorous snore when I step over her.

"Reyna!" Robin follows after me.

I keep going, tiptoeing around shards of broken glass, ignoring her pursuit.

"Please," she begs. "You *can't* go."

I stop, not bothering to turn and face her. "Why not?"

"Listen, I know it's a lot to take in all at once. It took me months to understand and even longer to actually believe in this stuff."

"What changed?" I swivel around to look her in the eye.

"This." She places both hands over her belly. "The world looks a lot different through the lens of a mother." She exhales. "I know it must sound crazy, hearing about ancient prophecies, and I can't really explain to you what makes me believe. I just do."

"I get it," I admit with a heavy sigh.

"You do?"

It's the same type of blind belief I feel in the pit of my stomach when I look up at the sky. I can't prove it, but I know Grandmommy's up there, somewhere, watching over me.

Another rumble from Mrs. Cane's nostrils reminds us that we're awkwardly standing with her sprawled body between us. I step over her for the second time and join Robin on the other side.

When my eyes meet hers, I see the softness in her face, the way she looks genuinely concerned for me. I decide she isn't a threat, convince myself that my life's not going to be in danger if she knows about my dreams, that she's not someone I need to run from.

"Promise not to tell?" I swallow. There's no point keeping my secret from Robin any longer. The rest of my friends already know. I might as well tell her, too.

She creases her forehead. "Reyna, what are you talk—"

"I'm a dreamer."

She gasps. "You mean ...?"

"I've already met Elolam."

"Reyna!" she squeals, then quickly covers her mouth. "You have no idea what this means! The prophecy says a dreamer will arise ... You're the one we've been waiting for! You're the one who's going to lead us! We *have* to go back and tell the others!"

"Whoa." I raise both hands in a "calm down" gesture. "I'm not ready to tell anyone else. Enough people already know."

I think about the boy from 111 and what his confession cost him.

"Wait." Her eyes narrow. "Who else knows?"

"My entire unit and ..."

"Who?" she pushes.

"The Admiral."

Robin groans. "This isn't good." Her gaze drops to the floor.

"You don't understand." I grow defensive. "I *had* to tell her."

"How long has she known?"

"She found out yesterday."

Robin grabs both of my hands and leans in. "I know you don't want to, but we *need* to tell the others." The look on her face matches the seriousness in her voice.

I don't know what she's thinking, but I can tell it isn't good.

"Okay," I agree. "I'll go back."

My heart rate spikes. I immediately regret my decision to tell Robin, to tell my friends, to work with the Admiral. Life was a lot simpler when the only other person who knew about my dreams was Geri. *But what choice did I have?* As much as I want to take it all back, I can't rewind time.

I take a deep breath. I have to do this. I have to face the consequences of my actions. I have to accept the fact that I can no longer keep my dreams a secret. There's no escape. Robin already knows. I have to go back to the meeting. Besides, it would be pointless to leave now without having enough information to share with my friends about the escape. That was the whole reason for coming. *Wasn't it?* I don't really know why I'm here anymore. The evening's been so hectically jumbled with the shock of new information, it's hard to keep it all straight. But if I left now, what would I tell my friends? How would we get out of here? I need to do this for them. I need to do this for Geri.

Another deep breath calms my racing pulse.

Robin wobbles toward the open door of the study, and I scurry after her. When we enter the room, everyone but Ruby is hovering over the map on the floor. They're all too fixated on the browning roll of paper to notice us when we enter. I'm a little annoyed by how credulous everyone is. Apparently no one else is worried about Dark Guards breaking and entering, and seemingly the only threat in this house is an inebriated Mrs. Cane. I probably shouldn't expect more from this peculiar crowd of people. Professor Diaz easily engrosses himself in whatever he's talking about, and since he's the one speaking right now, it's no wonder he doesn't stop to acknowledge us. It's possible Bernard can't even hear us. Walter's in his own house, and Ruby seems too interested in licking her plate clean to care that we're back. And I convince myself that the reason why the Warden's not bearing her usual watchfulness is because she's still recovering from her injuries. The only one who bothers to steal a glance is Clancy, but he turns right back to the map as soon as he sees his wife standing in the room.

"If we can somehow manage to stagger the explosions a few minutes apart, the panic from the blasts should create a large enough diversion for the rest of us to escape through the opening in the wall," Professor Diaz says. "After that, we'll be traveling blind."

Walter shifts onto his knees. "Not completely," he argues.

"Right." The professor nods. "We have a basic idea of what things will look like outside the wall from the intel you've gathered. But we should still prepare for the worst. It could take us weeks to reach our destination on foot."

"Ruby and I have already started gathering your supplies," Bernard rasps.

Robin clears her throat, and the entire group snaps their attention toward us. "Reyna has something she needs to tell us. Something that might change the pace of our plans."

My pulse throbs in my neck. I twiddle the stiff material of my uniform between my fingers and gulp. Once I confess this to them, there's no going back. They'll think I'm some kind of savior. But I'm not ready to lead a rebellion. I barely understand what's going on now. I'm starting to wonder if this is all a mistake, if Elolam visited the wrong person. My breaths quicken, and I look to Robin for support.

"Go ahead," she encourages me.

"I'm ..." I dart my eyes between them. Do I explain myself or come right out and say it? I choose to do the latter and inhale deeply. "I'm a dreamer."

Immediately, I'm met with quiet gasps and wide eyes. Ruby nearly drops her plate and fumbles to keep it from crashing to the floor. The Warden twists in her seat and smiles. She doesn't seem stunned by my announcement. Then again, she already knew about my journal. *What if she already knew about my dreams, too?*

Walter's the only one who doesn't look up. He keeps his chin down and his eyes buried in the maps. Shaking his head, he scoffs quietly to himself.

Bernard teeters on his cane. "Are you the one we've been waiting for?"

I was afraid this would happen if I told them about my dreams. His eyes are longing, like he's been waiting for this moment his entire life, but he's expecting more than I can offer. I'm not who he thinks I am. I can't lead a movement. I'm not strong like Erika. I'm not smart like Laude. I don't care about other people the same way Geri does. There's nothing about me that qualifies me to be their leader.

Besides, if the boy from 111 could dream, then that means there's other dreamers out there. Someone else could be their chosen one. I try to convince myself that it's not me, that I'm not the one, but my stomach twists into knots when I remember what Elolam said in the forest: *"You will lead them back to me."*

A lump forms in my throat. I can't bring myself to answer Bernard's question. I came here to learn about a movement, not lead one.

"I believe she is," the Warden answers, a look of pride in her eyes.

I blink in surprise. Never in all my life have I ever thought of her as someone who would be proud of me. But whatever she experienced at the Medical Center changed her. This isn't the Warden I remember.

Bernard sways to his feet and straightens his hunched shoulders.

"'And it shall come to pass,'" he quotes the prophecy, "'a daughter will rise in days of calamity when iron and ash have bound the earth. Breath of the Eternal One will stir in her sleep, and the light of the First Garden will return in her dreams. She shall remember what the world has long forgotten; the voice that once walked among mortals, a soul that has no beginning nor end.'" Tears fall down his wrinkled cheeks as he recites the final stanza. "'Tyrants shall tremble and sleepers shall stir, for the dreamer has come, and with her the end of all forgetting.'"

22

"The Chosen One," Bernard whispers, his bright eyes beaming, "It is a blessing to witness the prophecy with my own eyes." He sniffles. "And now I know for certain that the time has come for us to reunite with Elolam, to make pilgrimage and join our fellow believers in the wilderness. My only regret is that I am no longer a young man. My old bones aren't strong enough to join you on this journey to freedom."

My confession causes quite a stir among the others. Ruby stands to her feet and squeezes me. The last thing I see before I disappear into her fleshy bosom is Clancy wrapping his arm around Robin, both of them snickering.

"I've always hoped to see the day," Ruby sniffles in my ear.

My back cracks in her strong embrace, and I squirm to uncover my mouth and keep myself from suffocating in her well-endowed breasts. When she finally releases her hold, I let out a nervous laugh. I've never experienced this kind of acceptance from a stranger before. Sure, it feels good to be wanted, but the attention makes me uncomfortable. Besides, as soon as Ruby gets to know who I really am, I'm sure she'll be disappointed. They all will. There's no way I can live up to their expectations, let alone an ancient prophecy.

The Warden comes to my side and presents me with a firm handshake. Her stiff grip reminds me that, regardless of her altered physical appearance, she's still the same gruff woman who supervised my unit over the last decade.

"I always knew there was something special about you, Reyna. I'm proud to serve at your side."

This isn't the type of conversation I'm accustomed to having with the Warden, and I'm not quite sure how to respond. I flash an awkward smile, but honestly, I don't know what else to do. It's hard for me to think of her as anything other than my superior, and here, it almost seems like she's attempting to pledge her loyalty to me. Unfortunately for her, I'm not convinced I'm actually the Chosen One. And despite Bernard's enthusiasm, Walter doesn't seem to believe it either. With his upper lip curled, he gawks at the others, clearly unimpressed by their excitement. He pinches the bridge of his nose and clamps his eyes shut.

Professor Diaz scratches his head. "If this is true, and Reyna really is the promised daughter mentioned in the ancient texts, then we have to prioritize her safety."

"Yes," Ruby agrees. "The prophecy only comes to pass if she's alive to bear it."

Walter sighs and scoops the stack of maps off the floor. The meeting obviously isn't going his way, and I'm sure he's frustrated knowing he only has a few days left before his family is transferred to another base and our compound submits to the Admiral's administration.

This evening isn't exactly going how I envisioned it either. The last thing I want to be is a burden to these people. I don't need them risking their lives trying to protect me. All I want is a chance to get me and my friends off this complex.

Bernard clears his throat. "It will be my honor to serve as a martyr for your exodus." He stomps his foot in a salute. "I will volunteer to detonate the explosives."

"I'll stay behind, too," Ruby offers.

I'm overwhelmed by the fact that these people are willing to die for me. I want to scream, tell them they're not allowed to place their lives on the line for my sake, but I stop myself. The look on Bernard's face says he's been waiting for this moment his entire life, that he's finally found his purpose. His wrinkled cheeks curve into a satisfied smile. And I can only assume that my being here is cause for Ruby's sprightly and youthful burst of energy. Even still, my heart is weighed down by the seriousness of their proposals. Chances are, Walter's plans already called for someone to sacrifice their life, so I convince myself that I haven't really changed their trajectory. The only thing I've actually done by exposing my dreams is given them a reason to believe the cost is worth it. It's humbling to witness a faith so strong, but it would be unfair to let them continue on without telling them about my arrangements with the Admiral. She already has me in her grasp, and they have no idea what they're up against.

"There's something else," I confess, scrunching my brow and looking at Robin. She nods for me to continue. "The Admiral knows about my dreams. The only reason why I'm here now instead of locked away in some underground laboratory is because I agreed to work with her, willingly."

Bernard crumbles to the couch, holding a hand over his heart. Ruby sits next to him and shakes her jowls in disappointment. Their zeal deflates. Professor Diaz strokes his beard, partially covering his mouth, hiding his expression beneath his hand. Walter's eyes are wide. I don't understand why. This entire time, he's made it seem like he doesn't care at all about anything I say.

"Does she know you're here now?" After an evening of sending his passive-aggressive cues, Walter finally addresses me.

"I don't think so," I answer, but I don't really believe what I'm saying. I wouldn't be surprised if the Admiral had eyes and ears on me at all times. With a nervous swallow, I glance around the ceiling, expecting to find some kind of camouflaged surveillance cameras.

"There weren't any soldiers in the courtyard when we came," Clancy says, coming to my defense. "I would have known if we were followed," he assures Walter.

"None?" Walter seems puzzled by the thought. "And did you see any drones?"

"Nothing," Clancy confirms.

"What *exactly* have you agreed to?" the Warden asks, stepping backward to stand beside the professor.

"She asked me to come in for testing," I answer.

"What kind of testing?" the professor chimes in.

"Dream testing," I admit. "She thinks I can help her stop Elolam."

"History repeats itself," Bernard rasps under his breath. "This isn't the first time the government has tried to pit dreamers against Elolam."

"Sage." The Warden reverts to the stern tone I'm familiar with. "Whatever the Admiral does to try and convince you to work with her, whether it be threats or torture, you *cannot* allow her access to the City of Life. The future of the entire Earth depends on it."

My knees wobble. *I need to sit down.*

Settling myself back into an antique chair, I try my best to gather my thoughts. *As if my friends depending on me wasn't enough pressure, now the entire world is?* This isn't the first time the fate of the whole planet's been brought up. It's not like I haven't been paying attention. I just haven't accepted the weight of what my situation with the Admiral actually entails. Regardless of what I believe about this prophecy, I'm in an influential position—one that could go very badly if I say the wrong thing at the wrong time or slip and expose a sensitive truth.

"The Admiral already ran one of her tests on me, administering a dream serum that sent me into a sleep-induced coma."

"And did it trigger a visit from Elolam?" Bernard's fragile voice falters.

"Yes, but it wasn't—"

"Then we're all as good as dead," Walter blurts.

I see the shock of sadness gut Bernard as he slumps further into the couch. Ruby places his withered hand in her plump fingers.

Robin sinks into Clancy's side, attempting to hold back her tears of defeat. He pulls her head into his chest and leans his forehead to hers. I guess she didn't realize how involved with the Admiral I already was.

Guilt weighs heavily on my chest. *I didn't know the stakes. I was only trying to keep my friends safe.*

"You don't understand. Elolam knew the Admiral was watching. He wouldn't allow me to enter through the City of Life. He brought me somewhere else. He disguised himself as a hunter."

"*Where* did he bring you?" Professor Diaz combs his fingers through his facial hair, then relaxes both of his arms at his sides.

"I was taken to the top of a tall mountain overlooking a thick forest. At first, the dream was pretty empty of interactions. Other than leaves swaying in the breeze, I didn't see a single thing. Then a small bird appeared out of nowhere. It led me down a path marked with perfect circles carved in the wood. I traveled down the mountain until I came upon a campsite in the middle of the trees. That's where I saw Elolam. He never turned his face to me, but I know it was him. He showed me this place for a reason. I think it might actually exist." I pause for a moment, remembering what he told me. "He told me to find his people near the mountains."

"Omicron." The Warden directs her statement to the professor.

"My thoughts exactly," he replies. "Maybe there's hope for us yet." Professor Diaz spins around. "Walter." He claps his palms together. "Get the maps out. We'll chart our path to Omicron."

"What's Omicron?" I puzzle as Walter rolls his stack of papers back onto the floor, careful not to rip or damage the edges. Slowly, he reveals a map of a large continent. I've heard enough of Professor Diaz's history lectures to know it's a picture of the old world, the one that existed before the war. The landmass is divided into countries. Lined borders swerve between provinces and states. Names of cities are plastered in black ink. Waterways, rivers, and lakes are printed in blue. Walter unrolls the final crease, and I read the faded words at the top of the chart. *North America*.

"Omicron *was* our weapons division," the Warden answers. "The base was bombed over a decade ago when a rebel revolt managed to seize the complex from within. Rather than risk an uprising, the United Regime ordered an airstrike to flatten the compound."

Professor Diaz kneels over the map, dragging his fingers through several borders. "There's a rumor that survivors from the base began a coalition—a hidden community in the mountains." He jabs his index finger on the page. "Here."

"We think that's where Elolam wants you to lead us," the Warden explains.

Another mention of the prophecy triggers an inward groan. *I can't take this anymore.*

I'm flattered that they see me as their chosen one, but I'm not going to lead an army of people across the barren continent of North America. I don't think they understand that I've never even been off this base! I'm not qualified to be a leader. Besides, I'd be surprised if, after all of the damage caused by the Last War, the country still resembles the picture I'm staring at now. Unfortunately, there's no way of knowing for certain.

Before I have a chance to refute their mission, the Warden, Professor Diaz, Clancy, and Walter start working together to plan our route. Walter jots down notes while Professor Diaz spits out longitude and latitude markers, estimating the distance between each point of interest. Ruby and Bernard whisper words about the prophecy to each other. I won't pretend to know what they're talking about, and since the others seem rather engrossed in their plans, I shift into the empty seat beside Robin and collapse with a sigh.

"I'm proud of you." She smiles, then winces, clutching her stomach.

"Are you okay?" Her discomfort shifts my attention away from my own dilemma.

"Yeah," she hisses through gritted teeth, then relaxes her pained features. "It's just a contraction."

My eyes bulge. She lets out a little laugh.

"Don't worry, the baby's not coming anytime soon," she assures. "I get contractions when I'm extra dehydrated or spend too much time on my feet."

"Let me get you some water," I offer, recalling where Walter retrieved a glass for Bernard.

I make my way over to the counter and spy a silver sink sunken in behind the bar, a line of identical glasses stacked along the basin. Rounding to the other side, I notice a variety of brown bottles sealed in windowed cabinets underneath. They look like the ones Ethel snuck into the washhouse, so I think it's safe to assume I've found Mrs. Cane's collection of alcoholic beverages.

Holding a glass to the faucet, I lift the shiny handle and scoff as a clear stream of flowing liquid rushes out. There's no sputtering spray or spewing chunks of mud. My fingers curl tighter around the cup as I think about all the years I spent desperately sipping from the splattering spout of Bunker 112, only to throw it up as soon as it hit my soured stomach. My tongue coats my chapped lips as I lose myself, staring into the smooth, flowing fluid. I take advantage of the moment and fill a second glass for myself.

When I look up from the sink, Bernard is sitting on a stool on the other side of the counter. I nearly drop the glasses when I see him. My attention was on getting water for Robin, and I didn't even notice him approach the bar.

"Do you mind refilling mine, too?" he asks.

I take the glass out of his shaky hand, accidentally letting the water rise to its brim while watching the old man flip through the pages of a book he's brought with him. Some of the water spills when I place the cup down on the counter. My heart drops when the perfectly clean droplets splash against the marbled surface. I wish I could scoop them up and place them back in the overflowing vessel. Any of my bunker mates would have jumped at the chance to lick the tabletop and sample a taste. Even Lucile might risk the chance of catching the sickness if it meant relief for her dry mouth.

"Thank you." He smacks his lips.

"You're welcome." I grab the other two glasses and hurry to deliver a drink to Robin, but I can feel Bernard's gaze trailing me as I walk around the bar.

"May I show you something?" He waves his hand to stop me.

Robin sees what happens from her seat and gestures for me to stay where I am.

"Okay," I agree.

"This is my favorite book." He trails his wrinkled hand along the dark green cover, then turns the spine so I can read its title. The word leaves me motionless. Golden letters sparkle against the depth of the dark canvas. *R-E-M-E-M-B-E-R*.

"It's a collection of poems written by dreamers long before the war, before the arts of imagination were outlawed by the government." He chortles. "Most everything in this room is illegal, you know. It's a treasure trove of history, preserved by a long line of compassionate Commanders."

Compassionate? I furrow my brow. That's not exactly a term I'd use to describe Walter's dad. Selfish, detached, or irritable perhaps, but not compassionate.

"You see, on every other base, confiscated items from the old world are destroyed or turned over to the fire. Their leaders are too threatened by craftsmanship, believing it will inspire another rebellion. Yet every relic that's ever passed through the hands of a Commander on the Omega Compound has strategically avoided turning to charred ash." He taps the top of the book. "When the Admiral finds this room, I have no doubt she'll destroy everything in it." Bernard sighs. "I wish I could pack it all up and send it with you, but that's far too frivolous a request." He peeks at me from under his bushy eyebrows, then lets his gaze fall back on the book.

I stare at the yellowed pages peeking from behind the cover before turning my attention to the bookshelves that border the room. It's a shame to think they'll all be destroyed, but Bernard's right. Carrying thousands of books across the United Regime would be nonsense. They wouldn't even fit inside the truck Erika wants to steal. We have to pack wisely, and that means only taking items that will help us survive.

Bernard thumbs through the pages of his book and seemingly forgets that I'm standing behind him. I wait for a moment, wondering if he's done telling me about his prized possession. When he doesn't say anything else, I quietly shift toward Robin and finally give her the glass of water I've been holding onto for her. I take a sip from my own cup and relish the cool fluid as it travels down my throat. I watch as the others jot out notes, formulating our plan. They're conversing and arguing over which route will be best, and since I already know I can't help, I decide to peruse the bookshelves.

My eyes scan the extensive collection as I pace the floor. Books on science, history, and religion decorate the shelves. I read the titles, drowning out Walter's exchange with the professor. There're studies on philanthropy and politics, war and weaponry, and even a shelf dedicated to children's literature. It really is a shame that none of it will survive once we leave the base.

I startle when the tall clock near the back of the room rings with a loud, solitary gong, announcing the passing time. It then returns to the gentle tick of its hands and the low hum of the giant pendulum swinging back and forth in its chamber.

"I think I should go," I tell Robin. "It's getting late."

"Do you want to wait and walk back with us?"

"It's okay," I tell her. "I'll be fine on my own."

"No," Professor Diaz directs his disagreement at me. He must have been listening to our conversation. "Now that we know who you are, I simply can't permit you to walk alone through the barracks in the middle of the night." He dips his head. "Please, just wait a little longer. I'll go over the plan with you, then you'll be free to return to your bunker with Robin and Clancy."

The clock strikes two before Professor Diaz and the Warden agree on all the details of what's happening on Remembrance Day. They resolve for the explosives to be placed by Ruby's inside source and detonated by three volunteers during the afternoon address. Professor Diaz says the blast will simultaneously create panic and signal for us to convene at the machine shop. Since I told everyone about Erika's idea to take the truck, the location seemed like an obvious rendezvous point. From there, the Warden will drive us through the wall, and we'll make our way toward Omicron.

Professor Diaz makes me recite the plan to him over and over again until it's engrained in my mind. By the tenth recitation, the plan seems too simple, like we haven't considered enough of the potential hazards. *What if the bombs don't go off? What if the Dark Guards barricade us into the crowd and prevent us from getting to the machine shop? What if the Admiral actually discovers what we're up to and we never even get the chance to put our plan into action?*

My eyes are getting heavy, and the skin around my healing wound is irritably itchy. I need to get back to my bunker and sleep before I'm thrust back into the Admiral's tests. I don't bother bringing up any of my concerns, hoping it will get me out of here faster. When I head to the door behind Robin and Clancy, Ruby follows us. I bite my lip when she calls my name.

"Reyna." She cups her hands over mine, holding me hostage. "I just want you to know that I'm going to ask my friend at the medical center to look out for you." She offers me a soft smile full of sympathy. "I know Elolam will protect you, but it doesn't hurt to have a little help."

Her gentle eyes shift my attitude from annoyance to gratitude. Impulsively, I slip my hand from her grasp and wrap my arms around her ample shoulders. "Thank you," I whisper, overcome by what she's willing to do for me, for all of us. I have no doubt this will be the last time I see Ruby. It's true, I misjudged her usefulness and her bravery. She's proven herself to be a worthy ally. Now, I almost wish we had more time together so I could get to know her.

A heavy weight falls on my heart and stays with me as I walk with Robin and Clancy through the aftermath of Mrs. Cane's intoxication. Her body's still slumped on the floor in the same place at the end of the hall. Clancy's cheeks turn red when he notices her bare backside. He keeps his chin tilted toward the ceiling when we step over her and make our way to the nearest exit.

"What about the soldiers?" My gut feels uneasy. "Why weren't they—"

"I don't know," he cuts me off.

Robin shoots him a reprimanding glare, and he softens his tone. "Listen, I don't understand everything that's going on around this compound. A lot has changed since the storm, and I'm not going to pretend like I have a straightforward answer. All I know is that the professor said our meeting *had* to be tonight. I've learned to stop asking questions, Reyna, and maybe you should, too."

I stand stunned as Clancy swings the door wide and swivels his head in both directions before motioning for us to follow. Robin taps my shoulder, offering a silent apology for her husband's reaction, then trails out after him.

The night air greets us with stillness as we tiptoe onto the grounds of the Northern Sector. The eerie quiet sends a shiver down my spine. There's no scuffs in the gravel from patrolling guards, no howl of the wind. All I can hear is the amplified crunch of our boots when our weight shifts in the dirt.

I keep my mouth shut as we pass through the gate, but I recite the code in my thoughts while Clancy punches in the numbers on the keypad. Looking ahead, I see that there's still no sign of any activity among the barracks. We scurry across the open grounds to the Medical Center and press ourselves against the back wall. My breath catches in my throat, and my palms begin to sweat when I see them coming—a pair of Dark Guards following our path, approaching the barbed wire fence.

Robin yelps. Clancy covers her mouth. The Dark Guards haven't spotted us yet, but they will as soon as we shift away from the building. The only thing keeping us hidden now is the shadow cast by the ledge from the roof above us. With my body pressed against the cold wall, I strain to draw a clear path through the barracks. The nearest structure is too far away to reach unnoticed. We'd have to pass directly in front of the soldiers to get there.

We're trapped.

One look at Robin's trembling hands grasping her pregnant belly, and I know what I have to do.

"Stay here," I warn. Without giving them an opportunity to stop me, I sprint out of the shadows to meet the Dark Guards, trusting that Clancy will tighten his hold on Robin and keep her from revealing their position.

It doesn't take long for them to see me. Their red visors turn in unison as they raise their weapons, poised to kill.

"Don't shoot!" I yell, dropping my knees into the gravel. I raise my hands in surrender and pray they hold their fire, but I still brace myself for the impact of a bullet.

Their mechanical march beats the ground, growing louder as they swiftly approach. Next thing I know, the

Dark Guards flank me on both sides, yanking my extended arms upward, dragging me to the front of the Medical Center.

My body bumps against the rocks. They bruise my thighs and scrape my skin through the worn fabric of my uniform. I try to steal a glance at Robin and Clancy through the gaps in the soldiers' legs, but all I see is the bare brick of the back wall. An inward sigh of relief fills my lungs as I suck in air through my nostrils, then grit my teeth when the edge of a sharp stone catches my back.

The Dark Guards barge into the Medical Center and rip me forward, pulling me to my feet. I steady my shaky legs on the floor of the foyer and rub my burning eyes, which are still adjusting to the harsh fluorescent lights. When I manage to blink the room into focus, I see that the entire layout has changed. The front desk is gone, replaced by a series of smooth, rounded, white arches.

I saunter back, but one of the Dark Guards shoves me, pushing me toward the curved contraptions. Holding my breath, I step under the first arc. A bright red light flashes from inside the checkpoint, followed by a high-pitched hum. Shocks of electricity permeate my body. Burning pulses ricochet through my intestines. My bowels curdle with a deep ache. I coax my weak knees to escape the red light, but the beam holds me frozen in place. When the laser dissipates, I slump with its release.

A medical attendant sporting a long white coat is on the other side of the machine, waiting to stab me with a silver barrel that's shaped like a small handgun.

"What is that?" My voice quivers as the pinch of something foreign enters my skin.

He doesn't answer, only nods to the Dark Guards, signaling for them to take me. Without as much as a pause, the soldiers whisk me from the lobby, down an elevator, and through a myriad of white hallways until I'm thrust into a room where Doctor Ayad hovers over a tablet, tapping earnestly on its screen.

"You may go," he addresses the Dark Guards, refusing to divert his attention from his task.

With one last shove, the Dark Guards send me sliding across the floor. My head collides with the tile. A shockwave of pain rattles through my skull. The guards stomp out of the examination room, and Nurse Fukuda hurries to help me. She offers her bony arm for support and guides me to the chair in the center of the room. With a click of her tongue, she rubs her fingers across my forehead. Her delicate hand hurts to the touch, where a welt is already rising; a parting gift from my escorts.

"Imbeciles," she murmurs, then draws her attention to the brittle stitches snagging at my skin. "Someone should have removed these days ago."

Nurse Fukuda snips the threads with a small pair of scissors, then tends to my other wound, rubbing a glob of cold blue cream over the growing knot.

"There," she says. "That should feel better soon."

"You came early." Doctor Ayad steps into view. "I wasn't expecting you for a few more hours. Did you have something useful to report, or are you just eager to begin?"

I clench my jaw and stare into his cold eyes.

He snaps his fingers in front of my face. "Do you have any new information for me? Did Elolam come to you?"

"I couldn't sleep."

He narrows his eyes, seeing straight through my lie. I'm sure he has his suspicions, especially since I've arrived during the barracks' nightly lockdown. But, instead of asking me anything further, the doctor turns to Nurse Fukuda and tells her to prepare the experiment.

She straps my arms to the chair, and my heart rate rises. I dig my nails into the upholstery while she gathers the syringe, bracing myself for the burning sensation that follows the stab of the needle. My stomach turns when she tilts my head forward and forces the fiery fluid into the base of my skull. My tongue prickles with the taste of bitter metal, making me sick. Acid gurgles in my empty stomach, and I cough up bile before my eyes flutter closed and the room turns black.

At first, the images are faulty, skipping through scenes of Grandmommy in the emerald meadow. Each glimpse ends with her reaching for me, but when I extend my fingers for her hand, she dissipates and reappears in another spot. I let out a frustrated groan when I try, to no avail, to halt the tormenting loop.

This isn't a dream. It's a nightmare.

I try to move, but the dirt has swallowed my feet, cementing me in place. The grass doesn't laugh gleefully as it normally does. Sinister cackles emerge from the iridescent blades, amused by my failed attempts to touch Grandmommy. Pain courses through my feet. Razor-sharp edges have replaced the soft texture of the meadow. The grass cuts at my ankles, slicing my skin as I funnel further into the mud. The ground is sinking quickly. It's sucking me in. I claw back to the surface, but the serrated edges keep me from securing my grip. Grandmommy lengthens her arm to me, and that's the last thing I see before gulping in air and plummeting into darkness.

I hit the ground with a thud, landing on a mossy patch of woodland earth. Blurry treetops sway above. Bits of blue peek through the boughs. Leaves crunch under my body when I roll onto my side. A cool breeze runs across my back, delivering the scent of roasting meat to my nostrils.

I know exactly where I am.

Scurrying to my feet, I follow the smoke until I stumble upon Elolam's camp, only to find the site completely deserted. The only trace of him is found in the smoldering ashes of the campfire. I round the wooden structure, hoping to see him scraping an animal hide, but there's no sign of him anywhere. Not even the tools on his line are left behind.

I want to shout his name, call out to him. Instead, I bite my tongue. There's a reason why he won't show himself. *They're watching.*

The flit of little wings flickers among the branches, and for a moment, I think I can hear the seven-note song of the chickadee. I spin, searching for its little striped head, when the small creature emerges from the trees and gracefully lands on the roof of the makeshift home.

It bobs its head up and down and chirps its song. I whistle back, echoing the melody.

The bird flutters to the ground and flies into Elolam's shelter. With curiosity, I approach the front door to see where it's gone. Lifting the swaying flap, I peer into the compact room. It's too dark to decipher details, but I can hear the pitter-patter of tiny wings beckoning me to follow.

I step inside and sink through the ground. Another portal envelops me, spitting me out on a concrete floor. The shock of the impact bruises my hip, and I groan as I stumble to my feet. It's dark in the empty room, the only light emitting into the small space coming from an observation window. When I hobble to the glass, I see a man lying on a metal hospital bed, his arms and legs strapped to its frame. Tubes sprout from his skull, pumping fluids into his brain. My hands tremble as I bring them to my mouth.

Disfigured by pain, I barely recognize the face—the long jaw and smooth chin, the tight cheekbones and narrow nose. His bright blue eyes are drained of their light, replaced by tormented suffering—the same eyes that watched over me as an infant. My heart shatters into a million pieces as I bang on the glass.

"Dad!"

Two figures hover over his contorted body, immune to my cries. A younger student charts on a tablet while observing the procedure. His counterpart, an older woman in a knee-length lab coat, checks the nearby monitors. The screens burst with zigzagging lines tracing upward, peaking in succession.

"Theta and Delta waves are increasing," the woman says as she views the display. Her voice comes through the speakers set above my head. "Subject 11 is entering R.E.M."

The woman presses a button on the machine between them, releasing the remaining liquid from a long line of flasks. The bright yellow serum looks an awful lot like the one Doctor Ayad injected into my head with a syringe. I grit my teeth in horror and rub the back of my neck, feeling for the welt. It's sore to the touch. Just one vial burns my bloodstream, sending a flood of nausea to curdle my stomach. I can't imagine the unbearable agony my father feels with twenty doses of the poison rushing straight into his brain.

I clench my fists and sink my forehead into the glass.

"Dream state secure. Begin sequence capture."

A ceiling-mounted device lowers, locking into place above my father's head. A shiver runs down my spine. It's the same circular array of needles and humming diodes that Doctor Ayad clamped over *my* temples.

I gasp when a three-dimensional display flickers to life. Blurry and fragmented dream imagery appears. Even with an unclear picture, I recognize the petaled path that leads to the Source. They've infiltrated his mind, forced him to reveal the City of Life.

"There it is!" the woman cries. "Can we lock in a location?"

The young man swipes the screen on his tablet. "The connection isn't strong enough." His voice verges on the familiar, and when he lifts his head, he looks an awful lot like Doctor Ayad. He shares the same prominent nose and sharp jawline. *Could he be the doctor's brother? Or maybe his son?*

"Boost the signal. I'll administer another dose of the neural tracer nanites to enhance our chances." She works swiftly to replace the empty ampules, sending another wave of bright yellow serum into my father's brain. As soon as the fluid reaches his skull, he convulses, triggering a cacophony of alerts from the nearby monitors.

My own heart races while staring at the scene. I grab at my chest and scream in horror, but I can't peel my eyes away from what's happening.

"We're losing him! We have to stop," the younger man begs.

She ignores his pleas and chooses to release even more of the toxic formula.

"Turn it off!" he shouts louder. "He's going to die!"

"We're near a breakthrough," the woman insists, "on the brink of discovering a connection to the Eternal Realm. You will not end this experiment!"

"If he dies, you won't have a connection!"

The young man throws his clipboard to the floor and yanks the plug on the machine pumping poisonous serum into the patient's skull.

"No!" the woman shrieks. She rushes her assistant, attempting to stop him from removing the power source, but in her angst, she rams into the medical equipment, knocking the machine to the ground with a crash. Metal pieces and broken plastic flies across the tile.

"Now, look at what you've done!" she screams, her face full of fury.

For a moment, the bright yellow fluid stops flowing, then drains to the bottom of the lowest hanging coil, rocking back and forth within the narrow tube. A sigh of relief escapes my lips when the alarms quiet, leaving only the periodic beep of my father's monitored pulse to fill the room.

He's still alive.

I whip around, looking for a door or an exit so I can rush to him and free him from the machine. A single metal door waits on the opposite side of the room. I try the handle, but it's locked. I jiggle it harder, but it doesn't budge. I'm trapped inside.

An oscillating roar turns my head. Sparks spit from the engine of the wrecked machine as it sputters back to life. The woman shrieks in horror as the tubes reverse their function, sucking fluid from my father's skull. Thick blood oozes into the tubes, clogging the thin hoses that lead to the vials that once contained the awful serum.

"Oh my god." I cover my eyes and turn away from the scene as the assistant rips the lines from my dad's head, sending a shower of blood splattering across the room.

"He's destabilizing," the woman shouts. "Prepare for the extraction. Now!"

"But he's still alive."

"He won't be for much longer," she argues. "I want a clean imprint, and this is the only way. We *have* to find the tree."

Peeking through my fingers, I see an automated arm descend, wielding a second surgical halo. The clawlike arms replace the previous device clamped around my father's bloodied head. A hiss of gas releases, followed by a rising hum. The growing metallic whine becomes unbearable, amplified in the speakers overhead. I cover my ears and double over as one final shudder runs through my father's dying body.

"No!" I yell in protest, but my shouts fall on deaf ears.

A loud pop blasts through my eardrum as the top of my father's skull is lifted cleanly by the machine, revealing the hemorrhaging tissue underneath. Wrinkled flesh bubbles from the rim. Acid rises in my throat, and I puke bile onto the floor.

The woman snaps gloves over her wrists as the device lifts the severed brain from my dead father's head, placing it into a basin of milky, blue fluid. She plunges a long needle into the floating organ, connecting a series of wires. Another wave of bile spews from my mouth.

"Establishing a connection." The young man wipes clots of my father's blood from his forehead.

A crisp, high-resolution hologram of the Source materializes in the center of the room.

"We've done it!" the woman exclaims. "Download the files before they disappear."

My whole body trembles. The Admiral didn't need me to get what she wanted. She's already found Elolam, and she's sacrificed my dad to do it. His lifeless body is now nothing but an empty shell strapped to the table.

I hold my head. Panic seizes my mind.

What if I'm next?

I need to get out of here. My thoughts spiral out of control.

"Something's wrong!"

I snap my head to see the assistant taping hurriedly on his tablet.

"I can't retrieve the data."

The projection of the Source distorts with static.

"He knew," the woman groans. "It has to be him! He's running interference from the other side."

I shrink back and collide with the wall as shadows overtake the window. Black smoke envelops the room until it swallows me whole.

With a gasp, I'm thrust back into reality. Kicking my feet along the bed, I scramble to rid myself of the circular contraption encasing my skull. The tiny needles scrape my temples, burning my flesh with the sting of open wounds. I can't reach the machine with my hands. The straps tightened around my wrists cut into my skin as I attempt to rip them free.

"Reyna, stop!" Nurse Fukuda warns me. "You're hurting yourself." She twists her head and calls over her shoulder to the doctor, "I need help! She's awake!"

She presses her forearms against my chest. The weight of her body isn't enough to stop me from fighting. I have to get out of this device. I have to break free before they slice me open.

"Reyna," Doctor Ayad addresses me, "if you hold still, we can remove the Neuro Specter from your mind without causing collateral damage."

Collateral damage? Is that what I am? I've been caught in the crosshairs of a war I never asked to be a part of and my mind is the battlefield. I didn't ask to see my father's traumatic death, but now my memories are permanently seared with the visuals of his mutilated body. He was a prisoner somewhere down here in this underground laboratory. They kept him, tortured him, all the while I was left to believe I was an orphan.

My lungs rise and fall with erratic breaths, on the verge of hyperventilating. Flaring my nostrils and clenching my jaw, I allow the doctor to remove his device from my head while considering my window to pounce from the seat. Before the doctor lifts the Neuro Spector from my skull, he stares straight into my burning eyes.

"Don't try anything stupid," he warns, "or I'll be forced to sedate you and hold you as a prisoner."

His warning reminds me of the deal I made with the Admiral. If I cooperate, I go free. But if I don't, she'll still subject me to all of her tests. And now I've witnessed the result of what happens if I fight back. I have to get out of here, and compliance is the only way I'll ever see the surface again. I can't screw this up. I have to leave. I have to tell Geri and the girls about the escape plan.

I close my eyes and slow my breathing, releasing my clenched fists. The doctor lifts the Neuro Specter from around my temples and begins his series of questions.

"Now, tell me what you saw."

I scoff. "You already know."

"Excuse me?"

"Stop pretending. I've seen what your device can do."

"What did he show you?" Doctor Ayad asks firmly, his brow furrowing.

When my eyes meet his, I see the resemblance to the young man in my dream in every feature on his face. My lips part. *It was him.* Doctor Ayad was the young man in the room with my father. He was the one helping run the experiment. Elolam must have shown me an imprint of his past.

I inhale a sharp breath through my nostrils. It wasn't just a memory. It was a warning—a warning of what my future may become.

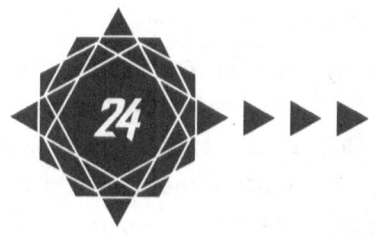

I do my best to pacify the doctor's questions by telling him about the twisted meadow and the abandoned forest, but I think he can tell I'm hiding something. Every time I stop, he asks if there's anything else I can remember, or if there's any more details I can share for his report.

"The more information you can provide, the more likely we are to keep these experiments mutually beneficial."

I don't see how I'm benefiting from these tests. The serum puts both my body and mind through torture. My stomach twists with nausea, and a cold sweat breaks out on my forehead.

"We have to flush her system," Nurse Fukuda reminds the doctor. "Her heart rate is elevating."

Doctor Ayad ignores Nurse Fukuda and asks me again, "Was there anything else?"

I blame the serum and tell him my dreams aren't as vivid when I'm under the influence, which isn't a lie. But since the Admiral isn't here to threaten me, which I'm assuming was at the doctor's request, we reach the end of our interview. Besides, my insides feel like they're roasting over Elolam's campfire, being cooked into a hearty stew. I don't think I can keep going without the antitoxin.

Reluctantly, Doctor Ayad gives the order to start the cleansing process. He exits with his nose buried in his tablet and leaves Nurse Fukuda to attend to my aching and weakened body. She releases my restraints, hands me another chalky white pill, and pushes fluids through my port. While she cleans the cuts on my forehead, I muster up the courage to ask her about the Neuro Specter.

"What do you see while I'm dreaming?" My voice is shaky, and it's tiresome to talk, but I know I'll get a boost of energy as soon as my treatment is finished. Right now might be the only chance I get to know what's really happening during these experiments while I'm unconscious.

She glances at me in her peripheral vision and continues working. "I'm really not at liberty to say."

"Did you see the meadow?"

She subtly nods her head, then sets the IV.

"And the forest."

Another nod.

I lower my voice to a hushed whisper. "Did you see the experiment?"

She shakes her head, then asks me to sit up so she can check my injection site. "We lost the connection halfway through the experiment and were only able to monitor your R.E.M. cycle through the spikes in your brainwaves," she whispers into my ear. "But the doctor knows you're lying, Reyna. Your data was indicative of a trauma response."

"I saw what he did to my father," I confess. "I saw what they'll do to me."

"The injection site is clean with minimal redness." She avoids making eye contact with me. "I'll have you escorted to the Education Center shortly."

Nurse Fukuda finishes administering my treatment in silence, bustling about the room while I wait for my discharge. When the Dark Guard arrives to deliver me to the surface, she hands me a packet of nutritional crackers and offers me a soft smile.

"Don't wait too long to eat something," she tells me, then turns to the soldier. "She's free to go."

I stuff the package into the pocket of my uniform and follow my guide through the underground maze. My head feels clearer now that I've received the antidote, but the sting of watching my father get sliced open hasn't left. This grief feels different than anything I've experienced before. It's not the same as when I lost Grandmommy. In some ways, I've already found closure in losing my parents, but knowing how my dad died stirs up a whole new wave of emotions. *I didn't know.* I didn't know he was still here, trapped underground, tortured. I didn't know he was a dreamer, that he had visions of the Source.

I hang my head as the guard pushes his key into the hidden slot on the elevator panel. It was dreaming that brought on this pain. My heart wrenches, and part of me wishes I didn't have the ability to see another world in my sleep. It feels like a curse. I never thought I'd wish for darkness instead of dreams, but right now, I don't want to be a dreamer. I want this all to go away—the pain, the hurt, the suffering ... the unbearable grief.

Blinking back my tears, I do my best to maintain my composure while I'm brought through the checkpoint in the foyer of the Medical Center. This time, I'm not required to walk through the shocking arches or given an unnamed injection. Instead, the Dark Guard marches me straight to the front door and across the empty courtyard of the barracks.

The sun is hazy in the sky, covered by a thin layer of clouds that stretches across the gray space in every direction. Judging by the lack of activity on the grounds, I'm guessing morning assignments have already begun and class is already in session.

When we enter the corridor of the Education Center, I can hear the faint projections of Professor Diaz's voice through the walls. The Dark Guard waits in the hall for me to open the door, then slams it behind me when I step inside.

Everyone, including the professor, jolts at the loud, sudden bang.

"Rey!" Geri jumps from her seat and runs to me, wrapping her arms around me. "I'm so glad you're okay."

I want to hold her back, collapse on the ground, weep into her shoulder, tell her all about my father's horrible death. But I can't. I'm standing in a room full of my peers, and most of them have no idea what's going on. So I just stand there, stiff in Geri's embrace, numbed by the shock of the Admiral's gruesome experiment.

"Gertrude," the professor says, interrupting our reunion. "I'm going to have to ask you to return to your desk." He pauses. "Reyna, thank you for joining us. I'll excuse the tardiness for today. Please, have a seat."

The professor's a lot better at hiding his thoughts than I am. He's acting normal, holding his postured stance at the front of the room as if he didn't spend an entire evening hunched over a map in Commander Cane's study. He doesn't even look tired.

I make my way to my assigned seat, managing to engage in silent exchanges between all of my roommates, but when I get to my desk, something's wrong. Walter isn't here. He usually sits behind me in class, but his seat is empty. Concern squeezes my chest. *What if they didn't wait? What if his family was transferred this morning?*

I shoot a worried glance toward the professor, who doesn't seem bothered at all by Walter's absence. He holds my stare for only a moment before clearing his throat.

"Now." He pulls his lapels. "Where was I?"

Why isn't he panicking?

I rattle my knee against the bottom of my desk. It's taking everything within me to push away the burning visuals of my father's open skull. And, here, the professor's giving a lecture, completely unfazed that I showed up late to class and that Walter's absent. Then again, he probably knows that a nervous breakdown in front of a room full of clueless teenagers wouldn't exactly be the wisest choice. The thought makes me self-conscious, magnifying my own panicked display. I slow my shaking leg and glance around the room to see if anyone's noticed my jittering body.

"You were talking about the Last War, Professor," Laude answers from the front row.

"Ah, yes. The Last War was a global catastrophe, causing more deaths than any other war in human history." He picks up the binder from his desk, a government-issued textbook, and flips it open to the first laminated page. "It was a last resort instigated by rebel attacks and destructive uprisings against government leaders. Yet, in a time of great peril and chaos, it was the United Regime that brought the world together, saving our Earth from complete and utter devastation."

Professor Diaz portrays his usual enthusiasm while reading from his script, but now that I know he's part of the rebel movement, I see past the ruse. This is his Remembrance Day lecture, the one he's *required* to give every year around the holiday. It's supposed to remind us of our history and force us into being grateful for our miserable existence. But it never works.

"The Covenant of Confinement was signed as a peace treaty, offering a way of escape and sanctuary for anyone brave enough to surrender their chaos for certainty."

He's reading from the same script he used last year and the year before that. I anticipate the next lines, quoting his lesson in my thoughts as he speaks, keeping myself from envisioning the horrors of my father's death.

"In good faith, the United Regime brought survivors of the war under their protection, opening twenty-four safe zones to shelter their loyal citizens from the aftermath of nuclear destruction. Here, humanity was given another chance."

I tap my fingers on my desk. The lecture isn't helping. It only makes me angry. It's all a lie—a cover-up for what really happened. The textbooks won't ever mention Elolam or the government's attempts to eliminate dreamers. They want us to believe the war was a necessary retaliation for irrational rebellion. But it was their weapons that caused nuclear waste to seep into the main water sources across the globe. It was their toxins that caused mass extinctions of flora and fauna. They're the ones that stuffed wounded survivors into insufficient complexes under the pretense of preservation.

My blood starts to boil, and I give up on trying to hide what I'm feeling. I don't care if people notice. I huff under my breath and curl my fingers into fists. The deception is so much more infuriating now that I've experienced it firsthand. I mean, there's an entire network of people working underground, right underneath our noses, and we're all expected to believe the garbage that gets shoved down our throats every year around Remembrance Day. Who even knows if the Earth is *really* in shambles or unable to be inhabited? If the forest I've seen in my drug-induced nightmares is actually real, then why are they still keeping people trapped as prisoners in their government compounds?

I'm tired of eating the lies they feed us. I can't wait to escape.

I look around the room, taking note of all of my friends. Laude's the only one who looks like she's paying any attention to the professor's lecture. Ronny's picking dirt from underneath her nails, Lu's coiling a strand of hair around her finger, and Erika's slouched in her seat with her arms crossed.

Geri's sitting right beside me, hunched forward in her seat. Her tiny body is looking thinner; the scar on her cheek is sunken in. When her stomach gurgles, she clenches her waist.

"Psst." I get her attention, and she leans in closer. "I have a pack of crackers left over from my tests. You can have them if you want."

"It's okay." She smiles. "They're supposed to feed us after class."

"No, really." I reach my hand into my pocket. "They're yours."

Before handing the crackers over to Geri, I look down at the package and see words scribbled out in ink on the crinkled plastic.

Hope is brimming.

My eyes widen. I remember Elolam saying this to me when he showed himself in the sky as the Great Morning Star. Nurse Fukuda must have left the message for me. *Did he say it to her, too?*

"What is it?" Geri whispers out of the corner of her lips.

Even though the professor's attention is fixed on his textbook, neither one of us wants to make a scene by drawing unnecessary attention to ourselves, so I hand her the packet in silence and watch her mouth the words.

"That's what Elolam said to me." I cover my mouth to hide our conversation.

"Reyna?"

Crap.

"Is there something you'd like to share with the rest of the class?"

"No, sir," I say, folding my hands in my lap.

It's a little strange interacting with the professor now after seeing him only a few hours ago at the meeting, knowing he's one of the people helping us form the escape plan. None of the other girls know it yet, and it's probably better that way. Who knows how long he's been able to keep his allegiances to the rebellion hidden. I wouldn't want to turn him in now by responding any differently than I normally would.

I sink down into my chair, and for once I'm actually missing Walter's snappy attitude stealing the attention away from these types of awkward moments. His sarcasm was a good distraction from the rest of us, keeping Professor Diaz tied up in petty arguments. If Walter were here now, the professor would be quarreling over some stupid fact rather than singling me out for whispering to my best friend. None of my classmates would be snickering at me, either. That, and my seat would have gotten kicked at least twice by now.

Where is he?

I can't believe I'm worried about Walter. I convince myself that it's not really him I'm concerned about. It's our plan. If Walter's not here, and his family's already been transferred, then who will give the Remembrance Day speech? Who will bring the maps? Everything else might fall through.

Professor Diaz continues his lecture, but I can't stop thinking about what might happen if Walter's gone and we can't pull off the escape. Before I know it, the buzzer's sounding, signaling our dismissal. Everyone must be hungrier than usual because a stampede of starving teenagers goes rushing to the door, eager to line up in front of the Dark Guards sent to accompany us along our short walk to the Mess Hall.

I catch the professor's eye while I stagger to the end of the line behind my friends. For a moment, he breaks character, and I see a look of concern flash across his face. He knows something, but he can't tell me. Not here. Not now. I should have asked at the meeting how they manage to communicate on the outside. Is it just through passing notes? Is there a secret code? A signal? *What is he signaling to me now?* I wish I knew.

When we reach the Mess Hall, the smell of bleach slaps me in the face. The bloodstains have been scrubbed clean from the floor, and all of the furniture has been returned to its normal position. But the stench of the cleaner only reminds me that they were once there. Flashes of Jones getting shot in the head surface unwelcomed in my mind, followed by the sounds of people screaming in terror, the look of Walter's bruised face, and the reek of soiled clothes that filled this room only two days ago.

I shake the thoughts away, only to leave room enough for the horrendous scenes of my serum-induced nightmare to surface. My father convulses. Blood splatters on the doctor's face. The machine cuts into his skull.

We settle into our assigned seats, and my mouth waters when I see the cube of mystery meat on my tray. I bite into the clumpy texture without thinking about the smell. Excessive salt stings my tongue. I guzzle the four-ounce bottle of water issued with my meal, triggering a coughing fit when some of the liquid drips down my windpipe.

Erika slaps my back, and I spew chunks of meat and water across the table and onto Lu's tray.

"Sorry," I manage to say while hacking.

She curls her lip and pushes the food away from her. "I wasn't all that hungry, anyway."

"Here." Geri swaps her tray with Lu's. "You can eat mine."

"Thanks." Lu's stomach growls as she spoons a morsel of meat into her mouth.

"I can't wait any longer, Rey." Erika leans over, attempting to keep her voice down. "What happened last night? Spit it out."

"Not too loud," Ronny warns. Several Dark Guards line the cafeteria walls while others flank the exits. Her eyes are nervously darting back and forth, measuring the distance between us and them. "Maybe we should talk about this later." She twirls her spoon on her tray.

I look at Laude, who returns my glance with pressed lips and a heavy sigh.

"What do you think?" I ask her.

"While the circumstances aren't ideal for sharing your evening events ..." she trails. "What if something else occurs between now and then? We can't promise later, but we can guarantee *now*."

As much as I hate to admit it, she's right. If there's one thing the past few days have taught me, it's that anything can happen, anywhere, at any time.

"What if you share some of the important things now and save the rest of the details for later?" Geri suggests. "I for one wouldn't mind a little bit of a bedtime story." She giggles, flashing a toothy grin, trying to lighten the mood.

I'll never understand how she manages to stay so optimistic.

"Okay," I agree. I decide to filter out everything about the prophecy and me being the Chosen One and skip straight to the escape plan. I tell them about the bombs and about gathering at the machine shop. When

I mention the Warden, everyone gasps. The tables near us quiet down, and I squirm when they all tilt their heads toward us.

Erika fakes a laugh and bangs the table. Thankfully, the unwanted attention shifts, and the blend of overlapping conversations swells again. I don't think anyone heard what we were talking about. The tables are pretty close together, but the one closest to us was for the boys in Bunker 111, and it's empty. A heavy weight falls on my chest when I think about their unfortunate fates. I swallow the last of my meal, but it hits my stomach like a rock.

"That was close." Ronny wipes beads of sweat off her freckled forehead.

"So, the Warden's okay?" Lu closes her eyes and gulps another clump of meat.

"She's ... different." I don't know how else to explain it without going into detail about the secret coalition and how invested these people are in their faith. "You'll know what I mean when you see her for yourself."

"I can't believe we're actually getting out of here." Lu shakes her head with a giddy smile.

"It seems too good to be true." Ronny tucks her red hair behind her ears. I'm surprised she doesn't voice more grievances about the plan. Maybe it's because she knows someone else devised our escape strategy. I haven't told them who, though. I wonder how they'd all feel about knowing it was the professor, or what they would say if they knew Walter Cane had his hand in on mapping out the route. I guess I'll have to wait until later to find out.

"I'm just glad we're doing it *together*." Geri places her hand over mine. I can tell by the way she's scrunching her face at me that she's hoping I don't disappear again without her, but soon we'll all be split up for our evening assignments. Sometimes I wish we worked in the same building, but thankfully Robin will be there tonight, and maybe we'll get another chance to talk about the hidden coalition.

The moments that follow feel strangely normal. Lu jokes about how hard it must be for the Dark Guards to remove their uniforms when they need to relieve themselves, and Erika nearly falls out of her seat in laughter. When a Dark Guard lurks closer, we quiet down, sharing our thoughts through hushed whispers. Laude points out that she noticed a change in Professor Diaz's script during class. I guess that's why she pays such close attention during the Remembrance Day lecture. Apparently, she's on error-detection duty. It wasn't a huge difference, but he slipped up and swapped out a few words during the part about encouraging ongoing trust and compliance with the United Regime.

"He actually implied not to," she adds.

Normally Professor Diaz slides his personal opinions into the history lectures, but not during his Remembrance Day lesson. It may have been one last-ditch effort to warn the student body about what's coming, but I keep my thoughts to myself because one of the Dark Guards is pacing two tables down. Even in the well-lit room, I can see the ominous red glow his visor emits.

I watch him march as the girls keep talking. Every time he walks in our direction, he inches himself closer to our table. I bounce my knee up and down, rattling my chair.

"Everything okay?" Geri flashes me a look of concern. Her lip trembles when she notices who I'm staring at.

The Dark Guard halts at the end of our row and turns his masked face toward me. Two more soldiers flank his sides.

I grab onto the table.

"Whatever happens," I spit out to the girls, "don't fight back."

"Reyna Sage of Unit 112," the middle guard says through his thick visor. "You're under arrest."

"No," Geri whimpers, tears filling her eyes as she grips my arm.

The team of Dark Guards pry me from my chair and drag me away. An awful ache rattles in my gut as I see the shock of fear on my friends' faces fade into the distance while they struggle to remain in their seats.

I've been taken away before, but this time feels different—and after seeing what I did during the experiment, I think I know why.

My father's fate will be my own.

Their tight hold around my wrists makes my fingers go numb. It's hard to find my footing, so I half run, half fall behind the Guards as they drag me across the threshold of the refectory and into the open quadrangle. The last thing I see through the closing door is Geri rising to her feet, only to be struck in the back by a Dark Guard.

When we reach the Medical Center, the Dark Guards don't slow down. They swing me past the checkpoint, avoiding all of the electrical archways, and move straight to the elevator. I slump on the floor of the metal cage and sink between my captors, heaving to catch my breath. The weight of sorrow overtakes me. I've lost all my fight.

I know I'm going to die.

The rubber stench of the Dark Guards' clothes mixes with the antiseptic of the hospital, making me feel lightheaded. I don't know if I'm ready to accept my fate, but I am ready for it all to be over, to leave the pain of this world behind. Maybe death will be my escape and I'll finally get to be with Grandmommy in that place beyond the stars. I close my eyes, hoping to remember the meadow, but visions of my tortured father invade my thoughts, reminding me of my unfortunate end.

Why did Elolam show me my father's dying breath? Why did he bother to bring me through all of this? Did he know it would end this way?

Anger rises in my chest. I wish I had my old, miserable life back. Tears well in my eyes as I relive the day before the storm; the day before everything changed. I'd do anything to go back to that moment of scrubbing the walls next to Geri, when the only real worries I had were whether or not a meal would come.

"Get up!" One of the Dark Guards yanks me to my feet when the elevator's silver doors roll open, revealing the hexagonal room with the Admiral's thought-detecting tile. She's waiting at her malleable desk, but this time she's wearing burgundy instead of her white tech-suit, and no one asks me to remove my boots. At this point, I don't think she cares to know what I'm thinking or how I feel. Why would it even matter? She'll be holding my brain in her hands before the day's over.

The Dark Guards push me forward, and I speculate what color my defeat would look like rippling across the geometric floor. They shove me into the lip of the desk, and the hardened surface pushes below my ribcage, knocking the wind out of my lungs. I immediately hunch over my knees and gasp.

"Leave us," the Admiral orders.

I don't bother watching the soldiers exit the room. Maybe the best part about dying is knowing I'll never have to see another Dark Guard again. Ever.

"The doctor told me about the results of your test this morning."

The Admiral sounds so casual, like she's catching up with an old friend. But the sound of her voice makes me sick. I unravel my crumbled posture to look her in the face.

"So?" I hope she feels the hatred in my tone, sees the disgust in my eyes. I loathe who she is and everything she stands for: the injustice, the deception, the manipulation.

"Well ..." She slides her hand across the stiff surface of the desk. The imprint of her molded palm is cast at the center, waiting for her to slide her slender fingers into their slots and activate the technology. "Perhaps you weren't aware of the breakthrough."

Breakthrough?

I narrow my eyes, still holding on to my aching middle.

"You did see the meadow, did you not?"

I think about the vision of Grandmommy glitching among the iridescent flowers, hear the sinister cackle of the grass as its sharp blades cut through my exposed skin. I don't know what she thinks I saw, but it wasn't *my* meadow.

"I'll explain it simply, since you don't seem to understand what this means." She puts both hands down on the desk and leans forward. Her green eyes burn a hole into my soul. Her sickly-sweet voice turns sour. "We've infiltrated the City of Life."

What? That can't be.

Rage replaces my apathy, and I ball my fingers into fists. If the Admiral's reached the City of Life, that means Grandmommy's in danger. And if the Eternal Realm gets destroyed, I have nothing to look forward to after death. That would mean ... this is it. This is all I have to live for. I can't let this be the end. Not for me. Not for my friends. Not for Grandmommy. I *have* to do something.

"Thanks to you, Reyna, we were able to establish a brief connection into Elolam's realm. And although we weren't able to keep it, it allowed us to map the pathway to an entrance. Unfortunately, the only way to get in is through a dreamer. Fortunately ..." She pauses. "I have *you.*"

The Admiral rounds her desk. I step back to avoid her, but she corners me against the curve of its edges.

Reaching into her pocket, she slides out a syringe. I dodge her stab and ram into her shoulder, knocking her off her feet. I dart for the elevator and rapidly press the button. I *have* to get to the surface. I *have* to leave the compound. *Now.*

Come on. Come on.

The circular button doesn't respond, and I realize it's because I don't have a key. I whip myself around, remembering the secret passageway, but the Admiral's already standing behind me. She stabs me in the neck.

The room spins. My vision grows blurry. My hands and feet go numb, then my arms. My legs. My spine can no longer support the weight of my body and I slink down, banging my shoulder against the Admiral on my way to the floor.

"Soon, this will all be just a dream." The Admiral hangs her head over my face, blocking the bright lights from the domed ceiling.

I hear the hiss of the hidden doors open, feel my body lift from the ground. I attempt to bite the hands that grab me, but my jaw slacks. Paralyzed and impaired, I can't fight my captors as they pick me up and place me on a gurney, wheeling me from the honeycomb room.

Through the haziness of my vision, the geometric panels slip away, replaced by hallway lights. Dizziness and nausea set in while I rock back and forth in transport.

The swarm of shadowed figures wheel me into a small examination room and abandon me there. I'm alone and unable to move. I desperately try to lift my head. Relentlessly I try, but nothing responds. I force my hands, channeling all of my strength into moving one finger, but nothing budges. All of my limbs are frozen. Trapped and panicked, I call for help, hoping Nurse Fukuda will hear me. A breathy squeal releases from my unmoving lips. I sink in defeat.

This is it.

Footsteps enter the room. My breath catches in my throat. No matter how hard I will my neck to turn, I can't twist my head to see who it is. Instruments clang on a metal tray.

Is it Doctor Ayad preparing to slice my head open?

A shadow passes over me. The footsteps grow louder. I want to squeeze the chair, scream, kick, anything.

Nurse Fukuda wheels a table next to me and straightens the supplies on display.

"Don't worry," she whispers. "The side effects will wear off shortly."

Her words don't comfort me.

"I'm going to take some samples of your blood before the doctor comes in."

She ties off my arm and sticks her large, hollow needle into my flesh. Even in my paralyzed state, I can feel the sharp prick pierce my skin. When she releases the tourniquet, a rush of bright red fluid flows from my arm and into the port. She fills vial after vial with my blood.

My fingers buzz. Tingling sensations zip through my body, waking my nervous system. My toes begin to twitch. Either the poison is wearing off, or she's removing it from my system.

"Do your best to hold still," Nurse Fukuda speaks softly, still gathering samples.

I hear her, but I don't listen. I attempt to lift my leg. It jolts upward, knocking into the metal tray beside the gurney. Nurse Fukuda leaps to keep the instruments from spilling to the ground.

"I don't want to have to sedate you before the surgery," she warns through gritted teeth. "Please, Reyna, hold still!"

She's here to prep me for surgery. Here to help the doctor slice me open.

I was stupid to think Nurse Fukuda was someone I could trust. If she was really Ruby's inside source, she'd be helping me escape, not ordering me to be still. I can't give up now. I can't let the Admiral have control of my mind. I *have* to get out of here. *Now.* I ignore Nurse Fukuda's requests to be still and make another desperate attempt to lift my arm.

Nurse Fukuda rockets to her feet and stomps over to a tall glass case positioned against the wall. I can move my head just enough to see her snatch the syringe from inside. My heart beats faster, pumping the will to fight, to *survive*, through my veins. It flares within me. I fling my head forward with all my might and sit up.

"Lie back down!" Nurse Fukuda gasps, her face full of panic. She grabs my shoulders and forces me down with her scrawny arms. The weight of her body pins me to the gurney. I'm still too weak to throw her off.

"I'm trying to help you." She hisses the lie through her teeth. Digging her forearms into my chest, she reaches behind her back with the syringe. I feel pressure against my hip.

It's over.

I stop trying to break free and close my eyes. I don't want the look of satisfaction on Nurse Fukuda's face to be the last thing I see before I go unconscious. The weight on my chest disappears when she climbs down from the gurney. I lie still, listening to her straighten the jumbled instruments on her metal tray, waiting for my mind to slip into oblivion.

Instead, prickling sensations start in my limbs. I stretch my fingers, then feel along my thigh for the injection site. My hand collides with the cool metal of a tubular object. I grasp it. Nurse Fukuda left the syringe wedged underneath my hip with the plunger fully extended from the barrel. I tug it close and conceal it with my hand.

I keep my eyes closed and my body still, taking steady, shallow breaths. The room fills with medical personnel. They're all here to witness my undoing—to help Doctor Ayad remove my brain. I listen to the footsteps and indistinct chatter, clenching my weapon, waiting for an opportune moment. If I'm going to make it out of this room alive, I need perfect timing. And aim.

"Has the patient been prepped for surgery?"

I hear *his* voice. The doctor's somewhere behind me.

No one responds, but I imagine Nurse Fukuda nodding in reply.

"Then let's begin."

Doctor Ayad calls for his assistants to move me into position. Someone tugs at my shirt, taping wires to my chest. Accelerated beeping fills the room.

"The patient's heart rate is elevated," an unfamiliar voice, quiet and raspy, remarks.

I inhale slowly.

"Perhaps she hasn't reached full sedation." Nurse Fukuda sounds confident, her voice unwavering. "Should I administer another injection?"

"Her blood pressure is raised as well." A flat comment comes from the scratchy voice.

My mouth pools with saliva. I fight the urge to swallow.

"Prep five more milliliters of the injection," Doctor Ayad orders. "We'll start with a small dosage. I don't want the patient bleeding out on the table."

I picture the explosion of blood bursting from my father's head when Doctor Ayad removed the tubes from his skull and hold back a gulp.

Retreating footsteps move to the other side of the operating room. A cabinet door opens, then closes. The click of shoes sounds against the tile floor.

I slide my thumb over the top of the syringe and listen for the doctor's voice.

"Begin the administration."

He's standing above my head.

"Her heart rate is climbing." The breathy voice sounds from somewhere near my feet.

I have to act fast.

My body surges with adrenaline. I thrust my arm behind my head and sink the needle into rigid flesh. The doctor's body hits the floor with a thud. The nurse at my feet screams. Nurse Fukuda drives a second needle into the assisting nurse's arm, lowering her gently to the floor.

I twist around to see a needle jutting from Doctor Ayad's throat.

"Quickly." Nurse Fukuda scrambles to the cabinet.

I roll on my side and swing my legs onto the floor, teetering to a stand, gripping the rails of the gurney while I attempt to find my balance. When I let go, I fall back, then catch my weight on Nurse Fukuda's cart, spilling the instruments onto the floor. The wheels tug, but they don't spin, and I somehow manage to stay upright.

"Take this." She hands me an elevator key. "When you leave the room, turn right, then left. Turn right and right again, then one more left. You should find an elevator shaft. It will take you to the back side of the Medical Center. The nearest exit will face the Northern Sector."

I space out.

"Did you get that?"

"Right. Left. Right. Right. Left," I repeat. "But what about you? Aren't you coming, too?"

"I'm going to sedate myself and make it look like you escaped on your own."

My forehead furrows. My feet waver.

"Don't worry about me," she insists. "I'll be fine." Nurse Fukuda urges me toward the door. "Just promise me one thing?" Her eyes fill with sadness.

My heart sinks. "Anything."

"When you hear the chickadees sing, you'll think of me?" A stream of tears releases from her eyes, running down her cheeks and dripping onto her uniform.

"Promise." My voice cracks.

"Now go." Nurse Fukuda pushes me onward and scrambles back to the cabinet to retrieve another syringe.

I don't wait to see her fall. I can't bear to watch it happen. Without looking back, I exit the room. When the door clicks closed behind me, I take a moment to lean against it and repeat Nurse Fukuda's instructions.

Right.

Wobbling on my tingling toes, I make my way into the endless stretch of white-washed walls. I saunter forward. I've never been drunk before, but I feel a lot like Mrs. Cane, wandering like a buffoon through these halls.

The first intersection comes sooner than I expect. I hold my breath when I approach the turn.

Left.

The hallway is empty. I force an exhale. My legs tremble, still shaking from the effects of the poison. My feet buzz with each step, but I push on, doing my best to keep a steady pace until the sensations peter off, returning the blood flow to my legs.

Right.

After I veer, another sharp turn follows.

Right again.

I continue through the corridors, relieved that every turn has found me alone. Another intersecting hallway appears. My heart pounds in my ears. There's only one last turn before I reach the elevator. I curve the final corner with a surge of excitement, then falter when I see a Dark Guard waiting near the set of silver doors.

My stomach twists. I swallow, but a lump wedges in my throat.

What do I do?

I scan down the hall, contemplating how long it would take me to find another exit. The problem is, I don't know where I'm going. I could easily get lost down here. Before I make a decision, I hear the elevator doors part. Holding my breath, I listen and wait for the Dark Guard to leave, to ascend to the surface.

My heart pummels my chest, and my hands start to shake when I hear two sets of boots marching my way.

There's nowhere to run.

I whirl around and dart down the hall, my feeble legs barely keeping me upright. Taking the next turn, I hurry down an unfamiliar corridor. I'm looking for a door. Any door. Somewhere to hide until the Dark Guards pass.

My breath quickens, and my side aches as I push myself to move faster. The increasing thud of my boots makes me slow down, but it's too late. I lose my balance and fall to the floor, smacking the ground with a loud slap. Nurse Fukuda's key slides across the tile.

"Freeze!" a Dark Guard orders.

I'm not going anywhere.

They peel me off the floor and haul me through the underground network of tunnels until we reach a room with a high-level security lock, some kind of scanner, and a screen that looks black, but the Dark Guard enters something onto its surface and a robotic voice responds, "SYSTEM OVERRIDE."

The door hisses, and I'm carried over the threshold. There's only a small space between the entrance and the chamber inside; a metal box with a plexiglass wall.

It's a cage. I'm in prison.

They throw me through a slender opening, and the walls move to close the gap. The mechanisms engage with loud grinding. Multiple locks clunk into place. There's no pincushion to save me this time.

I can barely see the Dark Guards exiting the cell room through the hazy glass. It's scratched and splotched like someone, or something, was in here before and tried to claw free.

Hours pass. I pace the floor until I can't stand any longer. Crumpling to the ground, I scoot into a corner, wedging my body between the metal, hoping the doors will slide back open. I bring my knees to my chest and rest my head in my arms.

Guilt eats at me as I think about Nurse Fukuda. She gave me a chance and I blew it.

What if the Admiral found out she was the one to help me? What will happen to her?

My stomach twists into knots and panic seizes my chest. I feel like I'm running out of air. I slide up the wall and throw myself at the glass, banging my fists until my knuckles bleed.

My vision starts to blur and shadows rim my sight. I hear muffled crackles and pops. It sounds like someone's stuffed linen scraps in my ears. My legs give out and I sink to the floor. The whole room spins.

Reality hits like a ton of cement crashing on my head.

It's over. I'm not leaving.

The Admiral's won.

I roll onto my side and nearly jump out of my skin when I see her standing on the other side of the window. Her green eyes look like they're glowing, but I must be imagining it. She presses a button on the outside of my cell, and her voice fills every inch of the chamber.

"You've betrayed me, Reyna."

I can't believe this woman has the audacity to say that *I'm* the one who's betrayed *her*.

"We had a deal, and you've broken our agreement."

I flip onto my knees. "You were about to slice my head open!" I yell, not knowing if she can hear anything I say.

She stares at me and cocks her head. "Now, who told you that?"

Nurse Fukuda's the only one who knows about the vision I saw of my father's death. She's the one who told me about the surgery. I can't admit that. I can't say it's her.

"*He* did."

"*Him*?" She raises her eyebrows.

"Elolam showed me what you were going to do—what you've already done!"

She pulls her finger away from the intercom and rotates from the glass so I can't see or hear her reaction. I expect her to turn around, to get in the last word, but she doesn't. I search for her through the scratches and see her leave without as much as a glance over her shoulder.

The door slams shut, sealing my fate along with it.

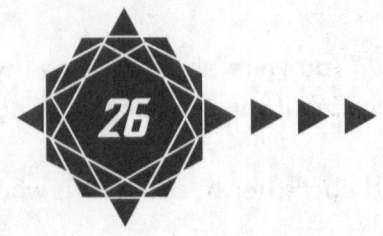

I've lost track of time. It's been days, maybe even weeks. There's no way of knowing. The lights stay the same. They never dim or brighten. I've dozed off once or twice, but I haven't been able to relax enough to enter into a deep sleep. No dreams come; no visits from the Admiral. Only two Dark Guards have walked through the outside door, sliding trays of food through a retractable slot near the chamber floor. The first tray had a dainty set of finger sandwiches accompanied by a teacup steaming with muddied liquid. I didn't care. The last meal I had was with my friends, and I wanted to keep it that way. Plus, I don't want to satisfy the Admiral by eating any of her fancy food.

I threw the tray across the cell, smashing the porcelain into bits. Unfortunately, the smell of sweet, earthy fluids is now inescapable. It's a constant reminder of my meeting with the Admiral under her synthetic sky. Hours have passed, and I realize I've only hurt myself because the concrete floor is covered in saucer shards, which limits where I can lie down when the dizziness overtakes me.

Kicking slivers of the Admiral's teacup away from my feet, I do my best to clear a space to sit. I stoop over on my knees, wondering why it's taking so long for her to come and get me, to finish me off.

Remembrance Day has certainly come and gone. I haven't heard any explosions, which means the plan either fell through or I'm too far underground to have heard any of the bombs detonate. All I can do is hope my friends made it, that they're all on their way to Omicron *without me*.

And, if not, who knows what the Admiral's done to the Compound. Maybe she's killed everyone and started transforming our homes into research facilities. Maybe Dark Guards are testing bigger, stronger, and more lethal weapons on the surface right now.

If anything, Walter and his family are definitely gone. I guess they're the lucky ones in this situation. They've been given a second chance at life. Even if it's under the pretense of working for the United Regime, I hope Walter takes it. Alive is better than dead, or locked away in a cage. Maybe someday he'll make it to Omicron, too.

I close my eyes and try to picture what it would be like to live in the forest near the mountains, collecting cool water from a fresh spring, hunting animals, and cooking meals over a fire. Elolam didn't show me the community of dreamers when he brought me into the woods, but I imagine they live in handmade structures similar to the one I saw at his campsite. I stretch my thoughts and envision a small village with people working together and children laughing as they play.

Cool air blows from a vent above my head, stirring up the stale air and spreading the stench of sweat and spoiled food. When I open my eyes, all I see is the mess I've made in my cell and a replacement meal. The second tray from my last visitor was brought hours ago, but I haven't touched it. This one didn't come with any special sandwiches, only a glob of putrefied mush. It's been sitting on the floor for so long that the meat has shriveled, and it's turning dark. The sight of it sours my stomach.

The only thing I want right now is water—something to keep my tongue from sticking to the roof of my mouth. Saliva starts to form on my lips when I think about how good the water from the stream in my dreams tasted. I wave my hands in the air like I'm sticking them into the clear fluid, pretending to drink from the spring. I stop when I notice I'm going crazy.

My heart sinks into my gut. I should have never agreed to take the Admiral's tests. I would have been better off burned in the incinerator. At least then I'd have a chance at walking among the stars, running through iridescent fields with Grandmommy. That, and the Admiral would have never found a way to infiltrate Elolam's city.

According to her, the vision I saw of Grandmommy under the serum's influence wasn't in a decoy meadow. And if it was the real thing, maybe sliding through the sinister grass was Elolam's way of kicking me out of the City of Life for contaminating his realm with the Admiral's poison. After all, *I'm* the reason she's found a way in.

Another wave of anger comes, and I wish the Admiral would just hurry up and end my existence. I've already accepted that there's nothing I can do to help the City of Life, not from here. I don't even know if Elolam would visit me if I willed my exhausted body to sleep, or even if he could now that the Admiral's found a way to manipulate our connection. At this point, I'm just waiting for the Admiral to run another test. I almost want her to. Even if it means slicing my brain out of my skull, at least I'd be doing something. Maybe then I could find a way to sabotage the link or create a diversion.

I curl up on the floor, begging my body to surrender to sleep. Even if I can't see Grandmommy, a dreamless night might do my overstimulated mind some good. I squeeze my eyes shut, trying to block out the bright lights in my cell, and do everything I can to forget where I am. Breathing in slowly, I envision the meadow as I used to know it, concentrating on the smell of purple blossoms, recalling the sounds of Grandmommy's laughter. And before I know it, everything fades away.

When I open my eyes, the lights are off. All I can see is darkness. I lift my head, expecting to find the faint glow of a Dark Guard's visor or light leaking in from the hallway, but the entire room has disappeared, replaced by what seems like an infinite void. I place my hand on the floor to push myself into a sitting position. The surface is icy to the touch and much colder than before. A waft of chilled air rattles my teeth. I wrap my arms across my chest and rub my skin to generate warmth.

I don't know if the Admiral's torturing me by freezing me in her cell, or if the power's gone out. Maybe the bombs did explode and the underground levels have lost power. If that's the case, the electricity-powered doors won't open, and the elevators won't rise. My breath quickens. I'm going to die buried alive, trapped inside the Admiral's prison.

Panic squeezes my throat. *I need to get out of here.*

I squirm to a stand with the intentions of prying the sliding door open with my bare hands. But when I reach for the wall, I fall backward, grasping open air. Either the wall's gone or I've somehow ended up in the middle of the room.

From nowhere, two illuminated arches appear in the distance. One is strobing with an array of colorful hues that remind me of Grandmommy's orb, while the other burns red like a Dark Guard's helmet. Woven vines and lush green leaves form the outer frame of the first, while pieces of charred bark weld the second together.

Am I awake? This must be a dream. Either that or the Admiral pushed her poison fumes through the air grate, causing hallucinations.

I step forward to investigate, but my foot drops into the void. I'm standing on a platform in the middle of nothing.

"Where are you?" I shout into the abyss, wondering if Elolam will even bother to answer this time.

The floor rumbles in response, extending toward the arches, splitting to form two separate paths with one leading to each doorway. Below the narrow trails, there's only vacant space. There's nowhere to go but forward.

I steady my feet on the slippery surface and saunter toward the arcs. When I reach the fork in the path, I consider my choices. The green arch's pulsing center captivates me. Across the threshold, emerald grass sways over a colorful landscape. Beautiful, cone-shaped blooms wave in the wind. It must be an entrance to the meadow—Grandmommy's meadow. I hesitate, wondering if it's a trap leading me back to the green knives that sliced my skin. I lean in, cupping my ears, listening for the valley's song. I hear the faint melody rising from the other side, and yet I'm not convinced that it's really there. There's no way of knowing whether or not I'm under the influence of the Admiral's serum. She could have transferred me while I was unconscious. I could be in an exam room with vials of her poison pumping through my veins, distorting my dreams. The only thing that I know for certain is that where I'm standing right now is *not* in the City of Life.

Maybe this is the connection the Admiral told me about—and if that's the case, and the City of Life really is through that doorway, then I shouldn't enter in. I'd be giving the Admiral full access to Elolam's realm. She would infiltrate the City of Life, destroying everything in her path and leaving a wake of destruction that matches the state of my world: barren and desolate.

Across the canyon, smoke floods from the scorched wooden frame, obscuring what waits through its threshold. I inch forward to get a better look, but the smoldering rot burns my lungs and sends me into a coughing fit. I'm struggling to keep my stinging eyes open, when I see a pair of floating orbs approach the archways. They look a lot like the golden souls that dripped from the Source's branches, except one's burning bright blue and the other's flickering dimly. In fact, all color is drained from the shadowy sphere, and it's sputtering much slower than its companion.

The small cyan light sails to the vine-covered doorway, burning brighter as it nears the entrance. A burst of golden light beams when it crosses the threshold, and I flinch and shield my eyes. When the intensity dwindles, I see a chiseled man with squared features standing on the other side of the doorway. His radiant, flowing hair drapes over his shoulders, framing the sky-colored orb sunken in his chest.

When the man moves out of sight, I turn my attention to the staggering orb, shifting awkwardly toward the second archway. A thin sliver of smoke slithers from behind the charred wood, snaking around the orb. I rub my stinging eyes, fighting to keep my focus on the gray sphere. The slinking shadow constricts and pulls the fading orb through the portal. For a brief moment, the swirling smoke parts and I can see an endless desert of cinders under a sky of burning liquid fire. The fading circle disintegrates into the ashen floor as the desert vanishes from sight, clouded by billows of thickening smoke.

I stumble back, my hand to my mouth. A heavy weight falls on my shoulders. Anger burbles in my veins, followed by a thick wave of sorrow. I don't know if it's Elolam manipulating my emotions or the Admiral's serum playing tricks on my mind, but watching the orb dissolve into nothing feels a lot like witnessing someone die, like holding bloodstained uniforms in my hands, like seeing Grandmommy's eyes go dull as she lies lifeless on her soiled cot.

My tears mix with smoke.

"Why are you showing me this?" The scorching haze burns my throat.

Elolam doesn't answer. And if the Admiral's hovering over my unconscious body, I don't think he will.

"What is this place?" I scream louder.

I startle out of my skin when the answer comes from inside my head.

"This is the Great Divide." Elolam's voice sounds like static in my ears. "The space between realms, where souls leave Earth and cross into eternity." Something—or someone—is hindering our connection. "Those who remember are guided by the light of hope into the City of Life. Those who forget..." His words fade.

"Forget what?" I yell.

Nothing.

"What?" I spin. "Tell me!"

I whip my attention to the vine-draped doorway, then back to the smoldering portal. *If one is the gateway into the City of Life, then the other must be an entrance to ... Death.* I gulp. Another glimpse of the wasteland peeks through the smoke. Mounds of ash stretch to an endless horizon. The desert isn't just a blanket of dust. It's countless crumbled souls. I stagger back. Entering over that threshold could kill me.

Fear chokes me. I'm not ready to die, but something shifts in my head when I consider the effects of my actions, should I choose to go through this door. Sacrificing myself could prevent the Admiral from establishing a permanent connection to the City of Life.

Stillness settles in my bones. I know what I have to do.

I take a step forward, when a low rumble bellows in the darkness. It sounds like a million drones whirling over my head. My heart races, thrashing my ribcage as the noise grows louder, rattling my chest. I teeter, but spread out my arms to keep myself from falling off the ledge. A sudden swarm of monochrome spills from the void, stampeding in pursuit of the open archways, channeling toward the smoldering entrance. I duck to avoid a collision and brace myself, flattened against the slick floor.

The crowd hurtles in the direction of the charred arch, and thousands of orbs cross the threshold, collapsing into ash. I can't do it. I can't die an eternal death.

Glimpses of color peek through the miasma of gray, aiming for the vined doorway. I crawl on my stomach, chasing after them, setting my mark on the meadow. I'm desperate to escape the stampede, to avoid being pushed into the doorway of death. I need to reach the City of Life.

Grandmommy surfaces in the vined door, her hands extending to me, beckoning me to come. I call out to her, wriggling myself free from beneath the mob. As soon as I can, I spring to my feet and dash among the trickle of glowing orbs toward safety. Breathing heavily, I pick up speed. To my left, a myriad of souls rush to desolation. The scorching sound of their disintegration sizzles in my ears. Death's clamor mixes with the loud thumps of my accelerating pulse. I cover my ears, squeeze my eyes shut, and yell as I dive into the portal. The horrific hum surges, louder and louder, until all at once, everything falls silent.

27

I wake up gasping, disoriented by the bright lights in my cage. I shield my eyes and search the small space. Nothing's the way I left it. The shards of ceramic are gone, and the crusted meat on the untouched tray is missing. The entire cell has been wiped spotless.

Who knows how long I've been sleeping? And what on earth did I just see?

I wish Geri were here. I wish I could talk to her about my dreams. At this point, I'd settle for Ronny's company, or Ruby's, or even Walter's.

Being left alone drives me mad. My mind warps in every direction, attempting to decipher what my dream meant, then combing through every possible scenario of what might happen next: life, death, and everything in between. I really don't know what the Admiral's waiting for, or why she's bothering to send me food. Maybe she's found another dreamer and she's holding on to me just in case things don't work out. A picture of the boy from Bunker 111 surfaces in my thoughts. I see his ashen face, his limp limbs. A shiver runs down my spine.

Just when I think I'm about to drive myself completely insane, the outer door swings open and a Dark Guard marches in. He's carrying another tray. I scoff and roll my eyes. *Again?* I've been offered more food down here than I ever have above ground. Either the Admiral thinks she can win me over with a meal, or she's trying to drug me through the food. Or maybe she's attempting to stick to our inconsistent meal schedule from the surface. That would mean I've spent at least three to five days trapped here.

The slot lifts and the Dark Guard removes the old tray from the floor, then slides the new one through the opening. To my surprise, there's no food on the tray, only a neatly folded black uniform—a Dark Guard uniform.

"Put this on," a voice spills through the intercom.

"Who are you?" I stand up, causing another burst of lightheadedness to overtake my vision. I'm seeing stars, but they're not the kind I want to see.

"A friend," is all he offers me. "Get dressed. I'll stand guard." He turns away.

I either stay here and rot or do as he says. I remove my boots. Drenched in sweat and filth, I peel my sticky uniform from my arms and slide into the sleek, shiny material. The clothes stretch to fit my body. I can't believe how breathable the suit feels against my skin. The outer layer bulges with padded armor, but the inner layer is smooth and flexible.

"Ready?" the Dark Guard calls from over his shoulder.

"What about my boots?" I ask.

The narrow opening in my cage whooshes as it glides open, disappearing into the wall.

"Here." He hands me a shiny pair that matches my new uniform.

I slip my feet into them, surprised by how lightweight the soles are. When I step, the bottoms don't give way; they hold against the floor with power and ease.

"Now this." He forces a weapon into my hands. The bulky firearm feels strange in my grasp. Like everything else, it's much lighter than I anticipated. I stare at the flat black metal in my hands and run my fingers over its barrel, feeling for the trigger.

"Strap it to your back," he says hurriedly.

I swing it around my shoulder. A magnetic force pulls it taut to my uniform. "Are you going to show me how to shoot it?"

He ignores my question and shoves a helmet against my chest. "Don't turn it on," he warns. "They'll find you."

I twist my hair into a knot and shimmy the dark mask over my face. A pop-up screen with red lettering appears on the visor.

NO SIGNAL. CONNECT TO MAINFRAME.

"It won't be long before the Admiral discovers you're missing. She's already sent orders for a secondary procedure to take place during the ceremony."

The Remembrance Day ceremony? I didn't miss it?

"Just follow me and let me do the talking. I should be able to get you to the surface before it's time." He does an about-face and heads for the door.

"Wait!" I call out, the visor fogging with my hot breath. "Why are you helping me?"

"You're a dreamer," he says flatly. "But I'm not doing this for *you*." He turns back. "I'm doing it for *him*. I couldn't save him, but if I can help you, maybe that's enough penance for his death."

At that moment, I think I know who my rescuer is.

"*Brenton?*" His name sizzles through my mask.

He nods. "Stick close and try to keep up."

Before he faces forward, I notice his visor isn't producing the same soft, red glow that all the other Dark Guard helmets emit. I assume that means his suit isn't powered on either, which means he probably stole both of them.

But how? Where has he been this whole time?

I want to ask him, say the questions aloud, but I'm having a hard time matching his pace. It takes me a few empty hallways to get the hang of walking in the suit. The anticipation of heavy boots throws me off, especially because the weight of the uniform is so light. I must look ridiculous, like someone who's got their feet caught in a slab of wet cement.

Between the blinking text on the screen and the condensation from my breath, it's really hard to look at anything farther than Brenton. I get the urge to wipe the visor clean, but that would really slow me down. I'd have to finagle my gloved hand through the impossibly small opening near my chin, or take the helmet off completely in order to make it worth my while.

The red words plastered inside my mask flicker faster, suggesting the suit be powered on. I'm tempted to confirm. There has to be a ventilation system embedded in these helmets. Powering the suit on might make it easier to breathe, which means I'd be able to see better, too.

I focus my attention on Brenton. If he knows where we're going, it doesn't matter that *my* vision's impaired. I watch his gait, the way he strides in the uniform. He looks so natural—so convincing. If he hadn't told me who he was, I would've been fooled completely into thinking he was a real Dark Guard.

I do my best to mimic his stance, the way he holds his arms at his sides, barely swinging them. I straighten my shoulders and widen my steps to match the timing of his walk. Before long, we're moving in sync, rounding corners, marching through the underground maze.

An intersecting hallway appears through the spaces in my steam-coated visor. Brenton puts out his hand, signaling for me to slow. My vision blurs with every exhale, but I can still make out the shiny silver doors of the elevator up ahead.

We're almost there.

Brenton slides his key into the slot, and the doors shift open. I'm relieved to see that it's empty inside, and I let my shoulders relax when we move up the shaft. A sigh escapes me, but I regret letting it out. The mugginess of my breath thickens the humidity in my mask. *I wonder if I have enough time to air it out and slip it back on before we reach the surface.*

I raise my hands to my helmet.

"I wouldn't do that if I were you," Brenton warns.

I think he's worried I might try to turn it on.

"It's impossible to breathe in this thing," I complain.

"Trust me, what you're experiencing now is a lot better than what happens if you power the suit on."

"What happens?"

"You lose control of your own body," he says quickly. "Now straighten up, we're almost to the surface. Do your best to stay quiet, and let me do the talking."

I correct my posture and match his stance, exiting behind him with coordinated steps. Even through my clouded mask, I pick up on the movement in the room. The foyer isn't crowded, but there's more people in here than I would like. A handful of medical personnel linger by the electrical archways. An elderly man makes his way up the center of the aisle, freezing under a wave of pulsating energy. Two Dark Guards wait behind him, forcing him forward when the machine stops.

I still don't understand what the purpose of the arcs are, or why the Admiral's installed them. When I see the man get stabbed in the arm with the metal barrel, I figure it has to be part of her new preadmission policies and procedures before patients can be admitted into the hospital for treatment.

"This is the third person who's come in today complaining of a headache," I hear one of the technicians say to the other when we pass by.

"Do you think we have a rising pandemic on our hands?"

"The neurological calibration didn't take," the third nurse interrupts. "His tracker was rejected."

"Let's send the patient to quarantine for a full evaluation."

Tracker? I fight the urge to rub my arm. *They put a tracker underneath my skin!* Panic seizes my chest. My heartbeat pounds inside my ears. My hands start to shake. I'm losing my coordination. My steps are no longer in time with Brenton's. I stumble into him when he stops at the front door.

"State your business."

The Dark Guard stationed by the exit won't let us pass. *What if he's seen through my disguise? What if he knows I'm not one of them?*

"The Admiral's caught wind of a possible rebel attack and has requested extra security detail during the ceremony," Brenton answers confidently, but I'm worried he's said too much.

Why would he give up our plan? Maybe he doesn't know about it.

The Dark Guard holds still, blocking the opening, staring directly into my face shield. I tremble at the thought of him spotting the information on the inside of my visor, or noticing the absence of the red light beneath the tinted armor. *I wish I could see through his mask.*

"Your orders aren't on file. State your ID."

Brenton spits out a laundry list of numbers, quoting his ID to the Dark Guard, who seems satisfied. We're allowed to pass, but I'm worried that if I really do have a tracker in my arm, it won't be long before the Admiral finds me.

The Dark Guard swings his fist in front of me before I cross over the threshold.

"Man your weapon, soldier."

I freeze.

"Yes, sir!" Brenton salutes.

I copy his response. We detach the guns from our backs and hold them to our chests. I tilt mine into my shoulder, mimicking Brenton, and hope to Elolam I'm not expected to use it.

The courtyard is full of people gathering for the Remembrance Day Address. Brenton leads me around the outskirts of the masses, pushing us toward the makeshift stage that gets erected every year for the ceremony. People part out of our way, motivated by fear, reminding me that I'm hidden under the ruse of a Dark Guard uniform.

When we get closer to the stage, I see the anniversary banner hanging as its backdrop. The red letters are barely visible through my clouded visor, but it's just enough to trigger my memories, bringing me back to the day Grandmommy died. My thoughts shift from the present to the past. One moment, I'm following Brenton, the next I'm trailing after the Warden on my way to Bunker 112. I shake the thoughts away just in time to notice a line of Dark Guards lining the front of the stage. Their formation continues, wrapping the entire multitude in a solid black rim.

Brenton slows his pace when we reach the steps leading to the metal platform. He shifts his feet in the gravel, does an about-face, and joins the other Dark Guards in their row. I do the same, trying my best to seem inconspicuous. Before I fully turn, I see Mrs. Cane at the bottom of the stairs straightening her husband's necktie. Her feathered boa slithers off her shoulder when she brushes dust from the lapels of his jacket.

The Canes. They're still here.

"But, tonight? She seriously expects us to be ready in just a few hours? And on Remembrance Day?" Mrs. Cane groans.

Tonight? They're talking about the transport. The conversation piques my interest. I tilt my head and strain to hear them better.

"After all we've done—" Commander Cane projects.

"Shh," his wife cuts him off. "*She'll* hear you."

"I don't care if she hears me through one of those blasted things!"

They must be talking about the Admiral.

"What she's turning this place into is unnatural. It's not restoring the Earth or rebuilding humanity! It's leaving it behind!" His voice grows louder. "It's only a matter of time before she turns everyone here into one of those brainless robots!"

A recording of the United Regime's national anthem blasts over the antique speakers, covering up the rest of their exchange. The song is only played once a year on Remembrance Day, but its eerie melody is hard to forget. Each line represents a fallen country absorbed into the United Regime—a fragment of past patriotism—a patchwork of pledges from deserted governments. The mounted speakers rattle on their poles as the final words ring out.

> *Land of the free, home no longer divided*
> *We stand on guard for the future and rejoice*
> *For we are all one ...*

The recording fades. Hushed murmurs in the crowd settle until the entire population of the Omega Compound—every man, woman, and child—is silent, and the only thing I can hear is the sound of my own breath as it coats my visor in fog. Squeaky bolts break the silence. The rickety platform rattles when Commander Cane steps onto it and approaches the single microphone at its center.

"Citizens of the Omega Compound, today we gather, not in fear or in mourning, but in remembrance—remembrance of the day our ancestors chose peace instead of war, mercy instead of heartache, unity instead of chaos ..."

I look forward, searching through foggy lines to find my friends. Our unit is usually placed at the back, but it's too difficult to see over the swaying heads of the crowd. *If only I were taller.*

"The Omega Compound, like many others, has become a place of sanctuary, a place where we have proven against all odds that *we are survivors* ..."

Someone's moving through the crowd, inching toward the outer border. I crane my neck as much as I can to get a better view without looking suspicious. It isn't just one person. It's two people. But I can't make out their faces through the fog.

Maybe it's Robin and Clancy.

My chest tightens as I remember the plan. *At what point during the ceremony are the bombs going to explode?* Nervous energy quickens my pulse. *What happens when the chaos erupts?* I'm on the wrong side of the strategy, dressed in a Dark Guard uniform. *If Brenton doesn't know, maybe I should tell him.*

"Once a divided world, we have found our refuge under the gracious hand of the United Regime and its leaders, governed by those who represent fortitude and strength ..."

I think I've swiveled my head back and forth one too many times because the woman in front of me is staring at me funny. She whispers something to the man behind her. *What should I do?* None of the other Dark Guards move. Even Brenton holds his posture perfectly still. He's had more time to practice than I have. *But how is he keeping himself from suffocating in the humidity of his own hot breath?* I feel like I can't breathe, like my throat is closing up.

The woman's secret gets passed from one ear to another. My breath grows erratic. I lose track of which direction in the crowd her words travel. Between the prompt to turn on the suit and the steam, it's impossible to see what's going on. The limitations of the mask make me panic. I want to rip it off my face, but I can't. Not while I'm surrounded by a web of Dark Guards. That would be a death wish. Not even Brenton would be able to help me.

"Together we stand for all mankind and remember the ones who have suffered before us …"

I shift my weight back and forth, unable to hold still. The gun slips on my shoulder.

"Let us offer a moment of silence for our ancestors: the ones who fell with rebellious pride and the ones who gave their lives for a better future."

The ground shakes, rippling shockwaves through the crowd.

"What was that?"

I twist my trembling body to see Mrs. Cane holding a hand over her mouth. Shock plasters her husband's face. He's grasping the microphone stand like it's going to help steady his shaking legs.

The first bomb. They didn't know about the explosives.

It must have been detonated deep within the tunnels of the underground sublevels, because the rumble was only enough to bounce the gravel in the courtyard.

Murmurs fill the multitude. I hold my breath, waiting for the next explosion. My visor clears enough to see that heads are swiveling in every direction. Mothers are pulling their children close. Hands are grasping for each other. Men are puffing out their chests, readying themselves for a fight.

I spot the couple still making their way to the edge of the crowd. It *is* Robin and Clancy. I exhale and lose them in the steam inside my face shield. I try to keep track of where they're headed. *That's where I need to be.*

"Everyone remain ca—"

A second explosion booms from underneath the ground, ripping a hole through the surface somewhere beyond the stage. Commander Cane dives from the platform. I duck and cover my head. His wife screams blend with the ringing in my ears.

"We're under attack!" someone yells from the crowd, inciting the panic. Some try to run. Dark Guards push inward, forcing the people to stay. I follow suit, raising my weapon and stepping in line with Brenton. We tighten the border, squeezing the already congested crowd into a more uncomfortably compacted space.

I can't bring myself to point the barrel of my weapon at the woman in front of me. Her eyes never veer from my mask. She's already spotted me as a weak link. My heart ticks nervously. Sweat drips from my forehead, stinging my eyes. I can't wipe them clear. I flinch, and she seizes the opportunity to push past me, creating a hole in our barrier. Others elbow their way through. Guns start firing. Complete and utter pandemonium breaks out.

"Run!" Brenton urges me.

I scramble from the stampede and sprint as fast as I can toward the machine shop, dodging clumps of debris. The sound of screams and gunfire mix behind me, but I can't bring myself to stop or look back. *Stick to the plan,* I remind myself as I swing my weapon, connecting it to my back. My feet pound the gravel as I pick up speed. I round the hole in the ground, the one caused by the explosion, and peer over its edge. Smoke pours from the opening. The harsh stench of toxic fumes gets trapped in my mask. I cough and wheeze and throw the helmet off my head, dig my heels into the gravel, and run faster.

The machine shop is just ahead. I can see it on the far side of the Compound, surrounded by the adjacent hangar. That's where our escape vehicle is.

The deafening grind of machines travels to my ringing ears before my feet reach the door. I burst through the entrance, met by a burly bald man with a grease-stained face. He's just as surprised to see a young girl dressed in a Dark Guard uniform as I am to see him leaning over the engine of a utility truck. He tightens his grip around a wrench.

I motion with my hands. "I'm looking for—"

"In the back," he hollers over the noise, tilting his head toward the rear of the room.

I walk past him, moving deeper into the shop. A bang from the nearby machinery sounds like the blast of a gun, making my heart skip a beat. It's no wonder the man in the front seems unfazed by the explosions. He probably couldn't hear anything through the racket.

No one's waiting at the end of the room when I get there, but I spot a set of doors and make my way through them to escape the deafening equipment. I can't believe Erika's not hard of hearing from working in here every day. Maybe that's why she talks so loudly.

When I push the handle closed, the noise nearly disappears. And I notice that safety warnings and hazard signs plaster the backside of the metal doors.

"Reyna?" Walter scrapes the legs of his chair across the floor and stands up from the table he's been waiting at.

"Are you the only one here?" I ask.

He nods.

"Why are you wearing that?" He notices my Dark Guard uniform. "Whoa, and how'd you manage to get your hands on one of their weapons?"

"It's a long story," I say, turning around to eye the door. "Is that what we're taking?" I gesture to the truck parked by the bay door.

"That's my guess." He rubs his hands together. "I've never actually been in here before."

"Me neither," I admit.

An awkward lull follows, and my mind races with reasons as to why no one else is here yet. I think of worst-case scenarios first, most of them involving getting stopped and shot by Dark Guards. I jump when the doors swing wide. It's Robin and Clancy. I exhale sharply and jog to Robin.

"I didn't think we were going to make it," she whimpers in my ear, holding on to my shoulders and choking on sobs. She tumbles back and grabs her stomach. The look on her face tells me she's having another one of those contractions, like the one she had in Commander Cane's study.

"You need to sit down." I help her into the chair where Walter was sitting when I first arrived.

She doesn't argue. "Thank you."

Professor Diaz and the Warden enter just as she situates herself in the chair. A swell of noise from the machines in the next room accompanies them as the doors open, then dissipates when they click closed.

"Is the truck ready?" Professor Diaz asks.

"Everything's loaded in the back," Walter answers.

"Good."

"Has anyone else come?" The Warden sounds hopeful. She's dressed more like the Warden I know, with a pressed uniform and polished boots, but there's a softness in her voice that I still haven't gotten used to hearing.

"This is it so far," Walter informs them before they venture over to check out our escape vehicle.

"I'll be right back," Clancy tells Robin, then scurries off to catch up with the rest of the group.

I ease myself into the chair adjacent to Robin, being careful not to knock my weapon into the backrest when I sit down. Robin has her eyes closed. She's concentrating on her breathing, sucking air through her nostrils and spitting out through her mouth. I lean my elbows onto the table and tap my foot against the concrete floor.

Where are they?

My eyes dart back and forth between Robin and the door. She clutches her belly and winces. I wonder if I need to get Clancy.

An engine roars, and the truck comes to life. The Warden shuts the driver-side door, and the professor climbs in on the passenger side. Walter hops in the back. Clancy makes his way back for Robin.

"It's time to go." Clancy helps Robin to her feet.

"But what about the others?" I say. "Aren't there more people coming?" I might sound like I'm asking about the rest of the coalition, all the people who were too scared to show up to the meeting at the Commander's house, but what I really want to know is why my friends aren't here yet.

"The professor says we can't wait much longer." He scoops Robin under his arm and half-supports, half-carries her to the truck.

I can't leave. Not yet. I have to stall.

I run to the driver-side door and pull myself up to look the Warden in the eye. If anyone will understand, I hope it's her.

"We can't leave yet," I tell her. "They're coming. I know they are."

Then I see it, the sadness in her eyes. She hangs her head.

"They're not coming, Sage."

"No," I let go of the cab and stumble back.

Professor Diaz leans forward. "Get in the cargo hold, Reyna."

I know I need to, but I can't move my legs. I can't leave without them. I can't leave Geri behind. *There has to be something I can do to buy them more time.*

"Wait!" I burst. "I think the Admiral put a tracker in my arm."

The professor's eyes bulge. He and the Warden exchange a glance.

"Where is it?" the Warden probes.

"In my arm." I point to the shoulder where I was struck with the silver cylinder.

"We'll have to cut it out." The professor climbs back out of the truck. He calls out something into the enclosed space where the other three are waiting, then makes his way toward one of the tool carts and rummages through its drawers.

The Warden gets out of the driver seat and tells me to pull my arm out of the suit. I show her the spot where the tracker went in. She rubs her fingers over the area. I'm caught off guard by the tenderness I feel when she presses down.

"I can feel it," she announces to the professor.

A triangular blade pokes from the handle in his grip.

I know what's coming and look away, focusing on the entrance, pleading for my friends to barge through.

A sharp pain penetrates my skin, and I suck in air through gritted teeth. The Warden shoves her fingers into my flesh, fishing for the tracker.

"Got it."

A pinch and then a pull. Blood trickles down my sleeve.

She throws it to the ground and stomps it to bits.

"If you're being monitored, Reyna, it's only a matter of time before they come here looking for us." The professor knits his eyebrows together. "I know you're worried about your friends, but if we don't leave now, we never will."

My heart sinks. I know he's right.

The Warden cracks open a first aid kit. It looks a lot like the one I found in the shed. She dumps something over my wound. The liquid burns. I wince.

"Come on." The Warden slaps a dry gauze onto the incision and helps me slide my arm back into my sleeve.

There's no time to properly clean up the blood or bandage the wound. But I don't care. The only thing I can think about is how I'm leaving without *them*, without my friends.

We were supposed to do this together.

The weight of my body feels extra heavy as I climb into the back of the truck. Walter and Clancy jump out to help the professor lift the garage door. When they scramble back inside, I know I've run out of time. We can't wait any longer.

The truck rolls forward, and I bite down on my lip to keep tears from streaming down my face. Leaving was supposed to feel good, but I feel gutted.

"Stop!"

My ears perk up. I swing my head out of the canopy.

It's Erika!

She holds the door open for Lu and Ronny. They're dragging Laude between them. Her face is covered in soot. My heart starts pounding.

"They're here!" I yell, banging on the side of the frame. "Stop the truck!"

The Warden brakes.

My eyes lock on the door, waiting for Geri to emerge, but the others press on without her.

Where is she?

Erika lifts Laude into the cargo hold, and Clancy helps me lower her to the floor.

"Erika?"

She avoids my eyes, and my heart stops.

Geri's not coming.

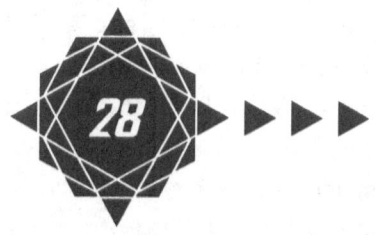

Two shots echo through the garage. I startle.

Lu's sockets stretch wide. Veronica hits the ground. They never make it past the tailgate.

"Get down!" Clancy yells, throwing a tarp over his wife as she crumples to the bottom of the truck bed and hugs her knees to her stomach.

Lu's stunned, frozen stiff. Erika groans and hauls her up by the armpits. There's blood pooling from her abdomen.

"Help me," she calls.

Walter grabs onto Lu's wrists.

I shake myself from my frozen state and help drag Lu next to Laude.

"You have to stop the bleeding," Laude rasps. She uses all of her strength to roll over and press on the wound. I drop to my knees and take her place, applying pressure to the hole in Lu's stomach.

Lu's eyes roll back.

"No, no, no, stay with me," I panic.

Another shot blasts. A bullet whizzes past my face, blowing a hole through the covered truck bed.

Walter rips the gun off my back and sticks it through the opening in the canvas to return fire.

"There's two of them," he hollers over his shoulder as he pulls the trigger.

A square window slides open from the cab, and Professor Diaz's face appears in the empty space. "We have to leave before the third bomb goes off."

Erika's eyes dart to mine. We're both thinking the same thing. *Ronny.*

I can't leave my post to help her get Ronny. I'm doing my best to keep blood from spilling out of Lu's body. Erika crawls on her elbows toward Walter, who takes another shot, then whips himself to the floor just as another bullet rips through the canopy. Erika jolts back to get out of his way. The truck starts moving. She scrambles to the ledge. Walter grabs onto the slack of her uniform and rips her back.

Erika's face is as white as the sheets they wrapped Grandmommy in, as drained as the empty cisterns we use for mixing cement. She shakes her head. *Ronny's dead.*

"No!" Grief wrenches me, squeezing my heart.

The truck jars. My hands slip. More blood seeps into Lu's uniform.

Walter unzips a duffel bag and pulls a blanket from inside.

"Use this." He gives Erika the grey covering. She shoves it into Lu's side.

The Warden accelerates, zigzagging the truck, rocking us back and forth. I can't see what's going on. I lift onto my knees and peer out the square hole in the cab, the one the professor's left wide open. The Warden's dodging people and debris, aiming for a gigantic black tarp that's draped over the wall.

"Hold on!" she yells.

Three more bullets zip over our heads. I hit the floor, wedging myself between Walter and Laude.

"I think I can get another shot," he says to me before lurching to the back of the truck.

I lift my head and catch Clancy's eye. He hasn't moved, guarding Robin with his body, using himself as a human shield against the Dark Guards' bullets.

"Rey! Get over here!" Walter shouts for me, firing another shot.

I shuffle my way to him and look out the back. Geri's running across the quadrangle, being chased by a Dark Guard who's lost his weapon.

"Geri!" I shout. "Warden, we have to stop the truck!"

The Warden doesn't stop. The distance between us grows. I can't leave without her.

"Cover me," I tell Walter, then launch myself from the back of the truck. The impact of the fall sends a shock of pain through my bones. I roll across the gravel, but the black suit keeps my skin protected from the rubble. When my body stops spinning, I gather my bearings as quickly as possible and jump to my feet.

"Hurry!" I yell to Geri.

She's barreling toward me, the Dark Guard fast on her tail.

Walter fires a shot that cracks his mask and throws him to the ground. Geri stumbles. I grab onto her, and we bolt after the truck.

The Warden speeds into the black tarp, taking the gigantic covering with her, revealing the gaping hole in the wall.

"We're not going to make it," Geri huffs.

"We're almost there." I dig my feet into the dirt, pulling her with me.

She slumps with exhaustion. Her pace slows.

"Come on, Geri. We can do this."

With everything I have left in me, I run faster than I've ever run before. We make it to the hole. I can see the truck up ahead. A blast sends us flying forward. I let go of Geri. Her body goes one way. Mine goes another. Something heavy lands on my leg. I scream out, but the thunder of the explosion masks my voice.

"Geri!"

"*Geri!*" My eyes frantically search for her through the flying debris.

Sharp pain sears through my nerves. I suck through my teeth, filling my lungs with smolder. Smoke from the crumbling wall overtakes the sky. Dust and debris shower from overhead, falling on my face.

"I'm sorry," I whimper as my back sinks into the dry dirt. We've finally made it outside the barracks, only to be claimed by the wall that's held us hostage all our lives.

All at once, I'm remembering the moments Geri's been by my side, the love that she showed me when we were just kids, the compassion she offered when I needed it most. Like a flood, the memories come rushing in. I see her toothless grin the day we met. I hear the sound of her laugh, the excitement she had when I shared my dreams with her.

"Geri ..." Her name barely escapes my cracked lips. Tears mix with dust.

I stare into the clouded ash swirling above my head, unable to move my leg, remembering my childhood and the days Geri brought me happiness. She showed me the sun when all I saw was the storm. Then, something strange happens. Contentment swells in my chest; thankfulness for her friendship.

Unexplainable peace washes over me the same way it did when I first tasted the Source's fruit. And here, trapped under the weight of cement, I feel hope, real hope, rising from within me. Somehow I know that no matter what happens next, when the dust settles, it's all going to be okay. *We made it outside the wall.* And even if we die here, at least I've kept my promise. *We're free.*

The rim of the sun peeks through the haze, and it's the last thing I see before the billows turn black.

I inhale the sweetness of the Source's blooms. A warm embrace holds me still.

"It's time," Grandmommy whispers into my ear. She pulls herself away, but keeps her translucent hands on my shoulders. Her diamond eyes sparkle as she smiles. The orb at her center pulses with a mixture of lavender and gold.

Beyond her beaming face, an entire multitude of creatures surround us, animals and people alike, gathered at the center of the island at the base of the massive tree. Their colorful shapes and chiseled features shine in the light of the Great Morning Star. They stare at me, their faces full of reverence, waiting for whatever comes next.

"Elolam has chosen *you* to mend what's been broken."

I pull my attention back to Grandmommy.

"And I couldn't be prouder."

A part of me wants to run and hide to escape the masses, but most of me wants to stay here with Grandmommy. I hold my stance and her gaze, letting everyone else blur in the background. Hot tears stream down my face, free of dust and debris. I let go of my composure and allow myself to sob. My tears, while gutted with sorrow over the loss I've just experienced, are full of relief. I'm finally back in the City of Life—and this time, I think I might stay.

Grandmommy wraps her arms around me and turns my shoulders to face the multitude. I wipe my watery eyes and take in the crowd. Thousands of colorful creatures sway back and forth. Their movements are subtle at first, but they build into a choreographed dance that imitates the flowers from my meadow swaying in the wind. Their feet stomp, building in crescendo like a drum. My heart races as the ground shakes.

Singing emerges from the masses with voices that meld and blend into an array of harmonies.

> *Bless the name of Elolam,*
> *Creator of the Universe*
> *All glory be unto his name*

Liquid light pulses between the bark of the Source in response to their song, turning my head upward. Its veins glow brighter as the melody from the multitude builds. A soft breeze blows across my cheeks, carrying their worship in its current. The leaves above my head shimmer as they dance with the wind. Blossoms release from the Source's branches, showering everyone who's gathered with fragrant petals. A strong smell of citrus and spice fills the air. When my mouth falls open in awe, the aroma sits on my tongue, making me crave the amber fruit that hangs from the massive tree.

The Source extends a limb to me, weighted with its ripe harvest.

"Eat and remember," Grandmommy says.

I pluck the rounded crop from the leafy bough and hold it in my hands. The skin sparkles, radiating with light. There isn't a single blemish or mark on its surface. I sink my teeth into the fruit and let the warm, thick juices drip off my chin, welcoming the peace that it brings me, the sense of acceptance and love that it gives.

Remember.

Elolam's voice echoes in my ears, not in a loud shout but in a quiet, clear whisper.

In an instant, I see *his* memories displayed before me. He shows me the expanse of the universe from the beginning of time, my dream world and Earth melded together. Mountainous cliffs outline vast, emerald meadows. Oceans of infinite waters lap the shores. Towers of trees create thick, thriving forests. Colorful creatures flood the skies. Powerful beasts roam the ground. Vibrant people inhabit a land yielding abundance.

My heart is filled with exuberant joy. I'm so overcome, I burst. My chest implodes and light radiates from my core. The fire burns a hole in my skin, but it doesn't sear me with pain. My flesh peels away, revealing a glowing orb at my center. The colors inside sparkle and spin like the shrunken galaxy that's set in the middle of Grandmommy's breasts. Rainbow swirls collide in chaotic patterns. I'm mesmerized by the scene, but a hint of doubt tricks my mind, combating the joy, convincing me it isn't real. The orb skips. Its colors hesitate, responding to my uncertainty.

You must believe. Grandmommy's voice wells from within.

I take a breath, suck in the wind.

This is real, I tell myself, and the joy returns, mixing with vibrant streaks of red and blue. I search for words to describe the happiness. Deep satisfaction. Absolute serenity. Unconditional love.

When I look up, a line of creatures has assembled before me, carrying gifts. A ruby-colored woman with white irises leans forward, placing a crown on my head, woven with yellow blossoms. "For the daughter of Elolam, Bringer of the Garden, Restorer of the Breach." Her melodious voice blesses me.

She bows out, making room for a pair of winged creatures with turquoise-colored skin and flowing feathered hair. They wrap me in a robe sewn with threads of gold. The weight of the material is carried by the wind, floating in the air like laundry in water, except without the dirty clothes or pungent odor.

At my feet, a child with translucent skin waits to hand me a small wooden object. He places it in my palm and curls my fingers around it before I have a chance to see what it is.

The multitude finishes their final refrain, and a hush falls over the crowd. They're still, patient, yet eyes eager with expectation. I only hear the trickle of the river, the rustling of the leaves, and the pulsing of the orb that's surfaced from my chest. Even my breath is silent.

Limbs from the Source entangle around me. Its glowing veins shimmer in the light of the Great Morning

Star as it gropes through the air to conceal me from the crowd. This time, I'm not frightened. I know Elolam wants to meet with me face-to-face in his secret place, under the shelter of his life-boughs.

I watch Grandmommy's eyes sparkle the way they have my whole life, and keep my sights set on her as the vines create their enclosure. This space is no longer a cage; it's a meeting place. My heart doesn't race with anxiety. It races with anticipation.

When Grandmommy disappears behind the leafy walls, I spin to see that Elolam is already standing in the center of our sanctuary. He widens his arms, welcoming me with an embrace. The warmth of his skin radiates through my hands and travels through my body. All of the hair on my neck stands on end. My orb pulses with streaks of orange and fuchsia, displaying colors that remind me of a beautiful sunrise. And just like that, I know this is the beginning of a new dawn. Hope, genuine and real, brims from my soul, painted in a portrait of something I love most: a sky full of color.

"You have done well," Elolam speaks. His approval fills my lungs with fresh breath, and I breathe in his scent—earthy and sweet, just like the Source.

Held in his arms, I think to myself, *I never want to leave.*

"But you cannot stay here," he answers as if he's read my thoughts.

I retract and look into his burning eyes. White flames dance around his pupils, but it's not the kind of fire I want to run from. It's the kind I want to warm myself by, the kind that invites me to sit and stay a while with my hands stretched over its dancing flares like the fire burning at his campsite.

"I don't want to go back," I admit honestly, but he and I both know he's already read my mind. I don't think I can keep my thoughts hidden from him.

"Your time on Earth is not yet finished. There is still much for you to learn, and a great deal for you to do."

An ache billows in my chest, like stormy green clouds swirling in my soul. "I want to stay here with you."

Sparkles of light leave Elolam's lips as he laughs. "My dear child, do you not know that I am always with you? I will never leave you." He takes me by the hand and uncurls my fingers to reveal what the boy-child gifted to me.

A small key made of twisted, golden vines rests in my palm.

"All you have to do is remember me." He smiles.

The key is remembering.

I recall the words he spoke to me the last time I was in the City of Life, before the serum-induced nightmares took over my dreams. At the time, I didn't think he was being literal. Yet here I am, holding a key in my hand—a memory key—and it looks like it's alive. The tendrils twist and turn like the branches of the Source, laced with lines of liquid light.

"I want to show you something." Elolam beams with childlike wonder. He grasps my hand, and before I can blink, I'm taken up, floating above the universe, staring down into an expanse so great my heart skips a beat and my orb spins with greying greens.

"Look," Elolam says, pointing into the distance. "The Great Divide is shifting."

I peer down into the darkness. My vision sharpens, searching past the stars and planets. Although I'm hovering miles above the scene, it's as clear as if I'm there. I witness a globe, marbled with blue and swirling with white. Millions of specks, like floating dust, emerging from the celestial sphere.

"Earth." The name rolls off my tongue.

"Look closer," Elolam instructs.

I stretch my vision farther and see the doorways of the Great Divide; one made from the Source's own limbs, the other crafted from charred wood. They're set in a chasm, deep and dark. Sorrow swells in my chest, spinning my orb with hues of midnight blue. Souls travel through the chasm, making their way to their final destination: eternal life or everlasting death. I'm tempted to wail for the souls that pour from Earth and descend into the gap, but something catches my eye and stops my heart from aching.

A leaf, single and small—a shoot of green emerging from the charred wood.

I gasp.

Hope is sprouting. The forgotten things are beginning to remember again.

END OF BOOK ONE

ACKNOWLEDGEMENTS

Thank you, God, for the gift of creativity and the hope of eternal life.

To my husband—you believed in me even when I struggled to believe in myself. You are my greatest supporter and my dearest friend. *Remember* would never have seen the light of day without your encouragement.

Thank you to my family, who have shown me time and time again what it means to persevere. I am eternally grateful for the generations of writers, artists, and musicians in my line who have paved the way for me to be the author that I am today. Mom and Dad, your prayers have kept me afloat and your example has inspired me to keep going, even when the dream felt out of reach. Thank you to my brother and my book loving sister, who spent long afternoons daydreaming with me about everything this story could be.

To my children—your unwavering confidence in me fueled both my early-morning and late-night writing sessions. Thank you for cheering me on. Leifram, thank you for letting me bounce ideas off of you. Torin, I'll cherish the day you told me my book was going to be so good people would request it at the library. Synnove, I hope your dream of becoming an author someday comes true. Freyja, your excitement for my story made my heart sing.

To Roman—the friend I never knew I needed. You were the first person who gave my story a chance. You helped me find my voice as an author and never held back from telling me where I needed to grow. Thank you for your honesty and for the hours you invested into helping me write Reyna's story. To you, I am indebted.

To my incredible editor, Caitlin—my story came to you in a time of grief, and still, you poured your heart and soul into making sure every line was polished to be its best version.

To Maria, my graphic designer—thank you for working with me to create an incredible book cover—one that truly encapsulates the story underneath.

To Peter, my life-long friend—thank you for putting up with my nonsense and ramblings, and for making my book look stunning on the inside. Your eye for detail does not go unnoticed.

Thank you to all of the friends who couldn't wait for updates on my writing journey. You'll never know how much your text messages, voicemail rants, and visits meant to me while writing this book. A special thank you to Emily, for gushing over my characters and giving me my first unofficial five-star review.

Finally, thank you to my church family, the wonderful community I found on Instagram, my beta and ARC readers—and to you. Without you, *Remember* would only be words on a page. So, thank you for reading my story and bringing it to life.

ABOUT THE AUTHOR

Cheyenne Cleveland grew up in Western New York surrounded by a family full of authors, artists, and musicians. With a master's degree in music education, Cheyenne has always found a sense of belonging in the creative arts—through songwriting, poetry, scripting musical theatre, and storytelling. When she's not daydreaming about dystopian worlds, Cheyenne can be found homeschooling her four children, exploring the outdoors, or making music alongside her husband. *Remember* is her debut novel and the first book in its self-titled trilogy.

You can follow her author journey on Instagram
@Cheyenne.Cleveland.Author

Thank you so much for reading Remember and joining Reyna on her journey. If you enjoyed the story, I'd be incredibly grateful if you left a review—it helps other readers discover the book and encourages me as an independent author. Your thoughts truly make a difference!